About the author

Tony Bryan was born in Liverpool, England, but has lived in rural Worcestershire for some years. Tony has enjoyed success as a playwright and theatre producer and his first novel, *99 Heyworth Street*, was published a few years back.

Tony has also had success with a screenplay of his version of a true story, 'The Decline of Daisy de Melker', which has been a finalist in several international Film Festivals.

Baltimore is the fulfilment of a promise made some years ago to his dad, that one day he would produce a 'searing, historical novel'.

Baltimore is the first of a trilogy with part two completed and part three 'under construction'.

BALTIMORE

Tony Bryan

BALTIMORE

Vanguard Press

VANGUARD PAPERBACK

A CIP catalogue record for this title is
available from the British Library.

ISBN 978 1 784652 92 0

*Vanguard Press is an imprint of
Pegasus Elliot MacKenzie Publishers Ltd.*
www.pegasuspublishers.com

First Published in 2018

**Vanguard Press
Sheraton House Castle Park
Cambridge England**

Printed & Bound in Great Britain

Dedication

My wife Pauline and my close family including Lauren, Hannah, James and Andrew.

To my dad Jim, mum Vera and especially to my sister Maureen for her unfaltering support.

My daughter Jo and son Kris, for the time I didn't spend with them.

My brother John for the time I did.

Ann, Dawn, Bill and Carole for their encouragement.

A special mention to Ashby Writers and Worcesterwriterscircle for helping to 'fine-tune' the raw enthusiasm.

Robert Graves, Ian Fleming, Wilbur Smith and Bernard Cornwell for their inspiration.

Claire-Rose Charlton for her endurance, Suzanne Mulvey for seeing the potential in my manuscript and all at Pegasus for making this possible.

Chapter 1

Baltimore, the southern tip of Ireland

The campfire lit up their faces. Expressions fixed, joyous eyes twinkled.

Behind, in the glow of the fire, young men, arranged two and three deep, watched the dancers with approving eyes. They laughed nudging and winking one another, before, every few moments, one would rise and show his appreciation.

When Daemon's turn came, he let out a shrill cry of encouragement, raising his arms, impersonating a twirl, drawing laughter and feigned approval from those nearby. His close friends collapsed in a heap amid the digging of ribs and playful backslapping.

Annie Figgerty pulled a blanket up around the ears of her month-old child, and passed him to her mother's willing arms. She rose and pulled the strings to her skirt tighter to accentuate her returning shapeliness. Shaking her long golden curls free she joined the dance.

The music throbbed. Tartan skirts twirled wildly. Rising in tempo until the skins were being pounded, bow strings shredded and pipes moaning, the band hit delirious heights until, exhausted, they let the crowd rest in an excited babble of whoops and ahs and much laughter.

Then Mariah stood, her back toward the fire, her cloak drawn up around her shoulders, long black hair gathered like a hood around her white face, she sang.

One long, shrill note, was followed by another, more gentle. The pipes blew, contrasting her note with a gentle lowing sound of their own. Eerily she lamented long lost lovers, the beauty of the valleys and a life, long veiled, by the mists of time.

The gathering hushed to her song, even the campfire quelled respectfully.

As if in response lambs bayed on the hillsides above them. There was peace all around and, as the lassies' eyes filled with crystalline drops, the lads' heads dropped knowingly.

Sitting astride a log, surrounded by her friends, Kirsten had not noticed his approach.

He stood, watching from a distance. A visitor from Donegal, and only two days in the neighbourhood of his distant cousins, he was smitten immediately his eyes fell upon her. He drew nearer until she could sense his presence.

She raised her eyes to meet his, turning slightly, until she was square on to him. His gaze was unflinching. He wanted her to feel his 'power', to feel uncomfortable. He expected her to blush and demurely turn away. But this, this was better! She looked him full in the face and smiled warmly. Her eyes drawing him to her.

Before she could drop her gaze he was standing within touching distance.

He reached out to take her hand and, she let him, but the push in the small of her back from a smiling friend Sinead, propelled her forward.

He walked her over, closer to the fire. Her friends watched as she went with him, her head high and proud.

The dull thud on stretched skins echoed, as the soft lyrical song gathered pace. The fiddler joined in as the couple swayed in each other's arms. They moved easily together, her head almost matching his in height. They matched one another for power and grace. The area cleared and others watched them as if the feelings of all of them were perfectly captured in their dance.

As the music again reached a pitch, and the twirling once more became furious and intoxicating, he took her away from the crowd and entwined her limbs within his own.

For long moments they writhed amongst deep grasses, stripping away any barriers, and felt the soft earth beneath them in their frenzied embrace.

They slept in each other's arms until the sun, rising above a misty dawn, signalled the call of day.

Pulling her things about her and straightening to her full height, she laughed as he rose to his knees to gaze at her. Her mood was giddy, his locked in a sense of wonderment. He preferred to remain at her feet even as she darted away. She turned just once to wave, and was gone from his sight.

Alone, Daemon lay back, arms cushioning his head, he gazed into the bright morning sky and breathed long and slow with such deep satisfaction as he had hardly known in his twenty-one years.

Out in the bay a North African, three-masted Xebek eased alongside the mooring and two brightly clad sailors hopped over the side and dropped hemp rope over well anchored posts. Above them, at the ships prow, dark skin glistening in the morning sun, white turban glowing above flowing black hair, the Moorish leader stood, hawk-like and watchful as other warriors quietly slid over the sides to fan out, beyond the rustic timber and away toward the hillside.

Surveying the scene before him, Ahmed Al Khan, satisfied as to the effectiveness of his timing, leapt from his perch onto the creaking boards and strode to the head of his forces.

Some fifty, decked in the brightest yellows and crimsons swirled shimmering steel above their heads amidst a muted howl of achievement.

Behind them thirty more remained at their posts, tending a gathering of bewildered white captives, and providing fresh water to rows of tethered oarsmen. They would be ready upon the return of the raiding party for a swift departure.

In the village the younger women were already at work when Kirsten arrived. She skipped down the hillside toward them as they herded milk laden cows into their pens. Looking up they waved in unison, demonstrating their own pleasure in her new found state of exhilaration. They gathered around her giggling and goading her until she burst forth a stream of information that had them swooning and open mouthed.

The well-drilled raiders fell in behind Al Khan as he quickened to a trot, upward from the bay, across the lush green fields before them.

Circling to avoid the cart tracks, they rose to the crest of Beacon Head before a single native was aware of their arrival. The village had posted no lookout. There had been no trouble for many a year and the day following a holiday was no time to be worrying about any 'damned-fool Englishmen or even the Spanish'!

The raiders looked down the valley at the sprawl of thatch covered cottages, the glistening, fast flowing river and as peaceful a scene of eighteenth-century Ireland as could be imagined.

***

A few villagers, mostly women, had risen to fetch fresh water and to start the breakfast fires going, but the day after Whitsun was always slow to get moving. The festivities of the previous evening ensuring that at least an extra hour would be spent amongst the straw.

Now even the sight of a hoard of strange fighting men drew no more than a casual inquisitive glance. Not until the hoard broke into a charge downhill, steel flailing and shrill screams splintering the air was the first alarm raised.

***

Having heard enough of Kirsten's tale, Annie Figgerty had wandered away from the gathering at the milking parlour and was making her way, two pails across her shoulders, to her father's cottage. Seeing the Moors she stopped in her tracks. Annie looked long and hard at how the brightly coloured garb of the charging line was strung out across the meadow, before realising imminent danger.

Eventually she abandoned both pails and ran toward her home. She tried to scream but nothing came out. Arriving at the cottage, she pounded away at the door, even though it was only on the latch.

Shaking with fear, she fumbled with the latch too long as the first sounds of terror could be heard in the village. Her assailant was on her back before she could squirm through the half-opened door.

Finally her vocal chords began to work but only a strangled sob emerged before a muscular arm encircled her throat and lifted her off her feet. A rope was looped around her neck and she was dragged away from the cottage toward the water's edge.

There, ten or more of the attackers had formed a circle into which Annie was thrown and snared with a hoop at the end of a spear. A terrified gurgling issued forth as she managed to raise a scream, 'My baby, my baby...!'

All around mayhem had broken out. Annie's father had risen, pulling his kilt around him and was outside the cottage flailing at the invaders with an old sabre. With skills beyond anything ever witnessed, the Moors stealthily moved through the village slashing their curved blades through the air and almost at will, through the clumsy, ill-prepared defences of the villagers.

Figgerty fought as bravely as any but within a few slashing blows a bloody, dangling mess hung where his fighting arm had been. He vainly flayed away with the other before a deep, chopping slash cleaved him from neck to waist. He fell face down into the river as his wife rushed screaming downhill toward them. The invader cut her completely, at the waist, her two parts falling insanely into the river alongside her man.

The village became awash with blood. The calm gone forever, screams and wailing echoed around the valley. The community devastated.

Away down by the milking parlour, the waiting feast, which was the group of young womanhood, was a gift to the Moors. Seven of them swooped on the five girls and snared them about the neck with consummate ease. They were dragged, kicking and screaming, to the ring where the other chosen were held.

The Moors were cold-eyed, ruthless and impatient. Their careful plan depended on speed and surprise. Any who fought or struggled too much were cut, with indifference, at the throat.

Young boys, women and teenaged youths were pinioned to the ground and snared about the neck until, in all there were some twenty-two captives.

Around them many of the villagers lay slain. Although two of the Moors had carelessly lost their lives, their bodies were not left behind. As if to remove all trace of their raid, all weapons and debris were carefully gathered up.

Leaving behind screaming babies, the groaning injured and the wailing of old wives, the raiders led away their captives to the top of the hill and down to the waiting ship. In all since the landing, the invasion had lasted scarcely twenty-five minutes.

Chapter 2

A Rude Awakening

For long moments, Daemon sat with his head cradled on his arms, unprepared to face the day, the delights of the evening lingering long in his thoughts as the morning sun soothed away the fleeting discomforts of a night on the hillside. Kirsten's lithe image when she rose to pull on her shirt, was played over and over behind closed eyelids.

Gradually noise from the village drifted up to him and broke through his dreamy consciousness, introducing new sounds into his mind. Shouting now disturbed him, shrieks of terror, then of rage. Metal clashed, the church bells clanged a stuttering warning. Horses galloped to and fro. Carts groaned along rutted tracks. Tentatively he rose, stretched and threaded his sabre into his waistband.

Another alarming shriek finally convinced him of imminent danger. He rapidly covered the ground to the crest of the hill. On reaching it he was able to take in the full panorama of the valley before him. He bit hard on his lip as each horrific sight in turn came under his gaze.

Rage thundered in Daemon's ears.

He saw the thin line of the invader across the far side of the valley, as it disappeared over the hill. Had he been able to sprout wings, he would have swooped down on them without a second's hesitation.

As it was, it was all his legs could do to keep him upright as he drove them into a frantic chase down the valley.

Breathless and aching from every muscle he surged upward to the crest of Clee Hill overlooking Baltimore Bay. Screaming inside, pain throbbing in his head and lungs, tears of rage filling his eyes, he reached the headland, only to look down upon the ship, with sail and oars, as it turned imperiously out of the calm waters of the inlet.

He watched as the distance between shore and hull increased yard by relentless yard.

No sound issued from the Moors, not even an exultant roar at the speed and efficiency of their victory but they began to respond to the beating of the drum that disciplined the oarsmen's every stroke.

Without even a hint of a sighting, he knew for certain that Kirsten was aboard that ship, captive and bound for a world he may never have heard of, and almost certainly would never see.

A feeling of utter desolation descended upon him. There was not the faintest hope, that he would ever hold her in his arms again.

***

For long moments Daemon sat again with his head in his hands, for very different reasons, unable to face the day. Eventually the sounds from the village again carried and penetrated his consciousness.

Painfully, shaking the dust from his clothing, he began to drag his way back to the crest of the hill.

Down below horses galloped to and fro, working horses, dragging bodies and debris away from the raging fires, away from the slaughter.

A cart disappeared into the distance, an old woman barely able to hold on as it jolted her from side to side. The prone figures of two injured villagers lay strewn across the back boards. Some of the older children were running between the river and burning cottages, with pails slopping back and forth. Younger children sat crying, bewildered, on the ground. Some of the old wives dragged bodies from the rock strewn river bed, laying them out on the grass.

Some of the older villagers were throwing pales into the smoking ruins of the Church and community buildings, at the heart of the village, but hardly a dwelling stood. Fire raged through the thatched roofs, and burning straw had collapsed inward, igniting everything within.

Hundreds of years of village life was destroyed in a matter of minutes.

Daemon, determined to help in any way possible, made his way down the hill. Suddenly, on sight of him a dozen or more stopped what they were about and gathered together before starting toward him. Carrying shovels and pitchforks, they charged up the hill until he drew to a halt. Throwing his hands in the air he yelled at them to stop.

Shrieking at the top of her voice, the first to reach him was a woman in her fifties, who made as if to take his head off with a shovel.

'Wait, Jesus, Mary and Joseph, I'm one of yous! Surely you don't want another body on your hands?'

Molly McCarthy poised over him, eyes bulging, and was quite prepared to slay him. Mercifully others arrived and gathered into a ring. An elder shouted

'Molly, be still!'

A three-pronged pitchfork was held under Daemon's chin by the greying elder. 'Who are yea? Speak your piece or I swear... '

'No need for that! I'm Daemon, Roddy's cousin, from Donegal! Has any of yous seen my uncle Sean? Jesus, doesn't anyone know me, from the feast... last night?'

'Where were yea? Why'nt yea come an' help when them heathens come down on us?' A voice from the pack demanded.

'For shame's sake, I was away over the hill! Didn't I leave the fire last night, to go.... walking with Kirsty... an...

17

well, I had hardly wiped the sleep from my eyes before I heard the commotion…!'

The old man fell to his knees. 'Did ye see? Did yea see what they did to the babies?' He wept openly, allowing the pitchfork to fall to the ground.

'Aye, I saw right enough… didn't I just chase them heathens across the Cree… and…!' he stopped, choked on his words, as their expectant eyes rose in hope.

Shaking his head, he finished – '… every last one of them was taken… on a ship…! It was out of the bay before I could reach the mooring! I'd have taken on the lot of them… Christ I'd have taken a few down with me an' all!'

His own eyes filled with tears, they dropped their weapons and he felt the well of sympathy. 'Please, let me help, is there anyone left? What can I do,? I could help you re-build…!'

One by one they turned and made their way back toward the village. None of his Uncle's family emerged. He found their cottage, a smouldering pile of embers now, and no sign of the three girls and Roddy.

He made toward the river, where he was handed two pails, pitching in where he could be of some use, he delivered water to a temporary nursing station and helped one of the old one's making a child comfortable.

Two days passed whilst survivors gathered about them a few valuables. Daemon had helped bury the dead. Thirty-four graves were laid, marked with bound twigs. Unable to get near to the burning chapel, a shaded area, near the tree line, became the new village graveyard.

Refugees left the village in a bedraggled line, strung-out as they reached the top of the hill. Tears flowed as they took a last look at the smouldering remains that had recently been a scene of peaceful co-existence. A village, to which all were welcome, had been so suddenly turned into a ghostly ruin that would welcome no more.

Chapter 3

Far and Farther From Home

For more than an hour they had stood, in a huddle beneath a canopy to the rear of the ship. Their neck restraints, looped so that any movement or attempt at release, resulted only in the tightening around their throats.

Standing, erect and still, each afraid the next movement may be their last, they held together in fear. Tears flowed copiously leaving trails on grubby faces, and many were unable to control their bladders. The deck became slippery under foot and the heat of their bodies, combined with high anxiety and the morning sun, meant the cloying atmosphere under the canopy became hardly bearable.

Kirsten barely opened her eyes for fear that a misdirected glance might re-ignite the hideous explosion of violence they had witnessed earlier.

In the gloom, she could make out fear-filled eyes, or a perspiring brow as the sway of the ship cast shafts of sunlight into the shadows. There were others, not only Baltimore people, but strangers, from other villages.

A whispered, strangled voice brought her head round sharply.

'Kirsty, Kirsty, is that you?'

'Sinead… Jesus, Sinead… are you hurt, where are ye?'

'Down here… so help me! I'm down here.' She pulled at Kirsten's skirt.

Stooping, Kirsten came within inches of her friend's face. She leaned until she could feel her sweat and tear-stained skin.

'What's happened?... In the name of God, what's happened to us?'

'Kirsty... these heathens are goin' to kill us, every last one of us so they will!'

'Listen... listen to me Sinead! It's not for killin' they took us! I don't know where on God's earth we are goin' but why take us... they could ha' killed us all in Baltimore Bay had they a mind to...!'

'Kirsty, they may as well 'av... I saw my father chopped in two, like a bullock in the slaughterhouse! I never seen anything like it in my life, an' I never want to neither! If the Lord took me now I'd go willin' so I would!'

Sinead broke down, weeping over again. Slipping down at Kirsten's feet, her head touched the deck and was content to lay where it was. Slops and urine ran freely into her hair and she cared not one bit as her knuckles whitened against her teeth and sobs ran through her slender body.

Kirsten stooped as far as her tether would allow and began to pull at Sinead's shirt.

'Sinead, get up – you can't just give up – please Sinead!'

Just then the canvas was flung back sending bright sunlight into the area and thirty or more pairs of hands shielded their eyes. Kirsten felt her arm dragged by a powerful hand. She gagged on the rope as it burned the tender skin of her neck. Suddenly it was freed.

A burly, black sailor pulled her across the deck and flung her down on to a pile of sacking. His free hand in one movement whirled a leather coil into the air and brought it sharply down across her back. The thin end bit into her flesh, leaving a bleeding, crescent shaped slash across her right shoulder. Kirsten let out a short scream in shock and pain, her head spinning round to see the sailors hand drawing back.

'No more talk, no more yelping... this will remind your friends...!'

Just that moment a shorter but powerfully-built stranger leapt up and held the threatening whip hand back. For a moment the two glared at one another!

'My friend... do not damage the 'goods' ... too much, hey? We want to 'maximise' our profit in the Barbary... No?'

A grin broke out on the other's face, 'Go ahead, you take her... but keep that rabble quiet!' He broke off and recoiled the whip while the other, a lighter-skinned, long-haired figure in the whitest blouse, stooped to help a bewildered Kirsten, back to her feet. Almost apologetically he re-tied the noose at her throat, leaving a little more slack than she had experienced earlier, so that it draped almost comfortably around her neck.

His eyes sought hers, attempting reassurance, but Kirsten's had settled back once more into the gloom and she failed to notice his attentions. With more room to manoeuvre, Kirsten brought Sinead up to her knees and held her in a long embrace, failing to notice the vivid red of her own blood as it ran down her back into her shirt.

Chapter 4

The Long Voyage to the Abyss

The bucking of the Xebec on the six and seven foot waves had become rhythmic and the captives managed to balance their weight sufficiently to deal with the swell but as the morning wore on, there was a perceptible change and the roll of the ship began to unbalance even the sturdiest of them.

A rise in the voices outside, both in volume and frequency told them that preparation was under way and the Moors were having to work hard to keep their course.

Now the excrement and vomit on the deck were diluted by sea water. Thrown this way then that, it slopped against the hull and back again swirling past their feet as they shuffled from side to side.

Sinead grabbed onto Kirsten's arm, then her other came around pulling the folds of her tattered skirt. Kirsten held her close to steady them both.

***

The wind blew loudly and snapped at the canvas around their heads. Now there was harsh frequent flapping and the timbers groaned out on the deck, where the slavers were frantically leaping from beam to rigging at the sides of the ship where there was more to grab hold of.

One of the captive girls lost her footing and suddenly they were all grazing knees and banging into one another. The deck bucked again and threw them untidily into a corner.

More water rushed through the gratings and a barrel thudded to the deck outside, rolling like thunder into the bulkhead beside them, it spilled it's contents of fresh water into the brine.

Now their murmurings became louder, turning to screams and groans. Outside, beyond the flapping canvas, Kirsten could make out the desperate heaving on ropes and a gang frantically snaring the tiller. Sailors were high in the rigging clawing at billowing sail. The canvas above the captives pulled so ferociously to one side that it snagged against the rail and left them open to the now teaming rain as the heavens opened.

'Jeez! We're all going to die!' someone shouted. 'Holy Mother of God please, please spare us!'

Kirsten turned and pulled at her neck restraint in vain. She could neither free herself nor disengage herself from the other captives. Sinead was on the deck again, her skirt obscenely around her waist revealing her pale, glistening limbs as she fought to regain her feet.

The sea crashed around her and her legs began an ungainly dance as she was thrown backward, having to hold on to her neck restraint with both hands. Three of the villagers went crashing down with her and Kirsten felt a vicious tug on her neck and was hauled headlong as a new wave crashed over them.

'Hold still. Jesus, Mary and Joseph, hold onto the rail. I'm chokin'…!' Mairie was howling but it came deep and throaty as the ropes tightened around her slender neck.

Chaos reigned all around now as the waves crashed mountainously over the side and swamped the deck. The formerly graceful warriors had become a clinging, baying rabble as the roaring seas threw the Xebec around like a cork in a fast flowing stream.

None paid any attention to the captives now as all were thrown together.

Around her Kirsten could see death was waiting. Some of the captives began to turn blue. Their faces twisted and vacant, tongues hanging limply to one side.

She turned to Sinead and tried to pull both of them upright but her strength was sapped and her charred hands pulled vainly on the cold, hard ropes. Their friend Mairie was on her knees but limp, seeming incapable of holding herself upright.

Around them the skies had turned a dark swirling mixture of grey and black and the rain slanted in like a hail of spears. The mainsail had been grappled into an untidy ruck around the transom and the oarsmen had ceased any attempt at propelling the craft forward and were tugging at their own shackles and smashing vainly at their seating with splintered oars.

Fear struck Kirsten like a dagger. She knew the helplessness of their situation. Another wave swamped them and although their collective weight prevented them being tossed around she knew that just behind her the relentless jerk of the rope had just drained the life out of another of her friends. All she could do was keep her own head out of the swirling water and hold her breath when the waves crashed in.

The ship keeled low now to one side. 'Another wave and she's gone!' Kirtsen knew the end was near. Now the ship began to spin, crazily around, all control now handed up to the Gods.

A crashing wave sent the vessel back almost upright again as a dozen warriors threw themselves headlong over the side and into the swell. She bucked viciously again up-ended from front to back before crashing down toward the bow, deep into the base of another wave.

Screams rose against the roaring noise of the sea as one, the group of captives were thrown collectively toward the bow. Roped together they became a string of gangling paper dolls before the sea took them into her merciless depths.

Again tugging fiercely on her binding, Kirsten stretched a long bare limb around a timber post to steady herself. All shame was eliminated from her thoughts as she struggled to keep her head out of the swell as another wave broke over the side.

Frantically she flung out an arm, she knew though that if she resisted she would surely be throttled or beheaded as the other captives were ranged across to the far side of the deck. Another swell and the post was torn from her grip, she was dragged headlong into the swirling sea and felt others limbs kicking and flailing around her.

Everything was suddenly calmer. Weightlessness took away the pressure from around her neck as the light faded and deep blackness surrounded them They plunged deep into the abyss.

Chapter 5

The White Moor

Blood throbbing, almost bursting out through her ear drums was suddenly curtailed as she felt a release of the tether from around her neck. She kicked out strongly with her long legs and thrust upward. At her side, knife firmly held between pearly white teeth, Banoldino, the 'light-skinned' Moor, put a strong arm around her waist and propelled them toward the surface.

With an unseemly loud gasp she sucked precious air into her deflated chest and became dizzy at the impact as pure oxygen filled her lungs. She sobbed loudly and retched into the sea, but her tears also flowed with relief. The realisation that she might not die! That all the nightmares of the past few hours had not put an end to her!

She suddenly felt strong and sure of herself. She began to swim through the deep cavernous waves with new strength found from she knew not where.

Banoldino flashed her a smile as he himself began to thrash at the cold sea. But suddenly, taking off at a tangent, he left her side and swam strongly away from her. Half turning Kirsten felt sudden panic, her own new found resolve suddenly sapped. She twisted to see him disappear as the peak of another wave drove between them and a torrent from the skies blurred her vision.

Minutes went by as she pushed out her arms in a semi co-ordinated but rapidly tiring attempt to weather the harsh seas.

A new fear settled upon her as she realised that on her own, she was surely doomed.

On the edge of new despair she heard him yelling desperately. 'Hey. Hi… Senorita, Senorita! This way, here, this way!'

Turning she could make out her saviour, pushing a timber in her direction. She knew then that the ship had foundered completely as she recognised the shape of the bow sculpture. The image of a dragon's head bobbed intermittently on the waves as he gradually gained on her.

She thrust out a hand and hauled herself on to the figure whilst he pulled at the tight string at her waist that had gamely held her coarse woollen skirt.

Working together they managed to pull her into a secure enough position as a new heavy wave battered down over them. She offered prayers to the Holy Trinity as she realised that the heaviest of the seas had begun to recede. The swell all around began to roll where it had once been an angry snarling thing.

Rain soaked and freezing they held on for a seemingly unending hour as they were tossed around on the powerful rolling swell. The harshness had long gone and they knew that there was hope if only there were other survivors or perhaps a coaster or fishing boat weathering the storm more readily than the Mediterranean Xebec, that had found the open seas too great a challenge.

Banoldino spoke to her, quietly, assuringly. He had been watching her for some time 'My name is Banoldino! I am a Spaniard by right! I hope you are not hurt!'

Her hand went to her throat as she remembered. Feeling the tender skin around her neck she wept openly. Tears streamed back into her hairline as she stared ahead across the rising and falling seas.

'Are you hurt?'

'My friend! All of my friends! Sinead… Oh God, I don't even know if my Ma and Da are alive or dead!' She turned and looked into his eyes. Her lips drew back and she sobbed again! 'What do you care!' It was a statement and she waited for no reply. Her head turned again to the horizon, now mercifully visible. The day had begun to fade and the skies, although now cloudless, were dark and foreboding.

Her head dropped and he knew it was not time to try to justify himself or his chosen path. Instead he suddenly raised himself and almost too loud he yelled 'Land – by all that is Holy, land'!

Almost too afraid to look up she turned and saw for herself a dark rise above the calming seas.

She knew it was Ireland – her home! She knew salvation was in their grasp. She thought of Daemon and his strong arms. She thought fleetingly of their coming together and rolling in ecstasy in the long grass. Her skin blushed although Banoldino would not have noticed as her colour returned from the ghostly pallor she had worn as she emerged from the sea.

Now he turned to her and grabbed her arm. 'My God! We're going to survive! Only moments ago I wouldn't have given a fig for our chances! But now look, girl! Look – we're going to live!'

She was captivated by his enthusiasm and his almost childish joy! It was unexpected. From a fierce warrior, a terrible foe, she now had a companion, who grabbed her arm like a friend would. Who looked at her with shining eyes. She was puzzled and at the same time suddenly afraid!

This was her captor, the enemy – he would be suddenly thrust back into the fray when they landed, he could be taken and strung up for piracy. The strife was certainly not over for one of them – perhaps it was only beginning.

Chapter 6

Land on the Horizon

Paddling frantically with bare hands on either side of their makeshift raft they struggled to turn in against an ebbing tide. But merciful yard by yard they made toward a rocky shoreline.

The swell of the surf smashed hard against a jutting rock formation but away to the right a beach, where the calmer waves ran their full course, they could see their route to safety. But the night was rapidly falling and progress slow and painful. Tired muscles cold and lifeless, they fought their way to within a hundred yards of the shore.

Shouting above the noise of crashing waves he called toward Kirsten. 'We will have to swim for it – I don't think our little vessel wants to be washed up on this shore! Can you make it?'

Kirsten hesitated she looked toward the shore then back at him! She felt heavy with her soaking skirt and her shirt clinging to her and her arms screamed with pain. Biting her lip, all she could do was nod in response.

Before she could think again he had grabbed her arm and plunged them both into the surf. Instinctively she began to swim and prayed to herself incessantly whilst the water swirled over her. Her head came up momentarily for air and his powerful arm once again reached out and took her around the waist. She could feel the forward motion, helped now by the rhythmic waves, they were propelled toward the shore.

She could feel him gripping her arm and then the pain as her knees scraped over broken shells and stone.

Eventually she was pulled over the shale surface until he released her and they both lay face down at last beyond the foaming edge of the water.

For long moments she pressed her body to the earth. Exhausted she fell into a dreamy sleep where a giant eagle swooped down from the skies to pluck her from a still pond and taken her soaring through white cloud against a deep blue star-speckled sky.

She awoke, wrapped and warm in the glow of a campfire. Her heady thoughts were of the festival of only days before and the warmth of her lover's arms.

Now she caressed her naked belly beneath the temporary covering afforded by a yard of old sail cloth, before she bolted upright, remembering Banoldino and that, as the only other survivor, he must have seen her nakedness as he made her a bed by the fire.

Looking all about her, she could see only the immediate area that was lit up by the fire and other than that, a covering of thick bushes and trees black against the night sky.

He was nowhere to be seen but her clothes had been hung over some twigs arranged on the opposite side of the fire, and she could see an awry shape sizzling inches above the flames and smelling of delicious roasting meat.

Calming, she mused at the fact that she really had survived and was now in the hands of a stranger who had indeed proven to be heaven sent!

She settled again and drew her knees up under her chin. She wallowed in the warmth for some moments and sent her thanks to the Virgin Mary.

Within minutes she heard rustling away to her right and he appeared, naked to the waist, a heavy gold chain and cross swinging from his muscular neck, and cupping a bowl of sorts, between his hands, he flashed her a smile before handing over a large leathery leaf, cupped to contain fresh water. She poured some into her throat, which she would have noticed was cracking like old parchment had she been obliged to try to speak. With the fresh water inside her, she could whisper her thanks as he retired to the other side of the fire.

He sat astride a log and tested the meat with the dagger that had hours before saved her from drowning. Now he pulled off a large smoking slice, from the spit, which he offered her on the point of the knife.

She took it gratefully, placing it down on a rock at her feet whilst she swilled her mouth and throat again with the clean water. Finally she reached for the meat and ate ferociously until grease dribbled down her chin as she chewed and swallowed to the accompaniment of approving groans of pleasure.

'Senorita! Please, slowly! We have time – lots of time!'

'I beg your pardon, but for most of the last day I thought I would never eat meat again! Please forgive my bad manners!'

He laughed! 'No, Senorita! Please the lack of manners is all mine! Please allow me to get you some more!' He reached again over the spit and speared another large chunk of rabbit. She took it from him with more decorum this time but ate it down with equal enthusiasm.

Pulling the back of her hand across lips that she now realised were full and swollen, she lay back with one arm cradling her head against a large boulder.

'So, mister! What is it you intend to do with me now that you have dragged me back from the bottom of the Ocean? Am I to be sold as a slave?'

Laughing again, he replied mockingly 'Senorita, I have neither the means nor the desire to sweep you away again from your native land! Indeed it is I who is more the captive now! Perhaps even as we speak your villagers may be armed and raking the countryside for me!'

'For Jesus sake!' She sobbed 'How can you believe that, when you left hardly a soul standing? The only people not with their heads split open I think were the elders and bare-arsed babies!'

He left her to cry out her anguish, but spoke again after a few moments. 'Senorita, I am at your disposal! I regret every moment, every injury, I can only beg you to find some forgiveness! I am deeply ashamed of having been a party to such barbarism, but I did what I could to curb their evil actions that morning! I deflected some of their sword strokes and directed some of them to more profitable actions, curbing the blood lust in doing so! I had not anticipated such savagery!'

He stared into the fire! 'Had I known their intent I would not have sailed with them! It was a foolish gamble, born out of boredom and idleness which has overwhelmed me for several years since my father died! In an attempt at putting some meaning back in my life I joined up with Ahmed Al Khan on the promise of a search for treasure! I had not realised until too late that the treasure was to be of the human kind!'

He looked toward her seeking her eyes, but he found only her beautiful face glowing lustrously in the light of the fire, and her hooded eyes and their long lashes as she once more plunged into sleep!

Chapter 7

Daemon's Journey

Daemon leapt from the cart leaving the old woman, Maura Figgerty, slumped over the reins as the old nag caught its balance and hunched its shoulders against the hillside.

Her family devastated, her granddaughter taken and her son and his wife dead, she had almost lost the will to go on. Daemon had tried to comfort her and she responded intermittently, but he felt his own deep anguish gave a hollowness to his words, that he could not fully cover up. 'Son! Wait, here! My boy will never wear this again God rest his soul!' She threw a long coat in his direction, which he caught before it could hit the dusty road.

'Here, missus, I can't take this, you might need it, you could even get a few bob for it!'

'Ahh away with yea, I'll not get much for an old coat, by the time I get to market, the nag will have chewed it tae pieces! Yea take it, I hope it brings you great fortune!'

At first Daemon did not exactly count his blessings. The coat was heavy and he could not quite make out its shape! 'Aye, well, I'll cherish it, and think of you every time I wear it.'

At that moment he thought to toss it into the bushes, he hesitated, holding it out in front of him. He realised it was a waxen jacket, with cloak attachment. Once turned the correct way up it hung very well in wide pleats. With a shrug Daemon pulled it around his shoulders and slipped his arms through the wide apertures before pulling a toggle fixing into place. It was lined with a fleecy materials and gave him instantly a feeling of warmth, well-being and importance!

'That'll do me nicely'!' He mouthed to himself! He felt quite the gentlemen when he strode off down the lane!

Turning left at the crossroads, he took the Wexford road as the trail of carts and weary refugees turned toward Killarney.

He expected to reach the coast within a few days and from there, perhaps he might find passage to England or France. Either would do! Maybe he'd even get started in pursuit of his beloved Kirsten. The image would not leave him, of her rolling beneath him in the long grass, her whisperings of encouragement in his ears, her writhing softness...!

He shook his head for momentary release from the pain. The thoughts that raced through his mind now, of her tethered to a mast and a brutish captor tearing at her clothing, he could bear no longer.

Unconsciously he gripped the handle of his sword until his clenched fingers began to ache. Opening and closing he made the mental note to work hard on his sword skills and seek a master who might fine-tune his own powerful, though palpably unsophisticated, style.

The day wore on as he walked, his thoughts were of his own family, away up north in Donegal where he had left his mother and Tam, his elder brother, some weeks before.

With Tam in charge of the croft and married now, his mother needy, since his father died, had been given new purpose with Tam's first born. With times hard and not really enough food on the table for four, there had seemed nothing for him in the little fishing port as, restless and unfulfilled he decided on taking a trip south.

Many years before his mother's brother, Sean, had taken two boats out to sea and lost both in a storm. Rescued by a passing vessel from Kinsale he was so thankful to the crew who saved and befriended him, that he pledged his future to their cause.

A skipper, short of a full crew, the three became four and he made his way south with them. Twelve months passed before word came that he had settled in a village known as Baltimore, married to the sister of one of his new shipmates.

Almost fifteen years later it became a loose thread of an idea that Daemon might seek out his uncle and spend some time in his adopted domain.

Leaving his mother had not been easy so soon after the passing of their father. But he kissed her fiercely, took the offer of a rusty old sabre from Tam, with a handshake, and with a hop he was over the dry stone wall and away.

As soon as he was on the road feeling his first taste of independence he felt exhilarated and excited at the prospect of new lands and new acquaintances. In a series of brief encounters with a variety of farmsteads, he cut through the centre of the Irish countryside in a matter of weeks.

The final few miles from Kinsale, along the coast toward Baltimore, had been mercifully uneventful, until he encountered three lusty young lads, returning from a day's hunting in the forest. They joined the road some half mile ahead of him and although his instincts told him to be wary, he had no hesitation in stepping up his own pace, that he might pull alongside and engage them in a little banter to pass the time.

As he neared them he could see that a small deer had been straddled between two of them, tied to a pared branch. The other led their jaunty march a few paces ahead. There was a spring in their step that made it difficult for Daemon to catch up.

Eventually tiring he called out but their reaction was not what he expected. As, half turning, the leader shouted an expletive toward his comrades and they dropped the deer and fled off down the path. The more he shouted to hold them back, the more desperate their flight became.

It dawned on him after a moment or so, that they must have been hunting the local landlord's deer, against the law, and he felt a terrible guilt come over him as they left their prize lying in the road.

He could see nothing else to do but pick up the deer and haul it at least to the next village to try and establish contact with the lads again. With the deer across his shoulders he set off at a steady ambling pace, amused as he considered the position in which he found himself.

Some half a mile or so further on his heart sank as he heard the thunderous hooves of what must be half a battalion of soldiers behind him on the road. Looking from side to side he could see nothing but high hedging and thick bushes barring his way from any reasonable cover. He could see no other option than to turn, hold up his hands and beg for mercy.

Two riders, one on a grey and the other a seventeen hand stallion gained on him in a matter of seconds. 'Caught! Red handed! A haughty English accent accused him!'

'Sir!' he replied swallowing hard, 'I have found a deer lying in the road, and thought nothing more of it than to return it to its rightful owner!'

'And whom indeed do you imagine to be the rightful owner?'

'Well as I am finding my way west to a little town, I was hoping that the rightful owner would emerge when I get there!'

'Impudent dog!' said the first. But the other put his hand out restraining him from what could only have been a motion toward running down the youth with his mount.

'Wait, Tar – his accent is indeed strange – perhaps he tells the truth and he did in fact find the beast in the road! Where are you from boy?'

'I, er well Y'r Lordship, I'm from the north!' Daemon responded. 'I'm visiting my distant cousins in… the south!' He thought better of mentioning exactly whom his kin folk were or where they came from, as he began to appreciate the extent of his dilemma.

The first, noticeably younger of the two did this time, alight his grey mare and stepped up to within a few inches of Daemon. 'I suggest you put down My Lord's deer immediately and hand over your weapons before you get yourself in real trouble!'

Standing the same height as his affronter Daemon, heaved a heavy sigh. Considering his options he slowly unwrapped the deer from around his shoulders before suddenly thrusting it toward the other.

Whilst the young man wrestled with the animal in an effort to keep its blood soaked flanks from making contact with his long riding coat, Daemon pulled his sword and offered it up to the others throat. The older, sitting astride his bay had been unable to move against Daemon on the narrow path where Daemon made sure that he kept his young opponent between himself and his companion.

Dropping the animal, the gentleman's son, realised his vulnerability and raised his arms above his head.

His Lordship spoke. 'Careful, sir! You do not know what you are about! Whilst I admire your spirit I must say any further action would be foolhardy! I am Lord Caister, the deer was bred on my estate. You are holding at the point of your sword the son of my estate manager and... well hot headed as he is, I would hate to have to return to his mother with an explanation that he had become skewered on the end of a peasant's sword, in pursuit of a half-grown deer!'

'Now, sir, I mean … Your Lordship… I beg your pardon, and I get the feeling you might be a reasonable man, but I say again that I found this here animal on the road and so far, I believe myself to be innocent of any crime!'

'Look here, put up your sword and I promise I will consider your statement truthful, and there will be no more said of it!'

'May I take it that the young gentleman here will abide your decision and allow me to go on my way?'

'You may indeed!'

Daemon ceremoniously sheathed his old, rusting sword and took two healthy strides away from the younger. With a flourish something akin to a salute, Daemon turned and made increasingly swift strides away from the pair, on down the road toward the west.

Collecting his tricorn hat from the dust where it had come to rest Tarquin Rickards growled a pledge of revenge that although Daemon did not exactly hear the words used, they left him in no doubt that he had made an enemy.

Restrained as much by the failing light as by his master's admonishment, Rickards wrapped the deer in a light blanket from his saddlebag, and laid it across the neck of his mount. 'At least Your Lordship has no decision to make as to what joint of meat will appear on the table these coming few days!' Turning their mounts they trotted away in the opposite direction to that which Daemon had taken.

It was no more than a moment that they had disappeared from view that Daemon was brought down heavily to the side of the road, ending in a ditch with a well-built youth sat astride him.

Two others held an arm each as they glowered down at him!

'So!' the first said. 'Yae plainly give up our prize to their Lordships right in front of our very eyes!'

'Ay!' said the next 'Took all mornin' for us to catch, and two minutes for yae ta give up!'

'What... er... exactly would you have had me do?! I called after ye's but ye ran off –from me – an' me on me own – on foot! At least I was run down by two fine soldiers on the biggest beasts ye ever did see!'

'We saw everythin'... you just gave up our supper! In fact we was goin' tae feed the entire village with that wee' animal! There's tae be a feast on the morrow! Now we'll have tae eat ye instead!'

With a hefty shrug Daemon unseated his attacker and toppled him head over heels into the ditch. Caught by surprise the other two were knocked sideways momentarily and he was able to scramble free!

'Now I don't think anyone will be eatin' anyone else... not tomorrow for the feast – or for the day after that!' Once more the old sword was noisily unsheathed and he held the larger of them at bay with its point!

'So – ye be bit handy with the ould sabre are ye? We saw it all – we was watchin' from the bank as you held the master's boy at point! Ha ha! We almost laughed out loud an' give ourselfs away! It was about time someone took that one down a peg!' He started to laugh and in no time the three of them were guffawing so much that Daemon had little option but to sheath the sword yet again, and join them in laughter.

'We're headed for Baltimore!' said the first. 'Come with us and get some supper!'

'I was hopin' for more than supper!' answered Daemon 'As a matter of fact I was hopin' to stay for a while! I'll be seeking my uncle... Sean... from Donegal! Do any of yous know of him?'

'Be Jeezes... I'll only be y'r cousin... if my Da' really is your uncle, then you'll be his sister Noula's lad from the north! Be Jeez... would ye b'lieve that... me own cousin with his sword at the throat of the ould Lordship's man! Ha! Would ye b'lieve it?'

With some sense of pride the lad took Daemon's arm and led him off down the path with the other two trying to edge alongside where the width of the road allowed. It was in this formation that they entered the village and introductions were made.

Uncle Sean and his wife made Daemon more than welcome and during the next few days a camaraderie was established between the lads. Roddy introduced his three sisters whom each in turn took to swinging on Daemon's neck.

Preparations were well under way for the Whitsun feasting and despite the lack of a deer to roast, they made ready with great enthusiasm.

The day held such an array of pleasures that the lads in particular had scarcely time to catch their breath. An old bladder, much patched from previous abuse, was produced and two 'sides' ran themselves to a standstill booting the thing from one to the other and eventually between two sticks. After ale and steaming pastries, they were off again throwing bales of hay over a strung out line.

They took to bowling down skittles in the afternoon but the girls joined in boisterously and showed the lads a thing or two.

The feasting started and refreshed in the stream, Daemon joined the other lads around the campfire.

***

Now very much alone and walking at a pace down a rutted path, he forcibly pushed the memory to the back of his mind. Quickening his pace he decided 'the sooner I get to the coast, the sooner I can start searching for her…!'

Dusk began to fall when he next took in the landscape, considering his progress. The road ahead was lined by forest and nothing of any advantage could be seen until suddenly in the distance a wisp of smoke gave him a target.

Breaking into a trot for some minutes brought him around a bend in the road where a warm and well-lit Inn roared a welcome.

Almost skipping the last few yards toward the door he straightened up his attire before pushing on into the lounge.

Daemon standing just over six feet tall, his fair hair roughly brushed back, even eyebrows and square jaw set on a well-muscled neck and square shoulders, should have brought at least a few glances in his direction. The dimple in the centre of his recently shaven chin, should have aroused a modicum of interest, if all else failed his dashing new coat, surely would turn a head or two!

Alas, not so much as a hair turned at his arrival, and for the ensuing five full minutes, no attention was afforded him. Standing in the centre of the room, he dodged about allowing comely waitresses to pass on either side, but failed to grab as much as a courtesy!

Hungry diners and those merely pursuing the pleasure of a few ales were noisily, merrily contemptuous of the new arrival!

Deciding on a course of action he pulled at the arm of a girl about to deliver two large platters to a table of mixed company. Her unintentional reaction to the tug on her arm spilled the contents of one of the trays into the lap of another diner!

Not exactly pleased at the sensation of warm soup penetrating the area around his private parts, he leapt from his seat and began angrily berating the innocent girl!

'You stupid, brainless slut, what the hell do you think you are doing! Have you seen what you did!' He stood, legs apart pointing toward his groin! A grey, slushy mess was dripping from him onto the timber boarding.

Raising his hand he considered swiping her across the face, but the entire room hushed and awaited the outcome! 'Damn and blast you, girl, I ought to…!'

'Please, sir, no… I… my Lord, please… ' Her hands went to her face and she broke down! She started wiping and scraping away at the mess down the front of his pants, with her apron, but he held her at bay, almost pushing her to the floor.

Daemon had witnessed enough and could remain silent no longer! 'Er, pardon, Your Lordship, apologies, if I may! The girl is innocent, and… ' Having bowed his head for the irate gentleman, Daemon's eyes now raised sufficiently to look into his face!

'Ahhhh! Your Lordship... it seems we meet again!'

'Well, well! If it isn't our friend the poacher... and this time no-one to protect him....!'

Staring back at him was no other than Tarquin Rickard, of Lord Caisters estate!

Drawing his sword, slowly with all attention directly focused on Daemon's eyes, he spoke again!

'Captain Rodney, this is the vagrant I was telling you about, only a few days ago I caught him stealing His Lordship's livestock! Only that time I was restrained from extending him the beating he deserved! Now? Well the moment has arrived! By pure chance he stands before me!'

Daemon immediately threw his hands up in the air! 'Now, sir, Mr Tarquin, was it? Surely we can let bygones be bygones, I never meant any harm then, and I meant no harm just now! It was an accident, completely, not the girl's fault, if anyone's, perhaps, it was mine, but not intentionally to...!'

'Eee'nough! You, sir, you owe me, and I will have retribution!'

'Now, sir, er Your Lordship, let's not be too hasty... I am not prep...!'

'Outside! You lily-livered coward, outside!'

Daemon shook his head, and downcast, turned toward the door, looking longingly at the contents of a recently delivered platter, he considered swiping a leg of chicken from it and racing off into the woods, but reconciled that his stomach would have to await the outcome of the next encounter.

Outside the Inn, Tarquin swung his rapier, back and forth causing the air to emit a swishing sound. Daemon was not entirely thrilled at the achievement.

Drawing his own sabre from its scabbard, he reluctantly stood guard and awaited his fate.

He knew nothing of the blow to the back of his head, administered by a shillelagh, attached to the arm of one of Tarquin's companions!

In fact he knew nothing at all for some hours before awaking, blindfolded and tied, on the floor of a rocking, noisy coach, being drawn with some distinction by at least four sturdy mounts.

The rolling and bucking, which had caused him intense pain and discomfort, finally stopped. His companions opened the door to the carriage and, slipping down on to the cobbles, were chatting merrily as they walked away into the distance.

Left alone, Daemon righted himself and eased some of the pain by flexing his ankles and wrists.

He considered every possible option then settled upon biding his time before extending himself further.

The glow from burning braziers along the edge of the harbour flickered light upon the inner walls of the carriage.

Daemon twisted until he could see through a gap between the sagging carriage door and its post. Pushing his eye right up to the crack he could make out in the distance Tarquin and his colleague engaged in conversation with another officer and port official.

The conversation was raucous as the group enjoyed a light banter.

Suddenly Tarquin stood erect and offered a salute, and turning he marched swiftly toward the carriage.

In the distance a sailing ship stood at anchor, gently bobbing on the returning tide. The smell of the sea was everywhere and a fresh breeze permeated through the gaps into the carriage.

Daemon filled his lungs and sank back into position, prone, on the floor of the carriage.

Tarquin threw open the door and noisily roused him. Daemon played along as though being awoken from his unconscious state.

He allowed himself to be guided toward the pier, where a boat knocked against the harbour wall. Again allowing himself to be lead, Daemon was soon sitting upright to the rear of a dinghy whilst two sailors rowed the party toward the ship.

Tarquin pushed Daemon ahead of him. Once comfortably astance on the deck, with polite introduction to the bosun and his mate, Tarquin welcomed him to his Majesty's warship. '*Warrior*. Your new home!'

Tarquin concluded by pushing him roughly into the first mate's arms and turning his back he strode away toward the galley steps.

Daemon smiled inwardly, realising he had been pressed into service aboard a ship in the English Navy, he mused that things could not have worked out better.

Chapter 8

Somewhere Along the Coast

Kirsten was running up Cree Hill, Tommy Mahon chasing after her. Tall for her age, athletic, almost boyish, she easily kept him at bay.

There were butterflies in season and dozens flickered away against the lush green swathe.

Kirsten knew Tommy would never catch her, unless of course she wanted him to!

She started to giggle for no particular reason, but the more she giggled the more she slowed and Tommy was, after all, very determined.

Collapsing in an untidy heap she was suddenly pinned down and Tommy's head came threateningly down toward her, blocking out the bright sunlit sky.

She felt his breath on her face and his lips brush against hers but with a jolt she flung him off and sat up sharply.

Wiping her hand across her face she blurted 'Tommy Mahon, you're disgutin', eeuccch! Don't you do that again!'

Tommy was by now writhing on his back, his dirty knees over his head and his bare feet rotating, it was his turn to giggle uncontrollably!

'Whyn't yae let me kiss yea? You let Joey Carney!'

'Didn't, I never let that eejit come near me! D'yae think I'd have Joey Carney even in the same field, he smells of... well somethin' like the cows in our shed!

'Well Joey told me yae kissed 'im, twice, an' he had his hand on yea…!

'Don't you dare Tommy Mahon… if you dare say another…!' Kirsten rose and pinned Tommy to the ground. He tried to buck her off but her dead weight was too much for him.

Taking a handful of grass she forced it into his mouth and as he squirmed and retched, spitting out the contents, he finally dislodged her!

They both sat up as Kirsten giggled again, at his discomfort!

'I wouldn't do that to you…' Tommy muttered almost to himself.

'What are you on about?'

'Well I wouldn't… I…' suddenly Tommy was on his feet. 'Come on, race yae to the church!' But Kirsten didn't take his challenge for once and lay back on the grass.

***

She slept soundly until she heard a buzzing around her ears. Sitting sharply up, she realised how stiff the cold, hard ground had made her. Pulling the sail cloth tightly to her chin she peered over to the smouldering, ineffectual fire, and beyond to where her new companion lay in a deep sleep.

She watched him for several moments, considering her options but not failing to notice his rugged, leather brown features and his lustrous black mane, which had been released from its bandanna.

She considered her options carefully. She could run! Immediately! No shoes, or clothing, but a square of cloth to cover her. She might get some distance before he roused. She could grab her own clothes, try to dress and still get away whilst he slept. She could waken him now and talk him into letting her go free. Or, she could wait and remain his captive and see what fate had in store for her.

She remembered again the screams and the death rattles in her friends' throats, she thought of them disappearing into the waves. Her spirits sagged. Despair enveloped her. She let out an audible groan from her dry throat and he woke, easily, without alarm.

He raised on one arm and looked toward her. 'Did you speak? Forgive me, Senorita, I momentarily dropped off and deserted my watch! I am glad to see that no harm has befallen you!' She could not manage a reply but 'half' smiled acknowledgement as it occurred to her that he may indeed have sat watch over her during the night.

She felt some gratitude and comfort in the certainty that he must have, at some time in his history, been a gentleman. Standing and shaking away the dust from his britches, he pulled his white linen shirt from a branch overhead and in easy movements pulled it into position and pushed the tails into his waistband.

Reaching down he lifted the dagger into position and also made it comfortable at his waist.

'Senorita! With your permission, I think we should try to find a place where I may leave you safe. Perhaps we could find our way back to your village before nightfall. Either way, I hope to find some nourishment for both of us within a short time! Are you fit enough to walk?' He made toward her with arms outstretched in a gesture which suggested he might lift her and carry her through the forest!

Immediately conscious of her state of undress, she raised an arm to shoo him away. Standing behind a bush she grappled with her clothing. He mercifully turned his back to her whilst she struggled, again, confirming to her that he was no barbarian. When he was finally ready to depart she found him rubbing animal fat into the soft black leather of his boots.

Catching her eye, with a shrug he offered an explanation 'Senorita – apart from my dagger, and this chain,' he touched his throat, 'these boots remain my only possession on God's earth! I think it only right I try to preserve them!' With a faint laugh he was on his feet again.

She smiled at him again in gratitude, and he understood without seeking to gain from her situation. Leading the way he made upward away from their encampment in a direction opposite the rising sun which was just beginning to slant through the thickly arranged trees.

For some miles he led the way through forest and across open moorland. He perforated the journey with light conversation asking frequently of her well-being and ability to continue.

They had two occasions to stop and take water from a stream, but saw no sign of life other than circling gulls. Kirsten found that her limbs were still shaky from the exertions of the previous days drama. All too quickly she became tired but resisted telling the Spaniard. She did not want to risk being abandoned.

At last a farm house came into view and they plunged on down the last few hundred yards before coming to a halt at the open rear door.

He allowed her to approach in the knowledge that the native tongue she would use would put the occupants at ease.

A moment or two passed before a wizened old woman emerged from the shadows of the doorway, she looked hesitant at first, eyeing Kirsten's companion with great suspicion. She had never before seen a man with virtually black skin and, well so rugged looking, clearly not a man of these parts.

Turning to Kirsten she said in a dry squeak, 'How now pretty one! What can I be doin' fer yea?'

Kirsten bit her lip, 'I ...we've been near drowned, when the boat went down...! Yesterday...!'

'Heaven above girlie... There was a bit of a storm right enough! But the boats come back alright... I've not heard of anyone missin'!'

'It was terrible so it was... the ship turned over, an'...!'
Her voice tailed off, partly to strangle a sob, but also to give
herself time to think. What explanation would she give?
Should she reveal her companion's part in the whole saga?

'I'm sorry but we lost some of our friends... this
gentleman saved me... dove right into the depths of the sea
and... well dragged me out. We were afloat on a piece of
wood for hours 'n hours!'

'I'm sure the magistrate would like to hear yae story!
Who's boat was it... was it from these parts?' Responded the
old one.

'Baltimore Bay!'

'Baltimora? ...t'be sure...I never heard of it?'

'Where is this? Where have we come ashore?'

'Why Slea Head o' course! Dingle Bay!'

'Oh God!' Was all Kirsten could manage as her hand
went to her mouth! She knew Dingle Bay to be miles from
home! No-one from these parts could possibly know of her
plight!

Suddenly Banoldino stepped forward, secure in the
knowledge that at least here he was not a 'wanted' man!

Taking Kirsten by the shoulder, he pulled her away.
'Senorita, you may be far from home but at least I may still
help you! Were we indeed near Bal..ti..mora, I would be
hunted down!'

'Baltimore!' sobbed Kirsten. 'At least learn the name of
the place yea destroyed!'

The old one leaned closer to catch what they were saying
but did not manage a clear understanding. 'Bring her in...
I've some stew that will go a long way! The poor girl looks
out on her feet!'

Kirsten half turned but her legs gave way and Banoldino
had to catch her up in his arms to prevent her falling to the
cobbled pathway. Laying her in a rocking chair in front of the
fire he turned to witness the old one stirring a cauldron with a
long-handled ladle!

As she stirred she began to mutter. 'I see... wait, no ... it's... a strange vessel! Not a fishing boat! It bucks and breaks on the waves! It founders and all aboard are thrown into the sea! I see ropes and... shackles? And...!'

Banoldino was at her side 'Shhh old one... you see too much!' He raised his hand to his throat and with one finger traced a slit from ear to ear. The old one looked at him knowingly and half smiled!

She turned back to her steaming cauldron and brought up a ladle full of stew. Depositing it onto a large, oval plate, she set it down in front of Kirsten. Dry and without having broken her fast, Kirsten took up the plate and fed herself in quiet solitude for several minutes.

Banoldino also took a plate from the old one and pulled on the fleshy parts of the stew with his fingers before drinking the liquid down straight from the plate.

'It seems we were blown well off course before we floundered. Can you tell us which direction we are to take in order to reach 'Baltim... *more*'?' he asked.

'Well I can only advise that you head across the mount until yea reach St Pat's Church! Speak with the heathen 'brethren' there and one of them will help you find the way back to whence yea came!'

'St Pat's? A church? Will we be able to find it? Across the mount you say?

'Aye... yea can't miss it if yea press on with the settin' sun at yea back! Yea should be there before nightfall!'

Within minutes they were only tiny dots on the horizon leaving the old woman with her face set in a twisted smile.

After two or three hours of steady climbing a plateau stretched out before them when suddenly Banoldino doubled in pain clutching his abdomen. He keeled over and gasped a long low groan. Then turning on his back he gazed up at the clear blue sky and jerked once, violently, before becoming rigidly still and letting out a hiss through clenched teeth.

Kirsten immediately dropped beside him and held his head in her arms. 'Sir... please... sir... are you...?' She felt his brow and it was slick with sweat. His face pallid and waxen yellow. She thought him dead and put her ear to his mouth for confirmation. She held her own breath and listened for his breathing.

Nothing happened for a long, long moment but just as she was about to pull her head away she heard a crackling from deep in his throat. 'Death rattle,' she thought. 'Surely it is his dying breath!' But as she waited and watched for many minutes she heard it again.

She knew he was alive and in desperate trouble but she felt completely helpless, holding him there with nothing to administer to him.

She could think of nothing that could be done to help him except to sit and await his inevitable demise.

With darkness settling all around, new fear racked her and she sobbed again at the hopelessness of the situation. The noise of her sobbing drowned out the rustling and scraping of the approaching sandals over nearby rock. She gasped, startled as she felt a hand on her shoulder. Her eyes swung upward where she could still make out in the faint light the shape of a monk, his hood in waves around his shoulders and a large crucifix dangling from the rope around his waist, she let him reach down to Banoldino.

'Your companion is very ill!' he confirmed. 'Do you know what ails him?'

She shook her head quickly. 'Allow me.' He released her and laid Banoldino down putting a rock under his head before offering fresh water from a leather bottle to his lips. She heard the groan as Banoldino sucked in clean water. His hand reached up for more but fell back limply after a moment.

'Can you think of anything that could have brought him down like this?' Kirsten continued to shake her head, but said 'He was well this morning and we walked many miles unhindered! We stopped at a fisherman's cottage where the old lady gave us some stew…!'

'An old lady you say, from across the valley – is it from Dingle Bay you have come?'

'Yes! She was kind and gave us direction after we rested…!'

'Quick – not a moment to lose… take this and make sure he drinks plenty!'

In seconds he disappeared into the forest. She heard him set about his task, twigs cracking and bushes rustling, but then for some moments there was silence. He burst back into the clearing and ran toward them. He held some leaves in his hands and a mound of paste had been contained in them. Moving with the skill of a physician the monk laid the paste onto Banoldino's tongue and forced his digestive system to take in a good quantity over a period of several minutes.

Exhausted he sat back and watched. Kirsten was fearful for Banoldino but at the same time fascinated at the monk's actions, stayed quiet but vigilant by his side for some time.

Eventually, stiff and cold, she asked the Monk what had happened.

'Poison!' he replied bitterly. 'The old one is a witch…! Woe betide any to whom she takes a dislike! The amazing thing is that she poisoned your partner but left you completely untouched! Can you imagine her motives?'

Kirsten was stunned and could only shake her head in disbelief. Tracing the hours since their arrival at the cottage, she found it hard to accept that the old one had been responsible!

Suddenly the quiet was broken by Banoldino jerking upright and violently vomiting the substantial contents of his stomach onto the ground. The effort obviously draining him, he then stumbled to a position of kneeling forward resting on his two hands, whilst he continued to retch up the poison. He eventually looked up sheepishly at his companions, seeing the water holder he reached out a hand without a word, took the water and drained the contents.

Groaning several times, he sat back on his haunches and, half smiling, gripped his stomach gingerly.

'Oh Lord, I appear to have made something of a mess! Alas, I do not recall either the amount or the quality of the drink that almost drowned me, but I can only hope I was not a bore in the consumption of it!'

Kirsten unhurriedly explained what she could though she remained incredulous at her own story. After some moments Banoldino felt strong enough to gain his own feet and with a little help from the monk on one arm and Kirsten on the other, he was able to cover some distance.

Within half an hour they had arrived at the old Abbey and were shown some bare rooms where each found the comfort of a cot with blankets and dropped into real restful sleep for the first time in several days.

Chapter 9

Return to Baltimore

After two more days at rest, the generosity of the inhabitants of the monastery and improvement in her health, Kirsten suddenly announced that she wanted to return to her origins, to Baltimore. The friar offered to accompany them on their onward journey.

Arranging some basic necessities across the back of an old mule, and making what preparations they could, they set off for a two or three day trek across the moor. Kirsten's mood for the first day or so maintained but as they drew nearer, and finally reached the outskirts of the village, the true horror of all that had taken place overwhelmed her.

She walked determinedly ahead of them in the direction of the church. Intent on searching she passed from headstone to headstone, pausing fleetingly to glance at the names.

Her watchful companions feared for her. Then she turned away and broke into a run upon seeing something against the darkening tree-line.

As the Spaniard and the friar followed in her direction, they saw her as she came upon the makeshift cemetery and knelt, draping her arms about a wooden stake. They knew she had found her mother and father's grave and felt the horror as all her hopes were crushed.

***

Banoldino watched, her shape in silhouette against the fire. Her head covered in a shawl and stooping, there had been no movement for more than an hour.

He knew that she was going through pain. He knew there were no words to console her! Both he and Friar Benedict had made some attempt earlier that evening, before the fire was set and their decision to stay had been finally agreed. But nothing seemed to get through and her sad face told them all that was needed for them to retreat and leave her with her thoughts.

Now, finally she moved. She stood, turning she looked in his direction and again her expression was enough. Her tiredness palpable, her eyes despairing, her shoulders slumped. He reached for her hand, which was limp at her side and led her from the rock she had used, away a few steps, to a place he had laid a blanket against a mound of straw. He let her find her own position and simply covered her, letting her drift into a sleep of low, almost inaudible breathing.

As the fire dimmed, he caught a look from the friar which seemed to reassure him, that perhaps she, was about to begin her recovery.

Still, keeping a watchful eye, until sleep eventually overcame even the Spaniard, he settled down a few yards from her.

He awoke, some hours later, a scream of frightening volume penetrated the dark curtain over his mind and brought him upright. In the dim glow from the dying embers of the fire, he could see Kirsten had risen and was standing, pulling at her clothing and calling out in delirium!

Friar Benedict was first to reach her, with strong, protective arms, he managed to hold her when she looked ready to bolt into the forest. Banoldino took a position in front of her, so that Benedict could ease his grip as her struggle for freedom quelled, and he attempted to bring her to her senses with soothing words.

For many minutes they restrained her as she sobbed and moaned, before he eventually drew a long piercing look from her unnaturally fixated eyes. As though failing to recognise him, she simply looked at him with her mouth twisted as if in disgust.

Then, almost in one movement, she folded into a heap on the ground and clawed at his knees as if praying to a mighty idol. She was there, back in the village, there was carnage all around her, she was straining against her captors strong shackles. She fought her demons until, exhausted, she could do no more than curl into a foetal position and lay still.

Again bringing a blanket, but this time, holding her head on his knees, he soothed her until merciful sleep returned!

When morning broke, she raised herself on one arm, and gave him a faint smile. She was grateful for a jug of fresh water produced by the Franciscan, and politely acknowledged him. They knew she was over the worst, and though, her eyes still told of the terrors of the night that had passed, she was at least comfortable in her surroundings.

Her companions knew what she had suffered, they knew well the horrors that had flashed through her conscious and unconscious thoughts and that only time and tender nurturing would restore her to herself.

'Mistress, is it your wish to stay here? To try to salvage something of life in this village?' Asked the friar when he felt the moment had come.

She looked up, puzzled at first, as though such a thought had not entered her head before. 'Why, … I suppose, there's nothing here, nothing at all… I just don't know where to go! Where do you think they are? Where is everyone?'

Banoldino rose from his squatting position near the fire and paced off into the distance, as if to search the horizon for some sign of life. He somehow knew her eyes would follow him. He felt that in doing so he might urge her to conclude that nothing was left of the community.

'I might suggest, perhaps you could walk to the next village, maybe try to find one or two of your friends, perhaps try the next, until you find a place where you can stay for a little while?'

'But... I've never travelled before! I don't know what's over the next hillock, never mind go on... to God knows where...!

'I... er... we Franciscans, we travel. That is our 'destiny'! I could help or... it would appear that our friend, has set his heart on protecting you! I feel also, somehow, that you would be safe under his guidance, for the time.'

His sentence was cut short by her unexpected burst of hysterical laughter.

'Father, if only you knew... he... how can I explain. He was one of them! He destroyed Baltimore... it was him and his... black savages!

The friar looked around swiftly to establish that Banoldino would be unlikely to hear her outburst, and his hand went to his mouth impressing upon her to be quiet.

'Oh, don't worry. He saved my life. I don't think I am in danger now, but how can I just... how can I think of going along... tying myself to him... the horror of...!' She tailed off, tears again filling her eyes.

'Child, I know how your heart aches, and what you've been through but I would urge you to perhaps give this man a chance... a chance to redress some of the hurt he has inflicted... my instinct tells me he would do anything, even lay his life on the line, to save you from further harm!'

'Father, if only I could be so sure!'

'I am sure. In fact I would venture this. I will accompany you north as far as the monastery at Cashel. It is some seven or eight days from here. There is a fine community growing up around the castle and you may find it a place where you could meet friends and settle. If there is any reason, whatsoever, that I feel a change in my opinions about our Spanish companion, I will in an instant, find a way of distancing him from you. Of course, I can only guess that he will want to make the journey with us... it may be his first desire to return, by *any* means, to the seas from which he came...'

She looked up... surprised at first, but she had become used to the sort of 'insight' the friar had shown since their first encounter. She had certainly begun to trust his instincts above all. The thought that at least he would be with them for another week gave her some comfort.

Banoldino returned from his foraging, declaring that they should soon 'move-on' as this community had become a 'ghost town!' He immediately regretted his turn of phrase and busied himself with preparations, and with the mule, avoiding eye contact with his companions.

They progressed all morning north, inland and away from the desolation of the abandoned community. For some miles cart tracks and trodden grass, at least proved that some survivors had managed to assemble and make a co-ordinated retreat. Kirsten's hopes of meeting up with friends encouraged her spirits to rise with her appetite for the journey.

Banoldino proved ever attentive, and despite long periods of contemplative silence, the friar also proved to be an experienced and cheerful companion.

Brief encounters with strangers, passing information in fleeting, sometimes contradictory anecdotes, pieced together a picture of the flight of the Baltimore survivors and the probable points at which 'crossroads' were reached and which were taken.

It was clear that a concerted 'body' of refugees had held together and was pressing north. One or two names, Feaney and Finnegan, Hurley and Shields became more frequently repeated, so that a picture of some leadership perhaps, even a hierarchy had been established, and was heading with some purpose for the prominent Port townships. Queenstown or far north to Dublin, were assumed to be their objectives.

***

For the time being Cashel seemed to Kirsten, to be a long way from home. The thought of venturing further afield was out of her imaginings.

They were happy with the food they managed to catch or accept in charity, which seemed to be the god-given right of any travellers of the 'cloth, or with the 'cloth'.

Two days passed. Benedict and Banoldino between them had fashioned a passable 'habit' by cutting and stitching old blankets and gathered rope ends. It was deemed safer and eminently sensible, that the dark-skinned stranger be passed off as a 'brother' Franciscan, recently arrived from 'Italy', that he might *follow the footsteps of St Patrick,* and 'discover' the emerald green lands, which had been so captivating those many years before!

Banoldino acquired some typical affectations and was mildly amusing in role-play as a Franciscan friar. The charade providing many moments of light heartedness which eventually raised Kirsten's spirits.

It was with such ease and bonhomie that they reached Cashel just seven days after leaving the ruins of Baltimore, that found them in good heart and eager for a good rest even if only a barn could provide it.

Chapter 10

Inland to Cashel

The castle had until recently been a garrison town for English forces. Since William of Orange there had been a sort of peace established between the native Irish and their English overlords, but trouble was never far away and 'tolerance' was their only option. King George II was settling into his role, although pre-occupied with his European conflicts he was careful not to completely turn his back on Ireland.

Many Englishmen settled in Cashel and certainly there seemed to be no animosity at least on the surface, when 'strangers' appeared. Nonetheless, they were obliged to introduce themselves to the local magistrate who assumed responsibility for law and order when the military moved out.

They were anxious to complete this task and make the last two miles north to the monastery before nightfall. Benedict was certain they would find good clean accommodation, and the best 'table' in the county.

The monastery, although bereft of much of their collection of precious artefacts after James II rebellion was put down, and Protestants established rule over the island, but they still had all the capacity to lay on a sumptuous table with fine ales. These were the fruits of their labour and no change of 'policy' or doctrine, could take away their ability to work the fields and vineyards and harvest highest quality produce.

But all in good time.

Firstly they had to deal with the formalities in visiting the Magistrate and telling their version of the events in Baltimore that fateful Whitsun.

Major Bostwick, a landowner originally from Renfrewshire, had settled there some years before and helped the locals over a crop virus which for two years saw the potato harvest ruined and starvation threaten the surrounding countryside. Now rewarded and embellished with titles, he had become established and trusted as a leader in the community. His integrity and ability to achieve the best deals with the English Navy for local timber and produce, he had risen to eminence in the county.

He listened intently to Kirsten as she told the story as far she might without incriminating Banoldino, and the Magistrate's response was genuinely sympathetic.

Explaining that this was the first news of the fate of the Arab craft and the reality that many souls were lost for ever! The information up to that point had concluded with the ship's disappearance over the horizon, allegedly witnessed by ten or more of the survivors.

Bostwick advised them of that a number of other refugees had passed through the town. He was able to tell Kirsten that an 'elder', Missie O'Connor, had been taken on as a laundry worker by his wife.

'Despite being wearied by recent events, she had shown a deal of skill in her sewing, and was upright and still had her own teeth! Therefore promising good service for at least five years, whilst costing very little by way of food and other necessities, making a fair arrangement for both sides.'

Kirsten asked for permission to speak to the old lady and had the opportunity to spend ten minutes, mostly in sympathetic murmurings from one to the other. Missie told, however, of the young man who had accompanied her for several miles, 'most courteously' helping her at every turn. That he had 'set off at the crossroads, toward the south', but that she 'could not recall him saying where he was headed'.

Kirsten was at once both relieved and disappointed, that, it appeared, Daemon might have survived the attack, but there was little promise of their paths crossing.

She made her decision to continue with the group at least as far as the monastery and give further thoughts to pursuit when she became more acquainted with distances and the difficulties of undertaking such a journey and the unknown that lay ahead of her.

The Magistrate had enquired politely of the origins of their companion, and had appeared satisfied that here was a man of the cloth 'on a journey', travelling with Friar Benedict and the refugee, and that Horth Abbey was their destination.

The Magistrate offered some Porter and some bread and cheese and had them directed to the kitchens where they would rest before the final trek up to the Abbey.

Just as the party rose from their supper table, four armed guards arrived and discreetly requested that Banoldino followed them 'back' to where Major Bostwick would wish a further interview before their departure.

***

The three companions rose together intending to return to the waiting Magistrate.

However, one of the guards placed himself in between them. Forming a circle around Banoldino they were able to separate him from his two travelling companions!

Banoldino caught the friar's eye to indicate that he should offer no resistance. The friar immediately understood his meaning, leading Kirsten away before gently lowering her to her place on the bench.

She waited a moment until distance had been established between the guards and themselves. 'But what's happened?' She swung round to look into Benedict's eyes. 'Why have they taken him?'

Friar Benedict raised his finger to her mouth, intending to quiet her. 'I can't imagine what has happened to change the Major's mind, or why he should want our friend back for questioning. It's all I can think at the moment, that he must have had some misgivings about our 'story'!

'Unless of course, he mistakenly imagines *we,'* he quickly gestured toward Kirsten and himself with a determined forefinger, *'are his* captives, being 'forced' upon a journey against our will to cover up some 'plot'!'

'We must wait awhile to see if he is returned to us! If not, then we move on to the safety of the monastery for this evening and decide what we must do come the morrow.'

An hour passed and the evening descended into darkness. Also a cold wind blew in from the north, making them uncomfortable and stiff. 'I think we have to assume that Major Bostwick knows more about the attack on the village than first appeared. We have to move on! Come!'

Reluctantly Kirsten accepted his hand at her elbow enabling her to raise from her seat, and take the first tentative steps in the direction of the North Road! It was with some trepidation, having lost her genial companion, that she ventured forward, wrapped tightly in her shawl, astride the back of the old donkey.

Benedict did his best to shield her from the elements whilst determinedly forcing the pace to make a significant assault on the journey that was likely to take them the best part of two hours, in deteriorating conditions. The rain started to fall steadily until there were streams running in the cart tracks, and swilling about their feet as they forged toward the crest of the hill and onward to Horth.

***

Meanwhile, Banoldino could also feel the rain. He had been left in a small room, no better than a cell with a wooden cot and some straw. Toward the outside a 'window' opened out of the north side of the tower. But the window was just a hole, a large hole with no glass, and no bars. Beneath was a drop of some sixty feet, down the outside wall and the cliff face which formed its foundation.

For some moments he looked out toward the hilly outcrop to the north, the thick tree line at its base and the darkening skies. The rain slanted in and the temperature dropped making him pull his makeshift 'habit' with its rough woven hood, all about him. He reflected on his recent fate, of the sunken ship, his near fatal dose of poison and now, captivity! The walls of this castle, and the strength of its garrison could not frighten him in the least, but the recent hand of 'fate' troubled him greatly.

At the heart of it all was this 'girl', a peasant, no argument, but with something about her, something, at that moment, he could not articulate, but he felt that they had somehow been thrown together but that this was only the beginning. He could not shake her from his mind for long moments while the rain spattered on his forehead.

Turning, he lay down on the cot but a future, plausible and attainable, formed in his mind, which saw them together, hand in hand, in a life with opulence and style!

Fatigue eventually overcame him as thoughts of Kirsten, in a fine gown, leading a graceful dance across an impressive brightly decorated hall, eased him toward a deep, satisfying sleep.

***

In what seemed like moments he felt himself being dragged upright by rough hands. His head cleared very quickly of all thoughts of future as the reality of captivity returned.

'Come on my fine friend' a mocking voice was breathing heavily into his ear! 'You're wanted. In the Great Hall, they're waiting for you!'

Banoldino, shook the sleep from his head and rubbed his eyes until clear vision allowed him to take in his surroundings.

Despite the bright early morning sun colouring the far hills an unnaturally bright green, the dark red of the sky across to the right and the sharpness of all distant images on a soggy landscape foretold of heavy rain to come.

Offering no resistance he allowed the two guards to lead him through a myriad of low ceilinged passageways until he felt they had arrived on the lower level where the entrance to the Great Hall opened out in front of them. A huge stone fire surround, with a log burning merrily in the grate, created a cordial atmosphere, which eased his immediate anxiety.

Major Bostwick sat behind a large oak table and feasted on roasted fowl and biscuits, warm ale in a pewter goblet occupied one hand. Quickly wiping the back of his free hand across his mouth, he smiled and looked askance at the figure in front of him.

'Veo que usted es un largo camino desde su casa!' Ahh! I see you are surprised that I address you in your native tongue?

'Senor, yo estoy muy viagado!'

'I too am much travelled I have served in His Majesty's ships, therefore my experience of the Mediterranean and its peoples, has proven advantageous on occasion.

''Est de Cervantes Don Bosco de Cervantes!' Banoldino, answered in his native tongue, having decided against trying to play games with his captor.

'You are posing as a brother of the Franciscan Order, your manner and piety threw me for a while, but I suggest the retention of those fine Andalusian leather boots peeping from under your skirts, was something of a giveaway! Throw off that ridiculous robe and talk to me – what is it you are trying to achieve with this deception?'

Again Banoldino, affording due respect to this clearly experienced adversary, decided a wisp of truth may go down better than a hastily prepared lie. 'Why, my small boat foundered in a storm, and I was lucky to survive and make it to dry land. At the same time I found a lady in distress upon the shore and she told me her story. I did what I could to help her, and we were both comforted by Friar Benedict when we reached the Abbey at... how you say... Kilkenny The friar simply suggested my disguise as a member of the Franciscan Order may save a lot of explanation... such as this, Your Lordship!'

***

'I see... you favour me with an almost faithful account, for which I am grateful. However, there is the question of which vessel you were occupying when you ran aground. What would you be doing in those waters off the southern Irish coast, and what a coincidence lies in the coming together of yourself and the... er, young lady.'

'Mine was a small fishing vessel of course, your honour. We had been blown off course and my two companions were lost.'

'Er... yes well... blown off course, by perhaps five hundred miles? I find this a little disconcerting! Particularly in the knowledge that I believe I have before me a most experienced and capable seaman!'

Banoldino had run short of patience and verbal jousting, at this time he merely threw his hands in the air in an expansive gesture which translated would have expressed 'such is life'!

Mildly amused, Major Bostwick, smiled accordingly, but suddenly became businesslike! 'Sir, a peasant fisherman you are not, nor are you likely to have been blown so severely from your course. Indeed, I would suggest you are a privateer and that *you* were among those whom attacked the village of Baltimore, foundered, but somehow found it within you to save yourself, and a drowning captive, from the depths!

'Quite what your intention might be, and ultimately what I am to do with you I cannot quite decide. But the penalty for piracy in all civilised nations, is death! The penalty for enslaving is also death and I cannot simply leave you to roam the countryside until you have found a way to return to your chosen profession!'

Banoldino summoned his resistance once more. ' But your Honour, you have mistaken me, I helped a young lady in distress, I am determined to continue to help her until she finds her friends or a place to call 'home'!'

'What interest have you in this young peasant girl?'

'Why... merely, that she was destitute and alone, and she had lost everything! I could not just leave her in a desolate village with no means to survive!

'Has she been your captive?'

'Not at all, your Honour... I have simply guided her! In fact, when I fell ill myself some days ago, I was at her mercy!'

Bostwick returned with seemingly less appetite, to his breakfast, finishing off with a flourish, he wiped his hands on a 'napkin'. 'I believe you mean her no harm... now! But what of your original crime? How long have you been engaged in this heinous trade?'

Banoldino shrugged with again an exaggerated gesture! ' I have no profession, indeed I am not a slaver as you would have me. I found myself aboard a ship which I took to be a trader and expected nothing more than passage back to my homeland! But this turned into folly when the captain confided that he was bound for Britain and what his true intentions were, I confess I had no way of turning back!'

'I am obliged to consider your version of the truth, in the lack of witnesses or corroboration, I have the burden of judgement. I am returning you to your cell whilst I consider what to do with you! Meanwhile, I shall provide you with some sustenance!'

With a gesture the two guards reappeared and took Banoldino in hand. A third ran off in the direction of the kitchen and soon joined them in the cell where he presented a plentiful breakfast for Banoldino to chew upon, whilst in the Great Hall, the Magistrate chewed upon his fate.

***

About an hour passed before Bostwick was disturbed by his manservant. 'My Lord, there is a visitor from the Abbey, asking for an audience.'

'Bring him forth, I will see him.'

The Magistrate pulled his coiffured wig over a greying, wispy head of hair, and straightened himself in readiness.

Benedict stood before him. 'My Lord, I have been given permission to return by Abbot Stephen, to entreat with you to deal kindly with your prisoner. As your worship is aware, there have been many Spanish seamen washed up onto our shores. Many of them prove to be hardworking, Christian souls, and very rarely of trouble to the State. We... er the Abbot and I, we believe this man to be of good character. That he may prove himself if given the opportunity of your Lordship's merciful consideration!'

'I am well aware of the possibilities that such a man may prove himself, yet I have a responsibility to maintain peace and protection of this domain, and I am not at all certain that when the refugees of Baltimore discover him, that there will not be confrontation! Indeed, only the vigorous intervention of the old lady now in my wife's retinue, alerted me to the fact that our friend was not indeed a companion of the cloth! She was most agitated, having recognised your fellow traveller, that he should be brought to justice! I was also a little uneasy about the brightly shining booted footwear of your companion, I have come to expect more modest attire!' Glancing down at Benedict's well-worn sandals.

An expression of understanding spread cross Benedict's face.

The Magistrate continued, 'At which point I would impress upon your good self, I do not appreciate a deception of the kind you practised upon our first meeting. I am still not certain that, perhaps, you were under the duress of a dominant captor when you first came to my court!'

'I take leave to assure you, with my humble apology, we travelled under no duress! The girl was lost. Indeed when I found both on the road, they were in dire need of attention. Banoldino was on the verge of death! The girl recovered quickly when provided with some nourishment, but only some medication, administered with great care and diligence by herself, brought about his recovery.

'These are not the actions of people under duress! Indeed I have noticed in him, a great deal of determination that the girl comes to no harm, with your Lordship's benevolence, they should be allowed to continue upon their journey.'

'Indeed? Perhaps you are right, Friar Benedict. I will weigh all you have said and mine own instinct against the possibilities that this man is playing an evil game which could induce me to a grave, and propitious judgement!

'May I see the man? Please, Your Worship? I would like to let him know that... er... well that he is not 'alone'! That we have not 'abandoned him'!'

'I am of mind to consent to your request.' Bostwick half turned, troubled by these events but not completely determined to bring about a conclusion. I will grant you a short visit, but please, Friar Benedict, do not make any attempt to compromise my authority. It would be foolish, and unnecessary!'

The Magistrate raised his hand and a waiting guard signalled that Benedict should follow him toward the entrance. Within minutes they were outside the cell and the door was cranked open.

Banoldino rose from the straw pile he had arranged in the far corner. 'My friend,' he took Benedict's hand and shook it in both his own. 'How is Mistress Kirsten? Did she manage the journey well?' He showed his real concern for her welfare and was relieved to find that, although soaked and tired from their efforts, Kirsten had enjoyed a good night's sleep, but had showed no inclination to rest until he, Benedict, had undertaken to mount a mule, and return to Cashel to establish that nothing untoward had befallen her friend.

'I am glad to hear that she was concerned for me! I am also very relieved to hear she has suffered no ill fortune since we were parted. But I am greatly troubled that this man, His Lordship Bostwick, has a great sense of duty... that he may feel bound to deal with me 'by the law' rather than by even his own instinct. Did you speak with him?'

'Yes, I spoke at length, I am inclined to think he will apply common sense. But I know him not! Abbott Stephen also implied that there was not sufficient 'history' yet, in his rule, by which to pre-judge his actions. We simply cannot be certain!'

While Benedict spoke, Banoldino moved unnoticed behind the friar and with as much care and tenderness as he could muster, he delivered a chopping blow to the back of the monk's neck, and lowered the now unconscious form to the straw.

Quickly removing the habit from his friend, he wrapped himself from head to toe and grunted toward the guard he knew to be positioned outside the cell. The cell door swung open and the guard ducked his head inside. It was positioned at a perfect angle for Banoldino to bring up his knee and catch him in the temple, the only part not covered by the metal of his helmet.

The guard slumped to the floor at his feet, and was easily manhandled into the cell before Banoldino eased the door into position and duly bolted it tight shut.

Applying some instinct and some experience of fortress buildings, he made his way to the outer wall of the castle and assumed a pious sobriety whilst hitching a leg over the mule, the makeshift rope harness of which, had been tossed toward him by one of the guards currently lounging at the gate.

Applying some gentle pressure to the mule's haunches, he stirred it into a bobbing trot, which had his body shaking and jangling across the wide open expanse toward the Abbey leaving the township behind.

He knew by letting the mule meander he would eventually end up on the road to the Abbey. The Spaniard was content to allow the mule to convey him for as long as he felt more progress could be made than by foot.

Constantly glancing over his shoulder he expected that, at any moment he might catch sight of mounted guards racing up the hill toward him.

Meanwhile, back in the cell, Benedict stirred and rose to a sitting position rubbing his neck tenderly whilst he cleared his thoughts and his slightly blurred vision. He fully appreciated the situation when realising that he was naked, and that he found a guard slumped at is feet! For a few moments he could not think straight he opened his mouth to cry out, but hesitated, changed his mind and stood in the middle of the cell with a hand to his head!

Considering his position and the possible interpretations that may be formed as a result, he decided, however unwisely it may prove, that he should delay raising the alarm.

He knew that Banoldino would be bound for the Abbey with the intent of collecting the girl! Having considered the potential for an unfavourable outcome to the Magistrate's deliberations, he decided to do all in his power to give the couple a chance of affecting their escape.

Considering that the first intervention would arise with the guard's recovery, he wrestled with the idea of hampering any attempt at alerting the Captain of the guard or the Magistrate himself.

First he must allow the situation to remain as it was for as long as possible, then when the moment arose, to apply some means of restraint.

For some time yet, Benedict sank back into the straw, pulling some of it into a position that would not leave him completely exposed, he lay in waiting for the guard to stir.

Chapter 11

Able Seaman Daemon Quirk

Daemon's first day at sea held several surprises in store for the new arrival.

Firstly the discovery that he was not naturally blessed with 'sea legs' suffering nausea almost from the moment the ship pulled anchor. Secondly that the crew of HMS *Warrior* were not much more than a gang of cut-throats, society's 'dregs', thrown together by accident and mis-fortune!

At every turn he was met with threats or disdain. He was treated like unwanted baggage. Pushed to the back of every queue, and left with next to nothing when the food was dished up or fresh water ladled out.

He was given every menial task imaginable. He thumped his head a hundred times on low ceiling supports and doorways, throttled himself and burned the skin from his hands handling rope.

He swallowed gallons of salt water as the ship bucked and plunged through what he considered to be mountainous seas, which in fact were perfectly normal for a mild spring morning.

He sank into a hammock as the sun set on the Atlantic horizon, tired and aching beyond anything he had known.

On his first night he was twice startled awake when upturned in his designated hammock by obliging shipmates, his last and undisturbed relief came upon finding a dingy, unwanted corner, where he managed to rig up his own bed from a patchwork sailcloth and two discarded nails.

He knew it was going to be a tortuous climb for him to gain any form of foothold in the 'pecking' order, or some recognition by those that mattered. At that moment his final coherent thoughts went to the first mate, a man of sixty, carbuncled and creased by a life of attrition, gnarled of hands and feet, weather-beaten of face, crooked back and all, who for the foreseeable future would be lord over all of Daemon's entire existence.

***

Several days passed in now familiar pain and discomfort before anyone spoke even a word to him. When it came it was not so welcome. 'Oy...! Paddy. You lazy Irish *bastard*, get for'ard and help those damned fools with the lashings!' Surprised and at first unsure that he was being addressed, Daemon hesitated, long enough to be given a kick in the pants, which helped to propel him in the appropriate direction.

Arriving, he grabbed hold of the end of a thick rope, a link in a human chain, and began to heave. 'Not that way imbecile!! Bring it round the bloody capstan, not that way!' Completely at a loss Daemon began pulling in the opposite direction and upended the last three seamen in the chain.

All three turned on him, cursing and snarling at him. Again completely at a loss, he threw up his arms and muttered apologies until they grasped that as a complete novice his capabilities were limited.

The bosun stepped forward and, despite lacking three or four inches on Daemon, managed nonetheless to grab him by the collar and make him feel like a scolded puppy as he thrust him toward the gathering throng of his shipmates.

Stumbling for two or three steps, he tried vainly to get his balance on the shifting deck where he was intentionally bumped from one to another! This process continued for several minutes as the hapless newcomer pinged around in circles, helped on by each thumping shoulder or body check which kept him in continuous motion.

The gathering became animated and amused at the fledgling's floundering and in some way they began to acknowledge that complete inadequacy may provide a sufficiently attractive trait to engender laughter and pity rather than derision.

After a few moments there was nothing more to be gained from adding further to the youth's discomfort, they left him and even added the odd friendly thwack across his shoulders to imply that he had played the game with spirit.

Daemon, panting and grappling with the side rail to gain some stability, a grimace of self-amusement evident at his own plight, decided upon a course of action that he hoped would turn things a bit more to his favour.

As the sun set and the crew went below for dishing up, Daemon took up a space alongside some of the familiar faces that had earlier formed a ring around him. He drew one or two sidelong looks but feigned to ignore them.

Soon the lumbering ship's carpenter came toward them, stooping and awkwardly bungling through the cramped archways. Without exchanging as much as a word he heaved himself into position alongside Daemon, forcing Daemon to dislodge the sailor seated at his left hand side, firmly planting him on the deck. The dislodged neighbour came up off the deck swinging with intent to mete out a beating upon his assailant.

Anticipating the blow Daemon pulled sharply backward and allowed the thrust of the punch to gather momentum before landing firmly behind the ear of the burly carpenter.

The carpenter rose and grabbed the other by the hair before thudding his fist in an 'uppercut' which lifted his assailant from his feet, before planting him down onto the several slop-filled dishes in front of the other nearby diners.

Mayhem ensued during which Daemon, weighing himself against the other protagonists, chose to take the side of the carpenter, fighting off attacks from three sides, the two, joined ultimately by the carpenter's 'mate', fended off the attack of six or more others.

Two officers arrived, one of which was none other than Second Lieutenant Tarquin Rickards. Both proceeded to roar their disapproval for several minutes before the mayhem came to a heaving, breathless halt.

Tarquin glowered at the men. 'One more display of this sort and you will all be keel-hauled! Fighting is to be preserved for the enemy! If any of you prove unfit for his duties as a result of this melee, ALL will be held responsible!' Turning toward Daemon, 'And, particularly you my friend! Give me cause to bring you to punishment and believe me I will strip your back... without hesitation!'

Daemon looked levelly at his tormentor before dropping his eyes, he nodded his acquiescence in the familiar way, marginally avoiding further admonishment.

Despite having taken two or three blows to the chin, and suffered a split above his left eye, Daemon had displayed enough resilience to have commanded respect from both sides, and was invited to join in the laugher that ensued as they all downed a rum, at the conclusion of the meal!

There is nothing like a good fistfight to bring a crew together. It seemed to be the great 'leveller' when win, lose or end up in the infirmary, the blows inflicted and taken, achieved some sort of 'bond', between the men. It gave each an inkling of what another may be capable of when the inevitable encounter with an enemy would come to bear.

Daemon had declared himself for the carpenter – 'Barka' as he was known, and was accepted as a dependable 'standby' whenever lifting or positioning or modifications to the ship's structure demanded labour. The carpenter and his mate 'Retard' made him welcome, although few words passed between them, he would respond to a call or jerk on his sleeve.

Eventually he told them his name, but settled for 'Demon'. Which was as much of a concession as could be expected! To the others he remained 'Oirish' or 'Paddy' either way he knew when someone wanted his attention.

In the first week his encounters with Tarquin were limited, but the more the voyage continued, the more opportunity arose.

He learned gradually when to pull or not to pull. He took his first tentative turn aloft, when given the crow's nest duty one fresh morning, from which he was able to watch not only the horizon, but the activities of the men in working the masts and handling sail. He knew it would become him soon enough that his role would involve scaling, at speed, the knotted rope ladders and webbings, and he knew well the dangers that lay in waiting.

One morning, when threading a lanyard around a brass stoop at the rail, Daemon ventured to speak to Tarquin, whom he found standing nearby, in typical naval fashion, hands withdrawn and crossed behind, and looking intently out across the mist-laden waters.

'Sir, er, may I speak, sir? I… er!

'Quiet man!' was the first response. 'I cannot imagine why I would engage in conversation with the likes of you!'

Daemon shrugged, 'Please yourself then, I was only going to ask His Lordship where in God's name we were bound for! Er… no offence meant!'

'Be still man! You are fortunate not to be already in irons, so do not provoke me further.'

'Well… to be sure, I have a tongue in my head and it's had little enough exercise, God knows! Being as you and me are from the same…!

'Go on. From the same…?'

'Well, you know, from, I just thought we might, you know …!'

'You, my friend, the lowest scum from the leftovers of galley slop, why you imagine yourself to have something in common, with myself, is beyond my comprehension. Indeed it is almost worthy of mirth, were it not so downright insulting. I've a mind...!'

'Well you know, how I see it... from my lowly point of view of course, is that, one day when encountering 'the enemy' whosoever that may turn out to be, His Lordship might be at the wrong end of a sword, (not for the first time I might add) and I myself, minding my own business of course, might have a free arm with which to offer assistance, thereby saving Your Lordship's person from pre-maturely becoming minced meat! I just thought that maybe... we might at least pass the time of day without offence... given or taken!'

Tarquin turned and for the first time stared directly into Daemon's eye. Slowly but surely a half-smile broke out on the Officer's countenance. Daemon returned the smile adding a sardonic twist to his lips, and a shrug of the shoulders. He returned dutifully to his task of winding rope, and felt certain that 'ice' had been broken.

Second Lieutenant Tarquin Rickard, strode one or two paces across the deck and resumed his watch, amused and reflective, that indeed the tasks that lay ahead may be faced the better for the gaining of one or two allies along the way.

***

Another day or so passed before Daemon and Tarquin were again thrown together.

'Beggin' your pardon, sir. I wondered if my question from the other day might meet with an answer... to beg your pardon again, sir. Where are we bound?'

This time Tarquin's voice had lost its edge when he replied that although he 'could not see the point' as 'where ever' it may be, was all the same to the likes of Daemon, but he obliged that 'the Mediterranean' was their destination, and another two days would see them 'pass Gibraltar'.

'Is that by any chance, near Africa, sir? Are they in the same direction?'

'Why yes!' Of course, man. Morocco is a mere thirty miles off the Island of Gibraltar. You can see it on a clear day when we first enter the Straits.'

Daemons eyes lit up. He could not have been more pleased that, so soon, he would have the chance to track down the slavers and search for Kirsten. Everything had gone perfectly since his first coherent thought after the attack upon Baltimore. Within weeks he had made determined steps toward reconciliation with the girl whose memory was indelibly embedded on his mind.

Chapter 12

Escape from Cashel

It was not the first time that Banoldino had used a mule as conveyance, but he could not remember a more painful and unpleasant journey. Indeed the ferocious seas that saw the demise of the Moroccan Zebek, had not shaken him more.

Nonetheless he soon found himself staring at an imposing fortress which he came to know as 'Hoare' Abbey.

His only thought was to locate Kirsten, and to remove them both, with as much speed as possible to make their way to the coast. He had no thought beyond that, but felt certainty in that she would wish for this outcome herself.

He again allowed the mule to reach its familiar resting place, inside the walls of the Abbey, in a wide courtyard, the stables distinguished by water troughs, straw and a mild stench, could easily be picked out among the outbuildings. A blacksmith was hammering at some farm implement though Banoldino, noting his full bearded head, well developed forearms, and the girth of his habit, determined that he would do his best to avoid an encounter with this individual.

Although there were ten or fifteen other brothers attending to their daily labours, he passed among them without incident, appreciating that indeed Benedict was as much a stranger to most of them as he himself would appear.

Noticing one venerable hooded figure, he approached with a casual air and enquired as to whether the 'young peasant girl' had been up and about this morning. The elder raised a crooked finger pointing toward the opening in the wall which lead into what proved to be a well-stocked garden.

Banoldino found himself in a carefully laid out area of about an acre. Clear pathways lead to the centre, where a stone fountain issued a continuous spray of clean water. Sitting on the low circular wall and trailing a hand in the pool, Kirsten looked, not for the first time, like a form from a religious painting, even the Madonna herself, thought the Spaniard.

He approached her quickly but without causing her to raise her gaze from the rippling surface. 'My child,' he said, half amused at the interpretation which may be brought upon this address. She looked up immediately and a smile broke out on her face that filled him with a strong urge to take her up into his arms. He raised a hand so that she may remain seated until he had conveyed his message.

'I am afraid I had no choice but to escape the hospitality of the Magistrate! At this very moment there may be ten or fifteen men in pursuit! If they are on horseback I have little chance of making a complete escape unless I act quickly.'

She immediately rose to her feet, and was almost in his arms. The concern on her face immediately encouraged him to continue.

'I will ask only once, and I will be gone forever if that is your desire, but I want you to come... escape with me... I will take care of you, and I pledge my loyalty for as long as I have breath in my body!'

Whatever thoughts came to her at that moment, she could find only one possible response which was to take his hand and race toward the gate at the far end of the courtyard. She pulled him along and burst through the gate. He realised she must have explored the ground earlier because of her familiarity with the layout!

Beyond the gate were rows and rows of planted fields and a dozen monks at work in them.

However, their interest in two figures cavorting through the crops, toward the hills which rose sharply away to the north, was mild, even though one of the figures was a comely peasant girl and the other to all appearances, a brother of their own Order!

Their flight continued for several days, when, though they felt they were always within seconds of re-capture, in fact there were no encounters of any kind. Their journey covered hills and valleys, streams and thick wooded areas. They scavenged among vegetable plots for anything edible, plucked berries from trees, and drank from streams. There was great discomfort, dank, drizzling rain, and cold as a constant companion.

Yet the feeling of excitement and exhilaration completely motivated Kirsten to keep going, and her complete trust in Banoldino, to do the right thing and keep them safe, never left her.

Navigating by instinct and the occasional glimpse of the rising or setting sun, guided them north and eastward toward the coast that Banoldino knew must appear sooner or later. His limited knowledge of the geography of the British Isles gleaned from prosaic naval maps told him that Ireland could be no more than two hundred miles from east to west, and that they had begun their flight somewhere in the mid-southeast of the landmass! The coast could surely not be far.

Some four days and nights after they fled Cashel, they came to the crest of a hill in a wooded area, but the sun shone through the trees and drew them toward a bright clearing. Beyond the clearing the forest opened out on to the beautiful rolling hills and deep ravine that formed a picturesque valley of stunning beauty. Way down on the valley floor lay a beautiful stone coloured lake, into which a cascading waterfall danced merrily in the bright sunshine.

It was a breath-taking, captivating sight which drew them to abandon all concerns. By the time they had reached the lake they were bounding hand in hand toward an uninhibited plunge, which brought forth bursts of laughter and shouts of triumph! They wallowed in the cool, fresh waters for long moments, throwing off heavy, restricting clothing as they bobbed beneath the foaming surface.

In minutes they were both naked, diving and plunging, rising and breaking the surface with leaps and lunges, they laughed like children, but when they inevitably slipped into each other's arms they clung on and locked into a passionate embrace. Kirstie threw her head back and he held her, arms wrapped tightly around her hips as he buried his face into the soft warmth of her belly.

Kirstie slid down as he loosened his hold and she in turn wrapped her arms around his neck, their bodies, beneath the surface came together, her legs around his waist, he thrust into her, and her head flew backward again, in ecstatic shock. They writhed together back and forth, water splashing over their faces and renewing their energies, they became as one, in tumultuous union.

She rode him as she would sit astride a dolphin. They simultaneously groaned, gasping for air in a climax of perfect timing then sank beneath the surface, soundlessly, swaying as cool water caressed skin, heightening sensations, swathing their satiated bodies.

They made their way lazily toward the shore, where Banoldino stood erect in the soft muddy riverbed and swept her into his arms. She clung to him and, to his surprise and delight, showered kisses on his face and neck. He dropped her down on to warm grass, and returned her kisses, running his lips all over her body as she threw back her arms and lay in ecstasy at his every touch.

Time passed, they knew not whether quickly or slowly, but instinct told them that other things had to be attended to. They cast around, giggling and communicating with smiles, whilst they gathered their clothing and arranged what they could to dry them off.

Again instinctively, Banoldino gathered a little firewood, some sticks and rocks and began a long and deliciously funny fire lighting episode which resulted in a triumphant shout when the kindling finally sparked into life.

Banoldino disappeared into the wood and searched around whilst Kirsten continued to dry out her shirt and the heavy woollen skirt that had been her constant companion since the days of the Whitsun gathering.

She briefly reflected that she had been disloyal to Daemon, but making the 'sign of the cross' across her naked breast she shrugged and dismissed the thought. The warm glow of satisfaction and awe at the sheer physical delight of her union with Banoldino would serve to cover her lingering regret for many years to come.

Chapter 13

Lucky Daemon's Battle

Daemon absent-mindedly swept the horizon, his mind clouded with thoughts of Kirsten and her captivity, before a piercing yell broke the moment, and turned his insides to out.

Up in the crow's nest, the lookout was screaming down toward the bridge, 'Ship on the horizon, ship ahoy!'

Two hundred thundering footsteps could be heard along the decks, upper and lower, as men scrambled to position. In every direction, officers and men came running, criss-crossing one another as they attempted to reach their station. Daemon was grabbed by his top coat and pulled in the direction of the galley. He followed the carpenter's example and took a position below the bridge at the head of the galley steps.

'What am I supposed to do?' he begged of Old Barka. The other grunted his response and patted his cutlass which had appeared from beneath his leather apron.

Orders were bellowed out by the officers, followed by the first mate, then the gang leaders, The guns were run out. In minutes the ship had become battle ready and the men, breathing heavy and crouched in readiness, awaited their commands.

'Report, Mr Belton!' the captain bellowed across even though Mr Belton was no more than a few feet from him.

With telescopes raised, three officers almost simultaneously with great pride declared sighting 'the enemy.'

'She's a Spaniard! Third class, forty guns'. Can't make out her name but she is rounding on us.

'Give me that Mr Belton' The captain roared as he took up position at the rail. 'By God that's a fair description, Mr Belton. We are looking straight at the bow of the *Santa Theresa*. Spanish she is and currently making life very difficult for our merchantmen to move in and out of Cadiz. This is a golden chance for us. There's a prize here all right. And if we can take her, we can turn six months of oppression completely to our favour.'

'But, sir, we may not be as prepared for the encounter as we would like. We're only a few days at sea and with much more training of the men… '

'Nonsense man – you never have to train an English crew for a good fight. They're born to it! Full sail! Steer two points off east, southeast, let us take her on the full as she bears down on us.

'I want every man to listen for my command – let her think we are trying to avoid her and take flight, then come around, swiftly on her starb'd side. Nobody fires a shot until I give the order! Got it?'

'Ay Ay, sir!' was the response in unison.

Twenty red-coated marines lined up along the mid-ship's rail and cocked their muskets.

***

In the following hush, Daemon looked around, for familiar faces, watching to identify each in his role, he was surprised to find many of them praying, muttering the words of the 'Though I walk through the Valley of…' bowing and crossing themselves, kissing talismans.

Their mutterings became a hum, and before long drew the attention of the captain. 'Quiet, you men! Get your eyes up and watch! The only guidance you need for the next few hours is from your superior officers and your knowledge of the enemy. Watch him!! Watch him!!'

The spray of the sea became the only sound now as the bow plunged on through white crested waves. The ship leaned starboard as the sail filled with the warm south westerly wind. The topsail stretched and the timbers creaked as the ship seemed to form herself into an elongated projectile shot from a cannon.

The deep blue sea raced by beneath the straining hull and every man held fast onto some rope or rail to make sure of maintaining his station.

Suddenly a thundering came from off their port side and a fizzing sound preceded a splintering crack that saw the top of their foremast break away and bring down its topsail.

'Steady, men,' roared the captain. 'Steady! She's found our range but we're a swift moving target. It will be two or more minutes before they can sight us up again. Come around,' Mr Flood, come around. He urged the wheel-man to get full lock on the rudder. 'Help him! Help him, Mr Rickards! Hold this line!'

Minutes went by when all but the plunging and breaking of the waves, was silence. Another thundering this time from much closer, and another fizz. A searing hot ball of iron ripped through a sail but plunged harmlessly into the sea beyond her starboard. The sail briefly flickered alight, but extinguished by spray, it settled down with a bucket sized hole, but held its rigging and shape.

'Steady, men! Steady, standby to open fire.' Another long pause, voices could now be picked up, shouting, perhaps alarmed, and the rumble of military drums from the Santa Theresa could be clearly heard by all.

The enemy suddenly took on human form and their desperation could be clearly felt by all as the *Warrior*'s crew awaited their turn.

'Ready on the gun deck, prepare to open fire. Await my call.' A cannon grumbled angrily her recoil all of ten feet. Down toward the beam-end a melee broke out. 'Wait I said, Mr Strapp, get those fools to re-load.'

The errant shot had missed the bow of the Spaniard by thirty yards, and in truth may have given the captain a very good 'sighter', because within twenty seconds, he screamed at them, 'Open fire – open fire!' from the bow and, as each gun on the *Warrior* fired in turn, a raking, splintering result could be heard and seen along the starboard side of their adversary.

The salvo had hit home along the gun ports and deck rail of the Spanish ship, perfectly positioned to do most damage to the superstructure, which would doubtlessly have the most disheartening effect on the receiving crew.

They saw their gun ports shattered, some of the cannon disabled, the utmost damage to personnel and smoke belched from the hold as a result of fire on the decks, falling through the gratings.

It was a prefect opening salvo, and determined the tide of the conflict almost in one stroke.

The natural course of their own ship was to round the *Santa Maria* at the stern as she passed. Another salvo from reloaded guns ensured that a great deal more damage would be inflicted to the castle of the ship, beneath the bridge, which in turn would disable the bridge and its controls.

There was mayhem aboard as the *Warrior* expertly manoeuvred into position alongside the stricken Spaniard, and the boarding party readied itself along her rail. There was much excitement now as the full ship's compliment steeled itself for the battle, with the scent of victory firmly in its nostrils and the enemy on its knees.

As grappling hooks were flung into her lines and came thudding into position across a divide of no more than twelve feet, the marines took up a covering position, picking off sharpshooters in the enemy ranks whilst the boarding party made up of three officers and fifty sailors, yelled out a stirring range of abuse and tirade of terror upon their adversary.

On the *Santa Theresa* men ran in all directions, tending to wounded, putting out fires, A few presented themselves as a line of defence, but it was ramshackle and uncoordinated, only one officer, with cutlass drawn swung from the rigging and urged more men into the line.

A group had assembled at an upper gun port and was readying itself to fire into the British ship but the marines had the gun crew firmly pinned down and was picking them off at will, it posed little threat as the two ships ground together.

The boarding party coming in high off the rigging to make up for the discrepancy of several feet to the height of the Spanish rail, but this merely added to the momentum of the attack and the fifty swung across and began hacking and slicing into the awaiting defenders. A British musket shot brought the Spanish officer flailing through his own rigging and rendered him upside down, bleeding from a hole in his temple.

Meanwhile a secondary line of defence had formed behind some of the shattered timber on the far side of the deck, and opened up a volley of fire from primed muskets and pistols. Some damage was inflicted and British sailors hit the deck, but the onward motion of the assault drew them into hand-to-hand combat with their assailants preventing reloading and diminishing the threat.

Nonetheless, the Spanish fought bravely. Captain Delgardo turned and yelled more orders and another two dozen men armed themselves and made for an assault. The line of marines this time fixed bayonets and led the charge.

Daemon, from his position beneath the bridge, watched in fascination as his shipmates threw themselves in to the fray with clear abandon, and was not surprised when Barka grabbed him by the scruff of the neck and thrust him into the line with the boarders.

Shoving a cutlass into his hand the carpenter bellowed, 'At 'em lad.' Before he had time to think Daemon was swinging at the end of lanyard onto the Spanish deck and flashing a blade toward a cowering seaman.

There was mayhem all around, but Daemon felt good. The action appeared to be in slow motion, he could see what was going on, he could feel the adrenalin forcing him onward, he felt his reactions were sharper than those of his foes. He could see what they were trying to do, blocked them and forced on them his own blows and thrusts which found their target with ease.

He did not stop to think about his actions, but let them flow as if involuntary, mechanically, his arms and legs did what they had to do and he felt assured, confident that he could do it.

Loud shouting penetrated his hearing, and his attention was drawn to the bridge. Mr Belton, the ship's first lieutenant, had the Spanish captain at the end of his sword and there was a general quelling of activity until silence pervaded.

Daemon released a Spaniard he had taken by the throat and moments before had disarmed. His own sword, poised above his head in readiness to deliver a death blow on his opponent, now fell limply to his side as he felt all resistance drain from the other.

Daemon watched until the man had sunk to his knees and drawn his hands up as if in prayer, and satisfied that he was in no danger of retaliation, was glad not to have to cleave the man who was now begging for his life.

A roar of triumph bellowed from the *Warrior*'s crew and grew to a crescendo within the ranks on the *Santa Theresa*. Watching now as the Spanish officers, followed by all the remaining crew, accepted their fate by throwing their small arms onto a pile on the deck, the marines took control by marshalling the prisoners and rendering harmless all remaining weapons and ordnance.

The Spanish captain was obliged to alight and join Captain Rodney Nash aboard the *Warrior* and many of the crew returned to their positions to begin the task of clearing up and returning order to their respective stations.

There was much work for the carpenter and his two mates, and Daemon, whose adrenalin rush had hardly subsided, found it strange to be focusing on hacking away at a splintered turret, rather than at a swarthy, bronzed adversary.

'Lucky for you,' the carpenter muttered.

'Lucky?' Daemon looked at him askance.

'An encounter like that, so soon after you joining the ship. Some waits years before they gets a chance like that. I think you have the luck of the Devil in yee... Demon... I'll be awatchin' you from now on.'

***

So several days passed when the men talked in groups about their triumph. There was laughter and much ribbing of their comrades and the atmosphere of bonhomie was infectious, drawing all into a kind of brotherhood. They had become a 'unit', working for one another, striving for success, for the 'ship' not for themselves.

Second Lieutenant Hardacre was obliged to 'man' the Spanish vessel with a small crew, and steer her back to Plymouth. So their numbers were depleted and distraction hard to find. All was good with the *Warrior* for a time, months rolled by and Daemon became an enthusiastic and valuable crew man, turning his hand to many tasks.

His burning ambition in seeking news, or any word on the fate of the Moorish raiders and the destiny of his lost love, became a distant and remote memory.

He threw himself into life aboard a naval vessel and all the variety and excitement it brought.

He became familiar with the major sea ports, he won and lost at dice, won and lost in brief though memorable encounters with the opposite sex. He became a good friend of his former tormentor Lieutenant Tarquin Rickard and experienced many a skirmish.

Chapter 14

Another World for Daemon

The Port of Gibraltar stood before them. This was to be the first time Daemon would come to love a land other than Ireland. He was impressed by the sheer size and the sharp angles of the massive outcrop of the rock island. Then the sandy dryness of the lands that lay beyond. It had never occurred to him that 'land' could be anything but green.

Then the waters beneath, shades of deepest blue, and yellow sand on the shores beyond. All this appeared a thing of beauty which filled him with excitement. When the ship anchored some hundred and fifty yards off shore, the next thing to impress upon him was the warm persistence of the rising sun. Without a sea breeze constantly cooling the skin, the natural warmth of this place brought to mind a rare day, back home, one late August, when, with the sun overhead and the air windless, in a shady hollow he shed his clothing and slipped silently into the mill pond.

But now, it was constant and it made his whole being glow. A film of sweat formed on every part of his body. It felt good, although he reflected, it would be hard to load out a ship with the sun at its height, something to which he would have to become acclimatised, as his life would inexorably move into new and unfamiliar territory.

Tarquin's sharp retort brought him to attention. He was obliged to man the longboat as the captain, Belton and Tarquin readied themselves for an excursion ashore. The captain wore his finest tunic and gold braid hung meritoriously from his shoulders.

Daemon pulled at his clothing and straightened up as well as he might and lightly dropped into position at a vacant oar.

Tarquin stood at the prow of the boat, and delivered his orders getting the party under way. Daemon pulled on his oar and found his rhythm with ease, following the more experienced sailors around him.

The boat soon pulled smoothly alongside timber moorings at the centre of a wide crescent. Bright coloured ship-lap buildings cluttered around a stone fortress beyond, all against the backdrop of the massive outcrop which soared into the bright skies above.

Their arrival drew interest from the hundreds on and around the quay. Soldiers, slumped against rails and shuttered, ramshackle buildings, suddenly drew to attention. Almost at one there was a clamour for attention. Local Spanish, ages ranging from five to fifty, selling their wares, sailors and merchantmen, hungry for opportunity, and petty officials clamouring with bunches of white parchment converged on the launch.

Captain Nash ignored all and proceeded, head high with a four strong personal guard, toward the stone built fortress that lay just back from the harbour. Daemon, was required to stand by, presumably guarding the long-boat and securing an escape route for the shore party.

Time passed and despite the constant clamour from the locals, things quietened down and the main distraction was provided by exotic dark-skinned ladies, dressed in dazzling loose fitting, crimsons and yellows, parading along the quayside with enticement written in every expression and every movement.

Daemon was happy to swap looks, and fulfil his not inconsiderable interest with visual delights which, he knew, could be rekindled on many a forthcoming sleepless night.

Word came back to the boat that they were to return to the ship, and would not be required until the following morning at 'ten – sharp!'. The captain had clearly found the hospitality too sumptuous to resist.

Pulling on the oar and taking in the landscape and layout of the busy port, Daemon was impressed that such a place, so far from home, could be considered by his current benefactor, King George, to be 'British', and he wondered that it could be defended during the current troubles with Spain. Taking in the sights his eyes fixed on a small outcrop far off to the right where a cannon as big as a barn with a hole that looked like a full sized barrel could be easily accommodated. Comfortably nestled, it pointed out across the inlet toward the Spanish mainland and provided some answers to his curiosity.

His days anchored off Gibraltar were among the most enjoyable that he could remember. Taking light duties, and frequent opportunities to bob in the cool clear waters where the Atlantic and the Mediterranean Sea merged, one with the other, gave Daemon ample time to reflect upon what might lay ahead.

He knew now that he would surely, one day, pull into a Moroccan harbour and would have opportunity to find out how the slave trade functioned. He considered his task in his determination to complete the search and release of the object of his entire future, and with a shrug, he heartily believed, time was the only thing that stood between Kirsten and himself.

For now, his thoughts returned abruptly to his next 'command'.

'Man the boats!' The words screamed at him with urgency upon which he did not spare a second. He was over the side and into the long boat before any of his shipmates appeared on deck. He stood awaiting instructions, oar at the ready, whilst the others clambered from the rail down the webbing and into position.

They cast off and were into their rowing pattern in seconds. Within five minutes, they pulled alongside the mooring and were in position as Captain Nash and his party, clumped determinedly along the jetty, and made toward them without ceremony. As they stood to attention the Captain , his adjutant, a marine, and a surprise guest hopped into the boat from the jetty.

The visitor happened to be a striking young lady with jet black hair framing an angelic face, which despite being partially hidden by a parasol, proved to be of wondrous proportions to Daemon, and undoubtedly every other male in attendance.

The 'lady' was assigned her position just back from the centre of the craft, and it endeared her to Daemon that she was within touching distance of his right calf, given that at each stroke, he would be almost obliged to stretch out his leg in an attempt to brace himself for the required level of effort in propelling the boat forward against the surf.

His attention frequently strayed from his immediate duty, that of pulling earnestly upon the oar, and that of catching the eye of the young lady. Eventually when their eyes met, his moon-faced trance was to be met with a sympathetic, but endearing half smile. He was certain she had been transfixed by his countenance and would duly fall madly in love with him by his mere proximity.

Such was his state of mind when Captain Nash, having been piped aboard the ship, proceeded to awaken him by the sheer power of his rhetoric, and the simple advice that as a loyal 'ship of the line' under His Majesty's command, the *Warrior* would take her place in escort to the fleet, under Admiral Fielding, and proceed to intercept the combined Spanish and French flotilla currently standing in the harbour at Marseille, in readiness to support a planned allied invasion of sacred British soil.

His orders had been confirmed as being to provide support at every encounter of the enemy, to the flagship and all ships of the line in their current endeavour. Forthwith the *Warrior* would attach itself to the fleet and proceed to bear close support in engaging her enemies sufficiently to deter its intentions.

***

Daemon knew this was genuine warfare, and that what was coming was in the lap of the Gods, but he could not understand for the life of him, what part the lady, recently joining their passenger list, could possibly be expected to achieve within the hospitality of the *Warrior*.

For several days the ship was a blur of activity. Cleaning, strengthening, tightening. The marines built bulwarks, from which they could give volley fire support. The gun crews ran out the guns for hour after hour repeating every action until they were honed to perfection in timing and precision.

Daemons role in supporting Barka and Retard, was attending to damaged superstructure, or in providing replacement timber blocks where canon in frequent use had worn or split its restraints.

The ship was battle-ready by the time they spotted the *Flamingo*, a sixty-two gun ship of His Majesty's line, which was bringing up the rear of Fielding s fleet.

Signalling commenced, frantically, to ensure that the *Flamingo* recognised the *Warrior* and acknowledged her presence, with return signals. For some minutes they collectively held their breath before finally a flag was hoisted in welcome.

Standing half a nautical mile off her larb'd side, the *Flamingo* confirmed their arrival to Fielding who in return sent his compliments and an invitation to Nash to join him on board the flagship for dinner at seven bells.

As Daemon suspected, he was called to duty with the boat crew to transport Captain Nash, and of course, his lady companion, to dine with Admiral Fielding.

Daemon spent a full ten minutes on his appearance, washing vigorously below decks, flattening his wayward curly mop of hair and pulling his shirt and jacket into order. He spat on his curled up strapless shoes and cleaned them off on the back of his calves where striped woollen socks showed below his pantaloons. With a despairing shrug, he abandoned his task and made hastily for the ship's waist to where the boat crew had assembled.

***

They held the longboat steady for the lady and she lit up an area all around with her dazzling smile and the glow from satin and silk that formed around her in ways Daemon had never seen clothing perform! An entire bench was required for her and the tiered skirts of her dress.

Nash, fawning and preening around her was the gentleman personified. Daemon could only gawp, and wonder at which planet in the firmament, could have produced such a creature and dispatched her down to lowly earth?

Polite conversation passed between them enabling Daemon to glean that the lady was in fact daughter to the Earl of Olney and betrothed to a Captain Dennis, commanding the warship, HMS *Resolve*, Fielding's flagship.

She was to be reunited briefly with her fiancé before being escorted to the the Palace at Naples where she would reside under the protection of her sister's husband. Her sister had married Baron Ramsbottom, assigned to the Court of the Duke of Naples, during the visit of Cardinal Boromeo, the British Papal legate. Such visits could be of several months duration.

Following the briefest of liaisons, the flagship resumed her place at the head of the flotilla, whilst the *Warrior* set a course east, nor' east for Naples.

This would require a detour of some five days for the *Warrior*, whilst the remainder of the fleet set a course to blockade the French fleet. *Warrior* would then rejoin the line, hopefully before any action commenced. It had been considered that Gibraltar might be vulnerable in the event that the Spanish, or French combined flotilla had broken through. Lady Daphne, would be safer in Naples.

Daemon took it upon himself to become Lady Daphne's personal bodyguard. Even if Lady Daphne was unaware of him to all outward appearance. He watched over her whenever she appeared on deck. He went out of his way to be 'available' if there was any assistance, of any kind, required.

Lady Daphne did appear on deck complaining that the water recently brought to her quarters, had been cloudy and warm. Before she had a moment to await a response Daemon was holding a ladle of fresh, cool water to her mouth. On another occasion she appeared, dressed for action and insisting that she be allowed to take the dinghy and exercise in the sea. Swimming for 'pleasure' had been taught to her during her stay in Gibraltar. She also insisted that the waters were refreshing and good for the complexion.

Captain Nash huffed and puffed for some minutes before giving in to the Lady's determined argument, agreeing to an hours' 'recreation'.

Again Daemon was on hand to manage the launch and steady her whilst lady Daphne slipped into the water. Although covered from head to foot in linen undergarments her feminine curves were evident from any distance. The crew enviously watched the proceedings from the rail and through gun ports but Daemon drew the envy of the entire ships complement by being allowed to assist the lady in and out of the water. He was ready with a bath sheet when she finally emerged, draping it around her shoulders before turning to the oars and steering the boat back toward the *Warrior*.

He was convinced she had nodded in his direction in the final exchange before Nash took her hand and guided her from the rail toward the cabin doors. As she disappeared the crew unanimously took up catcalling and berating Daemon until their combined taunts rose to a crescendo. They were oblivious to the actions of Lady Daphne who had playfully left the cabin door minutely ajar, so that she could watch Daemon's discomfort unobserved.

She chuckled merrily to herself as she descended the steps to her quarters, the captain's own cabin.

She had in reality taken a shine to the brash young Irishman and was happy to play the aloof 'goddess' to his earnest devotions. Her entire life had been carefully orchestrated, from the cradle to her imminent state, of marriage.

These last few months, sailing to Gibraltar, enjoying the attentions of the governor and the freedom to determine the content and length of each day's events had been a joy to her.

She had enjoyed walking along the cliffs. wallowing in the surf and calling a boat to conduct her on adventures around the base of the rock. She had taken a guide and scaled the heights to the summit of the rock, and taken in the astonishing views and dramatic impact of the sheer cliff face.

The monkeys, scrambling around the rocks at the summit, both alarmed and amused her and although their attentions fascinated, she was glad of the attendance of two of the governor's servants to resist their extreme interest in her flowing hair. Which, for a fleeting moment became entangled in the bony fingers of one of the furry inhabitants.

Her wanderings, barefoot, kicking the wet sand along the shore line gave Daphne plenty of time to reflect on the limited opportunities her life thus far had presented.

***

On the third day following separation from the fleet, a cutter was intercepted by *Warrior* and duly boarded to establish its itinerary. The skipper was obliging with information, anxious to divert attention from its cargo of opium illegally traded out of Nice.

The French and Spanish, eighteen ships of the line, had indeed left Marseille some three days hence and headed for Cadiz.

Nash called on Lady Daphne to advise her that he had no option but to turn the ship around and head back to support Fielding.

Daphne raised no resistance and accepted gracefully that Britain's interests superseded her own.

***

Within two days with *Warrior* under full sail, Nash plotted her course with the intention of rejoining the fleet just at the point where he anticipated the French would emerge.

On the third morning the mist cleared and they identified sail on the horizon. At that moment it was impossible to establish whether it was friend or foe but Nash plunged ahead, to make sure his timely return would have the impact necessary to be of assistance to his commander.

As the *Warrior* drew nearer, two lines of ships became clear and it was given that Fielding was bearing down on the French larboard side to intercept the line some three of four vessels from the head.

Nash raised a signal to alert Fielding of his presence, but the morning cloud hung heavy and it was difficult to establish whether their signal had been received or an acknowledgement had been raised.

Three midshipmen were placed in the Crow's nest to make any change in the situation.

Now within two thousand yards of the head of the French line a significant change developed which placed Nash in a vulnerable position.

The French made a move to resist confrontation. The head of the flotilla turned South and the line buckled mid way along its length. Clearly the French were refusing to be drawn into battle. The blockade was proving effective.

As Nash saw it, this was a disastrous move from the French point of view, allowing the first four or five ships to come under fire as they made a lumbering turn into a defensive melee.

Nash bore down on the third and fourth of the French line to block any retreat enabling the British fleet to pour cannon fire into them from the opposite side.

Suddenly, there was a commotion from the lookout. They relayed at the tops of their young voices that there was a signal from Fielding. The British guns fell silent.

'Withdraw! Withdraw! Do not engage the Enemy'

Nash gasped audibly at the instruction. It couldn't be true. He screamed at the crow's nest for verification.

How could Fielding withdraw and decline such an invitation. The French flotilla could be decimated almost without incurring loss or damage. The French could be sent back into port, battered and beaten and unable to recover for perhaps half a year. Nash was incredulous, but more important there were now five French vessels full ahead of him at six hundred yards. As Nash saw it they were there to be attacked and that is exactly what he did, firing off several volleys before the French either couldn't or wouldn't return fire.

Finally accepting the truth, that there was to be no support from the British fleet, Nash, immediately gave orders to head south, sou' west and to avert further action, sending a message to Fielding that he would demand an explanation.

The tide and currents, however, made the turn difficult and with only minor adjustment several ships of the French line soon came up broadsides with the *Warrior*. Nash was caught in two minds. Full retreat, or resistance. His unexpected arrival had placed him in an impossible position. He was unaware of the Admiral's intentions and clearly unable to establish the validity of the actions he had witnessed.

His only recourse as he saw it was to defend himself.

What followed was a tragedy which would have massive implications upon the British at sea, for years to come.

Fielding would be Court Marshalled, and the lines of communication would be improved beyond anything maritime warfare had previously encountered.

Nash was attacked on two fronts, and although he wriggled cleverly for hour upon hour, the three frigates and a Spanish brigg pounded the *Warrior* mercilessly. Fielding had withdrawn some five or six nautical miles and set out a defensive line which could only watch the proceedings. Captain Dennis was blissfully unaware that the ship being pounded by French and Spanish guns still contained his betrothed.

On board the *Warrior* massive damage was incurred. The fore and aft masts had been splintered and the sails shredded and the steering rendered useless. The guns, white hot with action intent on repelling the French, inadvertently caused fire to break out along the gun deck. Her superstructure suffered massive damage though she somehow remained afloat.

Down below, carnage, as forty or fifty cannon shot pounded into her. The wounded were stacked on top of one another, and the surgeon frantically dealt with the casualties.

Lady Daphne had immediately sprung to his aid and despite stoic resolve her resistance withered under the sheer carnage witnessed. She mopped brows and kept fresh water in supply. She tore at sheets making bandages, The roar of the cannon above and the pounding of the ship's hull shook her every fibre. Cut above the eye by a splinter of wood, she also bled copiously onto her braided gown.

Hauling a gunners mate down into the makeshift hospital, Daemon looked piteously into her eyes, she could not avert his gaze but grimaced and a tear ran from the corner of her eye.

His heart went out to her and he put a hand on her arm, she shook her head in anticipation, sensing he was about to talk her into withdrawing. He stepped back 'Milady… please…?'

She shook her head and bent toward a seaman gasping for water.

A sudden shattering thud shook the deck beneath them, and splinters shot in every direction.

A red ball lodged into the hull, but it's path had carved an opening under a gun port on the opposite side. There followed an explosion as a powder keg in the above deck exploded.

The hospital deck was thrown into confusion. All around men were dashed against the hull. A fire broke out in the mass of bandages. Amputated limbs were scattered around the deck.

Daemon turned to see Lady Daphne sink to the deck in a pool of blood, a sharp wedge had lodged in her side and blood soaked into her skirt.

Her eyes dimmed as Daemon lunged for her arm. Dragging her clear, he pressed her side in a vain attempt to stem the flow of blood.

His hand brushed the timber that had lodged in her side and she screamed out.

'Milady… Oh, God! I'm so sorry!

'No, it's all right, I can't feel the pain now. It's all right.'

She smiled.

Daemon put his hand around her neck and held up her head. Grabbing a sopping sheet he squeezed some water into her mouth. She swallowed gratefully.

'I don't know your name,' she said.

'Milady, I'm nobody… it doesn't matter.'

'No, I would like to know… please…'

'It's Daemon, ma'am. Just Daemon.'

'Well Daemon – I would like to have known you better.' Her smile faded and suddenly her eyes became serious.

'I believe you are seeking something or someone'. She managed thickly. 'I don't see you remaining in service for long…'

'I… I am set out to find a girl… she was taken by a ship, full of… black warriors… I may never see her again, but I've got to try!'

'Yes, you must. She will be taken to Morocco. The Barbary… you must see my brother. He is, in trade. He was in Morocco a year ago – he may still be there. John Standing… he doesn't use his titl… '

Suddenly she reared up, pain racked her beautiful, pale features, her black hair hung matted and loose about her shoulders.

She went limp and sank to the deck.

Daemon shook her gently at first, then vigorously. The surgeon, scrambling to his feet, came toward them.

He put his hand to her throat. His eyes met Daemon's. The pair pulled her toward the far corner of the cabin and covered her with a sheet.

'Did she say anything, were there any instructions?'

'Nothing, sir. Nothing of any consequence. She asked me where I come from....' Tears filled his eyes, a sob wrenched his gut. The surgeon put a hand on his shoulder. 'You're needed upside. Go on.'

Driving through chaos Daemon emerged through the hatch on to the deck of the doomed ship.

Amid shouts, screams and the now distant thunder of French cannon, orders were called out to the thin chain of command. Nash, bloodied and grounded, hung from the rail of the poop deck, roaring toward the bosun to 'Turn, turn into the wind, the fires will blow away toward the stern, heavier seas may douse the flames. Turn, man! Turn!'

Daemon rushed to his side, Tarquin quickly joined him. Between them they had Nash on his feet as fire crews sluiced water in every direction to restrict the flames and form a path which their captain and his attendants might take to the bow. Above the din, roars could be heard from the French frigates, a mixture of laughter and derision.

Warrior limped away toward the darkening skies of the east whilst the sun set away behind them forming a flaming backdrop to the skeleton masts of their pursuers. Nash was treated by the surgeon for many minutes, but recovered himself sufficiently to be able to demand a report on the ships condition.

Incredibly the enemy had withdrawn, the horizon was clear.

The smoking wreck was allowed to continue on her way, rudderless and without sail, she drifted southeasterly, as night fell.

Ordering boats to launch and what could be mustered of the crew to row, they were eventually able to plot a provisional course and direct her generally in the direction of the Algerian coast.

Tarquin was given command of one of the boats and commandeered Daemon to take the lead oar. Painful mile after mile was achieved until the *Warrior*, completely safe, was able to take full account of her condition.

Forty percent of her crew were dead, another thirty were badly injured. Acting Second lieutenant Glenister and two midshipmen were dead. Less than sixty good men remained to manage the ship toward a safe harbour.

A makeshift sail was erected on the second morning. Burials at sea were completed for fifty souls as the injured swelled the numbers of deceased.

Lady Daphne and the officers were wrapped and preserved for more dignified burial as might be achieved if they hit the North African coast within the anticipated time.

Daemon withheld his knowledge of the existence of her Ladyship's brother. He had resolved to seek him out and tell him in person, of the tragedy, but could imagine no benefit to either the lady or to himself in divulging a confidence.

Chapter 15

Algiers

When Nash steered *Warrior* into the harbour on makeshift lines, there was almost the air of the 'ghost ship' hanging over her.

What remained of her crew went about their business with a resentful, functional approach. Work had to be done to maintain their very survival, but none of it was rewarding, none of it profitable and none of it a pleasure.

Bodies had been condemned to the sea, battered equipment discharged overboard. At a gathering before the mast, Nash had spoken of courage and honour, but almost spat the names of 'Fielding' and 'Admiralty' as he defined the outcome of the encounter with the allied French and Spanish fleets.

Warrior was a wreck, virtually unseaworthy, but one hundred nautical miles had to be endured before she could make the North African coast without encountering any further conflict.

As mate to the carpenter, Daemon had non-stop commitment therefore avoiding sinking into the melancholy which shrouded most of the crew. He had held Lady Daphne as she declined and helped lay her to rest.

He had fashioned a stump each for two riggers whom had lost limbs. He had toiled away at repairs to the waterline breaches, shored up the mizzen mast and some of the upper railings. Day after day he sank into his bunk almost too exhausted to feel emotional or physical pain.

Now the ship thudded into the moorings, her timbers almost giving a hissing sigh of relief. Nash murmured a few instructions, Belton repeated them almost half-heartedly and the seamen dealt with the technicalities of securing the ship.

'Lend a hand there, Cleary'

Daemon turned to catch sight of his old adversary Tarquin pointing toward the gangplank, which swung into position at an awkward angle having split just above its ropelets. Daemon duly swung down from his temporary viewing platform and lashed the gangplank until it held securely.

Returning to the rail, he edged a little closer to Tarquin before addressing him a little more formally than of late.

'Beggin' your pardon, sir.'.

Tarquin acknowledged with a grimace.

'I would like to volunteer to carry the bodies ashore which are for proper burial.'

'You mean you would like to take Lady Daphne ashore.'

'Daemon dropped his eyes but Tarquin withdrew his probing comment, realising his remark had been a little tactless.

'I expect to take charge of the burial myself, I would be more than happy to include you in the party.'

Daemon, unable to respond with more than a touch to the forelock, stepped down onto the deck to seek out Barka for instructions.

Below deck Barka was engaged in smoothing off a finely shaped lid for a small, narrow coffin. Across the deck the base lay open with a ruffle of white linen draped over the sides. Daemon hardly dared move toward it but could not resist ultimately, in peering down on the pale, portrait perfect face of Lady Daphne. A lump rose in his throat as he took one last look, before turning toward Barka.

'Here, let me. You've been at it since dawn. Let me finish.

Barka looked up but slowly shook his head before dropping his eyes once more to the careful planing of the lid.

'I'll get on. Go fetch me a decent bit of brass to fix to the lid. Anyfin' will do, musket stock, gun halter. Find me somfin' nice I can finish off with. Polish it up a bit mind.'

Daemon turned away to begin his search.

***

On the harbour side, a gathering of traders of every possible description now assailed the ship. Guards with loaded muskets had been placed on the gangplank at the head and part way up. The two guards placed on the dock had been withdrawn having been unnerved by the crush and jostling from the crowd.

More armed men were positioned along the sides and at the beam, particularly where the mooring lines flexed up from the quay. Natives were intermittently trying to clamber along the ropes to gain access and although most floundered and ended up in the brine, some had to be forcibly shoved off.

The babble of mixed and hackneyed English dialogue rose and fell as all fought for attention. Arab garb in many varied and vibrant colours mixed with plain, head to toe Muslim blacks and browns.

A few tattered uniforms of various ages and denominations adorned others in the throng. Invalided mixed with able bodied, patched eyes, hooded, priestly and vagabond alike, all considered themselves viable providers of everything from fresh fruit, to powder and shot, to pearl necklaces and livestock.

Only force and steadfast attention prevented the ship from being completely routed.

***

Hours passed, with the throng constantly probing and attempting to gain advantage. The heat of the day enveloped the crew and Nash had not emerged from his cabin. Daemon, having polished up two gun halters and formed them into a 'cross' before presenting them to Barka, had been for some time watching Tarquin and awaiting some sign of direction or order.

By mid-afternoon, the main preoccupation being that of swatting the incessant attentions of mosquitos and flies, the crew were on the brink of mutiny when the doors to the poop deck flung open. Clutching his injured shoulder Nash, appearing overcome with fever, slumped to his knees before Tarquin or Belton could prevent it.

Raising his eyes to the bright sunlight above, he began a lament, begging the Almighty for help and deliverance. The seamen came rambling forward to form a ring about him as his rantings reached a crescendo. Sweat poured from his every pore and his skin reflected a pallid jaundice yellow.

Rickards forced his way through the crowd, reaching for the Captain as Daemon joined him in an attempt to bring Nash back to his quarters. Many of the seamen froze, failing to provide any help. A babble of resistance and complaint rose and only an air shot from Belton's pistol brought them under control.

They backed off as Tarquin raged his contempt.

'Back off you rabble – God forgive me but I'll keel-haul any man showing contempt for the captain... or demonstrating anything other than loyal commitment to this ship. Get back and return to your duties or so help me!'

Between them, he and Daemon grappled Nash down below and settled him onto his bunk. Cold water was applied to his brow whilst orders from Belton were levelled at the crew.

Tarquin murmured that something must be done to establish order and preserve the stability of the ship and its company. He nodded to Daemon his gratitude and bit his lip before uttering a plea for loyalty directly toward him.

'Can I count on you? If anything happens? I will arm you if necessary. Can I depend on you?'

Daemon nodded, and looked squarely into Tarquin's eye, giving his assurance the best he could.

Returning to the galley steps he yelled an order to Belton that the Surgeon was to be brought immediately. When he was able to hand over his ministrations, he signalled to Daemon that he was ready.

Handing a loaded pistol to Daemon, and arming himself, Tarquin clambered up onto the poop deck. Calling Belton to his side a quick exchange of words brought swift agreement. Daemon was stationed on one side and Tarquin the other. Belton leaned on the rail.

'Men, gather round. Richards, Carty, you and the others remain where you are and keep that rabble from the gangplank. You men – will stand firm. We will work together to make this ship seaworthy and to restock her for the journey back to Gibraltar.'

The men cheered at this point. All knew Gibraltar to be the safest haven.

***

'Captain Nash has suffered these few days, his wound, the fever and most of all the unpalatable position he found himself – the loss of his ship and its crew almost a certainty. He has achieved a miracle in getting us this far – don't you forget that my lads!'

Another short burst of approval.

'Now we are going to 'lay off' the harbour. With careful coordination we will bring aboard fresh supplies. We will keep this ship safe from boarders and we will endure! You will have all the food you can manage and we will restock with grog and fresh water.

'Let me hear it lads for the captain and the *Warrior*!'

Given their plight the crew managed a stirring response.

'Parties to go ashore will be formed, well-armed and supported. Let's get the ship into safe waters away from these hoards. We won't be bothered out in the bay.

'Barka, set your men to work on essential repairs. Tarquin, launch a boat to steer us away from the moorings. Irish, you stay with me Barka will have to do without you for the moment.'

Daemon duly stood firm, his cocked pistol resting on his crossed arms. Feeling faintly ridiculous he scanned the ship as if to keep 'watch'. The men proceeded paying him little heed, but Belton may well have felt that his words had been received with a little more enthusiasm for his presence.

***

With *Warrior* anchored in the bay, tensions lifted and a cooling breeze improved the conditions on board.

The boats were in constant use in rotation, never both at one time, being stacked with tradeable items and anything of gold, silver and copper that could be found. They returned with fresh fruit, a barrel of port, drinking water, sailcloth and timber.

Repairs were carried out around the clock, seamen hanging in harness and applying pitch to the hull. Timber repairs made to every splintered rail and deck board. Sailcloth was being mended and replaced and new hemp replaced the rigging and nets.

Belton returned late one afternoon, his launch full of supplies. Sacks of dates, raisins and coarse wheat which could be quickly made into couscous. During the unloading Tarquin called Daemon to his side.

'I have made contact with an Anglican Priest, he has offered to perform a ceremony and inter our dead.

We will form a burial party but I will provide an armed guard. Belton will lead the party and I am confident it will go without incident. I, however, must remain with the *Warrior*. If anything did transpire on shore, I have to be here to take full responsibility.' Daemon acknowledged and muttered his appreciation in having been taken into the officer's confidence.

The following morning they made ready to go ashore. They could put off no longer the arrangements for Lady Daphne and the two deceased officers. The burial party was organised. Nash had emerged into the bright morning of the third day looking pale but much more in control of himself.

The Christian chapel was on a rise outside the city and three coffins were carried across in the boats and mounted onto a cart. A formal entourage of six armed guards accompanied Nash and Tarquin and four hands to do the digging and handling the coffins, Daemon amongst them. Another four pulled on the oars and were to stand by the boat at all times.

It had been in Daemon's mind some days that he would be leaving the ship at the earliest opportunity. He knew that Morocco was attainable. His quest to find Kirsten would soon be under way. The opportunity with a depleted crew, difficult conditions leading to a regime far less formal than usual, gave ample opportunity for his escape.

He had toiled long and hard on the rights and wrongs of the situation. He had been 'pressed' into service, but this had suited his purpose. He had taken the opportunity which may never have emerged in a lifetime, to sail from Britain to North Africa. He had one objective in mind throughout all the difficulties and hardships. When he reached Africa, he would extricate himself from His Majesty's Navy, and find his way into the Arab slave enclaves.

Now he was troubled, he had found comradeship amongst these men, even friendship, for the first time in his life. He had fought with them, survived with them, learned about life.

Now in their hour of need, he was intending to slip away in the night and leave all that behind. Should he wait? Did he owe them his loyalty? Should he at least see the ship safely back to British territory, then take an honourable leave of the service?

For the moment he was torn, and would have to at least see his latest task completed before making his move. As the boat quietly slipped across the bay, his hand laid gently on the smooth timber of Lady Daphne's coffin, he felt a strange spiritual connection with the tragic figure within. Born to such a high society and a life of such finery, en route to a resting place in a parched North African sandstone grave.

Chapter 16

Kirsten and Banoldino

Travelling on, as lovers, made the hardships of the journey as nothing.

Kirsten felt safe and confident in her companion. Banoldino was transfixed, in love with his! He admired her straight back, wide athletic shoulders, firm breasts and soft, impossibly slender torso.

She in turn admired his immensely powerful upper body, his straight hips and sturdy thighs, she watched as he moved gracefully about every task. His every movement almost as a flamenco dancer, pulled up to his full height.

His skin had been lightening during the duration of their journey. It no longer had that deep 'orangey' tone of over-exposure to the sun. Now, despite the deep blackness of his hair, he was appearing more and more European by the day.

He held her hand at every opportunity. Led her safely across streams and lifted her down effortlessly from rocky terrain.

They heard numerous accounts of refugees, moving northward, with few possessions, come from Baltimore and trying to find a new home. On two occasions villagers explained how they had moved the refugees on. There was precious little to keep the locals in food and few opportunities of paid work.

They began to resent the people in the countryside, selfish, inverted people. Strangers were treated with a courtesy, as long as they kept moving.

Banoldino appeared impatient at the lack of grace and civility. He was deprived of conversation, or as he described them to Kirsten one night, under the stars, 'these people are unworldly!'

After weeks of travelling, the smoking chimneys of a larger township appeared, and beyond the mountainous outcrop, swooped down to the sea.

Drawing not a few inquisitive looks, they made their way toward the pier, where to Kirsten's delight she immediately spotted a group from Baltimore. Numbering seven in total, Grandfather O'Carroll, his daughter Marie, and her six-year-old twins, together with Kate Hurley, her daughter Aisleen, who was about eleven years of age, and a baby in arms.

Kirsten was so overjoyed at seeing them she left Banoldino's side and raced forward. As one they turned to her, there were cries of excitement, their greetings endless, with Kirsten twirling one, then the other of the boys in the air! She took the baby and cuddled her close to her bosom as if burning life into her.

Banoldino stood aside until minutes passed and Kirsten turned toward him. After a difficult moment she swallowed hard and called him over. She pulled him toward her and wrapped herself around a free arm.

'This is my friend, and he's... well, he has taken care of me! I would have died but for him! He rescued me when... '

Suddenly she realised they may not have known about the ship!

Questions suddenly poured out. What happened to you? How did you escape? Where are the others?

She blurted out, 'Did yea not know? The ship sank! Everyone was drowned! 'The slavers... everyone! I... I broke free. This man pulled me from the water. Since then he has been my guardian!

The gathering as one, eyed the pair suspiciously, waiting for further explanation.

'What about Sinead? Tammy? What about my sister?'

Kirsten shook her head, her eyes awash with tears.

'I can't tell you... the storm... the heathens couldn't handle the ship! They didn't know what to do and everything just went down! But Jesus, it was ferocious. I should have been lying at the bottom of the sea. But believe me, that would have been a better end than if we had all ended up slaves to those bastards, sold for whores and worse!'

Kate put her hands to Aisleen's ears. Looking admonishingly at Kirsten, she turned half away before taking the baby.

'Wait, Kate, please! I have seen so much these last few weeks. I returned with Banoldino, to the village. I saw the graves. The devastation... I nearly died, I was whipped by a slaver.' She pulled her shirt to show the deep red stripe that would be with her for life as her permanent reminder. ' I got that for talking out loud.'

Kate seemed to find some understanding within her. Accepting that their world had been turned inside out, she put a hand out to Kirsten and brushed her cheek.

O'Carroll looked toward them, 'Are you seeking passage? To the New World? Will yea go with us?'

Kirsten looked at her companion, no words had passed between them of the future, or what lay ahead but simultaneously they drew the conclusion that... 'Yes! Why not? We will go with you.'

***

Banoldino looked over at the three-masted galleon in the harbour.

'Is this the ship? *The Star of the Seas*? She looks sturdy enough. Have you met the captain?' Banoldino betrayed the Spanish origins of his accent

O'Carrol spoke. 'Aye we have paid our passage and we are convened here to board her this morning. We sail on tonight's high tide.' Turning to Kirsten, 'What about yea own passage, have yea the coin to pay?'

Kirsten looked up bewildered, ' Er... no, we've nothing. We barely had a stitch to cover us after the storm. We'll have to find a way... Banoldino?'

'I have an idea. You have to trust me. Please stay with your friends. I will find a way.'

As soon as he was distant enough from their hearing, O' Carrol made an offer. 'Kirsten, listen child. I don't know how this man turned up or what happened between yea, but if yea want to get away from him, I'll help yea. I can get yea passage, with a few coins I have left. You can come wi' us, ye'll be safe... '

Immediately and without hesitation Kirsten turned, 'Grandfather O' Caroll, that is very kind of you, but I know this man. Believe me, he is honest, and decent. He's a fine man. He would lay down his life for me... for us. I believe in him. He will return with the means to pay. He will offer us his protection.'

'Yea have faith in him. I can see that. But think again, do yea want tae tie yerself to this man? It takes months to sail to the New World. It will be hard for sure.' He looked at her, she was a sight for any man's eyes and he was only too aware of the trouble that could bring. Maybe it will be just as well if he makes the journey. 'I'm sorry darlin', but I haven't enough to pay his passage.'

Within minutes Banoldino returned carrying a pouch of silver. By this time the little party had settled down onto some old baskets and with sail cloth covering the children, they were exchanging stories about the last hours of the village and the fate of their families and friends. Kirsten was hardly able to add much in the end. She could account for five or six of her companions but the inevitability of their demise meant that her tale was cut short.

She turned and hugged Banoldino, and he held out his hand to let the sack of money drop into hers. 'I am certain this will pay our passage, I will seek out the captain.'

Kirsten's eyes were wide. 'How in heaven did you manage this? I hope yea did not hit someone over the head!'

'Er, no. Sadly I had to part with something very precious to me.'

He held open his shirt and showed his naked breast. Puzzled at first Kirsten suddenly realised, for the first time since she had set eyes on him the heavy gold cross and chain was missing from his neck. 'Oh you have traded your chain! That's a grand thing to 've done. I don't know how to thank you.'

His eyes were shining. 'For you, I would have given anything.'

The children began shouting hurray, hurray, that Kirsten would be joining them on the journey. They were all showing their delight when a coach and horses drew into the harbour and amid scraping and clattering drew to a halt on the cobbles.

Their attention, and that of all in the vicinity, was drawn immediately toward the fine spectacle before them.

Coachmen alighted from their perch, willing helpers drew around.

The doors were flung open and a finely dressed gentlemen stepped from the coach. Turning, he held out his hand and helped his lady companion down the steps. Two young girls and a well-tailored boy followed and an ageing, portly male in tricorn, attired in black from head to foot, followed into the street.

Showing his distaste for everything in proximity, the red-faced, businessman, huffed and puffed his way toward the harbour side, holding a kerchief to his nose the entire time.

Luggage was unloaded on to a handcart, and the party gathered into an isolated group, distancing themselves by the sheer size and numeracy of their belongings and their entourage.

Peering into the distance, His Lordship eyed *The Star of the Seas* and commented on her condition. His lawyer showed little interest, producing a sheaf of papers, passing various things of great import to his master.

The coach stood by, but the servants retreated leaving just the coachman and their immediate family in the group.

Banoldino and Kirsten looked on, the distance between them only a matter of ten to fifteen yards, Kirsten reflected on what a distance that was. That their worlds would never meet. Banoldino looked on and saw something very different.

'The New World,' he said slowly and deliberately. 'Even the highest of men would go there! For... opportunity? Perhaps, for a dream. I can make a promise to you, my love. Very soon there will come a time when I will dress you in the finest clothes, when I carry you on a fine coach. When men like His Lordship will invite us to dinner!'

Kirsten looked up at him. His eyes were moist, fixed and determined. For a moment she considered what he said. Suddenly a laugh burst from her lips.

'You are laughing at me.'

'No, not at all. I am laughing because I almost believe you.

Just then a fracas broke out. Two or three of the local chancers had gotten closer and closer to the well-to-do party, and despite being threatened by his Lordship, would not retreat. They held out beggars hands and pleaded for alms. But closer and closer they ventured until they stood near enough for one to reach out and grab the lady's purse, another blocked off His Lordship's attempt to restrain the lout and the other bumped him to the ground. The lawyer showing surprising stealth unsheathed his sword and thrashed one of them across the back, whilst His Lordship regained his feet.

The two louts grappled with them, as one of the boys joined in the melee and attacked from the rear.

A cutlass was drawn and the lawyer's rapier was shattered into three pieces at an attempted parry, meanwhile His Lordship was grappled to the ground, and his lady screamed for help.

Banoldino was on his feet and racing toward them in seconds. He bodily threw one of the louts into the harbour and smashed his fist into the side of the other's head. Helping His Lordship to his feet, he turned just as the lout rose from the ground brandishing a pistol.

He swung it into position and would have fired had Banoldino not kicked it from his grasp with the toe of his boot. The shot fired and flew into the air above His Lordship's head. Banoldino grabbed the man by the throat and thudded a fist into his grubby face, seeing him drop like a stone.

The lady continued to cry out. 'My jewels – they're everything I have… my family….'

Banoldino looked across the pier to see the thief disappearing around the corner of the largest warehouse. He looked over to Kirsten who by this time had arrived to comfort the gentleman and help the boy who had been grappled to the ground.

Her look in return assured him that it was her wish that he try to do something, and immediately set him off in pursuit.

A guard by this time had joined the group and offering his help he kept other brigands at a distance whilst taking the fallen one into captivity. He was soon joined by others and their protection was negotiated by the lawyer.

Meanwhile Banoldino had rounded the warehouse, saw the long stretch of open land between there and the next shelter of any note and realised the assailant must have entered the building.

Inside three ruddy faced men gutted fish and feigned concentration to the task. Banoldino stood in the doorway and surveyed the scene. Steps, leading upward, into a room across the warehouse offered a possible hideout. But a number of benches, piles of rope and empty baskets offered others.

Banoldino made to leave and the men began a sniggering exchange of expletives, but waiting just out of sight Banoldino was rewarded as another voice joined in and a pile of boxes disturbed, splintered and broke. Banoldino swiftly returned to the entrance and saw the thief swaggering toward the group with the purse open, showing his ill-gotten gains.

'Quick, y'eejit' get gone.' One of the workers quickly alerted the thief to Banoldino's presence and set him off running again the length of the warehouse. Banoldino gave chase but two of the fish workers made to block his way.

Immediately Banoldino pulled his dagger from behind his back and brandished it in front of them. The foot long, fine Spanish steel blade glistened in the light and his expert handling of it was enough.

They quickly parted and allowed him to pass through, shrugging their shoulders in a gesture that showed the preservation of the thief was hardly worth the risk.

The thief now returned to the harbour area and was caught in two minds as to whether to flee or to seek help from the local riff-raff. When Banoldino set eyes on him he had run into O' Tooles bar and then out again and was searching in every direction for a possible escape route. Banoldino walked slowly but determinedly toward him and, unable to make up his mind, the brigand drew his cutlass and decided to face up to his pursuer.

The contest lasted only seconds, two slashes and a misplaced lunge by the assailant found the hilt of Banoldino's dagger resting against the third and fourth rib of his right side.

He slumped to the ground allowing her Ladyship's purse to spill its contents onto the cobbled street. A number of locals made a motion toward them but the thief now lay motionless, clutching his stomach. Banoldino's eyes, never leaving the onlookers, retrieved the contents of the purse. He left the gathering, walking backward toward the harbour where the throng awaiting the voyage had grown sufficiently to separate those boarding, from the rest.

Passengers from every possible walk of life. More of the gentry had joined the group and others with even fewer possessions than the former Baltimore habitants, inevitably to be separated once on board. There were three classes for the voyage. First, second and steerage. Kirsten and her companions were clearly designated steerage.

Banoldino sought out the now becalmed gathering around His Lordship, and his Lady, and they were taking refreshment when Banoldino returned the purse to its rightful owner.

'Eternal gratitude to you my good man. Please allow me to reward you for your endeavour.' Her Ladyship, intervened, scolding her husband. 'My dear, you owe this man your life, and I owe him for the preservation of the few possessions I cherish. Please, my dear, reward him – yes – offer him anything he wants.'

'My dear, leave this to me, I am sure I can find a way to… Senor… er may I have your name…?'

Banoldino feigned a bow, first to her Ladyship, then toward her husband. 'Banoldino… Don Bosco. At your service.'

'Ah, from Espana. My dear chap. Please allow me to shake your hand. We truly do owe you a debt of gratitude. You have demonstrated that you are a very capable man.

'Indeed, I have a proposition. Clearly the passage ahead is going to be a difficult one. Of course when we arrive in New England, we have our connections, but, during the passage at least, I would propose to hire you to protect my family and belongings, and, may I suggest that, your good lady, could be of great assistance to my dear wife, during the voyage. Suitable remuneration to be agreed of course. What do you say? You would of course be obliged to share accommodation in the proximity of our quarters.'

Banoldino stood erect. A certain condescension in His Lordship's manner held him back momentarily but taking stock of the situation, the condition of many of the other passengers, he decided to take the offer with good grace.

'Sir, if I may consult with my er, companion, I will deliver my answer to you in a matter of a few moments.'

With a hint of a salute, Banoldino withdrew.

Approaching Kirsten, now reconciled with her friends, Banoldino had no hesitation in making the case for an alliance with the most respected passengers likely to be making this voyage. When Kirsten urged that she wanted to be with her friends, Banoldino pointed out that she would have ample opportunity to be of benefit to her friends, 'medication', 'clean water', 'food parcels'. As a much travelled individual, Banoldino was well aware of how difficult things might become once under sail.

Kirsten agreed, accepting the invitation to board ahead of the rest of the waiting passengers, at the behest of their new employer.

Chapter 17

On African Soil

Daemon considered making a run for it at the very first opportunity, but he stayed with the party wishing to see Lady Daphne properly buried.

The burial party made its way through the throng, a babbling, forest of mysterious silk and linen clad 'ghosts', gliding across their path and making narrow channels for them to pass.

From time to time the crowd's attention would focus on the party, under the snarling, rasping command of some irate individual, the gathering would sway one way or another, giving pursuit of the parade and forming a line of stragglers as it made its way through the narrow, twisting streets.

Occasionally rotting fruit would be thrown, so as to cause unease, it seemed, rather than injury. Some of the guard made to unshoulder their firearms but under Belton's steady command resisted for the moment.

Belton constantly sought the attention of the more venerable or prosperous types, desperate to make contact with the authorities. He called out in English, then in French to attempt to establish some dialogue. No-one responded and nothing remotely resembling authority intruded on their progress. There were no soldiers, guards or even clerical types to connect them to the local power base.

The progress to the Christian settlement was arduous but at least once through the gates leading to the very typical

Norman, stone-built chapel, the resident parson was more than helpful.

'Monsieur, if there is anything I can do, I am at your service,' Alphonse Le Clerk announced as they set the coffins down on hard, sandy ground. A swirling wind blew gritty sand into their faces, but the party was well disciplined and respectful of their task and bore the inconvenience with dignity.

' Monsieur, I am most grateful,' offered Belton. 'I must ask whether you would know if the local Emir is aware of our presence?'

'But of course, monsieur, Sheik Ram Damir has watched your every move since your arrival.'

'Is he aware of whom we are attempting to provide a decent burial? Does he know of the status of the unfortunate family involved? I was sure his curiosity alone would be enough to bring him out to make acquaintance!'

'I believe so monsieur, but the Emir is well aware that there is no leadership, no dignitary, ahem, 'alive' on board your vessel. The Emir has taken the stance that you will sail away when the refit is complete and your food and water refreshed. The Emir does not wish to make a 'commitment' of any kind on the grounds that the French are expected soon! Any 'courtesy' extended toward yourself maybe misconstrued!'

'Indeed? If that is his concern then it should also be mine! 'You men, proceed to the open graves and assemble for the ceremony! Your confidence, and indeed the freedom with which you have imparted the information is appreciated. You say the Emir has stood off, in anticipation of French disapproval. Yet, he has not attempted to 'take' us, and win French gratitude?'

'Au contreur! The Emir does not wish to favour any party above another. He would reside in indifference if that were possible. He wishes to preserve the status quo but considers that allowing the French to believe they are more welcome may be the most sensible way for the moment. At some time in the future, he may well feel the same toward the British. But for now, he will not interfere with your activities, if you do not place any demands upon him.'

'I see. I am intent on immediate departure We shall cause no further inconvenience toward his Worthiness, providing we in turn are not importuned in any way.'

'Meanwhile, you have indicated no particular regard for the French yourself – in advising that the French fleet will have a presence here very soon. You realise that such information could be used to great advantage.'

'I, sir, am an Anglican priest – no papist! My sympathies are entirely with the British Crown and all those whom represent it.

'Glad to hear it Father... ahem... shall we proceed with the matter in hand?'

The formal burials were completed and the gathering of twenty or more souls were duly respectful, none more so than Daemon who could not hold back a tear as he watched the lady's coffin lowered the three or four feet the hard ground had allowed them. Daemon looked up at the sky and scanned the endless blueness as if searching the wispy cloud where an ethereal shape might pass on its way to the heavens.

A sharp retort from Belton brought him to attention and he systematically fell-in with the guard as it reeled away down the hill toward the church gate.

Back on the fringe of town where the market stalls covered almost the entire surface of the area outside the castle gates, a pathway of just a few feet could be recognised, Belton immediately ordered that the cart was to be abandoned.

For some distance they managed reasonably well until, just about half way across the square, a soldier brushed the edge of a light timber trestle table which was adorned by a massed array of trinkets, accidentally spilling the pile onto the stony ground.

The stall holder leapt to his feet remonstrating, almost foaming at the mouth in a torrent of guttural, unintelligible insults. His neighbours rose to join in his verbal assault and pushing and shoving fuelled the general unease.

The first of the line had passed through and the incident affected the centre, Daemon and his shipmates having fallen-in behind the line, brought up the rear and were now in the centre of the developing melee.

Punches were thrown and suddenly there was a massed assault on the formerly controlled withdrawal. Belton shouted orders to the guard and shots rang out as they emptied their muskets into the air.

Many of the swollen crowd cowered away, but now some of the sailors were engaged in a desperate struggle to free themselves. Curved long bladed knives flashed and slashed downward toward unguarded shoulders and two of the sailors were immediately rendered wounded and defenceless.

The guard closed in having reloaded and Belton held two pistols at the ready, sufficiently to drive the throng backward, but Daemon and Rankin, the bosun's mate, became detached in the struggle.

The wounded were gathered and Belton fired shots again to clear a path. Daemon meanwhile had clambered up a wall and stood on the cracked tiles of a lean-to. Stooping low he held out a hand for Rankin but the crowd grappled the young fair-haired seaman to the ground, wrenched free of Daemon's hand.

Now the throng turned its attention on Daemon and began scrambling up toward him. Kicking and flailing at them he knocked two or three of them back but it was a losing battle, more clambered up the walls of the main building and were gaining advantageous positions where they would be able to drop on him.

Belton yelled at him from across the courtyard to get away, 'across the rooftops man!' Suddenly, one of his assailants arched upright and launched off the rooftop, toppling onto the crowd below as a shot from Belton caught him between the shoulder blades.

Now a sustained volley from the remaining guard saw roof tiles splinter and plaster crumbling from the walls around him. Another assailant slumped to his knees, holding an arm.

Desperate, Daemon leapt for a ledge on the opposite side of the narrow street to his right. The overhanging roof gave him plenty of purchase as he lunged for an adjoining parapet and swung upward to the next.

Very soon he was looking down onto the crowd in the throbbing marketplace, which was almost tearing down the walls of the building beneath him. Rankin had disappeared from sight. Stones and rotten fruit were thrown in showers up at him and a dagger clattered onto the roof beside him. Fortunately no firearms were within their grasp.

The main body appeared to turn its attention on Belton and the armed guards amounting to a charge toward their position at the mouth of a narrow alley. With one look of helplessness, Belton finally gave the command for the troop to retreat and assuming Daemon had half a chance of escape, sought to save the majority and retreat all the way to the harbour.

Now alone, Daemon was left to try to make his escape across the roof tops. Sufficiently deterred by the thunderous volley of the six muskets the baying crowd had lost some of its enthusiasm and Daemon leapt from rooftop to rooftop, he felt that the pursuit was less of a concern than the precarious loose tiles across which he must now make his escape.

Descending almost to street level, he was able to reach a quiet part of the township, where tightly-packed shacks and the odd brick-built structures lead away toward a line of low hills and the brown, arid countryside to the south.

Carpets and an array of white linen hung from a hundred sagging ropes where the townsfolk demonstrated their ability to constantly wash and dry clothing.

Much of it provided the cover he needed to skirt the town in his attempt to reach the harbour, that he might rejoin the ship. However, as night fell and he was able to rest amongst some boulders in a cool hollow, he reflected that what had happened was in fact at least as good as the best plan he could have formed for himself.

He had gained access to North Africa, he had not abandoned or deserted, he had found a way to leave the British Navy without disgracing himself.

Here he was. All he had to do was lie low, and eventually make his way safely from this hostile environment. There was nothing more for him on board the British 'man-of-war' – he had done his bit, even become quite attached to them, but now he had his own future to forge. He was on a mission after all.

Chapter 18

Crossing the Atlantic

When Kirsten was shown her quarters, a small area enclosing a 'cot' and a small chest for storage, upon which sat a blue patterned, ceramic wash bowl, she felt grateful for Banoldino's endeavours and the rewards they had brought. Across a narrow passage the doors of a salon provided roomy accommodation to Lord Ranleigh and his family.

It had not occurred to Kirsten that the little space she had claimed as her own, was to be shared, inevitably, with her 'husband'.

The realisation came over her causing her to blush self-consciously, and a little film of perspiration formed above her top lip.

Banoldino pulled off his shirt and lay down on the cot adjusting the straw filled pillows to enable him to raise his head sufficiently to look at Kirsten as she dabbed her forehead with water from the bowl.

'May I ask if you are well, my dear? You appear a little uneasy.'

'Er... I... er, it's just the whirlwind of the last few days, it's all left me a little bit... '

'Kirsten, please. If there is anything, anything in the world, I can do to help.' He raised himself on his elbows. 'My dear, I am your servant.'

'Please, don't worry. It's just, well, I need a little time… to get used to… ' she looked around the space and her expression told all he needed to know.

'You mean that cheating captivity and struggling for survival across a strange countryside is one thing, but to be suddenly required to behave as man and wife in enclosed quarters is another.'

'I have never slept in a bed, never mind sharing one with a stranger.'

'I understand completely and will make my quarters elsewhere for the time being.' He rose to his feet and made to edge around her.

'Wait, don't, that's not what I want, but, it's just strange and….' He put a finger across her lips. Pulling her toward him he leaned down to kiss her. Her arms reached up and held him.

'My darling, what you have been through in the past months has almost been a lifetime of terror, mixed with *excitement.* Do you not think I understand that. I want to protect you, I want to be there when you cry out in the night, but if you need time, then you have it. I only want your happiness and I am prepared to wait.

'Banoldino, I don't know how to say what I want to say. That's… '

'You know, that is the first time you have used my name.'

'*Banoldino.*There, I hope I will always have you close by, when I call out.'

'Kirsten, wait… we are aboard a ship, bound for a new world! When we arrive there will be hardships to face, but a great adventure also. I want you to go forward as … my wife. Once we set sail the captain can marry us.'

'You would make me your *wife*, in a ceremony, proper, in the eyes of God? Oh! I think I need to sit down.'

For some moments tears flowed and anguish showed on her face.

Banoldino stood by, silently watching but deciding it would be best to let her come round in her own time.

Kirsten was back in the village, in springtime, standing for her best friend Sinead, as the priest blessed them, in a little ceremony outside the village church, Sinead and herself with matching garlands woven into their hair. She remembered looking over at Sinead's mother who wept openly, then to her own mother whose eyes were fixed, shining and entirely focused on Kirsten herself.

A knowing look passed between them, it was enough for Kirsten to appreciate that her mother was looking forward to a time when Kirsten herself would be the bride, and how proud she would be.

For now, knowing that she would never see her mother, the rest of the family, even her own village, ever again, overwhelmed her.

For long moments she remained seated with a small cloth to dab at her eyes. Banoldino allowed her all the time she needed. He excused himself and left to seek out his new master.

Chapter 19

Abandoned in Algiers

Daemon awoke and immediately he could smell trouble. The sweat encrusted armpit of an overweight, silk-clad alien was inches from his nose. Attempting to right himself he felt the muscular arm tighten around his throat. Every attempt to free himself was met with equal force. Then when he felt that he would slip through the hold now that a fresh slick of perspiration formed between his neck and the arm of his captor, a second, more nimble than the first, took his arms and locked them into an unnatural and painful position.

Head pointing toward the floor and arms behind him, tied roughly, at the wrists, found Daemon scraping the stony ground with his face.

It was all he could do to spit away the dirt from his lips to prevent it lodging in his throat. With no freedom whatsoever, he had no option but to relax his straining muscles, lie in an untidy heap, and await the next element of discomfort to fall upon him.

After some time the light faded behind high walls, leaving him in virtual darkness. With no sounds coming from his immediate surroundings, he took the opportunity to turn and find a sitting position, where, after some effort, he could find a position where his aching limbs ached a little less, he could gather his thoughts and try to assess his predicament.

Exotic smells reached him from nearby habitats, and in the distance high-pitched wailing, emerging from the towns religious centres, pervaded the dusk and created a chilling atmosphere which matched his mood perfectly.

Aching and stiff as the night became cold and his discomfort found him beginning to despair, he began to call out, quietly at first, then louder until he quite surprised himself at the desperation in his own voice. The wailing had ceased and more normal sounds now permeated the night air, the odd dog barking, a child's cry, laughter.

Daemon was convinced his calling out would bring a visit from one of his captors, even if it produced a violent reaction, he was quite prepared for it rather than remain, in the dark, alone and forgotten.

His assumption proved right as within a few moments his turbaned gaoler appeared at the far end of what he had now decided was a straw topped hut. Approaching in his flat-footed, lumbering way, the guard emitted a horsey laugh as the sight of Daemon seemed to amuse him.

The guard lay down a wooden pallet upon which Daemon could make out the shape of a crusty, dark chunk of bread. A small bowl containing thin, cloudy liquid sat on the edge of the platter.

'How am I supposed to eat this you great oaf'?' Was all Daemon could think of to say. It occurred to him almost immediately that this may not be the smartest utterance he had made. But the gaoler just grunted and half turned making to leave.

Daemon shot out a foot, winding it around the leg of his captor in an attempt to gain attention. Almost stumbling, the guard angrily swiped Daemon across the face with the back of his hand. Flexing his jaw to detect any fracture, Daemon was able to at least realise the seriousness of his situation. Anther grunt from the guard satisfied Daemon that further dialogue could put himself into the realms of danger. Nonetheless he blurted

'Look, what's your problem? Who are you? Why am I here?'

Taking a handful of hair, the guard brought his face and Daemons into very close proximity. His foul breath through curling lips assured Daemon that 'You prisoner, you will be sold in slave market, two days from now, eat up your food – you must eat, the fatter the better!' The horsey laugh once again.

'What are you talking about? I am nobody's slave! I am a... an... officer, in His Majesty's Navy. I'm British. You can't sell me in any slave market!'

'Nobody want you. We offered you to ship's captain for ransom. Pity – he did not wish to pay. So now...'

'What, are you trying to say you offered me for ransom and they refused? What the hell! Jesus, who was it? Who did you talk to?

'Captain of the English warship, he told Hamden Pasha he no have gold.'

'That's a lie, a damned lie I'd say! How much gold did you ask for, for Christ's sake?'

'No, not Christ, Mohammed, of course! We ask for ten pounds of gold for 'brave' British officer!' They laugh!'

'Laugh did they? I'm not surprised – I'm no officer, I'm a friggin' ship's carpenter, self-styled to boot! Surely they made an offer of some sort?'

'They offer pistol and cutlass, but no gold!' At this point the guard laughed until his chest heaved.'

Daemon could find nothing amusing about the situation. He was unable to accept that his freedom had not been purchased, whatever the reality of the situation, he was left feeling sick and desperate at the conclusion of their discourse.

Indicating the difficulty with which he was likely to be faced before he could partake of the pallet of food, he tried to get the guard to adjust his bindings, but the guard simply demonstrated by prostrating himself on all fours and indicating that the way to consume the 'feast' that had been provided, was to take it like a dog, leading with his face!

His appetite waning, Daemon indicated that he had done with conversation for the night and the guard turned with a shrug of the shoulders and left him. Within minutes two rats, the size of young tomcats, had scampered over to the pallet and commenced to dine without him!

A virtually sleepless night passed during which Daemon had hallucinated, kicked out at rats and allowed himself to replay his recent past. The brush with Tarquin on an Irish country road, trussed and tied up in a coach bound for the coast. Mistreated by shipmates on his first voyage, thrust into combat and drawing blood of the enemy. Witnessing carnage and the death of a beautiful lady; grappling with a crowd of heathens in a marketplace, now tied in a rat infested hovel.

Most of all his mind wandered to Kirsten, he was beginning to find it difficult to recall her features, her lithe body was crystal clear in his mind, but her eyes? Shaking his head he resolved to do something come daybreak. He must press on, she herself may be lying in straw, being gnawed by rats or writhing in some fever. He would make the break – tomorrow.

***

Overcome by the cloying heat, sun beating down upon his head like a hammer, Daemon slumped to the rough timber. Feeling the soft, broken fabric of the beams which had once been solid timber appeared strange at first. Digging with a dislodged nail, he was able to split a quarter of an inch of the top surface free and pull out a piece two and half inches long.

It felt comforting to him to be holding a piece of timber. He recalled times on the Warrior when Barka would smash open a plank of wood, making five or six strands which could be stretched and curved and used to fill in gaping splits in the hull. For a big lumbering giant, Barka had such a delicate touch when using his tools, he could shape a piece of timber and plane it smooth, he could make a tennon joint or tongue and groove one plank to another, making an invisible joint.

Staring down at the timber beneath him, Daemon remained on hands and knees, as minutes went by. He watched the sweat from his brow land in small pools on the greasy planks which made up the platform which had supported an endless parade of human traffic over a period of what must have been a lifetime.

Lost in thought, a smile broke on his cracked lips, causing him to poke the tip of his dry tongue between them, in a vain attempt to spread the tiniest dreg of moisture from the inside of a parched mouth.

A dry cough emitted from his chest, hurting the lining of his throat, wiping away the attempted smile. Daemon felt, to lay his head upon the deck, and just close his eyes would be the closest thing to happiness that he could imagine. At the moment he was about to succumb to this overwhelming desire, a sharp whip-crack, followed by a stinging slash across his back, brought his head up sharply.

Squinting into the sun his tormentor of the previous few days leered down at him, his big round face and several stubbled chins, drew into a wide arching grimace. 'Stand up you cur! You human slop-waste! Vomit of a hyena, stand! On your feet! Remain on your feet!'

His hand drew back and was threatening to smash into Daemon's face, but pulled up at the last second, followed by a hissing guffaw of laughter from deep inside a sweating barrel- chest.

Daemon's head throbbed, he attempted to mouth a few words, begging for water when a pale full was released from a distance of three feet engulfing him in the sensation of a plunge in a fresh mountain stream.

Catching his breath, he inhaled, in a loud unseemly gasp, but instinctively, swept up the water with his tongue as it streamed down his face in strong rivulets. It brought blessed relief to his pain, easing his soreness and the throbbing overheated thumping in his brain.

For some moments he continued to gasp and suck in droplets of water until he felt quite restored. He tensed his arms, pulling tight against his bindings, but achieved no relief.

He again closed his eyes, but this time instead of a downward slump he threw back his head and sucked long, deep breaths into his lungs, refreshing his blood oxygen to a heady level, making him at least half human in ability to resist the next indignity or physical assault that his captor might bring down upon him.

Suddenly there was a blur of activity. An entourage filed into the square, others rose from their stalls and from open shop doorways to join them, creating a heaving mass. Voices were raised, trumpets blown.

When the 'leader' swept in to the melee, others cleared a path for him. His followers, whilst observing every nicety, pressed back the crowd until the Pacha was able to reach the dais without the inconvenience of human contact.

Standing legs astride, hands on hips and a riding crop beating the side of his leather riding boot he appraised the line of captives with a look of abject distaste.

His manner sharp and tone objectionable to those whom understood his Arab tongue, he called-out 'Bah! Is this the best you can offer? I waste my time coming to this poor excuse for a marketplace! Bring me water! Bring my horses water.'

He stood impatient, passing the moment by re-appraising the gathered human livestock. His eyes fell upon Daemon, still dripping from his dousing with cold water. The grime had been filtered to reveal small patches of his natural fair skin, whilst his sky blue eyes, gleamed back through the thick coating of grime.

For some moments the Pacha watched Daemon appearing to find something of interest in the Westerner. With a gesture he summoned one of his entourage and directed him to remove Daemon from the chain, indicating that his hands should be freed but legs remain shackled.

Daemon was guided toward a position a few feet away from the leader who was about to address his captive when the horses were lead into the square.

One, a striking black stallion, bucked and reared excitedly, stirred undoubtedly, by the swaying masses that spilled from every vantage point.

The stallion was clearly agitated and for a moment escaped his minder and thrust his head into the faces of the crowd. The leader raised his arms as if to quell the excitement in the animal's blood.

For a brief moment there was recognition, but almost immediately a shriek of pain emitted as the sandaled foot of an onlooker was crushed beneath the powerful rear hoof of the great stallion.

Seeing the distress caused and the angry reaction of the nearest placed of the crowd, the leader became irritated and lashed out at the horse with his crop! The reaction from the animal was even more dramatic, rearing high on his heels and thrashing at the air with his front hooves.

Suddenly the Pasha himself was in danger with nowhere to retreat, he could easily have been injured by his own prize possession!

Daemon stepped forward instinctively. Recalling from some distant corner of his memory the times back in Ireland when he would bring a tinker's wild pony to heel.

Daemon raised his hands in almost a motion of surrender. He allowed his head to drop to one side as in a sad repose, he did not move toward the animal but in a deep throaty burr he repeated the first line of an old Irish lullaby.

The Stallion caught his mood, bounced his forelegs twice more on the stony sand, but calmed to the point that his head eased alongside Daemon's, as if to hear more clearly the soothing lament. Although his feet were still tied restricting his movement, his hands were free to stroke the stallion along his neck and face.

The crowd, from swirling about, in panic, began to settle and a smile broke out upon many of their faces revealing broken, yellowing teeth as far as the eye could see.

The Pacha approached, gingerly at first, but his own smile, dazzling and lit with genuine delight, eased alongside Daemon and adopted the strangers soothing actions until Daemon was content to ease back and leave the Pacha clear space to regain the animal's confidence.

'Thunder'… 'Thunder' – you are my beauty… you are a wild one…! We must find you a friend… someone who can harness the 'thunder'… Eh?'

Head down and still under the effects of the heat, tired and aching from confinement Daemon slumped back against the dais.

Suddenly the Leader turned and spat orders to his guard, Daemon was swept up and bodily moved through the crowd.

There were a number of carts lined up behind a more finely draped wagon and Daemon was lifted into the second cart. A leather bottle was pushed into his face and the gate of the cart was closed and locked by an elaborate arrangement of ropes and pulleys.

Gratefully Daemon sipped on the fresh water, a dizziness engulfing him as it coursed through his system.

For several hours he waited. Bored and drowsy, he slept. He was disturbed, from a restless sleep, by the swaying of the cart. A number of captives were climbing onto the cart and the slatted, timber springs which afforded a level of comfort when the cart negotiated rough terrain, allowed a significant swaying movement when being mounted.

Four young Arab boys were ranged across from him and all eyed him with curiosity. Daemon opened one eye, surveyed the scene and decided to resume his restful repose. He began to realise that he was certain to invite curiosity from almost everyone he encountered. His face by now was sixty percent covered by the grizzly beginnings of a beard, somewhere between ginger and fair. His hair had long since slumped across his forehead and covered most of the remainder of his face. Bushed eyebrows and grizzly sideburns completed the shaggy visage.

Only patches of reddened, pinkish skin glowed through with his eyes the only other feature visible. He began to think himself 'hermit-like' and believed others must, likewise. He hunched himself up against the creaking timber poles and shut down any avenue of communication for the time being.

What ensued was a long, stultifying journey across the desert, in broiling heat, over a period of six days and nights.

The caravan consisted of six carts, two of which contained captives. Daemon and the four boys occupied one. Six females occupied another. As time passed Daemon was able to identify four young women, a portly older female and a child.

Three other carts were stacked with provisions, sacked meal, bales of silk, drums and barrels.

Four fine horses trotted along behind the Leaders carriage. The Black, a fine grey mare and two bays. Each in turn carried a rider, occasionally the Pacha himself. But for the most part they were left un-burdened. Fourteen or fifteen others, sharing six camels, in turn leading or riding, fulfilling the main entourage, which attended the Leader.

Beyond, stretching back for a quarter of a mile were a straggling band of merchants, some with camels, some with donkeys and others carrying their wares. They had joined the Pacha for protection. The very numbers in the train discouraging interference from wandering tribesmen or rival potentates.

Thus the encampment each evening brought smoking fires, strange rhythm-less music, and pounding upon small, skinned drums. The chanting of the Ayatollah was never far away. Each night at dusk the gathering would take to their prayer mats.

Lanterns, ranged across from tree to tree swinging in the cooling evening breezes, lighting the scene in a most pleasing vista. The babble of chatter and laughter filled the air, the odd shriek and altercation indicating ill-treatment of some of the lower calibre traders and on occasion, upon some of the newly secured captives.

For the most part Daemon was left to his own devices. His hands had been re-bound and his ankles restrained but he was lightly roped to a palm tree each evening and fed and watered in very fair proportion.

He genuinely felt signs of recovery from the former more brutal treatment and figured that his spontaneous intervention with the stallion had improved his stock.

Nonetheless the journey proved arduous, interminable and of great discomfort.

During the day the sun inflicted its own unimaginable punishment as it rose steadily to its height, maintained its relentless pressure for several hours and very, very slowly retreated at the end of each day.

The travellers began each morning in some degree of discomfort following the open exposure to the evening's chill breezes. This was soon replaced by the coarse dryness inflicted by the mid-morning sun. Some relief was sought as Daemon would join the four other occupants of the carriage on one side, seeking what shelter may be afforded by the raffia lid of the cart.

As the sun rose directly overhead the miniscule adjustments in position which were achieved were practised until the monotony and the degree of protection diminished in balance with the amount of concentrated effort needed.

Most afternoons were spent in silent defeat. Unable to raise the effort required to seek protection, depending on the angle of the penetrating rays, one or other of the occupants would suffer brutally. On numerous occasions Daemon would reach out a pull a comatose child across the cart into some level of protection when to leave them defenceless, could easily have meant the lifeblood boiling beyond endurance and certain demise.

The human spirit and the body's ability to recover, given the smallest encouragement, was tested to absolute maximum in the event, that somehow all survived the ordeal.

Their destination proved not to be the township Daemon had been anticipating. An oasis, a long dusty cart track between rocks. A residence consisting four or five alabaster buildings contained by a seven-foot wall.

Every surface was daubed 'white' reflecting the sun's rays. There was running water within the compound as attested by the impressive fountain in the courtyard.

There were six or seven children running around inside the complex dressed in fine attire suggesting that they were the offspring of the leader, his wives and concubines.

Forty to fifty people, clearly servile in the main, appeared to serve the leader and his family. The customary hareem ladies numbering seven or eight at that stage, kitchen staff, horse handlers, water carriers and others performing domestic chores.

Goats and scrawny sheep ran freely, around the complex, bells jangling and baying, skittish to movement and activity of any kind, which meant they were hardly ever at a standstill.

The fourteen soldiers forming his personal guard, appeared to be considered on a par with the family, and waited upon with equal alacrity.

The carts carrying Daemon's group and the females, were pulled to a halt alongside some low-lying sheds, across from the main buildings and separated by some fifty yards.

Ushered by three musket-carrying soldiers, they were herded into one of the sheds.

Daemon had to bend down to access the doorway and felt the butt of one of the muskets pushing him through the gap into the deep shadows within. There was straw laid out on the floor and a mound of it in the corner. There was the stench of animals inside the shed and Daemon fully accepted that cattle had been the previous occupants.

Finding a comfortable place on the coarse, sandy ground was difficult given the numbers inside. This was the captives 'lot'. Daemon looked around him and considered every avenue of escape, and there were many.

The shed was actually a lean-to. The timber of the gate was dry and brittle, the panels around the sides were flimsy and broken, allowing shafts of light into the gloom. The roof was holed in several places and the sand and straw compound which made up the inner wall was crumbling.

Daemon was convinced that he could achieve freedom from the compound.

But then what? He knew the many miles travelled presented an impossible escape route. Even with the finest animal, camel or horse, he could not hope to escape with sufficient sustenance to support such a journey. He would need a wagon-load of supplies and the acquisition of such made his situation hopeless.

He had to consider that, for the foreseeable future, he was going… nowhere.

Months passed. Daemon had been taken out of his 'group'. Assigned to a loose responsibility for the wellbeing of the horses, and fed to a level of quality and substance somewhere between that of the water-carrier, and the guardsmen.

He had little access to the other workers, and very limited acknowledgement of the leader. He did not belong to any group as such but had contact with some of the more eloquent of the soldiers and the blacksmith. He, in particular, presented a difficult and unworldly demeanour which Daemon found difficulty in dealing with.

There were few conversations spoken in the English tongue, he recognised the occasional Spanish phrasing and some French, but generally he spoke to no-one.

Nonetheless he was left to his own devices for much of the time. He became accustomed to the climate. Work in the afternoon was impossible. So, much rest was taken. The nights were long and he was allowed freedom of movement around the compound.

A female water carrier, Thewa, came to visit him one night, bringing some left overs and a leather wine bottle. She stayed, and although conversation was limited, they managed to achieve intimacy. The incident repeated itself, sometimes more than once a month. Nothing deep or meaningful was achieved but Daemon remained eternally grateful for such small blessings.

The occasional passing caravan brought interest in terms of festivities. It was always a moment of sadness watching them trail away into the distance when the business was done.

The soldiers prowled around the oasis, occasionally insisting or forcing a tariff from those partaking of the facility. It appeared that tribesmen of any connection with the Pacha and his family were able to use the waters free of charge. Other tribes, strangers or westerners were charged randomly. The more they appeared to be worth, the more they were obliged to pay.

Daemon eventually learned the names of his Pacha, being Rahman Al Soud,

And came to appreciate that as far as this region was concerned this was a highly respected leader.

Many times Daemon considered making a break for freedom. He decided upon a course of action that he was convinced one day he would have to take. He stored away all manner of things which might sustain him on a break for freedom. In a small hole beneath some shutters at the rear of the stables, he was able to conceal a head-dress and silken cloak, several water carriers, leather straps and a length of sail cloth which could form a hold-all.

Food was the most difficult thing. Nothing could be left around for long, above or below ground, it would be consumed by the creatures of the desert. Rats, spiders, snakes, ants, they could devour a pig leaving only a white skeleton in a matter of a few days. A bag or wrapping, with food inside would be attacked and pillaged within hours.

His nights were filled with dreams and restless conjecture. He had not forsaken his task. Kirsten was never far from his mind and he knew in his heart that one day, perhaps soon, his moment would come and another phase of his life would begin.

But here he remained, unable to form the plan, or make the move that would render him free. Indeed anything he might attempt could easily end in death.

Whilst he must eventually strive for freedom, in other ways, his situation was *tenable*.

***

Months became a year. He formed an attachment with the 'smith' and his wife, becoming like an adopted son. They spoke some English and he made every effort to make this achievement even greater.

His relationship with the Pasha never quite formed. There were not enough animals to make his role important. In fact there was very little use for the fine horses he kept. Much of the short, local journeys he completed in his elaborately decorated carriage or astride a camel.

The visits to the coastal towns and markets were more of an annual 'pilgrimage' and as it happened, Daemon was left behind on the anniversary of his arrival.

Daemon was treated with a tiny modicum of respect, and for that he was grateful and never pushed for more.

Between himself and Ali Darnati, the 'smith', they would take care of travellers in any repairs or maintenance their means of transport may require.

Horses were shod and groomed, well fed and watered. They were occasionally left to look after the livestock of visitors and guests.

During Daemons second year a great commotion began in the courtyard marking a time of great excitement. Soldiers and their supply animals were loaded up. The Pacha swung into the seat of his great Camel and the entourage prepared for departure. The Pacha spat a few orders in the direction of Abdullah, his second in command, who marched toward Daemon and quickly demonstrated that he was to mount Thunder, and follow the column out of the Fort.

Daemon could do little but fall in line but as he passed the steps just before exiting the gate, the Arab girl, Thewa, flung him a white robe and headdress and a leather bottle swollen with fresh water. Gratefully accepting the gesture he turned toward the column and allowed Thunder to take up an instinctive pursuit.

Camping that night there was a great deal of heated discussion within the main tent. The Pacha was clearly aggravated and did not appear fully in control. Abdullah lead the responses which appeared to try to calm him down. In all there were about twenty five of them, Daemon noted. He soon realised they were intent on some sort of raid, or joining up with another force.

There was little Daemon could do as his presence merely made up the numbers at that stage.

The following morning brought a fresh round of enthusiastic preparation. An out-rider brought news of a sighting and urgency in every action followed from that moment.

The small force made some progress through a rocky gorge and out into a sea of sand before some trees, an oasis, was spotted in the distance.

Damon looked on and a fist of fear clamped around his entrails as he saw the significant numbers camped around the oasis with at least forty horses strung out on line between the trees. Another seven or eight camels sat imperiously munching on their morning meal.

Abdullah turned his mount and with a swirl of dust circled Daemon holding him eye to eye for a long moment. Seemingly satisfied, he pulled a long bladed Arabic sword from his saddled bags and tossed it hilt first, toward him.

Daemon was taken a little by surprise but instinctively gathered in the weapon by the handle and looked back squarely at Abdullah! In a show of bravado, Daemon swished the sword in the air, with fairly impressive artistry, leading to Abdullah reigning in his mount and galloping back to the head of the column.

**

At every turn of events Daemon weighed up the opportunity of escape! As at the numerous other occasions, he could see no opportunity. He decided he would play his part in what was to come and trust in the 'gods'!

The battle was brutal but short lived, the word was given and the Pacha lead the attack, the element of surprise and the ferociousness of the onslaught immediately redressed the imbalance in numbers.

A dozen of those in the encampment were immediately cut-down. The remainder offered resistance which saw each of their own troop engaged in one to one combat.

Daemon, keeping to the edge of the affray encountered a native warrior whose skills may have been more accomplished at a distance as his weaponry consisted of a bow and a spear. Daemon, using the experience gained of a boarding party, was much too much for the man at close quarters. His blade slicing through the man's shoulder and leaving him rent across the sand. Daemon for a moment felt immense regret. The sight having an effect upon him in a way he had not expected. The golden sand, the bright blue sky and deep red blood spewing from the man's wound, all seeming out-of-place.

Immediately Daemon's attention was diverted by the strangled cries of a man Ali Darnati had by the throat and was just slicing through the man's neck with his dagger. Ali tossed the body aside as if it were a down-filled pillow. The two joined up and attacked a line of three more of the enemy. Between them they were able to disable two and ultimately brought another to his demise as he turned to flee.

All around an exultant cry went up as the Pacha and his men had completed the brutal slaughter of almost every one of the 'enemy'. Abdullah appeared, to relieve Daemon of his weapon.

***

Daemon with a strange sense of fulfilment returned to base with the others without ever having the satisfaction of knowing what had brought about the conflict.

***

As it turned out soon after their return a great feast was arranged and many visitors planned for. The Pacha's eldest daughter, having reached the age of twelve, was to be married to the son of a rival chieftain. It became a little clearer to Daemon over the coming weeks that the 'raiding party' had cleared the way for this arrangement, eliminating a rival for the hand of the chieftain's daughter.

The preparation lasted in excess of a month. The entire compound was bedecked with long silken drapes of every imaginable colour. Carpets were mounted on the walls. Torch holders were liberally spaced around the walls and the eaves of every building. Trestles were laid out and a great feast prepared.

The groom's entourage arrived and the numbers in the compound doubled.

Daemon saw this moment as the most promising of his entire captivity. He could make his move. Take two horses. As much food as his makeshift bag could carry. Ten leather water holders and a bale of straw.

He was determined to take the big stallion, knowing it would fetch a substantial sum at market when he reached civilisation.

The ceremony got underway and was destined to last three days. He would await his moment and begin his quest for freedom.

On the wedding day as the night drew in and the feasting got under way in earnest, Daemon visited the stables, as normal, ensuring the animals had sufficient straw and some water to last through the night.

Whilst retrieving the few possessions he had managed to hide away, he overheard an animated conversation proceeding in the courtyard adjacent to the stables.

By placing his ear against the vertical planking, he could barely make out what was being said from the far too quickly spoken Arabic he had picked up during his captivity. All he could do was piece together a version of events which ultimately gave him great cause for concern.

***

Stowing away his collection once again, he made his way to the quarters where he knew Ali and his wife would be enjoying their own small feast, contentedly remote from the throng of activity in the main dwelling.

Daemon spoke, with much 'sign' language and in suitable hushed tones, to his friend. 'I believe they are going to take the stallion on a journey...many 'leagues' from here. When the bride leaves to join her husband's family...they will take him I am sure I heard them say it....!'

Ali, shrugged his shoulders exaggerating the movement for effect. 'I don't know my friend! It is possible... Thunder may have been offered as part of the 'dowry'!

Daemon became downcast. 'That would make sense... err... it would be a good thing... for the 'Lady' Jasmina! But perhaps something would have been said to me?

'Do you think you heard the words correctly? Do you think they mean to steal away the Stallion?

'They used his name 'Thunder' they can't be stealing it, they talked about 'starting out early... with the rising sun... and... !' Daemon suddenly remembered his own plans.

A moment passed with both men scratching their heads, before Daemon rose to leave. Uncertain of his plan, perhaps it would have to be abandoned for the time being, he was lost in thought when the door sprung open.

'English... come, the Pasha would speak with you... come!'

'Err. I am not prepared... I am not ready to attend the festivities...'!

'Come now! There is no issue! You will attend the Pacha. Right away!' Daemon followed them into the courtyard where the festivities were well under way. The canopy overhanging the main tables was gloriously lit with lanterns and the music and atmosphere intoxicating.

The small procession picked its way through the decorative cushions and low slung tables.

Eventually he stood facing the leader, who was leaning quite resplendent against the high side of a chaise-longue. His attire glittering with embellishment, gold braid and gold thread woven in elaborate patterns throughout the crimson silk of his military-cut garments.

His bejewelled, turquoise, silken turban, sat atop his handsome visage and his jet black hair, like an imperial crown.

***

'English… we have news for you. Thunder is a gift made by myself to my son-in-law, on the event of the marriage. He will accompany the Emir and his family to their own dwelling in Bachtar, some distance from here.'

There was a pause, and Daemon felt some response was expected.

'I am sorry. Sir' he uttered, '… The Stallion will be sadly missed, by all of our family.'

The father of the groom, sat upright from his own cushioned chaise seeming surprised that the 'servants' were allowed such intercourse.

He looked toward the Pasha but shrugged acceptance when there was no response from his host.

The bride and groom were so entangled in their own love-nest that they failed to notice the confrontation.

Daemon quickly turned his position so that he faced the visitor. 'A thousand pardons Sir, I did not mean to speak out of turn.' Again the grand leader of the visiting family shrugged as if a small child had knocked over a goblet.

Daemon quickly returned his attention to his Master.

He laughed raucously. 'You may be required to remain with Emir Rachid Almansoor, if he considers your ministrations to the animals of some value. Either way you are no longer needed by my family.'

Daemon made as if to protest, although he was doing so for effect. He did not think his life could be improved or adversely affected either way. However, he did not wish to seem ungrateful for the life he had been thrust into, in the home of the Pacha.

Again, Daemon's immediate thought was that the possibilities of escape must improve, and that perhaps the location of his new Masters abode may well be more accessible to civilisation.

Nonetheless, he managed to utter some words which the Pacha took for sorrow, and he was dismissed and allowed to return to his lodging.

Daemon accepting his lot, said his goodbyes to the smith and his family and the few others with whom he had been allowed to establish a regular dialogue. Thewa did not appear.

So totally unprepared was he, that the turn of events may worsen his situation, that for some months he retreated within himself and was quite unable to plot or even contemplate an escape.

The Emir, whose establishment was the size of a small town, was in a more remote, mountainous part of the North African continent, which, Daemon found, was home to a slovenly, uncivilised, vile deceitful rabble.

His relationship with the family was entirely remote. He saw the comings and goings but was hardly involved in the preparation of the animals. His role seemed to be to muck-out the stalls and horse troughs and to change horseshoes albeit with the most primitive equipment.

He asked questions of any who might look in the least communicative, but was spat upon, pushed away and ignored on almost every occasion. There were dozens of slaves in the true sense, those who wore shackles by night. Daemon tried to spot a European among them to no avail.

The Stallion grew lazy and fat, unable to raise his enthusiasm to run or bounce around, he was ridden, hard, on occasion by his new master, but insufficiently to maintain his sleek muscular appearance. He was used to *mate* with a string of short, stocky-looking Arab animals and the offspring would eventually prove to be of a fine mix of work and play horses.

Daemon's quarters were in the stable above the horses, in a loft with a half bale of straw. He was frequently checked by the guards, although he was allowed to roam relatively free within the stable area.

His own well-being suffered to the extent that he was not aware of his actual appearance, had no sense of worth or ambition. His spirits sank. He had not the first idea of his location. Not the least hope of liberty.

**

Months passed and he lost account of his time, beyond the 'seasons'. He knew it was spring as distinct from the height of summer. He knew the nights turned cold in the late autumn. He appreciated the proximity of the animals in the winter.

A year passed and another was well under-way before anything changed to bring with it a new found determination. A battalion of soldiers arrived. They were Turkish at the farthest point of the Ottoman Empire and they appeared to exercise a seniority over the regime.

Theirs was a brutal, rigid and disciplined pattern of behaviour, to the extent that Daemon purposely kept a low profile avoiding direct contact with the garrison.

The new regime gradually increased its authority over the family to the extent that they required permission to go about their day-today activities.

There was less pomp and ceremony about the main dwelling. Soldiers took over the responsibility of managing and policing the settlement. Although the soldiers were 'guests' of the Emir, five of their officers took up residence in the main dwelling.

Tough, well drilled, well-armed and disciplined, the new authority gradually assumed complete control of the settlement and using the available male contingent, commenced the process of building a fortress.

Surplus activities ceased, the entire focus of the garrison was to complete the fortress from which this garrison would take control of the desert in the surrounding area.

A caravan arrived bringing supplies, refreshed and unburdened, it turned around and set off again. This time they harnessed a number of enslaved, former servants and employees of the old regime.

Daemon was among them and a new arduous, intolerable journey commenced.

This time however, journeys end proved to be a coastal settlement with a bustling harbour and busy marketplace. Towering black Africans worked under Arab masters to bring these chattels to market and ensure profit for the traders whom made the journey to replenish the supplies of the occupying forces.

Once again Daemon was intended for the slave market and put off any attempted flight for freedom whilst he accepted the food and water offered by his owners, intent on preparing him for sale. What choice did he have?

One morning an African arrived and unsheathed a threatening blade approaching Daemon from over his left shoulder. For a moment Daemon feared for his very existence but the arrival of a pail, and a small pot, which contained an oily substance. The African proceeded to shave the thick, matted beard from his neck and face.

Despite the rawness and unpleasantness of suddenly finding his face bare after many months of covering, Daemon felt like a new man by the time the exercise was complete.

Now he rested once more, putting off once again any thought of escape. He slept well that night with the comforting smell of the sea, fresh in his nostrils. Nonetheless when he woke he was blindfolded and led by a boy until coming to rest in the marketplace.

Still shaking the fog of belated sleep from his head, Daemon found himself being guided along an alleyway, although a rag had been tied across his face, presumably to blindfold him. Once he had adjusted to the daylight, he could actually see almost everything through a tear in the cloth.

Emerging from the alleyway he was pushed by the same strong hands that had manhandled him the night before, into a busy square where a number of frontless hovels were grouped along one side, framed by a raised platform. This formed a stage upon which a group of similarly snared individuals ranged, eyes riveted to the ground.

Daemon was obliged to join them and the gathering of local merchants began baying toward them where a 'ringmaster' returned their cackle with a sort of mocking banter.

Daemon was thrust up against a young dark-haired girl barely covered by a cotton 'shirt', her limbs shining with what appeared to be some sort of oil, the smell from which Daemon found nauseating.

As she lifted her face to a position where she could scan the crowd, Daemon could see tear stains running all the way down to her slender neck.

His 'blindfold' was suddenly ripped away and he caught the full glare of bright sunshine. Fingers were pointing toward him and a bargain was struck between the ringmaster and a colourfully garbed Arab.

Pulling at his bindings, out of sight of the crowd, Daemon realised that he would have to at least wait an opportunity before striking for freedom. There was nothing to encourage him there and then.

Further bargains were struck and as Daemon was led away he realised that he was one of a group of four that had been purchased by the Arab, a man whom boasted three well-presented assistants and two horse-drawn carts, one of which bore a bright crimson canopy with golden tassels. The Arab rested back on a cluster of pillows as his driver urged the stocky animals into motion.

The second carriage was adorned with a timber structure of palings which formed a cage. Daemon and his three new comrades, two young European ladies and a Latino boy were hoisted through a loose tethered gate at the rear and settled on the floor as the cart lurched forward.

'Does any of you speak English?' Daemon asked to no-one in particular.

All three looked up and the dark-haired girl responded. 'I... speak... I mean, I am English. I'm from Portsmouth.' She sobbed.

'How long since you were captured?'

'It was months ago. I have been on board a ship. Our boat was seized by these black people. They killed my father and threw him in the water like a dead carcass! I... I couldn't speak for weeks and still find my tongue getting stuck between my teeth. My teeth start chattering all the time until my jaw aches. I haven't eaten proper food for a month.

Daemon listened until she ran dry.

'I'll get us out of this mess. I promise you. I won't leave you behind.'

During this conversation the other two had looked on imploringly but unable to follow the language. It was soon established that the boy was Sicilian and the girl French. By communicating in expressions and a few words where languages crossed, they each brought some momentary comfort to the others. One of the attendants drew alongside and soon brought their dialogue to a halt by motioning first across his lips, then with one finger across his throat.

Daemon knew the threats were to some extent idle – they weren't going to pay good money for slaves to then damage them or do away with them. But the threat was at least enough to reduce them to whisperings.

**

Hours passed before they were offered bread and water through a gap under the gate.

The sun had broiled them and was so persistent that the Arab had ordered a cloth be thrown over their cage. He didn't want his 'goods' damaged after all.

The sun set dead ahead of their procession so Daemon knew enough to realise they were travelling west. He had the sudden fear that they would be travelling further from 'home' but this was a journey due west and he realised that, despite not being visible to them at that time, their road must be following the coastline.

'Do you know where we are?' he asked the English girl.

She shook her head but responded, 'I know we were taken to Algiers, or near there. We just left a town call Most-a-grem or Most-garem. My father taught me from some old books about the places where 'civilisation' began. Egypt and all that. I learned a bit about the Mediterranean coast of Africa'.

'If we are going to the west, where is the next place?

Well I know Morocco is in that direction, but I don't know how far. I think Tangier is a big City, but...'

'That's grand, at least you know more than me. If you remember anything else....

'I tell you one thing. I've seen slaves, white people from England and France. Hundreds, thousands.... There are lots of seamen. There are girls... children!'

'They sell them off and they're never seen again. I've seen them mutilated, mistreated in every way. De...debauched. Some want freedom at first but others, most of them, they would rather be dead or stay captive than go home and have to admit their shame to their families.'

'What happens to them all?'

'Some of them are ransomed. They return to their home-lands. I have nobody to come for me. My father and brothers were all aboard our boat when it was taken. My mother will be on her own, bereft, or dead by now. She depended on Father, the fishing and the rest. There's no-one for us!'

'But this is insane! How can they just 'take' people, how can they be allowed to carry on with this? What do they want after all? Surely there's enough of them to do the work, to satisfy their needs?'

'It's just like, well, they can use a person. They have total power over a 'slave'. They like white women... and boys.'

She looked pityingly toward the young Sicilian, shaking her head.

'How did you come to know so much?'

'I was taken, first by a wealthy man. This is the third time I've been 'sold'. He was killed. We had travelled for nearly a week. We arrived at this, well it was like a church – it was white, big, with high walls all around. There must have been fifty or more living there. There were ten or fifteen women, beautifully dressed, each one different. One day horsemen came. There were a lot of them. There was a terrible fight. Five or six of us, slaves, got pushed into a cart. We were taken to a compound and left there for days. After, we came to a place called Bolmerdas, then to the 'market' at Mostagram. That's where we just came from.'

'You managed to survive.'

'The Emir, or I think that's what they called him, he was a nice man really. After I arrived he, well, he looked at me. He, stripped me naked, had me washed. Washed in *warmed up* water with sickly smelling soap no less. Then he looked at me again. They dressed me in white cloth and took me to the kitchens. Strange, I felt sort of 'insulted.' Instead of being happy that, you know, that he wasn't going to do things to me, I felt ashamed.

'After a few days, I was happy working in the kitchen with the fat one and another girl, a bit pale and thin, like me. I think she was from Ireland.'

'I'm from Ireland meself. Donegal. I, listen, you don't know where she was from, the Irish girl? Was it the south? Was it...?'

She was shaking her head, stopping him. 'Sorry, I don't know exactly, but from what she said I think it was in the West, her name was Clodagh or something.'

'Are you sure?'

She shrugged her shoulders, 'What is it? Are you looking for someone?'

'A girl! It was Whitsun, two years since or was it three...? A ship came to Baltimore a little village in the South. They ransacked the entire village. Took away twenty young ones. The ship was out to sea before anything could be done!

'Kirsten, she was taken. I'm going to find her if it's the last thing I do.'

'You say it was what two years or so, in the Spring? They say a big ship went out but never came back. There was a lot of talk. Oh never mind, it couldn't be anything.'

'What talk, what were they saying?'

'Well they say one of the privateers, corsairs or whatever, an important man, one of the biggest ships. It sank in a storm, somewhere off the Irish coast about that time.'

'Sank. And what happened? What about the crew and...'

'No survivors, that's what they said.'

'How do they know about it then?' Daemon wrestled with the notion that the ship, the very ship that carried the Moors that sacked Baltimore, might have been the same this girl had heard about. 'I'd know.'

'What?'

'I'd know if she was dead. Kirsten. If she had perished at sea, I somehow, I would know! I'm sure she's alive. Sure of it! I'll find her.'

'I truly hope so. I'm sorry for telling you.'

'Don't, don't apologise, it's not your fault. Look, I don't know your name, I'm Daemon.'

'I'm Margaret, you know.' she smiled but Daemon fell silent for some time, lost in his thoughts. The girl respectfully left him alone. Nightfall brought them to an oasis where a dozen similar caravans, some trading in goods and others carrying slaves, were encamped for the evening.

Fresh water was brought. Fires were lit, and the four captives were ranged around and tethered to a tree.

Daemon had never felt more desperate, more miserable. The rumour of the ship that went down off the Irish Coast. The terrible reality that this was his third year in captivity.

Chapter 20

John Standing

Daemon turned, once again sleep eluded him. His arms ached, when that ceased his legs started. He felt twitching in his sides and a queasiness in his stomach. The need for relieving himself, always agonising, awaiting the right moment, waiting, waiting, then giving up and just getting it done, whomever was close or watching, it became irrelevant. The act had to be performed.

It was worse for the girls but at least their skirts covered them sufficiently to make only their squatting and positioning an embarrassment.

Now he knew he had to raise himself, ease the tension on his ropes, find a position in which the worse of the aching would cease.

He knew this new encampment was more structured, more permanent.

There was an orderliness about the proceedings. Commands were no longer bellowed by the captors as each had a role, a job to perform. One took charge of the allocation of 'accommodation', another took charge of the washing, another distributed clean clothing.

Nonetheless they were watched by the sharp eyes of well-drilled guards.

This was the fifth day since the auction, two nights further travel, always due west, had brought them to this substantial fort, on the edge of a busy township.

Daemon spent most of his waking hours assessing the options of escape. At least here he would not have the issues of 'desert', of long hours of isolation in tortuous exposure. Here his escape would be in the direction of the port, through the plentiful cover of the built-up areas. Here he would never be far away from vital supplies of water or bread.

All these possibilities had made his captivity more bearable whilst he awaited the moment when the bones of a plan could be meted out. He was sure in his own mind that it was just a matter of time.

Margaret had been taken in another direction, he managed to catch sight of her, cleaned up again, this time her clothing quite exotic. From the square openings, high on the outside wall, he could see her being led, reluctantly by two matronly types across the courtyard.

Daemon mused that perhaps this 'Emir' preferred his women a little 'leaner'. He had to admit to himself that Margaret had cleaned up nicely with her dark hair coiled with a variety of coloured ribbons. He chided himself, and felt an element of guilt, considered including her in his escape, then dismissed the idea as most likely impractical.

The noise and smells from hissing wood burners told of the dawn of another day. The chill of the clear night air would be vanquished by the rising sun, a red sphere which would be a burnished yellow mass above them within an hour. The relentless blue skies and the constant brightness, incessant heat, sweat-soaked shirts and headiness which sapped the energy and enforced afternoon sleepiness which could not be fought.

Daemon hung his head, hoping early repast may break up the tedium as the hours dragged slowly by. He took in the aroma of fresh baking bread. Flat and almost tasteless, it nonetheless provided abundant nourishment. His cracked lips cried out for the fresh water, his lungs working minimally in a deflated chest, he forced himself to occupy his mind to distract from these tribulations.

Suddenly the removal of the clamp and the loud creaking of the door to their compound, brought Daemon bolt upright from his self-induced trance.

Instead of a tray and breakfast, his guard displayed keys with which he released the anchor chain to which Daemon's manacles had been attached. He was brought to a standing position and allowed to flex his legs to get circulation going, before being led out into the courtyard.

They entered what must have been the main building, through a gated entrance and fifty or sixty paces brought them into a grand reception room. The Emir lay across several large cushions against a chaise longue to the left of a fountain. On the opposite side on matching furniture a well-attired European similarly relaxed, as he took a cooling drink from a bowl.

'Ahh, this way, if you please...' He looked toward Daemon but spoke in a quiet, respectful tone to the European.

'My dear friend, if it so pleases, would you like to look over our most fortunate acquisition?'

Daemon, almost smiled at the irony of this address. But not without looking behind him to make sure it was actually toward himself that their attention was directed. When quite satisfied that there was no mistake, he could not help but bring himself up to full height and acquire as cheerful an expression as his situation would allow.

The European rose and walked a full circle around the bemused captive. Standing just under Daemons height, at around five-ten, sporting a flowing Arab outer garment over his bright cotton shirt and black leather pantaloons he appeared cool and sophisticated.

His handsome countenance, lightly tanned and carefully shaven, beneath short, neatly razored dark hair, accentuated his aristocratic bearing. A rapier with bejewelled handle and stock, hung from a loose belt around his waist.

The overall impression markedly different from the bewigged, coiffured upper crust of which Daemon had recently become familiar.

He was nodding, as if to agree, that Daemon was, at least 'presentable', not too damaged and satisfactory by whatever measure may be appropriate to his captors.

'I think you made a good choice my friend. It was very good of you to consider my needs when quite clearly you had other objectives to your mission. I would be more than happy to take this ruffian off your hands.'

Daemon raised his eyebrows, but with obvious effort kept his tongue.

'Good. My friend, I'm glad I have been of service to you again in our happy arrangement. Our undertaking is blessed with good fortune, of this I am certain.'

'I believe so, indeed, I am very keen to get under way and make this enterprise, the most successful of all our dealings. I take it you speak English, old chap?' He asked turning to Daemon.

'I... I, of course, Your Lordship, I have been serving in his Majesty's Navy and... '

'Yes, yes, I believe so. Tell me, did you see any action?'

'Yes, your honour, I was involved in some, well, two really, massive battles with the French and...'

'Whom did you serve under?'

'Er, well, Captain Rodney Nash, and, er, I believe Admiral Fielding and... '

'Indeed. Tell me what about these rumours of Fielding's withdrawal.' Addressing the Emir, 'A couple of years back it appears one of our principal officers may have gotten himself into a spot of 'hot water'!'

The Emir shrugged, 'I have heard these rumours.'

'What can you tell us... Daemon?'

'Yes, yes, Daemon – what have you heard?'

'I can only tell you what I saw. We had been separated from the fleet and were conducting Lady Daphne of Olney to Naples, when... '

'Lady Daphne be damned. Lady Daphne, aboard your ship?'

He moved deftly behind Daemon, in a virtual whisper he continued, 'I will speak more with you later. Please for the moment play along with me.'

More distinctly for the Emir's ears.

'Well I'm damned if this fellow hasn't deserted a ship of the line!'

Daemon shaped as if to contradict, but catching the sidelong glance afforded him by the European, reverted to a obsequious acknowledgement.

'Nonetheless, he looks in good shape, and brings some experience, I will take him off yours hands, my dear friend, all as agreed, with your kind permission we will depart on the morrow.'

The Emir rose. 'Of course, Monsieur Standing, it is always my pleasure to have been of use to your esteemed self. I will have everything prepared for your journey and of course my soldiers will be at your disposal for the remainder of the enterprise. I have eight well-disciplined and appropriately armed men for your party.'

At the sound of the name 'Standing' Daemon mouthed the words 'Oh shit.' without any sound emitting from his lips. The Emir continued enabling Daemon to conceal the stunned surprise he was feeling.

'When you arrive at Sierra Leone, my brother Asif Agrand and his sons will be waiting with your cargo. I have given instruction that only the finest, healthy young Africans are to be selected for transport. I am happy to leave them in your capable hands and look forward to the rewards of our endeavour when you return in the new year.

'Meanwhile, may Allah bless every footstep of your animals and may the wind fill your sails. Shall I return our friend to the cells for the evening?'

'No, thank you Emir, for all your support, and indeed for providing this 'willing' pair of hands. I will take care of him now. I am more than certain of his constancy for the foreseeable future. Come with me, Daemon, I have some tasks for you.'

'If you are absolutely certain John, my friend, I humbly suggest you leave the 'bracelets' around his wrists, at least until your convoy is underway in the morning. One can never be too careful.'

'Leave that to me. I will make absolutely sure he will cause no alarm whatsoever during the rest of his stay.'

Leading Daemon to his quarters at the far end of the compound Standing released the manacles and offered Daemon his own goblet and a measure of wine. Grateful, Daemon grabbed it with both hands and yielded to Standing's motioning, he took a seat on a low, cushioned stool across the spacious room.

'I have to ask you, you mentioned Lady Daphne. I am John Standing, her brother. Tell me all you can. Is she well? Where was she bound?

Daemon struggled. He found it difficult to know where to begin.

Staring at the floor, he could think of nothing but to tell him the truth.

'My Lord, I take it you have not heard much about the fate of the *Warrior*. Let me first explain that I am no deserter, I promise you my Lord. I was aboard the *Warrior* when she, when Lady Daphne boarded in Gibraltar.'

Daemon's countenance gave away that there may be bad news to follow. He stuttered and hesitated, Standing waited patiently.

'I did everything I could to see that... well to make it easier for... anyway, Captain Nash's orders were to take her

Ladyship to Naples, but half way there we intercepted a vessel that had recently left Marseille and reported that eighteen French and Spanish ships had left the harbour. The captain knew that Fielding, with a small fleet, was in the path of the French, forming a blockade and, knowing the depleted numbers would find it very difficult to contain a much larger Fleet, turned around to rejoin them – of course he wanted to be of some use if an encounter developed.

'When we got within sight of the fleet, the French turned around and Captain Nash thought we had them at our mercy. But Fielding stood-off! Nash went in alone. We were battered and chased and God knows how we stayed afloat. We assumed Fielding had returned to his station to blockade the allies, whilst we were sacrificed.

'I have to tell you, sir, there are no words. Lady Daphne was killed, she died in my arms.'

Standing was on his feet, he paced the room. He held his head, momentarily turning toward Daemon.

'Poor child. I, she was just...' He put out a hand about waist high. 'She was just...'

'Sir, if I may. She was beautiful, full of life. She had grown, perhaps about eighteen years, she, she had a sparkle in her eye. Everyone...' He choked back emotion. 'We buried her in a Christian church at the place we moored-up in Algiers. The *Warrior*, she took weeks to repair. We marched up to the church, outside Mostgarem, and buried her with honours.

'I have spent over two years in captivity but a day hasn't gone by when I don't think of her....begging your Lordship's pardon.

'As we attempted to return to the ship with Lieutenant Belton acting commander – Nash was badly injured – our party were set upon by the Arabs.

'I was separated in the melee, chased across the town, but the others made it back to ship. I got captured and put in a slave market... Sorry, sir, I was going on about myself...'

170

'No, don't think about it, please, carry on.'

'Well that's about it to be sure. I got brought out for slavery. But it brought me here and...'

'Well let me complete the story. Emir Maktolla, is a 'friend', well let's say we've done business together. I'm taking a ship to the West Indies, loaded with African slaves, to work the plantations over there.'

'The Emir was paying his usual visit to the market, when he noticed you, and, guessing correctly you were a seaman, a deserter, as might be expected, he thought you would prove useful to me on the voyage. You can't have enough good seamen on such a voyage. It's a long way.'

'Your Lordship, I've no right to ask, but, I appreciate I am your slave and...'

'Please, allow me. You are not my *slave*. I have liberated you, as of this moment, you have spoken to me of my poor darling sister. I believe you have told me truthfully what happened. I am eternally grateful to know someone who was there when she... I must find a way to visit her resting place. You may be one of the few people who can help me. Please accept my apologies for your plight.'

'I am at your service, sir. If not your slave, then certainly your servant.' Daemon gave a short bow in salute. 'As it is I am on a mission myself, you may be able to help me. Her Ladyship said if anyone can, then it would be yourself.

'In the Spring. two years or so since, back on the south coast of Ireland, a little village, Baltimore, a band of Moorish warriors invaded and took half the villagers into captivity. They slaughtered half of the others mind. Anyway, a girl, my girl, was taken. I swore to seek her and free her, on my own life, if that's what it took.'

'I would of course be of help if I could. You say it was spring 1749, it was definitely Moors?'

Daemon shrugged, 'How could we know, they sailed in a large ship, three masts and rows of oarsmen. They were black and wore bright yellow and red clothing...'

Standing raised a hand 'It would appear we both offer only the worst news, you of my poor sister's plight, and for myself, I have to tell you that I knew the master well. I often encountered him in our various wheelings and dealings. Sadly, but only for your own personal concern, I have to say the world was rid of a great evil.

'His ship most certainly foundered in a storm. It never saw land again, and it is believed all aboard perished. Wreckage was found strewn along the Irish coastline weeks later. I am sorry my friend, but your quest may be over.'

For long moments Daemon remained silent. He held his head in his hands and wept quietly. Standing left him there, clearly anxious to make preparations for the journey ahead. Daemon, left alone, appreciated that it was in fact as a free man that he now found himself. Yet he had no mission, no goal, and nothing ahead of him apart from an arduous return to the civilisation that he knew.

Then the realisation that in fact there was nothing to which he was bound to return. His life suddenly had no meaning. Tossing around options, the life he had encountered, although truly dangerous, had at least provided excitement, had his blood flowing with a gut full of anticipation. He could return to the Navy, but now, what about Standing, bound for another world, the possibilities limitless. He liked the man. There was something of Daphne in his eyes.

When Standing returned, Daemon rose. 'I'm your man, if you'll have me? I would like to make this voyage with you.

Standing grasped his hand in both his own. 'It will be my pleasure to welcome you along for the journey. I will make you an offer for your enterprise, which I believe you will find acceptable. There is a lot of danger, a lot to lose. But if you come along and we achieve our goal, there will be no looking back. A place in society awaits the victors!'

The two shook hands vigorously. Standing slapped Daemon across the shoulders and they toasted each other with the fine Madeira, to which Daemon was now formally introduced.

Chapter 21

The Edge of the World

Alone that night Banoldino held Kirsten in his arms, her head just beneath his shoulder so that he could whisper into her ear.

The ship raised and settled rhythmically on an easy, gentle roll. Timbers creaked, ropes groaned, sail flapped in a pleasant 'clipping' sound.

'Where are we going?' Kirsten had asked with all sincerity.

Banoldino laughed quietly. She elbowed him lightly in the ribs, bringing a knowing smile to his face.

'I'm sorry, it's just, well, here we are, on a voyage to the New World, aboard a fine sailing ship with a hundred and fifty others. You now ask where we are going! I find that…'

'Stupid!'

'No, endearing. It makes me love you all the more.'

'What, that I'm ignorant?'

'No, that you need me. And even more so – that I really am able to help you. Let me tell you what I can, for the moment, accept that it is knowledge that has been proven, let's say 'accepted' in the civilised world.

'Across the great sea, 'Atlantis' they are calling it, there is another great landmass. It is many leagues, but, instead of dropping off the edge of the world, if you go far enough, you reach this land. 'The Americas'! A huge and wonderful place, with hardly any people. There are some, original inhabitants, 'Indigenous' – is what they are called because they were born there. Their ancestors before them occupied those lands for many thousands of years.

'They are different from us. They like to live on the land. Like gypsies, they move their habitation with them when the seasons change. So there are few buildings of any kind. The new settlers have started establishing villages and towns, not like ours. They are spread out because there is so much land.

'There… Kirsten… are you listening?'

He was met by a gentle, moan and a deep sigh. He knew she had dropped off to sleep. Smiling to himself he found his own deep slumber as their voyage to the New World commenced in earnest.

Chapter 22

Rough Crossing

The ship bucked and rolled and Kirsten felt panic grip her insides.

Her mind travelled back to the moment aboard the Xebek when she realised the captors' attention had moved significantly away from the enslaved, to their own survival.

Realisation that within minutes the situation could become desperate and the thought of the cold, swirling waters terrified her anew.

Gripping Banoldino she buried her head in his shoulder to smother a scream. Terror showed on her face and when he attempted to sooth her, she became angry and resistant, trying to pull away from him at the same time. He held her tight, limiting the resultant panic which he knew, in such a confined space, could be amplified into an unseemly drama.

'Hush now, my darling, hush, everything is going to be fine. This ship, she is built for these conditions. Don't think of that Mediterranean reed boat which almost killed us all. Don't be afraid my darling, Banoldino is here.'

'Banolo!' Lord Ranleigh had shortened his name for his own convenience. 'Banolo, quickly. Could you attend the children? My wife is terribly ill, I can't look after them all.'

Banoldino took Kirsten by the arms and almost shook her, such was the strength of his grip, 'Now look, my darling, you will be all right, I promise you, now I must go. Lay here, do not move, but hold onto the rail with both hands to stop you rocking. I must... '

As he left her he gave an assuring glance, but turned swiftly into the adjacent cabin, where the murmurings of the children could be heard above the roar of the seas. Banoldino pulled his dagger waved it in the air.

'The next person to scream will have his head chopped off and thrown to the fishes!'

The children instantly drew up from the positions where they had been propped by cushions, and stared back at him open mouthed.

'Ah haaa. You first, my friend.' Banoldino burst forth and speared a pretend pirate against the door frame. He quickly followed up by grabbing one of the straw-filled supporting pillows, where he thrust his dagger into its middle regions.

'There, I have vanquished all your enemies, now, what have you to be afraid of?' Young Ranleigh laughed with delight and the two girls, began clapping and calling for more.

'I hope this rocking about is causing you no discomfort. Ha! The only consolation is that it is much worse for the passengers below decks. Here we enjoy the excitement of a few little waves. Do you know that the bigger the wave, the faster we are propelled toward the Americas? Well, let me assure you – it is true! Every wave takes half a day from our journey.'

Young Ranleigh gave him a look of playful derision.

'Well, maybe not half a day, but certainly half an hour.'

Despite the rolling and sudden diving sensation, the children were now in good spirits. Only the younger of the girls looked genuinely off-colour, and Banoldino, now took her in his arms.

'My Lord,' he addressed young Ranleigh, 'could you please take care of Louisa and allow me to return to my quarters for a moment?' He carried Anabelle through to where he had left Kirsten but found that his companion had vacated the quarters.

Now, almost in panic of his own making, he returned the child to Ranleigh and made quickly for the steps up to the poop deck, fearing that Kirsten had fled in fear. The waves crashed over the sides and swamped the deck, but grabbing life lines he made his way along the deck to the hold area. Passing the Bosun he made a sign indicating that he was searching for Kirsten, which was returned by a pointing finger.

Down on the gun deck, Banoldino could make out shadows in the dark where he found Kirsten tending a sick child. Some of the friends from the village had claimed an area for their own, laying down their blankets and few belongings, which were encircled by stooping or reclining figures. Kirsten had realised that their well-being was more important than her own irrational fears.

Sea water had invaded the space long before, and hours of swell had made conditions almost unendurable. Lanterns were useless in these conditions, more so they could cause fatal damage if fire broke out.

A pail of fresh water, almost emptying, its contents swilled from side to side, but other pails, initially for washing and to stir in broth, had become receptacles for vomit. One after the other the steerage passengers threw up the contents of their stomachs as they encountered the swell of the seas.

Every day at least one fatality had occurred brought about by all imaginable means. The seas, the want of fresh food, the cold and simply being ill-equipped and ill-prepared for such a voyage, took its toll.

Each day the Captain would stand at the rail and arrange for white-sheathed bodies to be dropped over the side, to the accompaniment of a few pious words. This stormy passage would account for many more.

Kirsten turned to Banoldino. 'I thought, if I could just turn my mind from the... the dread of... well, I had to find something.'

'It's fine, I know you are doing what you can for your friends. My dear, please, we have our duty too. We have to take care of them first. Tell your friends you will return with some food later, but for now, please come, I'm sure Lady Evelyn is in need of you.'

Kirsten rose to take his hand, willing to be led to the upper deck, but suddenly she went into spasm and sank to her knees clutching her stomach. She let out an anguished cry before trying to retch her recently consumed broth, but nothing came up.

Reaching down Banoldino took her in his arms, 'My darling, what is it? What is troubling you?' He felt her stomach but she winced in pain.

Picking her up he strode onto the deck and staggered through more swirling sea water and pelting rain, until they had the shelter of the bridge. Helping her down into the galley he was able to manoeuvre her onto her bunk where he wrapped her tightly in a blanket. After a few moments, her expression changed. Now she relaxed and her beautiful features, free from distortion almost formed a smile.

'I'm fine,' she said.

'What do you mean, fine? How can one moment you look like a ghost and the next...'

'I think I know what it is... I'm with child.' She almost laughed.

Banoldino's eyes widened with delight. 'How do you know, what has been happening? Tell me, my wondrous girl, is it true?'

'Yes, I'm sure of it, I had an idea, a few signs, feeling sick in the morning, even when there was no swell. A little change, here and there, and well no 'show' when the curse, well, I'm with the new moon normally. Always.'

'This is amazing! Ha! Ha! I had better speak with the captain right away about taking our vows. What do you... ahhhh! Wait! I see everything now, you would do anything to get out of your daily chores. Isn't that it? You are going to fake this for the whole length of the voyage!'

She smiled at him, and put out a tender hand to his cheek. 'Believe me, feeling like I do and living through these conditions is about all I would ever wish upon myself, I would not willingly add to my burden. But I know you are just playing with me, you know it's true don't you.'

Banoldino nodded and pulled her upward until their lips met and he held her head in a long embrace.

***

The following morning Banoldino appeared with Lord Ranleigh before Captain Rouse. A black-clad, lay preacher whose mission aboard the *Star of the Seas* was more than just transportation, he quoted the Methodist Bible at every opportunity, held nothing back when addressing his crew when it came to bringing 'damnation' down upon them, and considered it his duty to deliver only 'good, Christian souls' to the shores of the New World.

His role as captain of the *Star* had provided a platform, where need and often desperation governed all things from life to death.

He revelled in his role and delivered his speeches and sermons with gusto at every opportunity.

'A marriage, you say. My Lord, I am certainly willing to exercise the authority invested in me for the benefit of bringing two Christian souls together in matrimony.' He stood, enjoying the moment. Then walked around Banoldino, nodding his head knowingly.

'I see before me a Catholic, no doubt, from the shores of Espania.

'Indeed, sir, I am of Spanish b...'

'I am sure of it, my friend, you do not need to impress it upon me.'

Ranleigh stood aside mildly amused.

'I have encountered many a Spaniard in my time, the vigour and enthusiasm with which you spread the extreme doctrines of your faith, particularly in the equatorial regions of the Americas is of some great concern to the more 'conservative' Christians of the civilised world.'

'Captain Rouse, sir, if I may, I have never thrust my beliefs, or my opinions upon any man, of any colour or creed. Until this moment I have in truth not committed myself to any cause. I...'

'A man with no convictions then, a man with no background or honour?'

'Sir, I...' Banoldino looked toward Ranleigh in search of some guidance, but Ranleigh was enjoying the intercourse too much to interfere.

'Sir, if I may, I have, in the past, may I say, been something of a soldier of 'fortune'. My path has not been, shall we say a truly straight one thus far.'

'Go on!' Rouse listened and continued to stride around the space limited by the presence of three full grown men.

'I met my 'friend' under the most difficult, er, circumstances. I have come to love her most dearly, I am determined to dedicate my entire life to her well-being. I am certain that my path from this moment will not be diverted again.'

***

'Lord Ranleigh, I take it you are prepared to 'stand' for your companion? Do you know the lady in question? Has she been in your employ long.'

'I am aware of her circumstances captain. We have taken her into our family, and I am confident of her good nature. She has no family, therefore I cannot think that she could be better favoured for a journey into what may prove to be a challenging new life.'

'In that case, bring the girl before me at noon. I will join them, in the sight of God Almighty, and thereafter include them in my vocations.'

Ranleigh slapped Banoldino on the back and withdrew to his quarters where Lady Evelyn sat with Kirsten at her knee.

Holding out his hand he drew Kirsten up and told her, 'Your marriage will be blessed today at noon. May you find happiness in your union, my dear.'

Lady Evelyn rose to join them and hugged Kirsten. A tear formed in Kirsten's eye as she thought once again about her own dear mother on the day of Sinead's marriage.

Lady Evelyn dressed Kirsten in a pale green, cotton gown, platted a strip of silk in a darker green into her hair, and draped a lace scarf over her head. 'There,' she said, 'so pretty.' She grimaced. 'There are many great and good ladies of my acquaintance who would give all their money and titles for looks like yours, my dear. Always be aware of it. Sometimes it is all a girl may need in life. You can gain the world with a favourable complexion, but also, my dear, be aware, many men will foist upon you their 'attentions'.

'Ninety-nine of every hundred would use you, and abandon you. I truly hope you have found one, *the* one, who will cherish you beyond one score years.'

'Lady Evelyn, thank you, so much, for everything. I know I am fortunate in having my companion, I believe in him, I am sure he loves me.'

Lady Evelyn stroked her face, 'And why wouldn't he, my dear.'

Kirsten looked down, a string of rosary beads was laid across her hands as they joined across her midriff. Kirsten held them close so that they would rest adjacent to the embryo of her child.

Rouse began, 'Banoldino Don Bosco de Cervantes, do you take this woman, Kirsten Malone, to be your lawful wedded wife?'

Chapter 23

The Voyage Takes its Toll

Days passed and the body count continued to rise. None were immune to the terrible conditions. The ship rose and fell, driving through roaring storms until barely a sail could be set. Then there would be icy stillness and the frozen temperatures made washing and freshness ever more difficult.

Lord Ranleigh himself became ill and fell into a coma. Following a sustained feverish state, he fell into a long sleep from which he failed to wake.

Lady Evelyn spent every waking moment by his side, talking to him, appraising him of any news and of their daily progress, but he failed to acknowledge a word even if he had taken in anything.

His skin yellowed and his weight dropped alarmingly making him appear twenty years older. Lady Evelyn prepared letters for the lawyer, Elliston, that he may join the family much earlier than was originally planned, to take care of their affairs in the New World.

They watched every day to find a passing merchantman en route for England to enable them to exchange mail.

Banoldino and Kirsten between them looked after the children although Kirsten's first responsibility, whilst keeping up Lady Evelyn's spirits, was to her unborn child, and to make sure she ate something every day and take advantage of the fresh goat's milk, brought in daily by the ship's cook.

One morning Lady Evelyn called Kirsten.

'Would you go to the surgeon and beg of him some unction which may be rubbed into the skin? My Lord has developed bed sores, despite all my efforts, the movement of the ship, and chafing his poor shoulders against the linen, I must try, would you mind?'

'Of course, Lady Evelyn.'

With a quick turn Kirsten made her way along the gun deck to the quarters where Wolfgang Otte would be found.

Otte spent most of his days in his quarters, most of his evenings in the dining room, almost constantly with a glass in his hand. Of German origin he had joined the *Star* following his return from Africa where he had been engaged on slave ships and made two trips to the Caribbean.

He maintained that two such trips was sufficient for any man's sanity and regaled his fellow diners frequently with description of appalling conditions endured, certainly by the slaves themselves but also the crew and paying passengers. Many times Ranleigh and Captain Rouse had to remind him that he was in mixed company and much of his rhetoric was of such a nature as to cause grievous offence.

On one occasion over cards, Banoldino, having been invited to join in with Ranleigh, Rouse, Otte and James Franklin, a timber merchant bound for New England, had to be restrained when the German's description of treatment meted out to a number of pubescent African slaves proved to be offensive, even to the males in proximity.

'My friend, you must contain yourself! I think my dear wife would prefer to know only the facts, rather than endure such graphic commentary. I implore you, show some restraint!' Ranleigh was compelled to intervene.

'Lord Ranlickk, I beg your pardon, my story is truthful to the last detail, I vould neffer vish to offend.'

'It is the truth of it we would really prefer you to leave out on this occasion.'

Lady Evelyn rose and took Kirsten's hand. 'My dear, and madam,' addressing a Dutch Countess intending to join her brother's family in New Amsterdam, as she preferred to call New York, 'please join me in my quarters, I would like you to advise me on some embroidery.'

With that all the men rose to bid a good evening but Ranleigh added, 'But, my dear, there is no requirement for you to leave us so early, I'm sure Herr Otte has concluded his story for this evening.'

At this point Otte swung back on his chair and waved a drunken hand in the air, 'Ahh let them go. Bah! Perhaps ve can haf some real conversation.'

Ranleigh responded. 'Sir, you are causing offence to the ladies, and now you are trying my own patience.'

Rouse joined in. 'Volfe, enough! You have overstepped the mark. Lord Ranleigh please accept my profound apologies, my associate has offended, and is clearly not his usual self.'

'My capitain, my friend and benefactor, as usual you are the peacemaker. Hah! Let men sort out their own issues, My Lord, I remain your servant – but surely ladies should be confined to their embroidery by eight bells, leaving the men to sort out… '

Banoldino did not like this supercilious, bombastic individual from the moment they had been introduced. He knew well that he slavered lustfully whenever Kirsten passed within touching distance.

Although his lips turned up as if in disgust, his eyes gave him away in that they fixed on her and followed every movement.

Rising and hovering over Otte, Banoldino slammed a hand down on the table. 'Enough, sir, I think you have offended everyone on this occasion and would strongly urge you to retire and desist from further comment.'

Struggling to right himself, Otte squirmed in his chair demonstrating the extent of his incapacity. He slurred his words. 'Spaniard, I suggest you crawl back to whichever primitif hoffel you came from, and leave the discourse to the gentlemen present.'

Banoldino took the German by the collar, inadvertently in the act, helping him to return to an upright position, and pulled his face close to his own.

'My friend you are coming very close to inflicting insult upon my ancestors which are innocent of all offence, and I assure you they have not kept a hovel over these many centuries.'

Rouse stood quickly to implore Banoldino, 'Senor, I beg you, my friend is the worse for drink, I do believe he would be swift and emphatic in his apologies were he fully himself, as I am sure he will be in the morning.'

Lord Ranleigh moved to put a restraining arm on Banoldino and calm the situation. 'Captain, my friend will make allowance, I am sure, for Herr Otte's condition. We take no offence that could not be put right with a simple apology.

'Come Banolo, let us play the hand and ease away the tensions of the day with one more helping of this fine brandy, what do you say?'

Banoldino released Otte who slumped back into his chair. With a white-toothed smile he shrugged his shoulders, raising both hands in front of him and accepted his master's offer.

Otte meanwhile had begun to straighten his clothing and sit upright to a more composed level than earlier. 'Your Lordships will accept my apologies I beg you. I did not vish to offend, in fact my attempt at humour was most clumsily managed.' Looking at Banoldino, 'I vill not be so careless on another occasion, I assure you.'

More than one of the company detected the veiled threat within the German's rhetoric.

Now Kirsten was at his door. 'Come,' he commanded. But Kirsten hesitated, not wanting to actually enter the cabin, she remained in the passageway.

'What is it? Do I haf to send a written infitation?

'Er, Mr... may I...I have come from Lady Evelyn to ask for some unction for His Lordship.'

'Ahhh! My dear, it is you. Enter. I have just vat you vant.

Kirsten wrung her hands but decided on at least opening the door to present herself properly. Pushing it inward she leaned forward and was able to see the bunk, a small chest of drawers and a long cupboard, but was unable to discover his presence in the room.

Adjusting to see if Otte might be further to the left she stepped half way inside.

Appearing suddenly from behind the door Otte took her arm and flung her toward his bunk.

Taken completely by surprise Kirsten found herself trying to regain her feet whilst he stood squarely with his back against the door.

She found him without a shirt, wearing just a pair of cotton, knee-length drawers. A thick ginger covering of tightly curled hair covered his upper body which was, she noted unexpectedly powerful around his arms and shoulders. Sweat poured profusely from his every pore and as usual his eyes were watery and lips slavering, his bald head shone where a coiffured, powdered wig usually rested at an incongruous angle.

'What is you want?' Kirsten could think of nothing else to say.

A harsh laugh emerged and his mouth smiled although Kirsten knew his eyes were coldly scanning up and down her body. She tried in vain to recover some calm and began frantically patting her skirt down to appear neat and orderly in the hope that he would be reluctant to disturb such a tidy demeanour.

'I haf vatched you, surely you are avare off my devotion.

'Please, Herr, Mr Otte, I do not wish to offend but I am a married woman and…!'

'Don't! I haf no time for such pathetic ramblings!' His right hand had eased into his waistband and he unashamedly fondled his manhood whilst he spoke! 'Ve haf and unterstandink, me and you, we both knew from the moment ve met this was goink to happen!'

'You are sadly mistaken, sir'

Kirsten attempted to pass him to reach for the door but he immediately became brutal, grabbing her around the neck and spinning her, he pushed her face down onto the bed. Such was his power and the speed of his attack, Kirsten could do little except attempt to catch a breath whilst her head was held in a powerful grip, with her face pushed into the mattress.

Behind her he tore at his own garments to release his engorged manhood and grappling her into position, pulled ferociously at her skirts holding her legs apart with his own.

He thrust himself closer and closer to her, pulling at her all the time to gain position. His manhood within inches of her, his mouth, breathing heavily into her ear, the smell a mixture of sweat and stale brandy. She relaxed and spread herself to bring herself up onto her knees. She felt his thrust.

Otte, convinced she was relenting and allowing him access, was poised to push himself firmly into her but Kirsten bucked violently in the air making him lose his balance and crash backward into the corner of the cabin.

To her great relief he was so intoxicated that he stayed where he was, legs gaping with his manhood exposed and commenced a high pitch hideous laughter.

'My dear, you haf out-manoeuvred me, it seems. I vas lining up, ha, for the kill! Ha ha!'

He seemed unable to control his laughter nor to be capable of summoning the strength to right himself.

Even as Kirsten kicked him viciously in the groin, he continued his high pitched laughter. Turning she left him lying there, a vision which would stay with her for many a year and would bring the bile of disgust rising in her throat.

On safe ground, she fell against the bulkhead and tried to throw up the contents of her stomach but nothing actually emerged. Her tears however ran indiscriminately down her face for some minutes. All the time she considered her situation and sobbed in frustration when reaching her decision.

She would not impart a single detail of the attack to Banoldino whom, she resolved, would surely stick his knife into Otte. Only trouble for Banoldino could ensue from such a response. She remained in a terrible dilemma, but chose ultimately to keep silent, unless of course, the attack was renewed, or even should Otte look toward her in other than a gentlemanly way, she would, she vowed, remain silent.

***

The difficulties endured during those bleak days made the time pass more quickly. Caring for the family, taking what they could down below to help out the Reagans and O'Carrolls, joining in the morning roll call and inevitable departures. A fresher wind and a general air of optimism eventually helped lift the spirits of all on board.

Even the crew became gradually more cheerful, this must have meant they were in the final throes of the voyage. The names of the landmarks which were cleared one-by-one, were passed around from crew to passenger. Greenland, Nova Scotia, Maine… each one was followed by a lifting of momentum and soon land sat permanently on the horizon and became the focus of their every waking moment.

Eight more days followed with land clearly visible off the bow, which brought such hope and yet much sadness.

A new born baby one day, an ageing grandmother the next, a once fit and vital youth, all perished in those last few days. All the more heart breaking with sight of the New World their constant companion. Many passengers below decks were now coughing a sustained and harsh barking sound, appearing physically on the 'brink', but still hope sprang eternal.

The ship plunging on through a heavy swell, and a fresh wind stretching taught canvas, the temperature noticeably warmer, gave one particular morning an atmosphere charged with excitement when Lord Ranleigh moaned audibly and brought Lady Evelyn to her feet.

'Banolo, Banolo, Kirsten, come quickly, my Lord, he's awake.'

Reaching the cabin, they rushed to his side and were able to confirm movement in his hands and feet.

Slowly, as an hour passed, they allowed fresh water to drizzle into his mouth and Lady Evelyn was able to bathe him, he weakly asked a range of questions, returning many times to the most important of all, 'How long have I been here?'

Lady Evelyn spent the following hours massaging his limbs and rubbing unctions into his skin. She helped him out of bed into a warm bath and draped him in clean linen.

He had come back from the dead, that is how they all felt about it, he was alive and they were going to make damned sure he would be returned to himself again.

Fortunately for Kirsten, the condition of Lord Ranleigh meant that food had been generally taken in their quarters and encounters with other passengers and crew, in particular Otte, were in the main avoided.

The routine of dining and playing cards in the wardroom diminished.

***

The day following Ranleigh's recovery, Captain Rouse visited and some of their dining partners were allowed a few moments with him. Lady Evelyn quietly cried into Banoldino's chest and allowed herself to be comforted before finally regaining her composure and thanking them both for all their support.

At that point she became faint and had to be carried to her own bed where merciful sleep enveloped her for a full twenty hours.

The remaining three days of the voyage saw the family regaining their health and strength walking the decks, watching the land slip by, the fascinating array of vessels that sailed close, exchanging signals.

Most of all the mood of optimism showed in the passing of lighthearted pleasantries between all within their class.

It had been a hard journey, the end was in sight and all of them filled up with fear and anticipation at what lay ahead.

Chapter 24

New York

The harbour at East Side, New York was visible through the morning mist. The ship was a hive of activity with all the seamen engaged in preparations.

There was great excitement in the air and many of the first and second class passengers with access to the deck stood along the rail and watched as the distance closed between them and the harbour wall. Finally, to a great cheer, they dropped anchor in the bay as a flotilla of small boats had drawn alongside and were bobbing on the waves.

Many opportunists were touting their wares. Accommodation, entertainment, places to dine, a wagon master, a lawyer, all offering their services. And, of course, a Quaker Minister, inviting any of the faithful to make their way to Boston, to join the brethren there.

Then there were relatives seeking their loved ones. Hopeful calls at first, then some more confident. They called the names, many typically Irish, 'Is O'Toole aboard?' The exchanges were mixed and often amusing, 'Now which O'Toole would that be?' 'Why? Does he owe you money?' 'He changed his mind and went to Bombay instead.'

If there was a sign of recognition, the chatter changed and became more determined.

'We're looking for Seamus O'Toole, me sister's boy from Derry, the one that lived next to the corner shop'.

'Tell O'Bannion that if he sets foot on American soil he'll be hanged from the nearest tree.'

'Any single women on board? We've husbands aplenty waitin' for yea!'

The first class passengers would gain great amusement at these exchanges enjoying some of the lighter moments of the voyage just before embarkation.

Only Kirsten was not at her most ebullient. Preferring to remain in the shadows to get on with her work and noticeably failing to join in the frivolity of the last remaining days at sea.

Otte had been a constant thorn in her side over those last days. He never removed his attentions unless right under Banoldino's gaze.

He furtively found opportunity to corner her, or to isolate her from the others in the party.

He sensed her determination to keep Banoldino in blissful ignorance of his attempted rape. He knew only too well that the Spaniard was capable of attempting retribution. He also realised that there was a good reason he had failed to take action against him. What was their secret? He cared not, all he knew was that she had not told him.

If the reason was that she wanted him to remain in ignorance so that he would not engage in revenge, then she was a strong character, oh yes. He was inspired to think of her as an independent woman, determined to keep her man safe despite her obvious vengeful state of mind.

This gave him power over her nonetheless and he was determined to exercise that power at every opportunity.

Finding her in the galley area folding freshly washed clothing, he moved up behind her in silence. Pressing up against her, he pinned her to the bulwark and through her clothing still managed to thrust himself unnervingly close to her.

His hot breath in her ear and sweat rubbing into her hair, he was determined to let her feel his power.

'My dearest girl, you have surprised me at keeping our little tryst to yourself. I expected at least to haf the gallant Senor throw his glove into my face.

'Leave me alone. I warn you.'

'Calm yourself, my pretty. You don't appreciate my attentions I know, but for some reason you find it preferable to bloodshed. Even should it be mine!' His lungs hissed reflecting the effort required to keep Kirsten under control.

'You are a fool, sir, if you think you can get away with this. My husband is a man you should not wish to wrong.'

'My dear, you haf given yourself avay, you vill not tell him.'

He was becoming breathless but she could feel his hardness against her thighs. 'Gif me vat I vant, now, just once, and I will leaf you to connive your vay into the New World with no shame or damage to your reputation. Come on. You know how to do it. You didn't get with child by clamping your legs together.'

'You know I have a baby inside me and yet you still... You're an animal!'

Kirsten somehow managed to turn to be facing him but he still held her rigidly against the frame of the sluice gate. She bent over backward to avoid his face coming into her own, feeling the rigid timber across her back and in great pain, she twisted her face and spat at him.

He held her but freed one hand to bring up to her throat, half around her neck and with his powerful thumb on her larynx he held her and for a moment she was convinced he would snap her neck or that he might strangle the life out of her.

Still struggling Kirsten resisted with everything she had and freed one hand to claw his face. Her nails bit into his skin near his left eye and he growled in anger before suddenly freeing her. Whilst she tried to wriggle past him, he grabbed the shutter door, he turned and took her by the hair.

Pulling her so that her face was twisted toward him he bent her so far backward 'You vill come crawlink to me von day my little colleen, unt von day I vil stick a knife in your man's heart.

Kirsten finally pulled away from him and did her best to tidy herself up before encountering Captain Rouse on the steps.

'Ahhh, ma'm. I trust all is well, you look a little flustered.'

'Er, no, I am well, sir. It is warm and the work hard in these conditio....Please, sir, let me pass.' At that point Kirsten burst into tears, and despite a hand on her arm, turned and left him on the steps.

Rouse with a shrug, descended the final few steps and was not a little perplexed at Kirsten's distress, when Otte emerged from beneath the staircase. 'Mine *Capitain,* I trust you are vell zis mornink'?

Rouse looked at him, long and hard, considered his ruddy complexion and a slight swelling at the corner of his eye. 'Herr Otte, I find you sober for once. I declare things are looking up.'

'My Capitain, do not berate your servant too much, you know the trials I haf endured. I am as always your devoted...

'Yes, my friend. Always devoted, but to whom?' With that Rouse ducked into his temporary quarters and left the German standing quite uncomfortably with a further remark unused on his lips.

Alone Rouse peeled off his jacket and the leather scabbard with its cutlass. Placing it on the cabinet beside his bunk, he sat reflecting for a moment on what he had witnessed.

'Surely' he mused, such a vibrant beauty as the young Irish maid would not dally wilfully with an oaf like Otte, surely she would not 'allow' him... and yet with one word the Spaniard would cut his throat, and who would stop him?'

His tiredness would not allow him to dwell too much on the issue, yet as he closed his eyes for a fitful few moments sleep, the image of Otte fawning over the beautiful, naked torso of the Irish girl invaded his dreams.

***

Days passed with only fleeting moments of discomfort for Kirsten.

On other occasions Otte gripped the back of her thigh hidden by her skirts as she passed his chair at the dining table. Otte, visiting at Lady Evelyn's behest, when once again Anabelle was off colour. On another he put his hand under her breast and squeezed her when her Ladyship turned her back.

But the mental persecution continued for Kirsten day and night.

She was tempted to reveal him on many occasions, biting off the words from the end of her tongue, she resisted. His spectre would not leave her and she longed for the moment they would be parted for ever once they reached their destination. She would step off into a new life and he would disappear over the horizon for good. That thought alone comforted her at night before sleep would envelop her.

***

Eventually the *Star of the Seas* was approached by a boat containing a representative of the Governor of New York, and the self-appointed harbour master, who knew Captain Rouse from earlier acquaintance. They all shook hands vigorously as they climbed over the rail.

Dawkins knew the waters 'intimately' he insisted, and agreed a small fee before guiding the ship safely through the shallows and alongside the mooring without incident.

The dockside and immediate development around the harbour was a maze of accommodations, built and half built, a continuous backdrop of banging and clanking confirming that construction and the use of timber in particular was the prime activity on the shores of the New World.

Shipyards were busily fashioning a range of sailing ships, some of most impressive design and proportions.

Beyond, across the narrow inlets, high rising ground, heavily forested at first then rocky and barren, an endless vista which thrilled the onlookers with its vastness.

Lord Ranleigh had his hand on Banoldino's shoulder. 'This is a land of opportunity my friend. New York is a metropolis – not inclined toward any doctrine. Puritans, Catholics, even Jews are welcome here. Freedom of worship and trade, is the important thing to these people. I'm sure you fully appreciate that. But I have connections! I know people! I have come here to enhance my fortune but for a man like you, given a foothold, there are no limits.'

Banoldino, turned to look his employer in the eye.

'I am your servant, I am also a very willing student. Your family made our voyage bearable. Without you, I know not that Kirsten and I would even have arrived here safely. I hope, in some way we can continue to serve, and again, even more that one day we will be able to meet as friends.

Kirsten was busy helping Lady Evelyn prepare for departure. 'Is everything well with you, my dear? I detect a little change in your demeanour lately. Have you not been content with me, and the children?'

'Oh, milady, don't think it. I have been happy, I love the children like my own brothers and sisters. It… it's nothing you could have done.

'But there is something?'

'I'm with Child!

'Kirsten, that's wonderful, starting out in the New World. Building a family is the best way to begin.'

'I'm not so sure, milady. I was thinking Banolo and myself, well we have to make our way, find work, a place to stay. I fear the future, milady, I know nothing of the world!'

'But we can help, perhaps you could manage the children for me, until your confinement, well so much can happen in a few months. Elliston has made arrangements for us to stay with Reverend Henry Jackson until our own residence is completed. I will make a case for you to be my personal maid and live in. Surely that puts the matter to bed?'

'That's very kind of you, milady, as always, but Banolo, he has grand ideas, I'm not sure what he wants to do yet.'

'Surely it would be a good thing whilst he is sorting things out?'

'I will talk with him, milady.'

'Do you have any idea what he intends? Which profession he might prefer?'

'I'm not sure, at all, milady. He talks all the time about 'horses', breeding and such. I used to help out Jon Smout, in the village – he was the only one who had a horse that wasn't for pulling a cart, so I'm not scared of them.'

'Well this is splendid. My husband is greatly involved in livestock, cows, sheep. Of course they have to be purchased and brought to the east coast, for the markets and for shipping. When we are fully established we will have very large facilities, and of course horses, lots of them. I will speak with Ranleigh before we go ashore.'

Kirsten smiled warmly and at that moment felt she had a friend in Lady Evelyn, a relationship which filled her with hopes for the future, just by association it would mean respect and position, whatever life had in store for them. Despite that she held back, she had an instinct that maybe Banoldino would want to be his own man, and she felt disloyal in pinning all her hopes on Lord and Lady Ranleigh.

***

Finally setting foot in the New World, there was much respect imparted toward Captain Rouse, his being a most difficult role, everyone had to agree. That Kirsten would be free of Herr Otte was the thing which was completely overwhelming her thoughts as the embarkation and farewell's were completed.

For a career ship's captain, there would always be difficulty, from the mere concept of two hundred people from different walks of life, some in the very throes of desperation and hardship, others with huge expectations, thrown together in a confined space, through awful weather for months on end, facing the cruel ocean. It was a recipe for disaster throughout the eighteenth and nineteenth centuries.

Thirty-two crew and one hundred and seventy-four passengers set out.

Twenty nine crew and one hundred and thirty-eight passengers disembarked in the New World. One entire family of seven and almost one member of each of the other steerage class had perished en route. When it was all over, the captain would restock his supplies, return with cargo and crew to his port of origin and begin all over again.

Knowing, after his eleventh voyage that to take the price of a ticket from many of the passengers would mean virtually turning him into the mythical 'ferryman' – he took their money to lead them to the 'other side', for some, their last journey in life. Yet Rouse departed with a hearty laugh and a long and sincere speech of encouragement.

***

Ranleigh and his entourage, which now included Banoldino and Kirsten were met by a carriage provided for them by acting governor George Clark, and conducted them to the Britannia Lodging House, Manhattan Island.

The quayside and the adjacent square were lined with locals waving handkerchiefs and small flags. An enthusiastic orchestra played familiar laments and Christian tunes and the atmosphere of a parade accompanied them on their ten minute journey to their lodgings. A second carriage brought their belongings.

It was understood that once rested and refreshed from the voyage, the governor would 'receive' the family formally before they took up arrangement with the Reverend Jackson.

Their rooms were clean and decorated with fresh flowers and a copper bath stood invitingly in a corner of the master bedroom.

The first evening arrived and the children were not alone in their fascination at finding the servants and many of the hotel workers of a most unusual variety, that being black African. Many indentured slaves, a small percentage freedmen, but one third of all people encountered were of this origin.

Banoldino and Kirsten dined at a long table with Ranleigh at the head, the dining room, cosmopolitan, with a range of classes, all dining together.

Men in fine costumes but of poor carriage and obvious ill-breeding, drank fine wines from crystal right alongside clergy and naval officers.

Ranleigh and his family remained highly amused, but Banoldino knew more of the origins of this mix of races than even Ranleigh himself.

'My Lady,' in answer to a remark by Lady Evelyn, 'if I may, the slavers have brought Africans in huge numbers to these shores. The southern towns and West Indian islands in the Caribbean are the first places colonised but the demand for labour in all parts of the New World requires the transportation to go on without sign of a recession'

'Well, it's all very strange, I have to say,' Lady Evelyn responded. 'We could not have this in England, I can assure you. They all look so unhappy, Ranleigh, what to do you think'?

'My dear, it is the way of the world, not for us to question how things are achieved, because we will not change the new order now. We must make damned sure our slaves are happy ones, eh Banolo'?

All the family smiled, as was usual with Ranleigh, he had a way of diffusing a situation, and his charm always came through.

'Banoldino, Kirsten, if I might, I would like to make a proposal. Tomorrow we go to the governor's residence and will no doubt meet a lot of people. I am expecting to find my friend Augustus Fitzroy, our families go back many years. He has married the former governor's daughter, Alice, I believe, and established himself very well here in the colony. Our introduction into society will be made easier by our association.

I would like to suggest that I introduce you as 'friends' shall we say, rather than, ahem, our retinue.' Noticing the look on Kirsten's face he quickly added, our 'servants'.

"Banoldino returned his look, amused and pleasantly intrigued."

'Look here, it's quite normal for my wife to travel with a companion, rather than a maid, and from my point of view, I do believe a 'man of the world', such as yourself Banolo, will fit in very well with the sort of people we're likely to be dealing with, particularly the military types. What d'you say?

Banoldino looked at Kirsten and the alarm which showed in her face told him he would have to be cautious in his response.

'My Lord, I am overwhelmed at your proposal, it would be a deception, but hopefully a harmless one. However, you have I am sure, taken some account at how difficult it may become when, shall we say, the conversation makes demands upon myself, and of course, Kirsten'.

'Look, my friend, and I do mean that, my friend. I would not want to put you in an impossible position, but I believe we can carry this off. Without too much embellishment, I am certain we could create a little 'history' for yourself and Kirsten.

'When Evelyn and I arrived in County Offlay to clear up the affairs of my late brother's estate, we encountered lots of families which would have been proud to boast a daughter as young and, may I say as beautiful, as Kirsten. Let's say, she could have been the estate manager's daughter?

"Yourself, my friend, had been in a Spanish Galleon which ran aground in the Sea of Ireland, and were washed up in Dublin, a town you found so to your liking that you remained, under the benevolence of Lord Stevens, whose estates ran west as far as the Offlay borders. It was inevitable that you would meet and marry, and seek to make your fortune in the New World."

'No more need be added. With my endorsement, I believe you will be accepted and time will do the rest. Perhaps we can discuss some prospects for a business venture when I have had a little time testing the ground with Fitzroy.'

Banoldino, squeezed Kirsten's hand and smiled, holding his glass toward Lord Ranleigh and Lady Evelyn, he accepted the plot in good heart.

'My Lord, I can do nothing other than accept your proposal. We already owe you a great deal, and will further rely upon your generosity before long. We will need to be dressed a little, for the occasion, and for some of the inevitable consequences of being involved in the world of commerce.

'We'll take care of all that in the morning, I'm sure we'll find a good tailor here abouts. Now drink up and lets settle in to our new surroundings.'

Glasses were raised again whilst Kirsten smiled benignly, her insides were turning over at the very idea of being thrust into society. 'After all,' she was thinking, 'what is society?'

Chapter 25

The Slave Ship

Daemon rose early, stretched and sluiced cool water over his face.

Great preparations were already under way and John Standing, looking every inch the English aristocrat that he was, in the courtyard checking the tac and the loading of the horses readying for the first leg of their journey.

There were seventy miles to negotiate between here and the Port of Agadir, where a ship was to be procured. Standing had briefed Daemon of the objective which would establish the format of their adventure.

The ship, largely funded by his Arab partner, would be equipped for a long voyage around the coast to Sierra Leone where the brother of the Emir Assad Agrande Maktolla would be rounding up Black Africans for transportation to the Caribbean. The enterprise would form the basis of triangular trade between there and Britain where they would deliver in exchange for the slaves, silver, coffee and tobacco.

Should the profits realised meet expectations, the process would be repeated over again. Either way, the first part of their adventure was sufficient to fill their attentions for the moment. Daemon, completely naïve in the ways of the world, in particular the world of slave transportation and slavery, had a lot to learn and only a very short time to learn it.

Nonetheless he could not get out of his mind a promise he had made to a young English girl, when he was in chains on

slave market! The things I've seen, I can't even think about without the shame! But by some miracle, here we are, travelling with an English earl ! Have you any idea what he intends, for me, or for yourself?'

'Well, it seems I'm bound for the West Indies, wherever that may be! We have to sail a cargo half way round the world! Strange isn't it? Two and half years since I never set foot on anything big enough to hold two pounds of fish! Now I'm going across the ocean with three hundred souls on board!' He smiled at his own rhetoric.

Margaret, however, gasped. 'A cargo, of souls, you say? Slave ships! Is that what you are about?'

Daemon shrugged, 'Slave ships, well I suppose that's what it is. Weird, I know, having seen what African slave ships do to people from *our* country, now I'm going into business. But it's 'cargo' accordin' to himself. He says we take them to a better life, where they will be paid for work, or at least get fed well and looked after. It's not like what *they* do. I don't think.'

'A slave is a slave. I only know what Jesus said about the meek inheriting the earth, and we're all supposed to be his children. I just think about what I felt like, when I was put in chains and lost everything, even the freedom to... to... use the privy.'

'Well I'll make you another promise. If you'll let me. I'll never treat these people like we were treated. I'll make sure it's like, well, like it should have been. The way John Standing is with me. It's almost like we were the same, you know, he doesn't want me bowing and scraping, he just treats me like a friend. He says that's why he decided on leaving the old country, he wanted to be in a world where there was no, what did he say, where there was no-one better than anyone else just because of who their father is, something like that any way.'

'He sounds like a good man. At least until the ship takes on its cargo. What do you think he will do with me? Do you think he will let me go home?' Again tears formed in her eyes, which she quickly wiped with the back of her hand.

'To be honest, I haven't asked him. I just assumed you would come with us until you were safe in an English town. Now you mention it that could be a long way off. I can't see how you could go with us. I mean, all the way. These journeys can be rough. Maybe he can find you a ship to go back to England. Mind you, who would you travel with? I better ask him when I have the chance.'

The animals stirred and John motioned to Daemon that it was time. Daemon rose and walked across to where Standing was tightening straps on the back of one of the mules.

Margaret rose and straightened her clothing, picking up a water bag and the headscarf she had briefly undraped. Just as she stood up John Standing appeared in front of her. Her natural reaction was to courtesy, and bow her head. Keeping her eyes to the ground.

'Margaret? It is Margaret isn't it? We haven't been introduced.'

He took her hand and his demeanour showed her that it was safe to raise her eyes.

She looked into his open, half smiling face and immediately became captivated by his sharp, deep blue eyes. Blushing she dropped her gaze again.

'I apologise, I haven't had the opportunity to make your acquaintance.

'My Lord...

'John, please, just plain John nothing else.'

'I... can only thank you with all my heart for taking me... for saving me... I'm sorry, I just don't have the words.'

'Look, enough of that. I'm just glad you could join us. I haven't had much time to consider arrangements as yet, but when we reach Agadir, I shall do my best to get the British Consul to look after you. I assume you would like to return home to your family?'

'Yes, if that were possible, or at least find work. I honestly haven't given much thought to my future. I have been... well I'm sure you understand... captivity.'

'Yes, I do. I would like things to change. Who knows, one day, we can all find our own 'space' to fill. Anyway, for now, you are travelling with 'friends'. Anything you need, please just ask and we'll try.'

Standing took her hand again, leading her to the grey mare. He watched her tuck her long black hair into the shawl and draw the veil across her face. Her eyes above it, looked up at him as his hand went out to help her. He could not help noticing how beautiful those eyes were, the long lashes, the long dark arch of her brows. She was slender, but graceful in her movement. Those eyes, now shining, he knew behind the veil, her mouth had formed a smile.

He made sure she was secure and with the best possible level of comfort for the next part of their journey, and felt genuinely, that the sooner night would fall the better, that he may sit with her, talk some more and, he hoped, get her to like him.

Chapter 27

Freedom

Waking up in a sturdy, timber-built hostel was strange enough for Kirsten. The quiet all around was startling in itself, then the stillness.

A few rumblings and a door closing here and there, told her she was not alone, but the luxurious straw-filled mattress was as comfortable a thing as she ever experienced. She writhed between the linen, adjusted her pillows and reached above her head to feel the solid timber of the bed post.

This was a new world to her in more ways than one. There was glass in the holes in the wall, like the chapel, back home. There was a smooth white ceiling overhead, between darkened oak rafters, and a wash basin standing on a cupboard.

Rising, she made her way to the window and felt almost giddy at the twenty-five feet distance to the ground.

She could see other stone and timber-built dwellings across a wide thoroughfare but no gaps between the buildings.

A carriage drew slowly to a halt in front of the building across from theirs and two men climbed down, stretched, and went in to collect supplies.

The storekeeper had barely opened the door when they were about their business collecting items. The idea of a 'store' was something also very new to Kirsten.

She stood watching as the morning developed becoming busy with activity. Carriages and carts of all shapes and sizes. People, nodding their 'hellos', stopping to converse and exchange goods. There was a bustle about the township and they were right in amongst it.

Almost forgetting, she realised her husband was missing, at least from the bedroom. They had spent so many months in close proximity, he watching her every move and she constantly seeking him and the reassurance she got from his presence, now it seemed strange that he was nowhere to be seen. She felt a sudden moment of panic, but chided herself at the idea that something was amiss.

She tested the water in the washbasin, clean, fresh, her skin tingling at its touch. Happily she sluiced the water over her arms and neck.

Turning, she looked around and found a clean dry cloth which she used to brush away the droplets. Spinning around she searched for clothing but found to her immediate surprise, nothing.

Pulling the sheet about her making sure that it covered her modesty, she propped herself against the timber headboard.

Some time passed when Kirsten must have dozed off, for the sound of creaking timber flooring and the swinging of doors brought her abruptly to her senses.

Banoldino strode into the room, smiling widely, he carried a bundle of clothing. Casting it down onto the bed in front of her, he stood upright and preened his long coat for her appraisal.

Laughing, Kirsten made sounds of approval whilst not fully appreciating the joke. But Banoldino would not let it settle there, he laid out two dresses which covered almost the whole of the bed. A green velvet gown with white fringe, and a deep purple smock type cloak that had black velvet around the edges and the collar. He also unfolded a range of white linen undergarments which were laced with pink ribbon.

Looking extremely proud of his acquisitions he awaited her approval. Kirsten was almost lost for words as again she laughed and squealed with delight picking up each item in turn, but just as she was about to pull on the first of the dresses Lady Evelyn's head appeared around the door.

'Kirsten, my dear, come, let us dress you – we are to leave immediately for the governor's residence. Come.

Lady Evelyn was clearly excited at the prospect herself so Kirsten had no option but to fall-in with her mood and gather herself for the challenge ahead.

'What do you think of my wardrobe, my dear? I trust we have your approval. Turning gracefully, Banoldino showed off his own new garments only this time he chose to return to his duties by turning on his heels and making for the door.

'If her Ladyship would be so kind, I have my… er… duties to attend to. The door clattered as it swung behind him and Kirsten was left with Lady Evelyn to prepare.

Finding Lord Ranleigh, Banoldino stood respectfully at the threshold of his quarters until Ranleigh summoned him inside

'Well, what d'you think, will the governor find what he expects when we meet?'

'Without a doubt, my Lord, you will not be found wanting in terms of nobility in actions and deeds.'

'I don't think George Clarke will fail in his support for the likes of us coming to settle in these backwoods. These colonies need the approval of the aristocracy in order to flourish. Without us they would be left to wallow in their own misplaced loyalties and disaffections.'

'I am sure you are right, Senor. There has to be order, I am sure you will find a place in this society. However, if I may, I sense a change in these parts. Something I can't quite explain, but the people here, they are keen to be your friend, but they bow to no man, they do not touch their forelock, nor beg for indulgence. From what I have witnessed they speak their minds and do not wait for permission.'

'My friend, I understand. I do. Believe me. I do not expect the old order to prevail, but I am sure the same people that lead the way in our land will lead the way here. I do not underestimate what lies ahead but I do believe we have come to this place at just the right moment in time.' He took Banoldino by the shoulders and looked him squarely in the eye.

'I do not believe a man can come here alone and reach for the very pinnacle of society. But I do believe a man, with friends, and with someone to watch his back, can take the opportunity that presents itself by the scruff of the neck and make a great fortune. You will be watching my back. I will be watching yours. Come, let us gather the family around us and show Governor Clarke exactly what we are made of.'

Chapter 28

Society

The occasion had brought out the best of society and carriages were pulling up and depositing the great and the good on to a wide platform adorned with flowers and a set of steps leading to open doors from which bright light shone wide and cheerfully into the dark and the strains of a small orchestra wafted through from the great hall.

Banoldino gripped Kirsten's hand and she held onto him as though he might fly off into the distance should she release her grip. Ranleigh ushered the children through the great doors as their arrival was announced by the maître d'.

The room beyond hushed momentarily as the gathering emerged into the light. The first sighting of the new arrivals had brought many of the ladies out when they would willingly have demurred in favour of their husbands enjoying a typically ordinary evening of cigars and Port wine.

Now they could see for themselves the cut of the newest titled family to join their community. A number of the British upper classes had previously alighted onto colonial society and very few had made a favourable impression. Indeed many had left in disgrace or filled their coffers and made a swift departure.

The music played on and polite conversation developed before Governor George Clarke approached across the bustling hall.

'Lord Ranleigh.' He bowed low with much ceremony and apparent sincerity. 'We are delighted to welcome you to the province of New York and to introduce you to our humble society.'

'Delighted, governor, may I present Lady Ranleigh, my dearest wife Evelyn.'

'Lady Evelyn, you will bring such elegance and style to our community, I dare not think of the influence you will have on the ladies here, why we may rival the court of St James itself.'

'My dear Governor Clarke, please, you flatter to a fault. May I introduce my companion, Kirsten Don Bosco, and her husband Banoldino Don Bosco De Cervantes.'

'Charmed I am sure, my dear, you are very welcome.' His lips brushed against the back of Kirsten's hand. It was all she could do to resist pulling it away. Banoldino clicked his heels and bowed courteously toward the governor who reached forward and joined hands in a hearty greeting.

Ranleigh then introduced the children who bowed and curtsied delightfully, before the governor took each in turn and welcomed them copiously offering all the delights of the music and fine wines.

There was a veritable crush as the crowd followed the enthusiasm of the governor's greeting and vied to be the first to present themselves. Ranleigh and Lady Evelyn were overwhelmed with attention and could scarcely draw breath until the 'leading lights' of the new world had made acquaintance and provided contact details for future assignations.

***

Kirsten and Banoldino remained in attendance, always ready to hold out a hand or perform a simple bow or word of greeting. They were most relieved to have escaped the kind of attention foisted upon Lord and Lady Ranleigh but grateful to be greeted by many without blatant prejudice.

Many were delighted to make the acquaintance of such a handsome couple and nothing untoward was experienced as the night wore on.

Dancing was encouraged but of course Kirsten declined every invitation. The dance was something they had thus far overlooked in terms of their evolution into society. It was only too obvious that this oversight would have to be quickly remedied should their introduction be a total success.

'Banolo, darling, when can we leave? I don't know how much longer I can go on with our pretence. If one more of these gallants asks me to dance I am going to have to accept. I think it only a matter of moments before both of us are squirming around on our knees looking for a place to hide our heads in shame.'

At just that moment a tall, straight-backed Englishman took hold of Banoldino by the arm. 'Sir, may I introduce myself? Anthony Rackham, I have a small business here, bringing timber into my mill and shipping it to Europe. I hope to expand in due course and compete with some of our friends in the Canadas.'

Banoldino listened respectfully and bowed his head knowingly at the information as it unfolded. 'I am pleased to make your acquaintance, I have noticed the shipbuilders alongside the harbour also consuming significant amounts of timber. Do you anticipate an opportunity for expansion in that direction?'

'Of course, you must have surveyed the coastline during your final few days at sea. You are right of course that there is a market for the finest timbers, the best, sturdiest quality.' He scowled at that point. 'Regrettably I was not able to find an opportunity with the shipbuilders. My esteemed colleagues in the Timber Association, carved up the business before my arrival. I have not been able to change the order of things and therefore found my own markets overseas.'

Banoldino bowed politely 'You may wish to meet James Franklin, a gentleman who sailed with us from Ireland'.

Rackham responded with genuine interest 'I would be delighted, perhaps I could depend upon you for an introduction.'

'Think nothing of it. Meanwhile perhaps in time, with a little persuasion, some of those shipbuilders could be encouraged...' He left the thought in the air.

Rackham stood erect and smiled warmly before bowing curtly. 'Should you have an interest in our humble trade, please call on me at my premises in Dale Street'. He turned to bow in Kirsten's direction. 'Your servant, mam.'

'Banoldino immediately realised he had failed in his responsibilities. 'Senor Rackham, may I introduce my wife Kirsten.' Offering her hand, again the recipient bowed to brush his lips across it.

'Sir, I must commend you on your beautiful spouse, a more handsome lady has not been seen in New York.'

Banoldino, whilst polite, was not enamoured at the attention afforded his wife on their first exposure to society, clicking his heels again he signalled acknowledgement at the compliment.

Rackham continued, 'If I may be permitted,' he turned to look into Kirsten's eyes. 'My wife, unfortunately, was not able to join us this evening, but I am certain she would be delighted if you could call on us. Millicent is very much involved in the well-being of immigrant families, perhaps those not as well connected as yourselves. My wife is tireless in her efforts to bring them to the church, and to help establish them in society.'

Kirsten's eyes switched to Banoldino's and sought support. 'I, er, would like...' Banoldino nodded, 'Yes I would be very pleased to offer my help.'

'I suspect you are of the Catholic faith, I am certain you will be pleased to celebrate mass at the new Catholic church of All Saints, in Long Island. Perhaps, yourself, sir, as of

Spanish origin will also admit allegiance to Rome? You would be very well received.'

Banoldino took control of the conversation 'My wife and I would be delighted to attend your church. We will contact you immediately we are settled.'

'Most gracious, sir, and now I bid you farewell.' Rackham gave a final bow and retreated.

'Jesus, I hope you realise how I almost fainted?'

'I understand only too well, my dear. I could see your discomfort, but it was admirable the way you managed yourself. You have proven how capable you are, in my eyes at least. You have nothing to fear. All you need to do is smile and agree with them.'

He bowed to kiss her on the cheek and could feel the tension drain away from her.

***

The following morning Banoldino sat with Ranleigh and recalled the events of the previous evening.

'I believe you have made a good start with Rackham, should we decide to look into timber. James Franklin may well know him already, or intend to get to know him. My only comment would be to suggest that next time such an opportunity occurs, you do not mention the 'acquaintance' before the meeting has been arranged.

'Should Rackham have a mind to, he could seek out Franklin on his own. Nonetheless, I do believe you have made a good start.

'For myself, I am pleased to have the governor's attentions, for the next week or so a number of other social engagements will be made and I will surely meet the cattle barons and establish a fruitful connection. Meanwhile, let's get Franklin over for a little soirée and find out his intentions.'

Both agreed to pursue the opportunity and made arrangements to put their plans into action.

***

Kirsten was spending her time with the children as usual. Lady Ranleigh, of good constitution, was inclined to rise late in the mornings, and enjoy social events to the full in the evening.

This enabled Kirsten to mix with the children before her duties to Evelyn got under way. The move to Reverend Brookes' accommodation was to be achieved during the following day so much preparation was to be instigated the day after the governor's 'get-together'.

By ten that morning Evelyn had called Kirsten to her rooms and a light breakfast was brought up.

'I thought you did very well last evening, my dear. You fitted in to society for the very first time as though you had been born to it.'

'Lady Evelyn, believe me, I could not have felt more uncomfortable. My knees never stopped knocking together! But I must say, I did enjoy it.'

'There, I knew it! The men were falling about your feet.'

'Hardly, my lady', she blushed. 'Goodness knows Banolo would not have been too pleased with me.'

'Nonsense, my dear, he must have been so proud. I am certain he was as pleased as the rest of us. I watched your encounter with that tall Englishman, Rackman, or was Rackham?'

'Er, well a man named Rackham did introduce himself, so he did, but I... '

'Well you made a great impression on him I'm sure of it.'

'Well he did ask me to meet his wife in the near future, and to worship at the All Saints Church.'

'Ahhhh! Did he indeed! All Saints, I am certain would be of Catholic determination?'

Kirsten nodded.

'Well do be careful, my dear, we will be residing with Reverend Brookes these next months. I don't think the Reverend will be overjoyed that you will not be joining *his* flock.'

'Oh dear, have I done wrong, milady? Should I have not spoken of....'

'No at all, not at all. You will not be under any threat in these parts for attending mass. It is not like England. There is freedom here to practise whichever religion your heart desires. I just would prefer that Reverend Brookes was not so soon given an opportunity to regret his generosity.'

'But, milady, I am sorry.'

'Hush, not another word. We will not let it distract us, not in the least. Now let us begin with the packing.'

'Yes, milady.' Kirsten was left with a feeling that perhaps, she should have not allowed herself to be so easily lead as to have agreed to meet Rackham's wife. She shook her head, aware that 'politics' or to her 'behaviour', was to be an area of much concern to her in the future.

Chapter 29

Agadir

The horses pulled up at a small trough and the weary group dismounted.

Standing called for his two Arab helpers to take them and make sure they were fed.

Waiting for a signal, Daemon and Margaret were ready when Standing called them.

Entering into the encampment they were halted by armed guards, but cleared to continue after a few words were passed down the line.

They were expected, and inside, reclining as usual another potentate was prepared for them.

Fresh fruit was served and sitting just behind Standing, Daemon and Margaret were invited to eat. It was all quite surreal to the two erstwhile captives, but John Standing reacted as though they had been lifelong friends, deferring to them, looking across for approval when his version of recent events varied into slight inconsistency.

He was happy with his two companions and they, becoming used to being treated as equals, were beginning to behave like the friends he needed for the tasks ahead.

He had explained to Margaret that she would be welcome to join them on the 'epic' voyage, that she could provide immense assistance in establishing a humane regime and to make certain that those being transported suffered nothing beyond what common decency would allow.

She enthusiastically accepted the offer on the basis that she would play a purposeful role. John Standing had no intention of justifying her inclusion to his Arab partners, he was quite content to describe her as the 'surgeon' for the voyage, avoiding any further questioning.

Now sitting with Hammed Al Barda he was describing the day's events having dismissed all other subjects as formality. Now he described how at eleven that morning, just an hour into their journey, a party of camel riding Bedouin had descended from high ground and surrounded the party.

Much waving of blades and howling, added to the two or three musketts that were fired skyward. They had made it plain that they were not impressed with the caravan, and its entourage, using their oasis, in particular the two 'effendi' from Maktour who were performing menial tasks for the party.

At one moment it looked as though they would attack and Standing armed Daemon and the two guides. Then Standing insisted on their leader coming to the fore.

A moment passed when there was a discussion going on within the gathering before one came forward.

'What is it? How have we offended? Please allow me to pay'.

The Arab, burly and heavy bearded, responded by grabbing a flowing part of his headgear and pulling Standish to the ground.

He stood firmly with a foot between the shoulder blades of his victim's back and shouted orders.

Daemon moved swiftly enough to support his leader but three or more of the Bedouin moved into his path.

The servants threw themselves at their opposite numbers but were quickly overwhelmed.

In the struggle Standing's headgear had come loose and drifted away across the sand. Now seeing a white man, bareheaded, the Arab's curiosity brought him to remove his foot and release Standish.

Climbing to his feet, the Englishman calmly brushed off the loose sand from his face and clothing.

'Effendi... who are you'? demanded the leader.

Standing responded in Arabic. Telling his adversary his name and rank, and current mission. The Arab moved an arm toward Standing to attempt to brush off his clothing but with one athletic movement, the earl took the arm and used it as a fulcrum with which to turn the Arab on his head.

Putting a foot between the man's shoulder blades he held him, face down in the sand for some moments. He had completely reversed the situation. The others all turned attention on Standing leaving Daemon and his companions now, to offer protection to their leader.

Standing however spoke again in Arabic. 'Stand back, effendi, your leader will come to no further harm unless you force me to permanently disable him, in a way that he would not be of any value to his hareem'.

Taking this weighty threat, made in the familiar tongue, as truthful, they backed off and raised their weapons above their heads.

Gradually releasing the fallen one, enabling him to come to his feet, Standing gambled that his humiliation was not too great as to make vengeance his only goal. The Arab rose slowly and laughed heartily when he reached eye level with Standing.

Then, bowing theatrically, he slapped Standing on the shoulder and invited him to dine at his encampment.

'My companions?' Standing motioned so that he impressed that it was unthinkable to leave out his entourage, the Arab responded by insisting that they all join the party.

Daemon looked over admiringly at Standing and awaited a response but the cool eye returned by his companion alerted Daemon that there remained a small possibility they may still have to flee or 'bargain' for their freedom.

In the end the dining completed, hospitality satisfied, they were waved off as they left the encampment with a small non-threatening attachment of warriors. Numbers sufficient to provide comfort during the last leg of the journey and see them part as 'friends' some miles from the city of Agadir.

The story told faithfully to their new host brought a torrent of abuse for the antagonists from the desert. Swearing vengeance in such vehemence and ferocity that had the whole party laughing aloud, especially the Emir himself when he realised the outlandishness of his tirade. What he was going to inflict upon the adversary's house, children, mother, horses, cattle and descendants was of such enormity that it might take two lifetimes.

Settling down to the real business Standing and the group were advised that the ship was fully prepared and manned with enough to sail the first leg of the voyage around the North African coast as far as Sierra Leone. It was always the intention to man the ship for the crossing with more able bodies on arrival at the mouth of the Niger, or from the ranks of the slaves themselves.

Chapter 30

Opportunity

Banoldino spent some days getting to know the area in and around the township. Familiarising himself with the complex layout of New York's harbours, on both sides of the channel, and the location of the bigger shipbuilders. He introduced himself to the port authorities, asked lots of questions and was provided with a great deal of support upon reference to his benefactor Lord Ranleigh.

Many of the shipbuilders enquired cautiously, as to the intentions of His Lordship, and the areas of business in which he might take an interest.

Most significantly, he rode out with Lord Ranleigh to the frontier boundaries of Philadelphia and New Hampshire, talking with the settlers.

It was quite clear, assessing the fortitude of their homesteads that hostilities with the Indian brethren were bubbling beneath the surface. There was hardly a day passing which did not bring news of some war party, or raids carried out on outlying homesteads.

The frontier settlers were of steely, determined stock. Many of them Irish. Many with larger families, sons of ten years and upward able to wield an axe and fire a musket.

Their sense of community only surpassed by their determination to live 'free' from the rule of others.

Many hours passed in the evening around the table at Reverend Brookes' establishment, where plans were outlined and options turned over again and again.

Banoldino had arranged a meeting with Rackham, following discussions with Franklin. They were intent on proposing a trading relationship which would provide Rackham with another outlet for his sawn timber and the opportunity for Banoldino to put his plans for increasing the quantities being brought down river.

The meeting had more or less sealed the relationship subject to a few legalities. Banoldino would have to spend some months in making his arrangements in the forests and organising teams for transportation.

With all arrangements in place, he could not wait to get the project under way.

**

Returning from the Franklin residence some weeks later his brisk evening walk came to an abrupt halt as he rounded the corner at the bottom of Wall Street, he was suddenly held up by a man springing from the shadows.

Unarmed, Banoldino, raised his hands in the air in an attempt to calm his attacker.

A pistol was pointing in his general direction, whilst the moonlight glinted from a long bladed knife.

'Mallachi's the name, just in case you was wondering sometime in the hereafter, who it was that brought you to this place.'

'My friend, please, I am carrying nothing of value. I have no weapons and I would urge you – check for yourself that there is no profit to be gained from this encounter.'

'It's not your purse I have come for'. Returned a calm, lyrical Irish voice. 'You sailed on *The Star of the Seas*'?

'Yes. That is true.'

'You fell in with His Lordship. Coming all the way across the ocean in his company'.

'That is also the case, yes, I admit it.'

'Well *my* brother. Yae see. He was a bit of a lad, but a young lad, perhaps not fully come into his senses.'

'I am sorry,' responded Banoldino, still holding his hands above his head, showing compliance, whilst calmly, he prepared for the next move. 'I have not met your brother, as far as I am aware.'

'Oh yes you have!' Mallachi, thrust his blade forward in an attempt at inflicting a slash across Banoldino's face. His evasive movement meant that only a scratch was achieved but it demonstrated that his protagonist had some element of speed and control.

'My friend. This is insane! I have no knowledge of your brother. You are making a terrible mistake. I would urge you...'

Mallachi moved around in a half circle then back again. Banoldino came to the conclusion the pistol was not loaded, that the man had intentions of using the knife only. He felt reassured that there was a reasonable chance of resisting the attack that was to come.

'You murdering bastard, you left my poor wee brother to die on the dock, whilst you boarded the ship with your fancy new friends and walked away.'

Sudden realisation came over Banoldino. The thief on the Dublin dockside. Who would believe his family in the New World would be bent on revenge?

'Please my friend. I would ask you to reconsider. Yes I may have encountered your brother. A thief on the dockside, attempted, with a gang, to assault and rob an innocent man. I felt a compulsion to recover the stolen goods but the offender was intent on putting a knife in me. Just as you are now. What was I to do?'

Banoldino began to manoeuvre now, left then right and Mallachi, the opposite.

229

'My brother's life was worth more than a few trinkets. You think we are just animals, the British think they can use and abuse us like pigs!'

'Sir, I am not British, I have come here to live a life of freedom, just like yourself. There is opportunity for both of us but this is not the way, I implore you'.

Banoldino had hardly completed his plea when Mallachi thrust again, this time with speed and accuracy toward Banoldino's midriff.

Catching the buttons of his waistcoat as the thrust was eluded, the knife became temporarily snarled up. Banoldino saw his opportunity and slammed a fist into the throat of his opponent.

Not completely successful, despite bringing a gasp from Mallachi, the knife was flashed close to Banoldino's ear and considerable strength was brought to bear, giving him no option but to put two hands to the task of preventing it entering his neck. Just then the butt of the pistol was brought down with some force onto Banoldino's temple, making him stagger backward.

He felt the timber walkway beneath him, wet with light rain, his two hands, trying to ease the impact of the fall, hit the deck first.

Mallachi was on top of him in a split second with the knife forcing it's way closer and closer as weakened, Banoldino fought to resist.

Allowing the weight and force of his attacker to commit to a last final thrust, he suddenly shifted his own weight so that Mallachi and the point of the dagger slammed into to the timber walkway. The knife buckled beneath him but with the broken end sticking upward, it lodged itself beneath the Irishman's rib cage.

Groaning he rolled over, clutching his stomach. Banoldino quickly regained his feet, though unstable as a result of the clubbing to his head. Blood ran into his eyes as he got to Mallachi to assess the damage.

Regaining some control, Banoldino wiped fresh blood from his brow, and quickly discerned that the blade was in reverse and almost completely lodged into the intestine of his attacker.

Looking around for any sign of activity, he saw the flicker of a candle on a door across the street from the incident. A brass plate shone in the dim light at the side of the door, just three stone steps from the pavement.

Grabbing Mallachi by the jacket, he managed to hoist him into a sitting position and finally to his feet. Unsteady as he was, the Irishman managed to stay upright. Emitting another groan, he allowed Banoldino to stoop under his free arm and half carry him across the street, and onto the steps of the house.

Banging firmly Banoldino determined to get attention, he made out the word 'Surgeon' on the name plate and prayed silently that the occupant might be a skilled man in handling knife wounds.

To his surprise Wolfgang Otte swung open the door.

'Herr Otte, I am astonished! Er, please please help me.

'Who iss it? Vat the hell are you doink banking on my door at zis hour? Ahhh Senor, it is you. Vell Vell, Unt who iss dis?'

'Herr Otte, please take his arm, the man has been badly hurt. He needs attention quickly.'

Otte stooped to take up Mallachi's arm, leading them in to the first door to the left of the hallway.

'Qvickly, brink him over here, lay him down, I vil get my things.'

Turning, Otte pulled at a wall mounted glass cabinet and removed some instruments. Banoldino tore at the Irishman's jacket and waistcoat. His shirt was soaked in blood and Banoldino balled up a cloth to attempt to stem the flow.

Otte was at his side in seconds. 'Vat has happened? How did he get like this? A friend of yours?'

'Not exactly. He attacked me in the street, an attempt at vengeance for some old offence. I assure you I meant him no harm.'

'I'm afraid the evidence does not support your claim my friend'.

A pair of steel grips retrieved the broken ended four inch blade from the gaping wound and blood flowed freely onto the table.

Within minutes the wound was cleaned with spirit, dressed and wrapped and Mallachi appeared to be sleeping, breathing steadilly.

Banoldino loosened his neck tie and collar, and slumped into a chair.

'Here' let me dress your vound.' You must haf taken qvite a blow.'

'Yes, he must have clubbed me with the butt of his pistol'.

'You say he attacked you? Some kind of vendetta?'

'Yes, yes, the less said the better. Will he survive? I don't want his death on my conscience.'

'I am sure you do not, Senor. What vould you tell ze authorities?

'I do not know. I suppose I just have to tell them what happened. When he comes around I will talk with him.'

'Here, my friend, take zis, a small potion for your head.'

Banoldino did not resist. He took the draught and closed his eyes.

***

Some time later feeling cold and stiff, Banoldino stirred and raised himself to a sitting position. The back of his head ached from the neck upward, and at the same time from a throbbing above his left eye.

He could hear talk coming from the hallway and a candle flickered across the room. Raising his eyes to discover his surroundings he could see the outline of the shape upon the table. So quiet and still was the figure that Banoldino rose, slowly at first, then grasping the head to turn it toward him, he realised the Irishman was stone dead.

Banoldino knew time had passed, he must have been unconscious. He staggered toward the door and found Otte talking to a dark cloaked dignitary flanked by two red-coated soldiers.

Turning, Otte was the first to speak.

'Ahh Don Bosco. The authorities have come to establish the facts about your Irish friend's demise.'

'What are you talking about? My Irish friend? Your patient, Senor. Some minutes ago he was sleeping soundly, unlikely to die from a flesh wound.'

'Sadly not so. The man died in my arms, his internal bleeding draining blood from his body. I am afraid his death is now a fact and that the Justice, here, will be seeking an explanation.'

'Senor Don Bosco, I trust you are well enough to accompany us to the Town Hall?'

'Well, I have to return home to my family. My wife will be anxious. Lord Ranleigh...'

'Yes, of course, Senor. I must insist though, that you accompany me first. A man is dead. A pillar of our immigrant community. Explanations will be demanded. Justice must be served.'

'Sir, I assure you, I was attacked by this man. He assaulted me with a pistol. Look you can see the evidence clearly. I took action only to defend myself.'

'Sir, might I ask you what your movements were earlier this evening? You say you were attacked and that the attacker had a pistol with which he assaulted you. The blade which killed him I assume was your defence?'

'No, no the knife was his, it broke in the attack, you will find it on the walkway across the street. There will be blood.'

'The knife and the pistol belonged to the dead man?'

'Yes, he was intent on revenge, he mistook me for someone else.'

'Why would he not shoot you? If he had both weapons why choose to use a knife?'

'Sir, I don't have any idea. Perhaps he did not want to make a noise. Even so, he was alive, he was not in danger, I do not understand how he can now be dead.'

'Senor, please once again, I would ask you to accompany me. I do not wish to use force. The dignitary motioned toward his armed guard and they stepped forward giving Banoldino little option but to accept the invitation.

**

Lord Ranleigh had bid a good night to Kirsten and was chatting with the maid. 'Senor Don Bosco is due back at any moment. Please be so kind as to await his arrival and lock up when he has gone to bed.'

A knock on the door brought Ranleigh around turning his back on the girl. 'Ahh this must be the Senor now, I will have a word...' Opening the front door Lord Ranleigh was taken aback when a clerk stood before him shielding his eyes from the glare of the hallway lighting.

'Sir, apologies, do I have the honour of addressing Lord Ranleigh?'

Receiving a nod in response he continued, 'I wish to inform your good self, that Senor Don Bosco has been detained by the chief justice overnight.'

'Please repeat your message young man.'

'Er, if I may, sir,...' He announced the message word for word.

'What is the issue? Why has my man been detained'?

'Nuffink I can be sure enough to confirm, Your Lordship. But I do believe it is related to a murder.'

'Stupid man! This cannot be the case, surely!'

'Beg your pardon, Your Lordship, I am a humble messenger – but I did overhear the conversation, a little.'

'You will await my return and conduct me to the Court House, forthwith. Stand where you are.'

Ranleigh quickly dressed for the late evening walk, and knocked gently on Kirsten's door.

Peering out of a narrow gap Kirsten was wide eyed trying to adjust when Ranleigh leaned forward and in a lowered voice, 'I don't wish to alarm you, my dear, but there has been some trouble and Banolo has been detained.'

Kirsten let out a stifled cry but hushed as his finger raised to his mouth. 'Please do not concern yourself too much. I am leaving right away for the Court House and I am certain I will get to the bottom of things.'

Kirsten attempted to protest but was quelled by his comforting gesture when he put a hand on her shoulder and insisted that he would return, with Banoldino before morning. 'You must rest and await my return'.

Ranleigh quickly disappeared and fell-in behind the clerk who with as much haste as he could manage without running, reached the Court House within a few minutes.

Being shown through a number of doors delayed Ranleigh's progress to the extent that upon meeting the chief justice he had become quite calm.

'Good evening to you, sir. May I have the pleasure of knowing to whom I am speaking?'

With a short bow of the head, 'Chief Justice Van Doren at your service, my Lord. It is my pleasure to make your acquaintance'.

'I wish I could say the same, sir! I would trouble you for an explanation of the circumstances surrounding my associate's detention'.

'By all means, Lord Ranleigh. Please be seated, may I offer you some libation? Please, I would do anything to spare your discomfort.'

Ranleigh accepted the seat. 'Please begin, sir'.

'I was called to an address just a short distance from here by a surgeon who had attended upon an injured man, whom we now know as Mallachi Driscol, an immigrant of reasonable repute, having arrived here from Ireland some six years since. The individual has recently died of his wounds.

'The surgeon explained that he had been brought to the premises by your associate, Banoldino... Don Bosco? Yes, Don Bosco.

'Your man had arrived at the premises and admitted an altercation during which the deceased was inflicted a knife wound, causing him to conduct the injured man to the surgeon. The gentleman subsequently died. Your man insists the injured man was in no danger when he himself was treated for a head wound inflicted during the same altercation.

'However, there is no evidence that any 'third' party was involved in the altercation nor that the death was caused other than by the wound inflicted by your associate.

'Therefore, I must conclude that the cause of death was the wound.'

'Yes, yes, but that does not prove that the wound was inflicted intentionally or with intent to kill.

'Quite so. Nonetheless, I have arrested Don Bosco on the evidence available, that he was the cause of the demise of Mallachi Driscol.'

'Sir, I have listened patiently to the chain of events as you have kindly portrayed them. I must be provided with a version of events from my associate Don Bosco himself. May I see him?'

Van Doren rose and lead the way. Upon turning into a passageway, Ranleigh looked up to see Otte, exiting a doorway and passing the group with his head bowed low and a hand covering most of his face.

'Otte! Is that you? I say, Otte, stand still man! I would talk with you!

The chief justice turned and looked toward Ranleigh. 'You are acquainted with the surgeon Herr Otte?'

'Yes, of course! What is he doing here? We left him aboard *The Star of the Seas* when we landed in New York two months ago. Herr Otte I would request an explanation!'

Otte eventually squared up and looked Lord Ranleigh in the eye. 'Your Servant, my Lord,' he stuttered with obeisance. 'I regret I am late for an assignation, a patient, you understand.'

'That will not do, Otte! What are you about, sir'?

'Why, Your Lordship, I haf made my decision to settle in the New World, just as you yourself haf done.'

'I trust Captain Rouse was given proper notice?'

'Indeed, Your Lordship, he gave me his blessing.'

Turning to Van Doren, 'Is this fellow in the employ of the justice department, sir?'

'Er, no, Your Lordship. He is a witness. He was gracious enough to provide a version of this evenings events surrounding your associate Don Bosco.'

'Good heavens, man, are you telling me this man has accused my companion? Do you not understand that the two have a history of disagreement, one might even say hatred?'

Van Doren turned to Otte, 'Herr Otte, you did not mention that you and Don Bosco were acquainted, or that you had history?'

Otte, fumbled about for a few coherent words. As usual he was the worse for drink. 'I vas acqvainted with Senor Don Bosco and indeed with His Lordship. Ve travelled from ze British Isles together. It is true that Don Bosco and I did not always see eye to eye.'

Ranleigh spoke more to Van Doren. 'Indeed we thought when we disembarked from *The Star*, that we had seen the last of our dear doctor here. I am not at all surprised at this evening's events. I imagine my associate was as astonished as I to find Otte here in New York.

'My dear chap, I suggest that Senor Don Bosco is released to my charge and I will take full responsibility for his whereabouts at all times should you decide charges are to be brought. However, I strongly urge that you consider the version of events provided by Senor Don Bosco as infinitely more reliable than those provided by Herr Otte. You can have my word on it.'

The Justice considered for a moment all that had been said and immediately summoned for Don Bosco to be brought from the cells.

'Herr Otte, you may be questioned further about this matter and I would stress upon you that to leave the township at all within the next two weeks, would be considered as an absconsion. Now I suggest you make a swift departure from these premises for the sake of law and order.

'Lord Ranleigh, I convey upon you responsibility for the whereabouts of our friend Don Bosco, should he be wanted further in connection with this incident. Gentlemen, I bid you goodnight.'

Otte was a distant figure at the far end of Wall Street by the time Banoldino and Lord Ranleigh alighted on to the pavement outside the Court House. A few moments later, Banoldino silently slipped between the sheets next to Kirsten and slipped a hand under her arm, wrapping it around her and pulling her toward him, where she nestled for the remaining hours until dawn broke on a new day.

Chapter 31

Prime Stock

The Durham pulled anchor at high tide. Two days after Standing's party arrived in Agadir. A crew of seventeen busied themselves with stowing the anchor and releasing sail, and a tropical breeze blew them into the Mediterranean at a healthy rate of knots.

Daemon stood alongside Standish and surveyed the landscape as it slipped away to their leeward side, whilst on the 'larb'd' the Rock of Gibraltar peaked out above a low lying, horizontal cluster.

The early summer sun began to close on the south western horizon and the red glow reflecting back from the cloud and bouncing off the surface of the calm sea, provided a heartwarming, almost sentimental backdrop to the drama of their departure.

Daemon's thoughts were with Kirsten, on her own glowing form as she swayed effortlessly against the campfire's own dancing flame. Her skin, warm to the touch, smooth, and dusky pink in the fire's reflection, her arms long and slender moving gracefully, her dazzling smile, her eyes! He could not remember the girl. Just her parts, just her wonderful, wonderful parts.

John Standing looked out, let the breeze ripple through the tight curl of his hair and breathed in deep, lungs full of sea air. This is what he anticipated when he set his plans in motion. This is what he dreamt of before sleep every night.

No rules, no etiquette, no 'pecking order'. He dismissed quickly images of his father, seated to the right of the fireplace in the great hall, the boys sat at his feet, Mother at a distance, with Aunt Alice, comparing shades of thread for the next needlework masterpiece.

A shudder ran through him, was it Mother? God rest her soul? Was it...? No he didn't begrudge George his inheritance. Nor Richard, his parish. He was only too glad none of that fell upon himself.

No, his nostalgia, was for a life that had gone for good. That the old ways would be lost and the new order, the commoners world was on the threshold of the future. The common people would own the land, the machines, the crops, the ships, the townships. The landed gentry would become outdated, isolated, remote and unloved. Of that he was certain. It was just a matter of time.

Now the sails filled with a fresher breeze, now the waves lapped and sprayed against the prow. Now the men moved without lethargy, but in harmony one with the other, each with the ship, she cut a swathe through the surf and thrilled the heart at her speed and her unrelenting progress.

Standing grabbed at the rail, Daemon held onto the rigging. They were riding the ocean. Alongside Standing, Margaret stood, her hair flowing on the breeze. Her face held to the spray, she closed her eyes, her exhilarated form cutting a fine line against the horizon, tasting the freedom, she looked almost as if she were about to take off. Their journey had begun in earnest.

Chapter 32

The New Arrival

Banoldino rode like the wind. A dapple grey mare, carried him, deceptively powerful, courageous and swift. She bolted through a wooded glen, leapt a fallen tree trunk and a stream. The long meadow ahead was cut down in a surge of powerful strides. She burst through the clearing, over his own fence and into the yard. Dante was waiting to take the reins, his powerful black arms glistened with sweat in the afternoon sun.

Banoldino slid easily from the heavy embossed saddle and dust spurted into the air from his heels.

Inside the house Minister Marchant sat on his haunches half way up the stairs looking worn out. High pitched excitement emanated from the first floor bedroom. Banoldino slowed only for the pastor to whack him across the rump as he passed.

In the bedroom Kirsten sat up against the shining oak bedstead. Her hair thick and golden, around her shoulders and high on her head. Her green eyes, heavy above her fixed smile, dimples on either side of her mouth etching happiness into her features.

In her arms, wrapped warmly in an ornate woollen shawl, the tiny form of their son peeped out at his world. His golden curls falling just above his ears, his own green eyes shining and oversized for his tiny head. The image demanded to be captured for all time. Banoldino recalled the endless, dramatic mother and child images of the multitude of churches of his homeland.

In awe of the little bundle he took it from Kirsten and held it high above his head for a long moment. Clutching the baby to his chest, he finally raised his eye in wonder at its beautiful mother, reclining with a tear in her eye and hand to her mouth, she could not take her eyes from the pair.

'I do not have the words,' mumbled Banoldino, holding back a short emotional gasp. 'You have never looked more beautiful. This, our Son, is... I don't know how to say, a *miracle*?'

He leaned to kiss her full on the lips and lingered until his balance threatened to bring him down on the bed with the child beneath him. He straightened again and held the baby firmly, seemingly unable to let him go.

'Banolo, I am so tired, I have to leave you to take care of the baby for a few moments. When I have rested... ' Her eyes closed and she wriggled down into the thick folded linen, her hair framing her face which he mused was like an angel's.

'But, what shall I...?' Banoldino appeared hopelessly out of his depth, holding an infant for the first time, he looked across at Lady Evelyn then at the crib at the foot of the bed.

She nodded her approval as he stepped toward it and lay the baby gently on his back, pulling the shawl in around him, making sure it did not cover any part of his little face. Lady Evelyn raised a finger to her mouth and shushed them both from the bedroom.

Throwing her arms around Banoldino she planted a firm kiss on his cheek and looked into his eyes. 'You are blessed, Senor Don Bosco. You have a beautiful wife and a wonderful child. I hope you realise how lucky you are.'

'My Lady, I could leap across the forge! You see before you the happiest man in the Americas! I have to thank you. Indeed, I have to thank Lord Ranleigh, Andrew, for everything. I have not been so blessed in all my life as to find such friendship!'

Releasing him, Lady Evelyn straightened her dress. Turning she made toward the door. 'I hope you know how much, I... *we* appreciate having yourself and Kirsten as our companions in this adventure. Our world is in the past. The confines and restrictions of society have been lifted since our arrival. Many of the things we have experienced have been so different, so alien to us, God knows how we would have coped. And here you are, so strong! Andrew should be thankful. I know he is.'

She turned and swiftly left him.

Although her outpourings expressed her friendship and were full of sincerity, he could not help feeling a little perplexed at the words and the uncertainty with which she conveyed them. Could it be Lady Evelyn, a pillar of civilised society was as vulnerable as any ordinary, common settler?

Banoldino shrugged off the moment and returned to the bedroom. Finding both his loved ones asleep, he made for the kitchen where Mrs Marchant was boiling water over the range.

'I have stoked up with logs, they will be burning brightly very soon.

'There is some fresh cheese and bread on the table and I trust you will make sure that Kirsty receives some of my broth as soon as she awakes. I will have to leave you soon, Senor Banoldino, my husband needs my attendance at the church this evening.

'However, I am sending over a young woman, to help Mistress Kirsty whilst she decides upon her arrangements. Should the girl prove herself, then I would urge you to take her on. She has a child of her own, and she may prove invaluable as a wet nurse, should Kirsten need help.

'Her own family were slaughtered when Seneca Indian attacked their homestead. You may find her a little morose, but I pray to the Lord she will find her way within a happy and prosperous household.'

'Madam, I thank you for all you have done, please do not trouble yourself further, I know your duties are many. We will find our own... hired help, in due course.'

'Nonsense!' The sternest of pinched faces, peering out from beneath her bonnet convinced Banoldino to hold his tongue. ' You know no-one as yet, where would you go to find capable assistance? Or is it your intention to employ slaves?'

'Absolutely not, madam. I assure you... '

'Good, that settles it then. You will take Allison Fairchild and give her a chance of recovery in a Christian house. Good. I will send her in the morning.'

As the door swung shut behind her Banoldino shrugged his shoulders helplessly, and smiled to himself. He knew it was the right thing for all concerned. He also knew not to tangle with Mrs Marchant, over anything, in the future if it was avoidable.

He knew how vehemently Mrs Marchant and the Reverend were against keeping slaves so he made a point of paying his two 'hands' ceremoniously on a fortnightly basis, providing them access to his horses and a cart to go into town and purchase their own needs.

Dante and his wife showed no signs of dissatisfaction with the arrangements and he himself was pleased that rather than awaiting instruction for each and every act, they thought out their own itinerary for the day. They advised him and provided an opportunity each morning before breakfast for Banoldino or Kirsten to rearrange or add their own needs to the list. The household had established a nice familiarity, easy going but respectful on all sides. Renata came in from the barn at just that moment and offered to prepare a stew for the evening meal.

'May I enquire as to the mistress's well-being, Senor? She and the child, they are well? Renata spoke with an hispanic

244

accent and what they had been able to glean from their story was that she had spent time with a Mexican family. Banoldino had tried Spanish on her but found she was slow to comprehend.

'Yes, indeed, I would suggest you go into the bedroom, as quiet as a mouse, you may let me know that they are both still sleeping soundly.'

Smiling and bowing toward him she set off for the bedroom, returning a few moments later to advise him that they were 'serenely sleeping' and the 'most beautiful mother and baby the world had seen since the Madonna'.

Reclining in his wide oak armchair with its Indian blanket covering the old leather, Banoldino smiled at her innocent delight. 'Be sure to call me immediately they awaken, even if I myself drop into a sleep.'

***

The hacienda on the outskirts of Grenada sprawled across fifty acres. Orchards in the immediate proximity, planted fields a little further up the slope, barren, dry hills with snow-capped mountains in the distance. The southern Spanish landscape contrary to the stranger's eye, but beautiful, rugged and welcoming to the natives.

There was a strange atmosphere. Father had been shouting at the men about the ranch. He was short-tempered with everyone these days. Banoldino had hardly had a word in his direction for months, other than 'return to your studies', 'do you want to live like a peasant when I am gone?'.

There had been unrest among the villagers and even further afield, but Banoldino had no idea what was behind it. But lately momentum gathered force and it was clear that a journey was inevitable, but for whom?

Blacksmiths battered away day and night, furnaces roaring, the clatter of steel fascinating to Banoldino, but he was kept away from that part of the ranchero. Horses were gathered in from surrounding areas, Banoldino watching in the early morning as they were corralled and tamed.

Because of the heavy armour and equipment they had to carry, only the sturdiest mounts were chosen. Carriages, cannon on wheels, sack upon sack of produce and dozens of reed-covered wine pots were loaded up. Each day the activity started over, each day the excitement grew.

Flags were unrolled, men assembled, they were being trained, fighting with wooden staves and swords. Young men flocked to their ranchero and camped around the perimeter at night.

Father had women working all through the night on livery. He had chosen scarlet and sky blue and it was reflected in the flags, drapes for the wagons and skirtings for the horses. Each new metal staff had a duo of red and blue ribbon tied to its hilt.

The morning came about when all was ready and Manuel Don Bosco de Cervantes, came into his room. 'Banolo, you will take good care of your mother and sister whilst I am away. I trust you to be a good son, to carry on the name Don Bosco long after I have gone. Should I not return in the spring, I want you to support your mama, study hard and become a great scientist.'

Taking Banoldino by the shoulders his father kissed him on both cheeks and turned away. A huge lump formed in his throat as he watched the sculptured oak door swing on its great hinges and settle in its closed position.

Banoldino was unsure what to do. At ten years of age, he felt he should be going with his father, he wanted to be on horseback, carrying a banner and waving to the people in the countryside. But here he was. Swallowing hard, he ran through the corridors, looking in every room. There was a state of abandonment about the entire hacienda.

He found his mother and sister sitting at a window seat, looking out into the courtyard, handkerchiefs at their faces.

Turning, his mother caught sight of him and buried her head sobbing afresh.

'Mama, what is it, why can't I go with father'?

'You stupid boy! Do you want to be killed also?' She sobbed again.

Marrietta came over to him and put her arm around him burying her head in his shoulder. She was a year older but he was the taller.

'What is it, Marie? Why won't anyone talk with me? Father says I must look after you and mama, but how? How can I do it?'

Now a roar went up down in the courtyard. Ladies wept and gave out shrill cries. Younger ladies waved and shouted evocative promises toward their loved ones.

The line was moving, fourteen horses at the head, a banner above each unfurling on the breeze.

The dazzling effect of crimson and blue filling the entire scene, a single 'tinnie' drum and the deafening, shrill bugles in high-pitched, monotonous long blasts filled the air. Six in all completing a marching band.

Eighty more foot soldiers, holding aloft their staves and pikes, followed up the small mounted force. Guns and carts creaked into motion and a dust cloud blew up over the entire ranch and surroundings. At the head of the column, his father on Rocco, the once untameable black stallion, prancing in time with the drum beat.

Banoldino knew they were going off to war. He just did not know why. He understood less than most because it had been kept from him.

Ever since he was born, the War of the Spanish Succession had raged across Europe but here in southern central Spain they had not been touched. Eternally bad news, battles, cities lost. The 'Grand Alliance', British and Dutch and a rogue Italian prince, had beaten the Spanish and sympathetic French forces, time after time with possessions lost in the Americas, Gibraltar and even mainland Spain.

Banoldino turned over what he knew in his mind, saw himself coming to the rescue when his father was down. But shuddered when it came to wielding a heavy sword at his opponent's head.

Calling for his mother, he was eventually placated that on this occasion, the combined force was being brought against the enemy under the command of Compt de Villier a great French general. This time they expected a great victory and his father and the troops would surely tip the balance in favour and bring the War to an end.

'Meanwhile, back to your work, study – the Medici, Da Vinci, Copernicus, Galileo…' Banoldino wanted combat.

When his father's body was returned on a canvas stretched out between two poles, and dragged behind the now thin and scarred stallion, Mother stood for an hour before she could bring herself to pull back the torn and bloodied banner that covered him. Banoldino and Marietta stood behind her and dared not move or speak.

The few companions returning with the body, all that remained of the force, waited patiently for a signal that they could take food or respite after their long, arduous journey.

When finally she did remove the covering, Consuela broke down and slumped to her knees. The children rushed to her side but were quickly gathered up by a servant and taken into the house where they had to remain with only each other for comfort.

Terrible times ensued after Senor Don Bosco's death. With few remaining servants and many peasants deserting the region altogether, their crops failed and lands deteriorated to ruin. They were left to eke out an existence by selling some of their possessions.

Consuela faded, ageing rapidly and losing all interest in her surroundings. Marietta was sent to a convent where her education would be completed. Banoldino never saw her again.

An ageing fencing master, an old friend of the family, also hit by the disastrous effects of the bloody campaigns in Catalonia, called frequently, at first in hopes of reviving Consuela to consider him as a suitor following many years as a distant admirer. He found her unresponsive and a shadow of her former self, but nonetheless persevered as an ageing romantic might.

He was intent on honing the skills of the unfortunate youth whose prospects now seemed destined to rely upon an inevitably long search for fame and fortune.

Under his tutelage, the youth developed, becoming stronger, taller almost by the day. Life was tough now, he had ploughed fields, collected fruit from the orchards, cleaned out stables and groomed the three horses that remained on the ranch. Banoldino was trained with sabre, rapier and foil and the use of a dagger. Giuseppe had been one of the finest swordsmen of his day attached to the Court at Grenada and Cadiz, he was much vaunted.

For a period of two years in almost daily visits he paid court to Consuela and almost all his time, his knowledge and skills were heaped upon the enthusiastic shoulders of his protege.

When fifteen years of age, Banoldino stood like a man, moved with ease and grace, could skilfully wield a blade and compete with fully-trained soldiers in the art of combat.

Before his sixteenth birthday Banoldino gathered his few possessions, rolled up a beautiful gilt-handled rapier in a leather pouch and pulled on the reins of the last remaining pony on the estate.

He turned once when reaching the top of the hill and with one last look down the valley which had been his world, without regret he waved farewell to his early life.

***

'Senor, Senor, wake up, your wife has called for you. Please, Senor.'

Banoldino had not realised how much he needed that sleep. He was vaguely disorientated, forced to gather himself before returning to the bedroom. There he found Kirsten sitting up, feeding the child at her breast. Smiling almost apologetically, 'Quick, Banolo, come and see, am I doing it properly?'

Banoldino, took a moment to look down once more on her lovely rose, pink complexion, and the baby almost matching her fairness.

His heart leaped.

'He looks contented my love. Who would not be? I think if you were not doing it properly, he would find a way to let you know. Ha! I am utterly amazed, and somehow yet, I feel almost useless. You are everything to that child, me a mere spectator. It will be many years before he looks to his father for comfort.'

'Silly, you will be a comfort to him, and me, every day of our lives. We will both be waiting for you at the door from now on.'

Banoldino briefly flashed back to his years of waiting for his father, first to communicate with him in any way, then to return from the war. Quickly he pushed those thoughts aside, but not before making a vow that this time, it would be different.

Chapter 33

The Niger River

The ship rolled slowly toward the mouth of the estuary. The air hot and stagnant. No breeze from the great ocean, nothing to propel the ship other than the two boats strung out forty yards off the bow.

On board one of the boats, with Daemon at the helm, the line was tight and the minutest movement of the great hulk could be detected.

The boat alongside manned by Olaf, the ships cook and a clutch of his Nordic comrades, the line ran slack back to the bow of the *Durham*. From the rail Standish was calling on them, 'Pull, you men, pull, for all your worth.' Heads were shaken and shoulders drooped. The sun beat down mercilessly. One of the men slumped forward over his oar.

'Get them moving, Mr Rankin – get them moving, throw some water over that man.'

Rankin responded but could get little improvement. Daemon's boat continued to make a little headway, but clearly they required a more competent performance from the other boat to achieve genuine progress.

'Drop anchor!' The command rang out and the combined crew in both boats slumped forward groaning with relief.

Daemon had long since abandoned his shirt, tied his hair into a tight ball and was in need of the reviving impact of cool sea to clear his head and soothe his aching limbs. He

251

slipped over the side of the boat and allowed himself to float on the surface as lukewarm water lapped over his body.

Several of the crew of his boat followed him and in Olaf's command, they acted in unison for the first time that day by sluicing everything and everyone with sea water.

In time they returned to the ship. Clambering with great lethargy up the rigging until they were able to slide down on to the deck. Forward motion seemed beyond each and every one of them.

The few crew not involved in this 'shift' although rested were almost equally as incapable. Margaret had done her best to arrange some rice and salt beef, acting cook whilst Olaf was occupied in the towing operation.

She had abandoned all pretence of propriety and wore a muslin wrap across her upper body and the lightest pantaloons in her limited wardrobe.

Her midriff bare to the elements was sweat-stained equally with the crew.

***

The equatorial heat of the mouth of the Niger was beyond the experience of almost every soul on board. There were flies, persistent little black shapeless things determined to land on and irritate every inch of exposed skin. They would fizz and buzz around the head before coming to rest on a suitable open pore.

There they would sit, presumably sucking up salt, until a movement of significant resolve encouraged them to take to the air again. This was a process unrelenting throughout the waking hours of the day.

Six days they had endured these conditions the hottest, most unsociable cloying heat that any had ever experienced. The loss of salt and fluids taking the power and resilience of each and every one of them.

John Standing stood tall at the prow of the ship almost the entire day, taking water only when absolutely necessary. He issued forth every form of encouragement, every possible form of abuse and every credible directive that could be mustered to galvanise the wilting crew into action.

But he knew only too well what limited effect it was having. What is not possible should not be striven for, because ultimately credibility is breeched, the impossible can not be delivered.

As the evening of the seventh day began to close, lanterns were lit and rations issued. A quiet settled over the ship interrupted only by the occasional groan or deep sigh. Men lay sprawled out, in shaded positions wherever possible. Little food was taken because there was simply not the appetite.

Margaret enjoyed generous quarters due to the small numbers aboard, and spent a great deal of time sprawled out beneath a muslin drape where she was spared the attention of the flies.

Sweat-soaked shirts hung from the rigging and comfort of any kind was achieved only at a premium, the cost being endless swatting at flies, endless attempts at achieving fresh air, and the slow deliberate visit to the fresh water barrel. Even the sustenance normally gleaned from a cup of grog or brandy, was not on the wish list of the crew.

Words were almost an unnecessary waste of energy, the thoughts behind them being the most sapping of all. Only Standing remained purposeful and resolute.

The sound of music, drifted across the consciousness of all on board. A sea shanty emitting from an old squeeze box. The light drumming of wood on bucket and a few unco-ordinated voices. Nonetheless the effect was energising beyond anything they had experienced for the past week.

Almost in unison they raised themselves up and made for the larboard side, where they could just make out the lanterns of an approaching vessel.

Gradually the music grew louder, piercing the heavy dank atmosphere of the night.

Almost alongside at a distance of eighty yards, more sounds could be heard. Moaning, wailing, low and muffled, but constant and persistent, making the hair stand up on the backs of the necks of the watchers from the *Durham*. The other ship hung low in the water, fully laden with cargo for a long voyage. On Board, lanterns illuminated a gathering of sixteen of more, eating and drinking, whilst the band played with equal persistence.

Shouts of 'Ahoy' greetings returned, some of them English, others in French and a mix of accents. 'Bon Voyage.' 'Welcome.' All manner of greetings were exchanged between the two crews.

Standing drew alongside Daemon at the rail. 'You hear that moaning, it's from the slaves, below deck. They play to drown out the sound.

There could be four hundred on board, judging by how she sits in the water.'

Daemon looked at Standing, disbelief on his face. He had formed his own ideas on how it would be. What a 'Slave ship' would look like and the conditions that might be endured, but the reality left him speechless, bewildered. He did not know what to say. Standish slapped him on the back meaning reassurance but Daemon was left with a heavy heart, full of misgivings.

Standing was at the prow, 'Ahoy there. Is your Captain on deck?'

'Aye. Who wants to speak with him?'

'I'm John Standing, captain of the *Durham* chartered to the Brooke Trading Company of Barbados. Identify yourself.'

'Captain Roderick Hart, out of Liverpool. You are heading for Lokoja? I believe your cargo is assembled, they are awaiting your arrival.'

'How far out are we?'

'Two days and nights if you get a move on.'

'Can we expect a full sail at any time?'

'Maybe dawn through until mid-day on the morrow. But you may have to pull yourselves in.'

'Thank you. May I enquire as to your destination?'

'Aye, we are chartered to the Blue Mountain Coffee Company of Jamaica. This is our seventh mission. Over three hundred and sixty slaves on board. We will dock at Liverpool and unload some ivory and some metals before crossing the ocean. How about yourselves?'

Standish did not want to reveal too much to a 'rival'. 'Barbados, of course, you say our cargo is assembled?'

'Aye, only the finest. I have not seen stock like it, I was quite envious.'. Your Moorish partners have worked very well on your behalf'. You must beware of the Dutch. They have a chartered vessel in the area protecting their interests. They still hold the Elmina Castle fort on the Gold Coast. '

'I thank you for the warning. We are not equipped for an encounter with a warship. I am glad to hear our stock is available for a swift departure. I wish you every success with your voyage. One last question. How many 'casualties' do you anticipate?'

'Ha! Good question. A lot depends on the quality of the merchandise at the outset. Good, well looked-after stock has the best chance of survival. But if we keep our losses to twenty percent, I will be well pleased.'

'I thank you for your candour and bid yea farewell.'

The music which had subsided respectfully during the exchange between the two ships, now started up again with fresh gusto.

The crew of the *Durham* returned to their discomfort and all on board had at least enough understanding to weigh the information, that many slaves would perish on the voyage and never see the Americas.

***

When morning broke, a breeze could just be detected from the west.

Sail was run out and with some element of enthusiasm, the crew made preparation.

The ship lurched into forward motion and an audible though muted cheer went through the ranks.

Daemon, into action and going through his duties, remained introspective. Contemplating all he had heard. His appetite for what lay ahead noticeably dimmed. Margaret had joined him at the rail and he spoke in a low voice.

'I trust you are well? I do believe this is almost as bad a slavery.'

'I'm fine, thank you for asking. It was awful, those last three days have been as agonising as any I can remember. But today, well, just look, we are making progress. John is all fired up. I am sure we will all feel happier when we arrive at our destination.'

'I only wish I could join in, but I am, well, a little uneasy about the voyage.'

'Ahh, you have got cold feet!'

'No, nothing like that, I am up for the challenge. It's just, the whole thing, slavery, you know!'

'Daemon, I owe you so much for your intervention, otherwise I would be in slavery to this day. But, I feel sure John Standing knows what he is doing. I believe in him, you said yourself, he is a fine man.'

Daemon looked at her, he did not speak for some moments, until she turned her eyes from the horizon and looked into his. 'What? You are looking at me! What is it?'

Daemon half smiled, 'Oh nothing, it's nothing! I haven't seen you this cheerful. Remember, all we saw of each other was between the bars of a prison.'.

'I know what you mean'.

'Anyway, pay no heed to me, I'll get used to the idea. Ha! I am so looking forward to landing in the Americas.'

'Me too.' Margaret smiled at him as he turned away. Daemon mused at what he had seen. Margaret with 'stars' in her eyes when she spoke of Standing. Daemon was not jealous, in fact he was pleased for her, that she had at least an opportunity to become an admirer.

He just felt that perhaps his 'ally' was not his 'ally', indeed she may be considered now to have joined the camp of His Lordship. Daemon laughed at himself. He had no pretensions, and no expectations, but it amused him that Margaret had so quickly fallen for John. Now he was unlikely to be able to exchange a confidence or seek an opinion. He felt that from here on in, Margaret would probably follow Standing were he bound for hell fire and damnation. He laughed to himself as he pulled on the out riggers and put his back into the morning's work.

He knew a discussion with Standing was necessary. On the other hand Standing knew also that his companion was full of misgivings and would need to be convinced all over again as to the merits of their undertakings.

The two avoided each other for most of the day. Performing what tasks they might to ensure that progress was made and that they would reach their goal within the deadlines set out. When Captain Hart had described the remaining distance in terms of two days, Standish gauged a distance of some ten land miles.

The river mouth became more defined, the banks closed in.

Now, settlements could be seen clearly, with the activities of the day being perfunctorily performed. Boats, tall sails over a small dinghy-sized vessels, swept in and out of the channels. Little heed was paid by the locals to their passing.

Water buffalo and hippopotamus wallowing in the shallows, some cattle and their attendants could be clearly seen. Strange sights to many of the crew, let alone Daemon who realised only too well, what a limited experience of the world he had achieved thus far.

***

The river was brown, green moss lay on the surface where it was undisturbed along the banks and reeds grew thick near the edges. The ship appeared to be slicing through mud as it progressed further up river. The heat, searing heat and suffocating humidity, pressed the crew until they became motionless. The ship lazily easing its painful progress through the last few hours to its destination.

Eventually a township could be made out following the line of a cluster of ramshackle huts along the banks. Smoke emitted from some rooftops. More boats appeared and many of them targeted the new arrival for special attention.

Landing on the dock there was a carnival atmosphere and the ship's company gratefully accepted fresh water and dates and figs. There were stalls scattered all around the harbour providing all manner of foods, mostly rice based, and multi-coloured garments. The aroma of rotting vegetables permeated the air all around.

Fish was the only variation, again rotting fish, and occasional fresh pilchard and what looked like haddock sizzled on crossed sticks propped in the ash of smouldering charcoal.

Standing immediately departed in search of his contacts and returned with two impressive Arabs accompanied by two camels and minders.

Walking with Standing, they hopped on board and swept around the *Durham*, checking out her superstructure before going below and checking the accommodation.

Daemon observed their behaviour and was encouraged that they appeared to be satisfied at the condition of the vessel. Standing joined him at the rail.

'Ashti and Amaoba are cousins of Ali and were expecting us.

'They will continue to check out the ship until they are completely satisfied that the 'merchandise' will be taken care of. They have dealt with some traders which had scant regard for the safety of the merchandise on previous occasions and badly eroded their profits.'

'Just what 'profits' do you expect from the enterprise, if you don't mind me asking?'

'Not at all. I will tell you exactly what we can aim for. We will transport two hundred and ninety men, women and children across three thousand eight hundred miles of ocean. They appear in fine health and in the main, are showing no obvious signs of resentment.'

'I would not expect them to be whooping with joy.'.

'You may be surprised my friend. The mortality rate of natives around the Niger delta, is forty percent. That is to die before the age of maturity. The ultimate life expectancy is thirty years. The climate, the availability of fresh water and treatment of ailments is very different here. You may appreciate that the average lifespan is fifty to fifty five in Europe, many live into their seventies.

'In tropical Africa, in other words, one in three can expect to die before reaching the age of sixteen. Two in three by the age of thirty.

'In the New World slaves can work plantations, eat well and receive medical attention when needed. Their babies have a better chance of survival, their young of reaching maturity. They will survive well past the age of fifty.

'You see, there is every reason to believe they are being given a chance of a better life.

'Anyway, on average we will pay the equivalent of eight pounds sterling, or the price of two muskets, for our stock. In the New World, we will sell for fifty pounds, on average. That seems to me a pretty compelling argument.'

'My Lord, John, sir. It is not for me to question you about your business. I don't know enough about the world, and about trade even less. That, to me, seems to provide a considerable profit and there are clearly reasons for you to go on with what you're doing.

'For myself, I owe you everything, my freedom, a debt of gratitude such as I can't quantify. But I do not feel good about taking people, however poor and hungry they might be, against their will, and transporting them half around the world.'

'I understand your feelings, what happened back in Baltimore must have been a great shock to you. The world is a mysterious place. Imagine, Moorish warriors set off across the seas to capture young Europeans, slave ships take natives from their shores across the other side of the world.

'It is the age of discovery, new horizons. Europe becomes heavily populated, areas of our own two countries have no free land whatsoever, and many thousands to find food for. A continent like the Americas has so much land, and few occupants. There are huge demands to feed the millions in Europe and huge potential in the colonies. The population is just in the wrong place at the moment.

'In Europe, people go freely to occupy other parts of the world. In Africa genocide is committed.'

'Genocide?' responded Daemon.

'Mass murder, to keep the numbers in check for the limited amount of food available in this hard-baked landscape. Daemon, I do not have all the answers. I have found myself with an opportunity and have never questioned the moral issues. The practical ones are the ones that occupy my thoughts.

'How do twenty seamen, get this ship full of human cargo across the great ocean in safety? I would not wish a single fatality, yet records would show that at least twenty will perish, and at least one member of crew. Does this mean we are wrong to undertake such a mission?

'What if we left this cargo for another, Spanish or Dutch for instance? What if they lost fifty or more? What if we gave the crew the choice of staying on land? For one of you will die during the voyage. Would they choose to stay?'

'John, you have given me enough to think about. I regret having taken up so much of your time with my meanderings. I will join you on this voyage and do my best to achieve what you want. I will also try to fulfil my duty to the other humans on board. Crew and... Well, I may wrestle with my conscience for eternity, but I will not let it get in the way of doing the job you brought me for.'

Standing clapped his friend on the back and drew his head toward his own. Fashioning something of a hug, Standing left Daemon under no illusion about his worth and value to the enterprise.

***

Leaping down the steps Daemon popped up in front of their Arab visitors. 'Is there anything I can do for yous? Would you like to inspect the ballast or the rigging?' Bowing to show sincerity the cousins nodded in appreciation and allowed Daemon to conduct a tour around the superstructure but this time removing gratings and sail-cloth to ensure that every inch of the ship could be checked.

Upon completion of the tour Amoeba turned to Standish, 'Please bring your young friend to dine with us ashore this evening. In the morning we will inspect the cargo and complete the stowing of supplies before you load out the ship. I hope you will be able to depart on high tide tomorrow.'

Bowing again they departed, mounting their camel, attendants trotting at the rear, they returned to their encampment.

***

At the encampment, an elaborate range of tents were set out to form an enclosure. Performers could be seen against the night sky, lit up with many lanterns and the fire at the centre. A whirling dervish had a tower of clay pots on his head and spun rapidly to music from short bulbous flutes, strings and stretched skins hit with batons. On one leg, the dancer whirled, and whirled, the monotony of the music thumping out a beat, his head went back but the tower did not topple.

Everything but the dancer remained still, transfixed now, watching the heavy fringed skirts spin out a rainbow of colour on a horizontal plane. The pipes stopped. The strings stopped, just the thud of wood on leather continued. Now the dervish increased speed, his non-supporting leg out, then in, then out, half a spin, half a spin. Daemon felt himself lightheaded as if drugged, his eyes followed the dervish's free leg, in-out-in-out, its white-stockinged, black-booted foot extended.

The spinning grew more and more trance inducing. Daemon felt dizzy, reaching down he felt a cushion beneath him and allowed himself to settle down on to it, unable to remove his eyes from the dancer.

A hush settled over the encampment, and still the drum padded out the monotonous beat and the dancer continued to twirl. Looking around, Daemon noticed other spectators, in particular the Bedouin and Moorish, their eyes closed and their minds locked intimately in the continuous, furious action of the dancer. Murmuring started up, one there, another over there, further, then another next to the fire. The Dervish went relentlessly on. The crowd moaned, like zombies rising from the dead, blank-eyed Arabs rose from the ground, and began twirling their heads in time with the movement of the dervish.

Twenty or thirty were on their feet, then others followed. Men called out, prayer like gestures abounded, sweat and feverish gasps emerged from everyone in the proximity of the encampment. Daemon, catching sight of Standing, watched momentarily as his mentor's eyes closed and his head hung to one side, appearing to be at one with the gathering.

He also noted John's hand enclosing that of Margaret though both their hands were then obscured from general view by the folds of their clothing.

Aside from dizziness, Daemon felt detached from it all, he simply watched and waited. Moments passed. The dervish closing on the fire, now dangerously close, he continued to twirl.

Around again and again, until completing a full circumference of the fire, eyes to the heavens, seemingly guided by some sixth sense, the dervish suddenly stopped, slumped and amidst a crescendo of noise, a number of the Arabs in the immediate circle, raised up and slumped forward, collapsing to the ground. The Dervish rose slowly proceeded to the other side of the encampment to retrieve some equipment. Returning to the fire he provided a salute that would have been acceptable to royalty, and departed without further leave, disappearing into the night.

A collective sigh emanated from the gathering.

Sheik Amoeba called to them to make their way to the head table. Once there, greetings were exchanged and room was made for them amongst the privileged around a low banquet-laden table. Margaret was introduced as 'our companion' and was obliged to sit beneath a separate canopy some feet away from the men. Standing was about to complain but Margaret waved to him in a way that showed her sensibility, that it was not an issue worth troubling over, she would certainly be contented watching from the side.

The food was lavish and full-flavoured, there was fresh juice to invigorate their bodily fluids, and much to freshen them. The conversation bounced around but the subject of the quality of the 'merchandise' assembled for this particular voyage was of high interest.

The men were broad at the shoulder and narrow at the hip. Almost all were 'well endowed', potential for breeding being very favourable. Handsome, broad foreheads, smooth skin and thick at the neck and well-muscled legs.

But the females, their descriptions exceeded all possible imagination. Tall, slender, high-cheekboned, silken of skin, bright of eye, white of tooth, limbs of finest shape, breasts pert and high.

These were indeed a special 'breed', assembled to reap the greatest possible return from their enterprise.

The conversation would simply not move on.

Finally a little high on atmosphere and not a little rum, the party began to make its way back to the *Durham* where all was quiet. Daemon felt a hand upon his arm, just as he was about to fall in with the others. One of the Arabs waved a friendly finger in his direction.

He caught Standing's eye, and was released from any duties by a shrug and a smile from his benefactor. He followed the Arab through the myriad of hanging silks to a tent with more subdued torch lighting. Inside, he was lead to a pile of cushions and just a small ripple of movement occurred as he was about to find a suitable place to recline.

Heady with the experience of the whole evening Daemon reclined with hands behind his head, a half smile of expectation on his face.

He soon noticed something disturbing the arrangement of pillows nearby, when a slender limb appeared, followed by an arm and then the bare torso of a stunning, bejewelled Arabian girl, whose movements were akin to a lithe, snake-like form approaching a feast.

Her pretty face, flawless skin, atop a long graceful neck, finely formed shoulders and full bosom, captivated his attention. A tiny movement released her breasts from their diamanté encrusted restraints and two deep purple nipples standing proudly from their equally purple aureole, pointed invitingly in his direction. Daemon was liquid in her hands, he lay back, thought briefly of Kirsten, then allowed himself to melt into the sumptuous, coffee-coloured form of his new companion.

Following an all too brief union, from Daemon's point of view, the girl introduced him to an intoxicating bathing ritual, using warm towels and exotic oils to caress every inch of his skin. His entire body was lathered, shaven and oiled as if he were royalty, and ultimately treated to hour after hour of intimate body to body contact, the consummate result of which was mind blowing at its climax.

Daemon walked back to the ship shortly after dawn that morning. His legs feeling somewhat weak, his heart pumping at an unusual rate, his head light and his breath being taken in short bursts. He felt very odd, and yet, the morning seemed beautiful. The sun and the surroundings seemed to speak to him. An African with a huge headdress passed by, offering a warm greeting, followed by a short informal bow.

Daemon had to literally shake his head, to begin to return to a normal conscious state. He had never experienced such a night in his life, and probably, he mused, was unlikely to do so no matter how long he might tread this strange place we call Earth.

Standing met him on deck later that morning and proceeded to mercilessly berate him about his reckless behaviour, whilst Margaret looked on, amused. Daemon did not know where to hide his face.

'Come, my young Stallion. Tell us all about your exploits then? I bet there is not a maiden left in the entire region who isn't longing to be next in line! I know not how to advise you for the best. Should you return and marry the poor unfortunate lady upon whom you poured your affections, not once but 'ten times' during an endless night of debauchery!'

Standing's barbed harassment continued for long moments whilst the crimson-faced Irishman wriggled uncomfortably in an attempt to depart the scene and seek a quiet corner in which to crawl.

The laughter followed as first Margaret then Standing found Daemon's discomfort all too amusing.

'I... I beg your pardon, sir, p-please, may I find some way to repay your indulgence, I... I should take on the first watch of this night and will not expect relief until the morrow. Indeed – perhaps the crow's nest should be my post for the next full... '

The laughter for the others continued unabated until he too realised the futility of protesting. He held up his hands at being caught out and was happy to take a pale over his head by way of both punishment and revival.

A commotion gave away that their cargo had appeared in the distance and was being shepherded through the streets of the town toward the harbour.

Daemon shook surplus water from his head and shoulders and joined Standing over by the rail. They watched as the line of captives was steered through the crowd. At one moment the slender form of a stately looking native lady leaned out of the crowd and put am arm on one of the males. He turned and a look of desperation quickly seized both of them. She dropped to her knees as the line came to a brief halt. Tearing at the shackles she tried vainly to release his bonds.

One of the Arabs moved toward them and the youth thrust the old woman back into the gathering and held his hands in the air to show compliance. He fell in with the others and they continued now down the last few steps from the harbour into the longboat.

Twenty males, looking remarkably similar and in fine condition, clad in a simple white loincloth, dropped into place along the four benches of the small craft. Three seamen, one armed with a cocked musket, steered the boat toward the *Durham*. A second boat was loaded up – twenty-two more collected and rowed toward the Ship.

An hour later two hundred and ninety had been loaded up. Sixty women and twenty-eight infants completed the numbers. Separate quarters were devised to keep the men apart from the women and children. Not one word passed between the parties of any significance at all. When all were secured down below the murmuring started. At first a low wailing from two or more children, then a chorus of young cries. Then the mothers and finally anguished cries from the males. The din created a solid sound, a backdrop to all other activity.

Standing turning to Daemon spoke quietly. 'When we are a day or two at sea, we will choose a dozen compliant 'blackies' and give them duties. If they perform well, we will provide a reward of some kind. Perhaps even rotate, so that all of them can have their opportunity. I think morale could be maintained if there was the promise of some freedom and fresh air on a regular basis.'

'I'm sure that would be a good idea, they all look capable of hauling in a sail. It depends how willingly they go to it. I don't see any point in whipping them into activity if they don't understand what we want.'

'Well, I think they will understand well enough. We will give them a fair chance. It will be obvious what they are capable of within a few minutes of being given an instruction'.

'D'you think any of them speak English?'

'Oh, I expect half of them can get their tongue around the 'King's English better than you my friend.'

'Hey, that's a bit mealy mouthed of yea! If I didn't think better of it I would think yea have a bit of the green-eyed monster about yea, considering it was only myself that got to enjoy the pleasures of the flesh last evening.'

Standish laughed. Just then Margaret came into view, taking a ladle of fresh water from the barrel. Standing's eyes followed her and a smile broke out on his face. Daemon looked at him, and slowly it dawned on him, his doubtful expression turning into a beaming smile. What? Surely not?

Standish tried to wipe away his own smile and the undoubted look of contentment that settled across his face, but to no avail, his happy countenance gave him away.

'You and…really?'

Standing smiled again, Margaret looked in his direction, and returned his smile before wandering down toward the prow of the ship.

'I have asked her to be my wife.'

'Yea're kiddin' me… no… seriously?'

'I'm finding it hard to believe myself'. I have met many a young lady in my time, as you can imagine. But none have come close, it's something I can't fully explain, but I just wanted her to like me. To think about me.

'Then I couldn't bear the idea of anyone else having, or being, with her. I realised I wanted… Well, to take care of her. But she's a strong girl, she would surprise you, if you have the chance to get to know her, as I'm sure you will.'

'No, I like her very much. She's tough all right, it's just, well it's only been a couple of weeks'.

'I know… I am very surprised myself. I don't know how it happened but I am deeply…'fond' of her…'

'What will you do? You can't surely want her to go through all this, to come to Barbados?

'No, I don't want to part with her. I will marry her, but then I think I could leave her in good hands. A friend of mine is very close to the ambassador at Morocco. He is the Manager General over the Fort at Rabat. She could stay in Government House, or take passage back to England. It's still to be decided.'

'Wow, I don't know what to say. But, well, good luck to both of yea. I think it's a good thing, a real good thing.'

'Thank you. Now, to business. Call the crew. We must set down some ground rules.'

'Listen, men. Those of you who can't follow my words, get your friends to explain fully. The 'slaves' are our cargo. It is like gold to us. We don't want it damaged.

'We will deliver it to the West Indies eight weeks from now with a good wind behind us. We will have our hands full to make the crossing. For those of you who don't know the Atlantic, it will test the best of us, with high seas, intense heat, and when we reach the West Indies, storms like you have never seen. But we have a fine ship. She will manage, the question is, will you?'

'Well, I have every faith in you. I know you will show yourselves able seamen, and reap your rewards when our mission is completed.

'I intend to choose ten natives to help with our daily tasks, this will take some of the weight off your shoulders. But at night – only the regular crew will have access to the decks.

'Now, every day, the natives will be walked around the deck, to enjoy fresh air and clean water. They will be fed three times a day on basic rations, and their chambers will be sluiced out every second day whilst they are on board. I will get them to achieve that much for themselves within a few days.

'No crew member will have personal contact with any native. Male, female or infant. No fraternisation whatsoever permitted with the females. Is that clear? Is that clear to all?' Standing looked from face to face, awaited an acknowledgement before moving on to the rest.

'That's it men, treat everyone as you would be treated – especially the natives. I don't want them sick, diseased or marked when they arrive at the auction rooms. I want them plump and prime and they will fetch a handsome price.'

'Go to it, men.'

Standish turned to Daemon. 'How was that, my friend? Do you think it hit home with them?'

'Absolutely, sir, no messing about, I think they took every word on board.

'Not a bit of it. You may think they would honour every word, every commitment, well not in a million years. Every one of them will already be planning how to get his hands on the women. How to steal their food, how to avoid the daily chore of having to wash them down. Oh, they will line up to sluice the females, at first, but even that will become a task to be avoided.'

'But why…?'

'Why did I bother to go through all that with them? Well, I now have a set of rules to punish them by. Had I just let them go they could claim ignorance of my wishes. This way they know they will be in for punishment. Let's see how it works out shall we?' With a smile he let Daemon go about his tasks and slipped below to spend a free moment with his fiancée.

The *Durham* made slow but deliberate progress toward the mouth of the Niger and within four days the ocean, its colour deep metallic blue a significant change from the muddy brown river. Their evenings were happy times, three friends enjoying each other's company, as if on an island, they chatted happily and made plans but only for the distant future. They knew that the order of things was about to change. One more stop, at The Fort at Rabat, before the Atlantic crossing.

***

The ship rocked and the swollen waves around them splashed almost playfully on the decks. The water ran through the grilling and below at first it brought some slight frivolity among the slaves. Hour after monotonous hour passed but the sound of their misery, though muted, was a constant companion. Without music, of any kind, an oversight perhaps experience would not have permitted, there was nothing for it but to bear the misery of their captives like one would a sick animal. Make it comfortable and leave it to nature.

Except this wasn't natural. Each slave had a space to lie in the width of its own body, next to, and with no means of separation from his partners on both sides.

Two slaves were each manacled together. When they were below decks their ankles were not shackled, when they were on deck they were attached by the ankles.

A large bucket stood at the ends and mid-point of the compartment where fifty or more slaves would lay on two bunks at night. When one required use of the bucket, his partner had to go too. The buckets were emptied each morning by the slaves passing them up to the next pair until they were emptied over the sides.

When emptied, a hose would clean out the bucket and it would be passed back down the chain.

Below decks the atmosphere was humid, the stench almost intolerable and the heat cloying so that every being was permanently covered in a slick of perspiration. Their fine bodies became marked, their faces a permanent scowl.

The sores on their wrists and ankles were evident within a couple of days. Steel is not friend to human flesh. They developed a way of carrying the chains so that the chafing would ease. The rocking of the ship, however, was sufficient alone to cause chafing, sores became more sore, they would bleed, congeal, then bleed again.

Standing showed them gun grease, and made them spread it on themselves. Margaret tended to the children. Her heart was heavy when she returned.

'John, we must do something! Surely hemp would be enough to restrain children.'

'I'll see what can be done,' he responded, not able to hide his compassion. 'Perhaps you could devise something. It may take all your remaining time you have on board to find a solution.'

***

'When emerging each morning the males would struggle in an attempt at modesty. Shuffling close in their lines to conceal their manhood until cold seawater diminished the problem, whilst the crew gleaned particular amusement at their discomfort. Their loincloths were removed and rung out over the side and each would do their best to cover up with their hands as the sea water pumps got to work.

The cloths would dry and be retrieved by the time all one hundred and eighty were processed.

The children would hop from one foot to another and would largely be ignored, the plight of the women was the next in the proceedings to stir the crew. They fought over whose turn it was to wield the hose, who would move them along or 'help' them with the task of 'showering'.

The natives would hide their faces, but their heavy breasts with their prominent peaks, high set, well-rounded buttocks would remain open to all eyes. The loincloth and the 'tie' used to bind their breasts, would be released, washed and wrung out, as with the men. They followed the same procedure daily. Shame for them was in their faces. Their nakedness was the cause, but their faces were hidden preserving their dignity, at least to themselves.

These were physically fine specimens, well-muscled, flat stomachs, long legs and long elegant fingers, their skin a bronzed, coffee in colour, tautly stretched to provide a healthy sheen over all surfaces.

'So different from most powdery, flabby, loose-skinned middle Europeans,' thought Standing, 'these are indeed beautiful and fascinating creatures.'

When the moment came to choose the first tranche of natives for duty, the choice was made simple in that physically there was little to choose between them, but there was in some of them an 'intelligence' that could be found in their eyes. Some clearly bore hatred, some resentment, some were like wounded animals, others appeared to accept the inevitability of their situation.

Daemon and John Standing together paid particular attention early on the fifth day. The sluicing and washing down proceeded normally, the natives moving toward the rail, then, forming a queue where rice was simmering on a hot plate, they took a bowl and ate feverishly as always, with their fingers, brushing their lips across them until every morsel had been ingested.

Each time the two men nodded agreement at the same time observing the same individual, they knew both of them had recognised that 'intelligence' they were looking for, and that the selection would be among those to form the first gang.

The first ones chosen cowered and hid their faces, they were terrified that they had been selected for some form of punishment. 'Ngah. Ngha... massah, ngah.' They were regaling at having been segregated and moaned at their fate.

Daemon was beside them soon, holding an arm, he would try to meet their eyes to convey that nothing was going to happen to them. But they simply cowered away. When twelve pairs had been stood aside, and all others had been ushered below, they stood nervously awaiting their fates until eventually they simply had to attend to what was happening.

Standing addressed them with a mild greeting. 'Ho there, ho! Look here!' He tried vainly to bring them round. ' Can we have, er, your attention?' Daemon went down the line getting each to lift his head and look toward Standing, but as soon as he removed his hand the head would immediately drop.

Eventually Standing took his pistol from his waistband and fired into the air.

The resulting 'crack' breaking the relative silence was startling, the regular crew jumped to attention, even Daemon came sharply upright.

The natives, as one lifted their heads and with bulging eyes as if on stalks, glared at the pistol.

'Now, you men – you must listen to ME.

Their absolute attention was now on what was being said.

'You men will be given tasks... tasks to do... swabbing... er, roping. Damn, how do I...?' Grabbing a long handled broom, he swashed away at the deck for several moments, unsure as to whether he had their attention. They were looking down at the deck, then back at him.

Daemon stood aside, quite amused.

Standing thrust the brush toward one of the natives. At first the slave would make no attempt to take it but with more and more prompting, and verbal encouragement, this time from Daemon, the fellow took the pole from Standing.

Now, again, further encouragement, Daemon took another and demonstrated alongside the native. 'Here, like this.' Slowly but surely the man began to follow Daemon's actions and sluiced a small area of deck. Daemon thrust his brush into the hands of the natives partner, though shackled at both ankle and wrist at this time, made an attempt at performing the task.

'I think, John, we had better release the shackles whilst they're on duty. I don't expect them to go crazy and run riot around the place. What d'you think?'

'Well let's take it a step at a time. Release their wrists first, they can move freely with their arms to mop side by side, but they will move their legs as they must when on deck, in unison.'

***

The first among them were released from their manacles and given a turn with the broom. Each took to their task with enthusiasm and began to show some capacity for work but it amused Standing and Daemon that after moments they began to slow down, to hold their backs as if under stress, and wipe away imaginary perspiration.

Their capacity for continuous application was left in some doubt when these antics were performed with much exaggeration. Both men resolved that they would have to drive their new crew members hard to achieve a decent day's work. They also resolved to come up with an incentive scheme a lot sooner than originally intended.

The following morning the same individuals were pulled out of the line. Washing down and the first meal of the day were completed before the process of selection moved on through various tasks.

They were shown hard stone and tallow, and how they were to scrub the decks after clearing away dust and debris. The same slow purposeful process had them bending their backs after an hour.

To enable the natives to move freely Standing ordered that their shackles and manacles be removed, the delight showed on their faces without exception, at freedom of movement. They began a sort of rhythmical dance planting one foot in front of the other then crossing over with the next.

The regular crew started up a sea shanty and the natives continued with even more enthusiasm. Without warning of any kind one of them suddenly turned and sprang over the side of the ship into the sea.

All rushed to the side and watched as the hapless African thrashed at the water, disappeared beneath the waves then re-appeared moments later. He started to scream, having not the slightest hope of propelling himself forward. He had been in ignorance of the sea, imagining that all water was to them, the same as the riverbed of the Niger shallows, that a man might stand up.

The *Durham* was making four knots through the surf at that time and within thirty seconds the man was being left behind in the wash. The other natives shuffled around the rail attempting to watch him and, it appeared, to keep abreast of him. But he was disappearing from view as the ship ploughed on.

Now one of them was on the rail and about to leap to join his friend. Daemon caught him by the ankles at first, in the struggle others began pushing and pulling. It was impossible to establish whether they were trying to restrain the man or to help him in his leap to certain death.

Once again, only the crack of a pistol shot from Standing brought order and attention and the natives back under control. Standing ordered a boat to be released and the Bosun to pull the wheel around full lock.

They were made to line the rail whilst their shackles were refitted.

Their faces were a mixture of disappointment and surprise. They stood watching whilst the *Durham* keeled low in the water making a three hundred and sixty degree turn. Bringing her about she followed the line of their original path and the boat was lowered into the water.

Manned by Standing himself and two crewmen they wove a zig-zag pattern across the wash in an attempt at finding the native in the water.

Half an hour passed before Standing ordered the boat to return and they emerged back on deck.

Showing his annoyance both for genuine reasons and for the purpose of a demonstration, he rounded on the remaining natives on deck.

'You men, you are damned fools if you think you can survive in the open seas! Look what you have done!' He rounded on each of them forced them to look into the depths of the seas and the space where their countryman had moments before been thrashing on the surface.

Forcing them to look until they realised there was no sight, no sound, no trace of the man that had stood next to them some moments earlier. Now one stood alone in his shackles, he was brought out to stand in front of the others.

'Do any of you know English?' He pointed to his lips. 'Do you speak my language?'

They collectively looked bemused and incapable of response.

Standing shrugged. 'Look – all of you. From now on,' – he held up the empty clamp and the end of the chain and the other's hand came up simultaneously –'look – no good. No good.' He shook his head furiously.

Eventually one of them murmured, 'No goo, Goo No Goo. No Goo-od.' The others joined in one by one until there was a chorus. 'No good! No good!' and furious shaking of heads from side to side.

'OK, you men. Back down below. Off with you, I'm sick of the sight of you!'

Standing made as if to wash his hands of them and walked away in disgust.

They mumbled among themselves all the way back to their quarters, then told the story to the others, whose exclamations could be heard at the other ends of the ship.

Later that night a single female began wailing, louder than usual, and more agonised than ever before. It was an assumption among the crew, and between Standing and his comrades, that this was the partner of the dead man.

Chapter 34

The Duel

Several days passed following the encounter with Otte, and the moment came when Chief Justice knocked on his door again. This time Van Doren was intent on his apprehension and succeeded in transporting Banoldino to the lock up.

Ranleigh arrived the following morning this time with a lawyer who quickly established that there were grounds for a release under bond.

Otte had been lying low to all appearances but had put his case in the strongest possible manner with the Justice. Banoldino had brought the man to him on the threshold of 'Death's Door' and nothing Otte could do could save the tragic figure.

***

Banoldino had paid his old adversary a visit two days before the hearing to try to refresh Otte's mind about the events of that evening.

'I haf nossink to say to you. Please go avay.'

'I will not keep you more than a moment. Surely we can talk man-to-man?'

'I do not vish to talk with you, Senor, my hands are tied, by the law.'

'Look – I have no interest in making you culpable for the death of the Irishman, I simply wish to clear my own name. I think you know I did everything under the circumstances to give O'Reardon a chance. There was nothing I could do. I had hoped you could save him but it wasn't to be'.

'You are trying to make me out a fool. Well, damn you..... I vil not been made a fool off. I haf nothing more to say until the trial.'

'There is no trial, you are mistaken my friend – there is a hearing and I know the truth will be told. Why are you putting yourself in this position?'

Otte swung the door closed and Banoldino had no choice other than to walk away.

The following morning, the troops arrived at Banoldino's home with the clerk from the justice. They escorted Banoldino into custody pending the hearing on the grounds that he had terrorised Otte.

That evening Otte turned up at Banoldino's home. Kirsten was sat alone by the fireside composing a short message for her husband. One which she wished to pass to him before the hearing. The maid entered and bowed quickly before announcing, 'Mistress, there is a gentleman at the door wishing to speak with you, he says he is a physician.'

Kirsten immediately felt a strong spasm in the pit of her stomach but managed to stand straight, with her back to the fire and smooth out her dress whilst gaining her composure. 'Show him in please.'

Otte, stood before her, bowed low with his 'tricorn' hat in his hand and came up to his full height.

'Madam, I am your servant. Please may I have a few moments of your time?'

'I don't know what you could possibly have to say to me, sir. But continue if you must.'

Otte approached three of four paces before speaking 'Madam, I er, regret very much the situation in which your husband finds himself. I… '

'If that is what you came for, you may as well leave right now. It is… '

'Please, Kirsten, I… '

'Mrs Don Bosco if you please.'

'Er, mistress, I know how you must feel but I am not your enemy, nor indeed your husband's. I…' Advancing further toward her Otte suddenly seized her hand, dragging her to him, he pushed hard up against her.

'Well, well, my dear, it has been some time since…' He sniffed at her hair and rubbed his nose deep into her shoulders, inhaling her scent, he almost appeared intoxicated. 'My dear, you must listen to me. Your husband is not here to protect you it is no use. Just stop, listen to me.' He was breathing heavily, perspiration breaking out in large beads on his forehead. He was engorged, his lust palpable, the atmosphere heavy and cloying.

'Please, let me be.' Kirsten pulled away with all her strength but it seemed she had little resistance, almost as if she were paralysed by his attentions. His hands reached for her breasts and his mouth closed on the skin from the nape of her neck, and moved sloppily to her shoulder, pushing her dress down so that it hung from her arms.

'Stop, stop, you evil bastard. Leave me, Let me go.'

'It is in your power – let me haf vat I vant… your husband vil haf his freedom within hours.'

'Never, never, I would rather die.'

'Vel, zat iss most unfortunate – it will be your husband that dies… hanging from a rope.'

'Stop, this is not happening. Why me?Why?'

'You know what I said before. I am goink to haf you… I vil haf my vay.'

'Banoldino will kill you. He will cut your throat for this.'

'You will not tell him. You haf seen vat I can do. I haf him behind bars already. I vil not be denied.'

The maid suddenly appeared with two well-muscled African servants.

In the confusion Kirsten managed to pull away and retreated behind the dining table, leaving Otte standing in the middle of the room.

'Please show Herr Otte the door. Quickly! He is very insistent upon leaving us.'

The maid shouted instructions and the two burly Africans took Otte by the arms and escorted him to the door. A red faced Otte was thrown down the steps onto the gravel path.

He regained his footing, turned and brushed down his clothing as he stood and searched the windows for Kirsten. His eyes locked on her as she appeared, determinedly attempting composure. Slowly Otte lifted one finger of his left arm. 'One day,' he mouthed, and the usual, smirk spread across his ruddy face.

Kirsten turned away quickly, determined this time that Banoldino would hear the whole saga, the moment she could get him alone. It was clear to Kirsten that Otte had arranged the entire predicament with one intention, that of gaining access to herself and pressing his vile attentions upon her.

***

Otte was supported by a strong band of Irish 'brothers' intent on retribution and their actions almost caused a riot on the streets. Armed troops had to be ranged outside the Town Hall to convince the rioters that a real attack would lead to untold bloodshed which meant for the time being, their protests remained essentially passive.

Time dragged by in the mid-summer heat and tensions rose.

The hearing was convened against all traditional constraints bringing the date forward.

Banoldino stuck rigidly to his version of events and Otte stuck more or less with his own. Otte put his reputation as a 'surgeon of great experience', on the line and the courtroom swayed one way then the other. Once again Lord Ranleigh held sway, in a speech of political proportions, he renounced Otte as a drunkard, a liar and a cheat.

Otte issued challenges to both Lord Ranleigh and Banoldino.

Banoldino was only too eager to accept the challenge and Van Doren, despite making it clear that this was an 'old fashioned, European style of justice', in this case could only endorse the proposal as fair and reasonable under the circumstances.

Once again, Kirsten hesitated when her ordeal with Otte could finally be told. She fought with her feelings unable to decide whether the story would inflame Banoldino so much that his judgement might be impaired. She was in turmoil over whether to reveal her tormentor until at last she came to the conclusion that her husband would certainly kill him in the duel.

Fearful as she might be that by some accident Banoldino might not fare well in the encounter, she held her tongue knowing that for justice sake, he would do all that was needed to rid them both of this vile individual.

***

The township was up in arms at the idea of 'duelling' and many protestations were heard before the official sanction reached the protagonists.

Ranleigh acted as second to Banoldino and a bible-bashing Irish Priest and former confessor to the deceased acted for Otte.

Prayers were said over both their bowed heads but only Otte received a spray of holy water from the ruddy-faced parson.

Mist swirled among the trees in the grounds of the Great Hall and pistols were chosen. Earl Drummond officiated in a most precise and gentlemanly fashion as the paces were counted out and order given to 'fire at will'.

In the distance, Kirsten hooded against the pale morning mist, and holding back as far as she might, but at least able to watch from the shelter of an overhanging willow, bit her hands in anguish now the reality of the duel was fully upon her.

She could just about make out the expression on Banoldino's face, determined, resolute, and she thought, 'Oh so handsome'. His dark hair brushed meticulously into waves behind him, the collar of his white embroidered shirt up around his neck.

She fleetingly glanced at Otte, his red, bloated complexion stark in contrast. Yet she feared him, she knew only too well his power and the evil driving him on. She firmly believed that if he survived, her own life would not be worth living.

***

Otte held out his pistol and his hand shook so violently that the shot fizzed into the air eight feet to the right of Banoldino. Silence settled on the occasion. Several men in black breeches and white blouses stood in the early morning chill. Around them some seven or eight ghostly figures, cloaks and tricorn hats held frozen in time in the stillness of the early morning.

A sound emitted from Otte seeming to come from his insides, rising through his chest to reach his sagging, open mouth. The anguished cry it emitted was unnatural in volume and unintelligible, expressing only extreme fear.

Yet he stood ready to take what was coming to him, without buckling at the knee.

Kirsten, held her breath.

Banoldino took aim and deliberately held his pistol firmly and directly at the head of his opponent. The 'click' of the hammer as he released the shot was almost as startling as the normal explosion of the firearm.

A look of complete shock overcame Otte as he dropped gratefully to his knees. The pistol had misfired, he was saved. But twenty paces away Banoldino held up his hand and between two fingers displayed the lead shot that he had removed from his pistol.

He let all present see clearly that he had no intentions of firing on his opponent. He turned and bowed to each in turn and strode toward Ranleigh and his waiting carriage.

Van Doran pronounced that Don Bosco's innocence had been established and yet, there was no 'reason to believe' that Otte's actions were anything other than those of any medical practitioner.

Kirsten, wept into her hands, partly relieved that Banoldino had walked away unscathed, but also because she knew that before too long Banoldino must face his opponent once more, otherwise there would never be a place for her to hide.

The case against Banoldino was duly closed. He returned to their home only seconds after she had squeezed in through the living area via the porch entrance. The maid took her cloak and scarf and whisked them upstairs as Banoldino swung open the door and called to Kirsten. 'My love,come, please greet your old warrior returned from the wars!'

Chapter 35

Morocco

John Standing convinced Margaret his return in five months would be guaranteed. Their marriage would now take place in the governor's residence in Rabat, and Margaret would be waiting unless a British Man of War docked, in which case the new Mrs Standing would seek passage to London, and await his return.

Rabat was another suffocating, hot, sticky experience, with a bustling community of infinite racial origins, and activity of every imaginable kind.

The aromas alone distinguished this as a significant port and centre of trade. Spices, coffee, jasmine, perfumes of northern origin like spruce. Many and varied stalls with trinkets and pottery, fresh produce abounded.

A message was sent to the governor's house and a carriage returned within the hour.

Port officials tied Standing up for hours before he was able to depart for the meeting with Gerald Sampson explained in his note. Gerald had expressed great delight in the visit of his friend. They had been neighbours when Standing and Sampson's estates backed on to one another.

The first Sampson, a cousin to the Duke of Northumberland, had bought a large section of land and a river basin, from Standing's father. A total of three hundred acres changed hands and Sampson became a highly motivated farmer. He produced wheat and barley, and a range of produce and exported on a large scale to the army and market traders.

Young Gerald Sampson and John Standing, just a year difference in age, became firm friends. Hunting and shooting around the estate and growing into young men of military training and deportment.

It soon became clear that Sampson would accede to his elder brothers and find an alternative career, and that a farmer's life was not for him.

He was commissioned into the Army, garrisoned in York, before catching the eye of his superiors. A fine horseman and shot, he was proposed for duties in the Household Cavalry.

His star was rising in the cavalry, with action at Dettingen, when he surprised everyone by accepting a post 'Aid de comp' to the General of the slave Fort at Rabat. Sampson was happy to throw off the shackles of discipline framing every part of his life in the cavalry. He was an individual, a free man, he was not going to spend the rest of his life under rules.

Taking a position overseas he intended to make his own mark, in the diplomatic corps, and find another way upward into society. He had married the general's daughter within six months of arriving at his post.

Lindsay Burkett was pale, short and prone to letting her head drop to one side. This made her look slightly docile and hardly desirable to the adventurous young men passing through the Moroccan township. Two previous visiting members of staff had reached the point of an 'arrangement' over the lady, but had not stayed around long enough to see through the opportunity.

Sampson on the other hand took his time. He made her acquaintance, found her funny and thoughtful. He had her smiling and in return she brightened up her countenance. She was transformed. Tying her hair in ever more adventurous ways, she scooped her necklines and paraded an impressive bosom whilst adding a little rouge to her complexion, she appeared healthier.

Sampson proposed. Her father was overwhelmed having been too pre-occupied to have noticed the change in her. He accepted the young man into his family and granted him a substantial dowry.

Standing was delighted when he heard of the significant improvements in his friend's fortunes.

'I couldn't be more pleased for you, it was some risk you took in leaving the army, we could hardly believe it when we heard.'

'It was a gamble, John, before I tell you about my news, let me say that I am deeply sorry to hear of the demise of your dear sister. Daphne was very special to me at one time, I am sure you knew. But such terrible news.'

'I hardly dare think about it. My friend Daemon, my 'lieutenant' on this venture, was with her when she died. He has given me a very personal account of events.'

'An absolute shambles I hear. Fielding is being hauled over the coals in the admiralty. He'll never get another commission. Nash is somewhere in the Antipodese navigating for some Yorkshireman.'

'Anyway, my friend, on with your story.'

'Yes it was a risk leaving the army to go my own way, I knew that, but look at it this way. There was serious competition when opportunity came calling, especially when you were in the cavalry. You know what life was, an endless round of social events, punctuated by war. If an eligible lady was 'out' in society, six hundred of us lined up to parade our assets. It was an uneven contest, so breaking away to 'go it alone' was almost sensible.'

The two of them laughed. 'Almost sensible for me at least.'

'And the lady? She is happy? What have you done with her?'

'I promise you, she is well, we have an idyllic life.'

'Will you return to Britain?'

'Eventually, I don't want to take her away from her family yet. But I would like to take her home. It is important that she understands our family, my background. We would like a family of our own. It would make good sense to settle in England.'

'I wish you all the very best, both of you.'

'And now, your turn, what would you intend to do? I understand you are bound for the West Indies?

'I am. My options are open for the moment. I am taking my first cargo but I had thought about establishing a management company, trading from Barbados, I would rather be handling the sale and placement of the goods, and arranging return commodities, than being constantly at sea. I do find being at sea rather tedious. I'm not a natural 'seafarer'.'

'I do understand, my dear chap, the days are too long and the conditions hardly comfortable. I do prefer my home comforts myself.'

'Look, I will manage, one or two round trips, but I don't see my future on the high seas. I do rather want to settle down, like yourself. This is the main reason for my visit. And I do hope you will forgive me but we need to be away on high tide tomorrow. I would like to bring a lady, my lady to stay with you, here at the fort. She is currently slumming in the galley of the 'dear-old' *Durham*.'

'Well, John, I am intrigued, who is this mystery package? I must meet her at once. Lead me down to the harbour and I'll give the old thing the once over. The *Durham*, I mean... not... '

'Ha! Same old Sampson, foot in mouth. Never fails to entertain. Come on we'll go down right way, or would you like to run this by the old boy before we go?'

'Not a bit of it. I'll smooth things out, don't give it another thought.'

The two rode down the half mile or so to the harbour where the *Durham* rocked slowly a hundred yards out in the bay. The dinghy was moored on the jetty and two hands awaited Standing's return. Within minutes they were clambering up the rigging and hopping the rail onto the deck.

All was ship-shape and Standing clasped hands with Daemon, complimenting him on the condition of the deck.

'Is all well below?'

'As well as can be. I think the sooner we are away the better. You know how restless they can be.'

'Yes, yes, absolutely. Daemon, I would like to introduce you to my old friend Gerald Sampson. I have told Gerald of my plans and he is keen to do everything he can for Margaret. Would you go and fetch her?'

Daemon hesitated a few moments. 'John, I'm a little uneasy about, well, Margaret has been a little downhearted, as far as I can tell. Maybe the reality of being left behind... '

Standing looked concerned and turned to Sampson. 'Give me a few moments, here, Gerald. Daemon will show you around the *Durham.*'

Immediately Standing slipped away to find Margaret and there, as Daemon had implied, she lay on her bunk, head buried in her pillow.

'John, I'm so glad.' She stood and threw herself into his arms. 'I don't want you to go. I mean, I don't want to... Well, I don't know what I want. I'm so afraid of you leaving, the whole enterprise worries me, but I have realised that I would rather be with you through all the danger, than to see you sail... '

His finger reached her lips to quieten her. 'Darling, please let me speak. There will be demands, great demands upon us on this voyage. But I don't believe I could make the right decisions, do the right thing, if your safety and comfort were compromised. You must understand, I could only continue with this adventure if I were sure of your situation, and I do believe the situation here could not have been better had I planned it.'

Margaret buried her head in his chest. 'Darling, please... '

'Come, trust me, this is best for both of us. Do you not think it is also painful, devastatingly difficult for me to leave you, having only so recently found you? Believe me, I don't want this, but I am sure it is the right thing. Please come, I will introduce you to Gerald Sampson.'

She allowed herself to be lead up on to the deck.

***

Greeting Sampson as he and Daemon approached. 'Well she is in fine shape, the ship I mean, and the cargo, well, I am full of admiration. It looks like a fine endeavour. Now enough of my prattle, please.'

Standing took the opportunity to introduce Margaret. She was wiping tears from her face and straightening her plain cotton shirt.

'Delighted, my dear.' Sampson took her hand and brushed his lips across. 'I am so pleased to welcome a friend of my friend, even more so, John is a very special friend and there... I do go on don't I!'

They all laughed and Margaret managed to utter her pleasure at making his acquaintance.

Sampson's eyes lit up. 'An idea.' he said. 'Why don't you make an honest woman of her, if you'll forgive my crude impertinence?' We could go up to the residence and arrange for you to be married in the morning. That way you can leave your dutiful wife behind with proper status, it could actually save a lot of 'explaining' which may otherwise be required. What d'you say?'

Standing looked at Margaret, her face brightened and a fresh tear found its way out of the corner of her eye. 'John, that would be...'

'Perfect! My friend has proposed for me. I think I ought to do it myself. Margaret, would you kindly consent to becoming my lawfully wedded wife?'

'Oh yes! Yes please!' came the reply.

Daemon unintentionally spoiled the moment by suggesting to Standing that the 'delay might make the natives a little restless'.

But Standing waved away the protest insisting that twenty-four hours was not going to make a significant difference. The ship would be well-guarded, extra rations for the natives and extra grog for the crew. The three of them would spend tonight at the residence and Sampson assured them he could arrange proceedings despite the short time available.

That night, after introductions, Lindsay and Margaret found such common ground. Their age, upbringing, Lindsay's fascination that Margaret had been enslaved. They formed an immediate bond and companionship which it appeared would stretch far into the future.

So excited at the prospect of a wedding, the romance of it all and the swift departure of the happy groom, Lindsay was swept along on the mood of the moment. She proved very helpful in organising things for the event to go off in fine fashion.

She fixed up Margaret with her own bridal gown, needing few alterations to fit her perfectly. She took Margaret completely under her wing denying Standing access to her for the entire night before the event.

This left Sampson, Sir Roger Burkett, the general, Daemon and Standing to enjoy a fine dinner and some very fine port. A more agreeable time could hardly have been enjoyed by a more amiable group.

Morning came and Margaret appeared in the chapel of the governor's residence looking serene and very pretty, dressed for the occasion as though the dress were made for her, and indeed the first time Standing had actually seen her in more than the plain cotton garb that had been hastily procured at the Bedouin markets shortly after her freedom had been established.

Daemon looked on, a little envious, his thoughts went to Kirsten. He saw her, as it should have been, had the raid never happened. The old churchyard back in Baltimore, a fine summer's day. Horrible thoughts invaded then, the village destroyed, the ship going down, the girl of his dreams, sinking deep into the rough seas.

He had to shake those thoughts from his mind. Looking up he found that the final words were being uttered. 'I now pronounce you...' and it was done.

They enjoyed a last meal, Standing and Margaret parted from the others and spent an hour and a half in their hastily arranged chambers. They spent the time talking, laying in each other's arms, there was no 'token' intimacy, it wasn't necessary to cement their already close bond. They would cherish each moment fully aware, fully focused and speaking with one another of the future.

A few tears followed but Margaret bore up very well. Lindsay assured everyone that she would be looked after 'like royalty, or even better'. They all swapped truly fond farewells and Daemon waited at the carriage as Standing said a final goodbye.

The carriage raced them back to the *Durham*, which thankfully stood where they had left her with no signs of interference. She rocked exactly as previously on the ebbing tide and looked every inch ready for cast off.

Despite the low babble and muffled groans from below deck, there appeared to be no significant change in the behaviour of the enslaved. The voyage was under-way within an hour of their return.

The sails filled with warm, tropical air and the ship, leaning to starb'd, sailed out of the harbour. John Standing stood on the bow rail, one hand on the rigging and one on his hip. He watched until the ship had rounded the mouth of the bay and the fort disappeared from view.

Jumping down, he joined Daemon on the poop, and put an arm around his friend. "I don't think I could have left her in better hands... and I don't think I could have a better companion to make this journey with. I am full of sorrow but convinced that all has been done as well as it could be. I know we are going to have the best of times my friend.'

Daemon returned his smile. 'A glass of port, sir?'

'Why not'. replied his mentor. 'Let's celebrate.'

Chapter 36

The Frontier

Banoldino stood at the foot of the hill. Rain fell steadily, and mist hung over the forested mountainside as far as the eye could see.

Logs, thirty foot in length rolled down the hillside, thudding into each other as they gathered momentum. Reaching the flattened out cart tracks they piled up and came to rest, mud, foliage and flakes of bark swirling into the atmosphere twenty feet over head.

Systematically, four well-muscled, bearded men moved into action.

They tied slings around the trunk of the uppermost log and, with the help of a hoist they swung the log across to the far side of the pathway until it hovered above a long trestle which had hardwood rollers ranged crossways, the full length of the table.

The men dug hooks into the trunk and pulled the log toward a timber-covered housing. Inside the housing a saw was set spinning by a long tiller, and began to sear into the log cutting it down the centre.

The process continued until long, square-cut lengths of timber were extracted at the far end and loaded on to a cart. The wheels of the cart were set at ten foot spacings front, middle and rear with a spare set of wheels slung under the flooring. When fully loaded, stacked four feet high, the cart was teamed up with four stout English shire horses, and the transportation of fresh cut timber lurched slowly into motion.

The hostler lead the team on foot and a guard mounted the uppermost timber on the load, with a loaded musket across his knees. The delivery of timber into the township six miles down the valley would proceed over a day and a half.

The continuous delivery of building timber had been in full process for more than six months. Banoldino's place in the commerce houses and burgeoning society was ensured.

Banoldino oversaw the work on a regular basis, but his operation was manned by well-rewarded and loyal immigrant men from England and Northern Europe, and proceeded in all manner of conditions become, a vital supplier to the ever increasing demands of the building of the new township.

He had begun to receive enquiries from further afield. His name, his reliability and no-nonsense, fair mindedness, had spread along the coast. The governor had become a friend and very consistent promoter of his business interests and was duly rewarded.

Finally, the shipbuilders were calling on him and gave him plans and designs for new craft with the opportunities he had long planned for.

His friend and patron Lord Ranleigh, having established the New York Bank of Commerce, now publishing a weekly news sheet and laying the ground for a breeding farm, was always available and a frequent consultant to his activities and the direction of his commercial interests.

He had landed firmly on his feet in the New World, and the future appeared as bright as the dreams of himself and his adoring wife might have hoped. Their joy in the daily development of their baby son, was a constant reminder that they had a lot to 'thank the Gods' for.

'I'm home, darling, where are you?' Banoldino pulled off his boots in the lobby and hung his heavy cloak over the arm of the great chair. Rushing out from the kitchen his housekeeper grabbed up the cloak and took his hat.

'Mistress is on the porch out back, Senor. Can I bring you some refreshment?'

'Nothing, thank you, I'll wait for supper.' Turning, he made his way through the double doors into the parlour and spotted Kirsten, gently rocking back and forth on the chair, young John Nathan on her knee. Her flowing blue cotton dress formed a circle around her feet and finished with white frills at the wrists and neck. She looked every inch the loving mother as she bounced her son on her knee.

'Look, young John Nathan, who's that? Who's come to see us then? Well it's a very handsome man indeed, he looks like a very important man. What shall we do? Shall we let him in?' She held up the child as Banoldino pushed through the swinging, lightweight doors that separated the living area from the porch.

Holding his son up in the air Banoldino was relishing every moment of contact between them, before bending to place a long kiss on his young wife's lips.

They sat with John Nathan for some moments before the maid turned up and, bowing politely, asked Kirsten if it was time for bathing the baby.

'Yes, please take him through, I will be along presently.'

'Ahh, please not so soon, I only just got him to smile, surely not so soon?' Banoldino protested.

'Please, darling, it is getting late. Besides, I need to speak with you.'

Banoldino reluctantly gave up the baby, and turned his attention toward Kirsten. 'What is it my love? I am at your service.'

'I'm a bit scared Banolo. I heard of settlements being attacked again, not five miles from here. The savages are in the province and I'm scared when you're not here.'

'Darling, I know, I have heard, but I am sure there's nothing to worry about. I spoke with Ranleigh only yesterday. He keeps abreast of everything that goes on within a hundred miles. He tells me that there is trouble brewing because the French are stirring up the Huron, Rock and Creek tribes, against British interests – it's all this because of this conflict in Europe over the Spanish succession, that reaches out to every corner of the earth.

'Ranleigh says if it threatens this area, or even comes close, the militia will be mobilised and King George's forces will be matched with our people and drive them all to the Canadas.'

'I know, darling, I'm sure Ranleigh is right, but you know how it is when you are not at home, waiting every day, with you out at your business every day, I'm left here with nothing to think about but the safety of our child. It weighs heavy on me. If we lived in the township I am sure I would feel a lot safer.'

'Kirsty, my love, I promise you, if I thought one moment you and John Nathan were in danger I would move you to a safe place in an instant.

'I will consider everything, overnight. Indeed we are due to visit Andrew and Evelyn tomorrow. I agreed to stay with them the night before the governor's ball. We will discuss everything then, please, my darling, feel safe. I am here for you, always.'

Kirsten held his hand to her face and brushed his skin with her lips. She held on to him tightly and he was under no doubt that she indeed felt vulnerable and, despite his encouragement, she believed the frontier was a dangerous place at this time.

***

The following day the carriage, pulled by two fine black mares, drew up outside Windale Hall and a finely dressed, dark-skinned servant, pulled on the handle of the door. Springing the footrest from its holding he stood aside and bowed lightly as Banoldino stepped down.

Turning, Banoldino reached for Kirsten's hand and lead her toward the steps of the Great Hall. At the head of the steps another servant, more mature and with a well coiffured wig atop his round, friendly face, announced 'Senor and Senora Don Bosco de Cervantes', at which almost all present turned to catch sight of the handsome couple.

Immediately Ranleigh crossed the room and reached out a hand, but unlike the occasion of their first introduction to the 'new society' many others lined up to welcome the new arrivals. Theirs had been a seamless introduction into the community, with unquestionable credentials, and close alliance with a peer of the realm, it was in everybody's interests to make their acquaintance.

Invitations followed, opportunities were put in their way. Banoldino rapidly moved upward in the commercial sector from the moment of laying down his plans and appreciating the timing of their arrival, he made a promising start. The unfortunate encounter with Malachie had done nothing but enhance his reputation, both as a man of integrity and a man not to be trifled with.

Governor Clarke, summoned the community leaders to a general meeting with the single subject on the agenda. 'What are we going to do about protecting the homesteads?'

The political situation in Europe, a treaty drawn up to establish peace after thirty years of warfare meant that there would be no concerted British effort to quell the Indian uprisings which, covertly, were fuelled by the French, still determined to keep North America their own.

The British had maintained their interests by shoring up their encampments in the Canadas but had kept their presence in the East Coast provinces fairly low key.

Clarke was determined that a militia be formed in the interests of all the colonials who were not going to live or die by the political inclinations of the British monarchy.

Clarke made it clear that he would return to Britain in a short time but on arrival he would lobby ferociously for a full armed response to these savages. The number of homesteaders slaughtered now ran into hundreds and a good number of families had packed up and headed south or to the coast.

Contrary to all that, two substantial Irish groups, the O'Regans and the Clearys based in Maine, had successfully formed militia and managed their defences so well that their countrymen flocked to join up.

There were major incidents recorded where the native Indians had been scattered by these forces, formed essentially with two families at their core.

Clarke made his intentions clear, a grand speech and a grand gesture, appreciated by most but recognised as a lot of rhetoric for a man who would soon be on the high seas waving farewell to the New World. Despite the emptiness of his promises, others realised that his intentions were valid. Something had to be done.

It fell to the recognised leaders to take what had been said and to organise the offensive.

Lord Ranleigh, naturally, was called to the fore and asked if he would lead a battalion drawn from the local community.

Without hesitation he agreed but gave fair warning. 'Gentlemen, I would crawl on my hands and knees to serve my country and my community, but I have to warn you that I suffered an illness during the crossing which has left me debilitated, somewhat lacking in stamina, shall we say? I would not wish to be a burden upon the volunteers. In fact, I would like to nominate my very good friend and companion Don Bosco here. A soldier of some repute and a damned good man to have around in a crisis. I would nominate him to lead the battalion, is there a second?'

The room hushed significantly, before Brunswick chimed up in support of his associate.

Charles De Villiers stood up and raised a hand to quiet the room. "I am afraid I would oppose such an appointment. Senor Don Bosco is of Spanish origin, I believe, and has throughout history opposed the interests of the British Crown."

'Sir.' Brunswick stood and took the floor. 'My dear fellow, Senor Don Bosco has himself never opposed the interests of the Crown. It may be assumed that should such conflict arise within the dominions then he may well have to choose sides. However the past thirty years has seen Europe at arms over the Spanish succession. I can assure you that Senor Don Bosco's family has indeed supported the British and Italian interests in preserving the succession for the young Spanish descendant and opposed France in its determination to see the Burgundian line enthroned.'

Banoldino stood next, thanking Brunswick for his support and Ranleigh for the nomination. 'For the sake of record Gentlemen, my father did indeed fight against the British in the succession, a sad and wasteful war which ended very much with the status quo exactly as it had been before. Nonetheless, I personally have no interest in continental politics, I believe I am now a colonial American.

'I would fight for my family, and my friends and they are all here. I hope you do not consider my statement revolutionary. It is not my intention. But I accept the commission only on the grounds that it is to protect the settlements, not to gain advantage for either of the European powers.'

Clarke took the floor. 'Gentlemen, I accept the offer of Senor Don Bosco, he would get my support if it were down to a vote, even though his loyalties to the Crown may be taken as somewhat challenging. If you are all in agreement say 'Aye' and let's get on with the business of equipping a force which will rid us of the enemy all along our borders.'

There followed a unanimous chorus of 'Ayes' and Ranleigh rushed across to congratulate Banoldino on his appointment. Promising to look after his business interests during the campaign, he wished his friend a swift and decisive outcome.

When Banoldino explained what had happened at the meeting to Kirsten, her mood starting in high amusement at the sequence of events and the words spoken, as related with some humorous twists by Banoldino, soon deteriorated to gloom and despair.

'Why us? Why you? Why now, our child, our business interests, our home?'

Banoldino reminded her that only days before she had expressed her wish to be relocated to the town for a while, until the uprisings had been calmed.

Now he had the opportunity to bring about an effective solution and saving many families, many homesteads, and indeed expanding the boundaries of the frontier.

Kirsten remained unconvinced. Surely there was a regular army to deal with these things? Surely there was someone else.

'My darling. I have been granted a great honour, I have been supported by the establishment, I am their chosen one. We should be elated at this rise in status. It will have great significance to our interests when I return victorious.'

'Banolo, my Darling, I am filled with dread. You have been chosen, yes. You have also been put out there to face the enemy where they would not go themselves.'

'Kirsten, my love, please, do not question the integrity of a man like Ranleigh who has given us a great opportunity to rise up in this community'.

'My love, don't be fooled, you deserve everything you have achieved – you are beholden to no man. I only hope Ranleigh's motives are as pure as you believe them to be.'

'I have no doubt my love. And neither should you. These are our friends. My interests will be taken care of whilst I am away. Surely you can see the sense in this. I will return before you know I have gone. Please give me your support, your blessing. I don't think I could go with a good heart knowing you were resentful. Come, let us talk over dinner. There are weeks yet before we will be ready.

'Banolo. Do not lie to me. I know preparation is already under way. I know you will be gone within two days. The meeting was called because the situation is desperate. They are not going to let you take this thing at your own pace! Darling, I am so fearful.'

'How can I convince you, all will be well? Ranleigh has asked for you to stay with Evelyn during the campaign. Will you go?'

'I would be foolish to stay here. How would it be, you are off protecting the homesteaders and your wife is captured by Sioux Indian. Besides I need to make sure I am out of … '

'What? Out of what?'

'Oh nothing, I… '

'Darling, what? You said you need to make sure you are, what?'

'Out of reach… of the natives… I… '

'That's not what you meant, I feel there is something. Perhaps you should tell me.

'How… can I, I, I have to… Please don't make me!'

'Kirsten, you must tell me what is troubling you, my mind is going quickly in many directions, is it me, is it the boy? Is there something I should have… '

'No, Banolo, no, please don't make me.'

Banoldino walked toward the large ornate cabinet which filled the wall on one side of the living area, he pulled out a bottle and two glasses. 'We are going to sit down and talk. However long it takes.'

Pouring wine into each goblet, he set one down on his side of the table and one on the other.

'Sit.'

Kirsten sat opposite, took a sip from her goblet and began from the beginning to unfold her history with Otte.

Tears flowed as she struggled to unleash her story. She left out nothing, but somehow made it so that Banoldino did not fly into a rage. She told him the worst, in her calmest voice. She told him the way she dealt with it in her most ferocious. She was still terrified that the outcome at the end of this saga would result in big trouble for her husband'.

Banoldino listened, stroked her face when she seemed ready to breakdown, held her hand when she found it difficult. He took it all very calmly, he was astonished that she had been present at the duel.

Even more that she had wished the man dead.

When it was all over he held her tightly, kissed her and reassured her that she had done everything exactly as he would want his wife to do it. Behaved in the very way that he would expect of her. He felt he had always known Otte, for the vile individual that he had proved to be.

'What will you do, dear?'

'I will handle the situation in a way you will never have to worry again. You will never have to deal with Herr Otte, ever again, I promise you.'

'But, darling, I have kept it all to myself all this time so that you do not commit murder.'

'My sweet, I do not intend to commit murder. On the contrary, I have a position for Herr Otte, surgeon. I intend to take him with the militia on our little sortie. I promise you something else. He will not return. But Banoldino will not soil his hands.'

Kirsten cuddled up to him. 'Banolo, kiss me, properly. I don't want you to go without the memory of your kiss, your body against mine. Come.' Kirsten lead him to the master bedroom.

***

Three days of intense preparation followed and the battalion came to readiness. Two hundred and eighty five in all, wagon drivers, hostlers, cooks. Two hundred foot soldiers, sixty on horseback. Well-armed, a carriage full of gunpowder, food to last eight weeks and a surgeon.

The force was mobilised and lead by Don Bosco, who rode at the head, part armour clad with a ceremonial rapier hanging from a blue and yellow ribbon at his hip. Banoldino could not resist the memory of his father's departure in very similar style some twenty years earlier.

The thought of his father's return, in very different circumstances, flashed into his mind and was dismissed with equal rapidity.

Half of the population of New York lined the streets to wave them farewell.

A carriage with Ranleigh, Evelyn, Kirsten and the children rode just behind the front rank for the first three miles before farewells were exchanged and a final wave saw Kirsten disappear into the carriage, blind pulled across, whilst Banoldino sat looking at the vacant square of leather for some moments before he realised that the occasion was simply too much for his wife, and that she had retreated behind cover to save further distress.

Astride a noble grey stallion sat Wolfgang Otte, a small black valise containing his instruments, slung across its neck. Otte pulled a wide-brimmed, felt hat down over his eyes and evaded the attentions of the throng whilst his mind raced in varying directions as to how he had arrived at such an uncompromising situation.

Having been cleared at the hearing of any influence on the demise of Malachie O'Reardon, he had made a point of maintaining a low profile in the community. German settlers had migrated toward him and his reputation had grown as a skilful surgeon, but with little to recommend him in society.

His disposition ensured two things. Firstly, that he was seen as a man of considerable intellect and knowledge in matters of injuries, diseased and infected limbs. Secondly, that he was isolated and generally excluded from social circles.

This suited him perfectly. He had neither desire nor need of interaction and the necessity to provide information. He had no intentions of having his past scrutinised. He satisfied his only other human requirement, unrecognised, as he trawled the late night taverns around the quayside.

The governor called upon him in response to Banoldino's request. It seemed perfectly reasonable that a surgeon accompany the militia and that Otte, a single man, a reputable surgeon, a man of experience should fulfil this requirement.

The governor approached him, independently, in writing, so that the petition was a matter of public record. Otte had formed a plan of his own. Once again, in the absence of her husband, he was intent on forcing himself upon Kirsten. He had already envisaged his approach and a tumultuous climax to his exertions on a dozen occasions, since the forming of the battalion had become public knowledge.

He considered and indeed perpetrated a number of evasive actions to avoid being embroiled in the undertaking. All of which lead to the conclusion that he was clearly suffering from cowardice and surely would not be able to remain a respected member of the community if he persisted with this stance. Only when he announced, through the local Chronical News sheet, that he was joining the 'party' and was always 'happy' to do so, only resisting briefly out of deep concern for the well-being of the community if the campaign proved of long duration.

***

Banoldino made it his business to keep Otte in his sights at all times.

The small force made its way northwest for a matter of three days before the first rendezvous was due. Meeting a force from Maine, which was organised by Major Doyle, a career soldier, under General Montgomery's British forces based at Fort Albany, was the first objective.

Up to that point no major encounters between colonials and Indians had taken place for a decade, the British having nurtured a strong alliance with the Cherokee maintaining a balance throughout the northwest frontiers.

Trouble stirred up by the colonial interests of the French and Spanish were at the heart of most of the encounters. The British had purchased the rights from Spain, to nurture trade with the indigenous population along the western seaboard and the determination of the French to enhance their interests and replace the British trading position was the undercurrent to the present hostilities.

Land rights were granted to the settlers. The land was 'purchased' from native Indians, many of which had no rights to make such deals. Many times this was the cause of flashpoints on the frontier.

Many of these attacks resulted in the slaying of whole families in their homesteads, or in vengeful and brutal raids on rival villages.

Now with more than two hundred raids wreaking havoc along the Pennsylvania borders, and the struggle to contain the numbers returning to townships in search of shelter, accommodation and sustenance meant that some action was imperative. There was also the loss of produce, timber and livestock which was the lifeblood of the large communities.

'Don Bosco de Cervantes, at your service, Major, I am pleased to make your acquaintance.'

'Not a regular soldier then, Senor? How did you come to be appointed?'

'Ahh, let me say a matter of necessity. There was nobody else.'

Major Doyle smiled, reaching out to clutch the hand of his new acquaintance.

'Well, you have brought fine body of men with you, sir. And I would venture to suggest that you are very well supplied and, I trust your ordinance is likewise plentiful?'

'We have only three cannon. I am, shall we say, experienced in the use of guns at sea. I certainly hope to prove the value of long range warfare during this expedition.'

'With Indians, I regret to say that much of the combat will prove to be close quarters. But we shall see.'

'How large is your force, Major?' Asked Banoldino, keen to keep the conversation going.

'I have one hundred and eighteen men at my disposal. We are aware that the township of New York has a thriving population and are hoping your numbers will exceed our own.'

'Two hundred and eighty, I would suggest two hundred and forty being combatant.'

'Good news indeed! Are they well disciplined?'

'I would not attest to that, but I have seen most of them handle their weapons. Particularly the musketeers, they are diligently cleaning and preparing their weapons each evening. This is a good indication for myself at least.'

'I agree, it is. I think, nonetheless we will set up some practise during the morning, before we encounter the enemy. We will have a better idea what to expect.'

'Would you join me in my tent this evening, after you have your men bedded down?'

'My pleasure.'

At that the two leaders parted and made to establish the encampment for the night. Lookouts were posted and duties generally spread among the two forces.

The New York county militia were by far the better served from the point of view of food and supplies and the regular soldiers were glad to accept some of their generosity.

***

Later that evening having dined on salt beef and ale, Major Doyle outlined his plan to Banoldino and Doyle's Adjutant Lieutenant John Connor. They would set up a chain of outposts, or 'forts', along a thirty mile front, each manned by thirty to forty men, with communication between them managed by riders, and signals from beacons.

The forts would have to be well chosen, hilltop locations. There would be regular scouting missions and alerts would mean the support of at least two forts, one from either side, coming to support sightings or attacks.

'This puts up to one hundred men in proximity at any given time.'

'I have to compliment you on your plans, Major, I cannot think of anything that would improve it. How long do you intend that the network remain in place?'

'I consider that within three to four weeks we will have established where the major threat is coming from. When we are certain, we will apply an attack policy intent on driving the major protagonists back to their own territories and establishing where the major French support is based.'

'In the event we are attacked with force, the French will get a strong response whilst they reveal their positions and leave themselves open to a more concerted counter-attack.

'My only concern is that the fortifications will require substantial engineering and labour, perhaps our resources are not up to the plan.'

'Irish labour, Don Bosco, don't you worry about how we bend our backs when we have to. We have built more roads around the world than the Romans did.'

Banoldino raised his glass and toasted the plan's success. 'I think the sooner we begin, the more convinced I will be. I drink to our success but no more tonight. I wish to be fresh come the morning.'

Rising, Banoldino shook hands with his two new comrades and took his leave.

'Senor, please accept the rank of acting Colonel for the duration of our enterprise. Your forces are more than twice those under my command.'

Banoldino bowed acceptance but added, 'I accept the title and will do my best to justify it, however, I will bow to the experience of professional soldiers whenever the situation requires. I bid you good night.'

***

Kirsten sat pensively looking from the window of the Ranleigh's town house. The square situated a hundred yards from Wall Street, was for access to small carriages, the gravelly pathways nicely flattened by regular use. Maidservants were busily tidying the fronts and beating rugs in the houses across the street.

It was a far cry from the 'wilderness' home they had built for themselves, the acres of trees cleared leaving a view of the nearby mountains, the river and tree-lined tributaries that made up the sumptuous views from their porch.

It was also a far cry from Baltimore, the village which, before it was sacked, had landscape of equal merit beyond a well-spaced row of cottages. The fast flowing river she now could never think about without it turning shades of pink becoming more red by the moment.

A shiver extended from her spine into her hair line and she had to shake her head to eject the reaction from her body. Now she wondered about Daemon.

Did he leave the south altogether? Did he even leave Ireland? Would he have tried to find her? No. 'Silly,' she thought. 'Our love lasted one night. Why would he think of her again anyhow? Where would he be? Where would he have put down roots? Perhaps like his uncle, he would settle in a small village, have his own fishing boat, come home to a pretty wife, two or three young ones.'

Her eyes fixed on John Nathan. His head tilting toward her, his fine green eyes shining in the light from the window. She saw a face she knew.

Could it be her mam's? She smiled to herself momentarily before her thoughts were clouded over by other pressing events.

Banolo was out there, sleeping rough. He had not really wanted to become involved. Would the rivers be turning red again? Would he return to his little family?

***

Just ten short years previously, the British forces clashed with Indians supported by Spanish crews from a great flotilla. He had listened carefully to the version of events that unfolded among the higher placed citizens. The British had brought peace, *bought* peace, and opened new trade routes with the Indian, the Spanish had released their holdings in the north Americas in favour of their South American interests, gold, silver, coffee, sugar.

French interests were in keeping their very profitable fur trading links open with the Huron Indian confederacy. This had flourished over sixty or more years and was not to be given up lightly.

So the Spanish had what they wanted, now the British also have what they wanted. Now there was a battle to preserve what they had gained. The French would not relinquish its interests in the north, but by this time were being eased toward the Canadas and more remote territories. Their spiteful legacy was to stir things up among the native traders and the British. There were hundreds of casualties along the frontier. They had to be stopped.

Albany, a stronghold at the moment under Dutch control, but more inclined toward the British than their perennial foe's the French, was too far away to provide adequate cover or protection to the homesteaders, many of which were in fact Dutch and German.

***

Banoldino made his way through the line of small encampments, some under strung-out sailcloth. One arranged around a spike as he had been told the Indians made their own homes. He was thinking of the morning to come, the setting up of squads for manning the fortresses. The work in establishing the bastions. Choosing if and when artillery would be required.

He passed a wagon atop which slept three or four non-combatants. Wolfgang Otte sat upright with a trail of cigar smoke lingering in the air over his head.

A hissing laughter was followed by 'All I would have to do is touch the end of a taper and you, our fine commander, would be blown to hell! Heh Heh, the thought is sufficient to send me to sleep with a smile across my face.'

'Ahh, Herr Otte. As always, the very last person I would wish to meet on my way to my place of rest.'

'Heh, heh, your permanent resting place. Indeed the thought cheers me even more.'

'Otte, I know you hate me, and now I understand exactly why you hate me. You considered my wife would never reveal your wretched animalistic behaviour. Well now I know all about it. Every detail. Had I known those months ago when I had you in the sights of my pistol, the led would now be in your head and your head would be in the ground with the rest of your rotting carcass, where it belongs.'

'Ahh, so the little birdy has been chirping has she? And all this time I thought you had chosen to include me in your little war games, on the merits of my skills as a surgeon.'

He sucked hard on his cigar and his lungs filled with intoxicating fumes. 'He began coughing as he released it and the cough once more turned to ironic laughter.

'It will be most interesting, to see which one of us, if either, returns home to be the next one to slip between the long, slender legs of your darling wife.'

311

'Otte, I would cut out your heart without another thought, and I may yet do it. But do not tempt me my friend, to do it before I am ready. I usually make a terrible mess when I am angry.'

Otte hissed once more, 'Heh, heh with that thought, I bid you a good night. I hope you manage to get a few hours' sleep.'

Banoldino was already ten paces further on up the line and did not bother to respond.

Before he lay down, he posted two sentries outside his tent, and reiterated his orders. 'Remain alert. Do not allow anyone to pass – not even Major Doyle, without acknowledgement from myself.'

***

The morning broke all too soon and Banoldino rose, quickly. He threw some cold water from a bowl across his face two or three times, and straightened with a long exaggerated stretch. It had been a while since he had spent time living rough, and despite these three days, was nowhere near to becoming used to it.

Sounds of pots, the low rumble of first communications, men clearing their throats and their heads, all emanated through the fugg as he gathered himself, brought his sentries to attention and asked if there were any incidents to report.

The negative response saw him immediately pulling on his cloak and light armour, sheathing his sword and passing through the ranks throwing a few acknowledgements as he went.

Within a few moments he was bringing the force to attention and confirming an outline of what had been agreed the night before that they would form into six squadrons of forty men, each commanded by a newly appointed lieutenant.

***

'Men, I would like you to choose your own lieutenant, initially, I do not know you well enough to make such choices. In the event of more than one proposed – I will make the final decision. Please align yourselves and provisions will be made for each group.'

An hour passed and much activity filled the time, but when he returned to the parade area he was pleased to find the men grouped as he had explained and in all but one case there was a natural, or chosen leader. Three men occupied the front and centre position of the first group. Banoldino approached them.

'My friends, I will lead this squadron myself until a natural leader emerges. No disrespect to any of you, I am sure you are all capable, but we have not time to work this out. Please fall in, all of you.'

They drew up behind Doyle's forces, similarly broken up, but into three squadrons, and the enterprise got under way.

Within another day's march they had reached a number of burnt out homesteads, found burial grounds and groups of settlers in wagons headed east.

Questioning and probing, they established the range of territories that had come under attack, an idea of how each war party was set up and armed. They had begun to come up with a number of areas where the springboard for these attacks might be located.

For the moment they went about their task.

The first of the forts was established on the left flank, around an area known as Lower Creek. An abandoned farm provided the basic structure of the fort and the forty-four fighting men and attendants were left under the command of Acting Lieutenant George Smith of Rhode Island.

Two miles north found them at the remnants of a small settlement, with an abandoned chapel, originally named St David's. The force set up their base and the process continued until there were nine links in the chain.

Hill top beacons were established. Good ships telescopes could make out each as it emerged from the position of the next.

Within two more days all the forts were ready and already two of them had begun to receive refugees. Homesteaders from the Pennsylvanian borders were landing at the new frontier line and more information was gathered up.

A mule train arrived at Benton's Mill, third in line from the southern-most point at Lower Creek. Banoldino had set up his adopted squadron there with St David's between them. They were able to establish that the abandoned village had been a well-used trading post and saw mill, until savagely attacked a year before.

Now the mule train, led by Cherokee Indians had to travel almost to the coast in order to make their trade.

The Cherokee offered much information about the other tribes and the French units. A certain Colonel Montpellier had initially led a force of about one thousand from Charlestown and gathered up all the tribes from South and North Carolina to join forces.

Local skirmishes, when tribes from the middle ground fought against use of passage or occupancy of their own territories eventually reduced the force by a third, but the intermittent reinforcement by hostile Indians kept up the overall numbers to around twelve hundred. With light artillery they had become a very mobile, hard-hitting force, causing havoc among the settlers.

Doyle had ranged his forces to the north of the ark, with himself at Reagan's Hollow, only five miles west of his own homestead. His father had established a settlement at Riley Station, with fifty or more families from Dundalk and Iniskillin. Now a population of two thousand strong, theirs was a settlement quite capable of mounting a significant defence of its own.

When a number of the original settlers felt the need for more space or had plans of a grander scale they ventured up to twenty miles further to the west and it was these families now finding that life out on the edge of the frontier could be very threatening. A number of families had lost children and young adults to the Indians, being taken captive and turned into slaves themselves.

At the end of the first week a beacon was lit on the hill over Reagan's Hollow and the forces from each side joined the centre within an hour.

Finding Major Doyle at the ready, one hundred men followed in quick time toward a point north east of their position. Fire could be seen for miles as a bridge had been set alight. Further up the hill a farm was burning.

A flat back wagon came into view At the reins a crusty old farmer, a boy of about twelve alongside him. in the rear, a mother and four young ones held on for dear life.

The wagon careered down the track across a wide rock-strewn, scrub area and distress was emanating from every expression. The wagon pulled up violently on sighting the armed squadrons and old man Conroy almost leapt from the buckboard in his enthusiasm to direct the force.

'You'd be Doyle, I assume. Heard you was coming. Only too late – my boy has just been cut down by them savages! Took three of 'em with him. God bless him. Took my granddaughter too. But this here's his wife and three other kids…only got away by the skin of our teeth and they was—'

'Sir, I would urge you to calm yourself, please tell me everything, but be accurate, I want our actions to carry the first strong message to these people that this attrition has got to stop.'

'There's fifty savages, they got four French Cavalry and they are burning up the whole county. You get yourself off toward the Santee area and you find them Frenchmen and give them hell, boy!'

'Sir, press on for the next two or three hours in that direction, you will come to Riley and find a township there where you can tend your family.'

'Goddam, I know Riley – I was one of the very first settlers – but we set out again eight years ago, maybe we went too far? Who knows, my boy would still be alive now if we'd stayed where we was.'

'Don't blame yourself, sir, go and seek refuge. We will deal with these savages.'

An hour later they were looking down on an encampment. Seven teepees had been hastily set up alongside the creek and fires were sending long trails of smoke into the windless atmosphere.

'Major Doyle drew up his forces, took the telescope and established the authenticity of the party. Pots and pans and clothing were being passed around among the Indians. The four Frenchmen had tethered their horses and were lounging next to a fire, a young white girl was kneeling before them as if being questioned, but the tone and merriment of their attitude suggested that the questioning was not of strategic nature.

Away in the distance the farm burning, livestock slain and fences strewn down the hillside was proof enough that they had been savagely attacked.

Under Doyle's command the squadron spread out, made steady progress toward the encampment and took up positions unobserved.

Dismounting, Doyle drew his cutlass and waved forward the full line of over a hundred men, muskets at the ready.

A lookout, having been posted some fifty yards clear of the encampment sat against a tree and chewed on salt beef, before pulling long and hard at the neck of a deep green, wine bottle.

One of Doyle's regulars came upon him and soundlessly speared him to the tree with his bayonet

The force moved in and from twenty paces opened up a volley of fire taking out half of the fifty or so warriors.

Mayhem ensued as the warriors ran scrambling in every direction, grabbing up weapons as they ran. The two remaining French cavalrymen immediately looked up for their horses only to find three of Doyle's men holding them steady whilst another two took aim and opened fire.

Some of the Indians gathered in the centre of the encampment and began spraying the air with arrows, some of which randomly found a target, but within minutes there were less than twenty, on their knees in the centre with their foreheads firmly in the dirt.

Doyle quickly formed up the detachment and with their prisoners strung-out, made for the fort.

After a debriefing, two men were assigned to take the entire story of the action to the fort at Benton's Mill, and were to return any new reports or any significant responses to himself by nightfall.

Doyle decided the prisoners would be placed in incarceration at his home town at Riley's. There was a strongly reinforced corral where they could be securely kept for a period of time until suitable justice could be meted out.

The young girl had managed to rise to her feet amid the chaos and was found slumped against a fallen tree on the edge of the encampment. Tearfully she accepted the hand of one curly haired soldier who took responsibility of seeing her safely back to her family at Riley station.

***

Meanwhile, the two messengers arrived at Benton's Mill to find only a skeleton detachment.

Banoldino had departed in haste when report of an attack on Lower Creek found its way to him. St David's had already gone ahead and they were to rendezvous at the southernmost fort.

During this time Wolfgang Otte, having been stationed at the central location of McCaffrey's Trading Post, was watching and waiting for an opportunity to bring a solution to his plight. He knew Banoldino would not let him return to

New York. He knew also that he would not allow him his freedom. At least that was the conclusion based on what *he* would do in the same position.

Otte was faced with a decision. He could slip away, go 'AWOL' and return in the night to New York where he knew very well where he would find Kirsten. He could also choose to slip away and put as much distance as possible between himself and the woman that haunted his sleep at night. He quickly dismissed the latter.

His other option was to await his opportunity to rid himself of Banoldino once and for all. To this end he would have to be near his opponent. He soon concluded that this was the better long-term solution.

Having dealt with the few casualties suffered by Major Doyle's action, and upon receipt of news that the southern forts were in action, he volunteered to swiftly relocate to support them.

Banoldino, meanwhile had raced his men to support the Lower Creek fortifications. As a seafaring soldier Banoldino knew the value of artillery and mobilised two of the three cannon under his command.

A minor skirmish engaging a dozen misplaced warriors attacking a homestead placed in the Seaton Creek valley, had turned into a major altercation with a French force of more than one hundred Cavalry supported by fifty or sixty Rock and Cord warriors of the Huron confederacy.

The French had quickly realised, through scraps of reports and rumours, that the British had organised a force to deal with the raids they and the Indians had openly perpetrated.

Now they had to be more coordinated in their attacks and be prepared for an increase in hostilities. This was their plan coming to fruition, they would soon amass the sort of force needed to drive the British back to the townships. But first they must test the resolve of the British by hitting their outposts, those of which they knew at the time.

Banoldino's scouts reported a small war party crossing the creek with two white captives.

Immediately diverting fifteen of his force in a sort of skirmishing unit to intercept the war party, he lead the main force toward Lower Creek fort where a considerable exchange of fire was under way.

The French with superior numbers clearly thought they had the upper hand, but would be completely unaware that reinforcements from the chain of forts could be quickly alerted and provide support.

Banoldino came on the rear of the French assault, hostlers were by now attending thirty or forty horses, whilst the French pressed the northern wall of the encampment on foot. A greater force was engaged at the main gates. Having apparently broken the line at that point by continuous assault Indian warriors were clambering over the outer barricades and engaging one to one.

Quickly Banoldino arranged the two pieces of artillery to be set up to provide a barrage which he hoped would unnerve the French that had dismounted, and bring them running for their mounts, which were now under his control.

The first cannonballs thundered into the soft escarpments leading up to the Fort, making a huge impact on the soft ground, throwing earth and rocks into the air to such an extent that the effect was immediate.

After three thirteen pound shot had landed in their midst, the French, in reality with only two men actually downed, turned on their heels and made toward their string of mounts. Banoldino had arranged two banks of ten loading and firing muskets to present a volley of fire which took a significant toll whilst pinning down the remainder, taking cover behind any boulder or mound of earth at the bottom of the valley between the fort and Banoldino's position.

Immediately some twenty or thirty defenders were released to reinforce the main gate. The Indians were thrown back, the French Cavalry suddenly faced intense fire and decided upon retreat.

Realising that their mounts had fallen into enemy hands the cavalrymen trapped in the valley tried to move out in pursuit of their own retreating numbers, but were now caught in crossfire from both the fort and from Banoldino's men.

Just at that point, having overcome the war party at the creek and released the white captives, the thirteen of the skirmishers still combative arrived having followed the creek and reached the place where the remainder of the French, scrambling away from the crossfire, were about to cross the creek. Another volley of fire from the skirmishers brought down what was left of them.

French and native casualties amounted to nearly one hundred. In the fort fifteen had been killed and seven wounded. The surgeon was sent for and Banoldino moved his men and artillery into a defensive position.

Between himself and Lieutenant George Smith, they decided that it was almost a certainty that the French would return with significant force. They had surrendered forty well-trained mounts, and suffered many casualties and great indignation. They would mount a swift retaliation.

The English set about defensive fortifications and prepared as well as they could for the imminent response.

The surgeon arrived and quickly set about tending the wounded.

Banoldino allowed Otte to go about his work and slotted the issue of his own security into a place in his mind where it could be quickly retrieved.

For now he sat down with George Smith and revisited all the areas they had discussed in preparation.

***

Smith was no more than twenty-two years of age. Had been born in Maine of English parents, newly arrived on the 'five ships'. The five ships had brought nearly two thousand settlers to New England some twenty years previously and established a very firm hold on the territories around Boston where the population followed English traditions whilst enjoying freedom to worship the Presbyterian doctrine.

Six feet tall and ginger haired with the obligatory ruddy complexion, Smith was of strong, determined nature. He had not intended a military career, but considered the Law the more interesting option.

His father was a cabinet maker and was producing fine furniture for the upper crust of society, around the province. His mother a tough determined negotiator, handled the merchandising and accounts of the business. Two sisters completed the family but the business was of more appeal to them than to himself.

George had proposed to the daughter of mill owner Daniel Theakstone, but her father had made it abundantly clear to him that George was not of the stock that he would have considered suitable to marry his only daughter. The new hierarchy was being established.

Somewhat licking his wounds, George volunteered for the army, where he found the Redcoat attire suited him very well. He had been sent to the Hudson Bay in his first posting and rose through the staff ranks on merit.

He dreamed of being commissioned, and pushed himself forward at every opportunity knowing that field promotions were his most likely route to his objective.

Now sitting with Banoldino he freely expressed his wishes for promotion and recognition, and left Banoldino in no doubt that he would be a good man to have around when the going got tough.

'Do you consider it out of the question to send for further reinforcements, the central forts will be back to full strength by now?'

'No, sir, I have been considering our position in exactly those terms,' responded Smith. 'I was thinking perhaps we have now located the source of the main French force, here around Lower Creek. Would it be sensible to concentrate our own forces now? Or, should we stick to the original plan, which was to cover a thirty-mile stretch.'

'You could say the original plan is working very well. 'Central' engaged in an encounter and we now have achieved a significant outcome to our first encounter. In both actions only the numbers collected from three of our posts, coming together, achieved our objectives without leaving other areas exposed.'

'I agree, so far so good, though we did not expect to encounter such numbers so soon. We set out our stand on the basis that a frequent number of small encounters was likely. Now I think we have provided the French with evidence of a much more intense response to their activities along the frontier. Perhaps we have created something of a monster.'

'I see your point. It may require a little more persuasion to get Doyle to abandon his plan so soon. For the time being, we will report our situation and confirm we have repelled initial attacks and are confident of holding the position.'

'Perhaps not abandon, but modify. We could easily revert to our original status, if the major encounter does not materialise, or indeed if it does and we do not bring about a surrender.'

'I think we will have to delay our decision, unless something happens to change our minds. We should see the strength of the French response before calling on Major Doyle. Do you agree, Senor?'

'I think it is the right course, given all that we know. We hold out until we are sure the northern forts are not under similar attack.

'As a regular British officer I suggest you assume command. I have some skills to offer, and can organise artillery. I put myself at your service for the duration of the conflict.'

'Senor, I accept your proposal and thank you for your confidence in me. I will do my best to justify it. Please consider yourself in command should anything happen to put me out of the front line.'

They both laughed.

'Seriously, I also have every confidence in your ability to hold this garrison. The men appear to respond very well to your command. Did you spend many years at sea?'

'Oh yes, under one flag or another. I tended to roam from place to place and only recently upon my arrival in the New World, have I put down roots.'

'You have a family?'

'Oh yes. My wife and child await my return in New York.'

'Lucky man!'

'Indeed, I am blessed. I only wish I were with them now.'

Smith rose and put a hand out to Banoldino. 'Let us hope within a very short time you are returned to the them.'

They were disturbed by a commotion nearby and both wheeled away to establish its cause.

Riders had entered their encampment and were intent on delivering their news at the earliest opportunity.

'Lieutenant Smith, sir, Colonel Banoldino...'

They reached the edge of the gathering in time to greet the messengers.

'From Major Doyle, sir.

Handing over a crumpled parchment, Smith immediately steered Banoldino toward the nearest campfire. 'Just about make it out. Doyle says he is moving north. Three more homesteads under attack. We are to hold until the full extent of this action is understood. Please report exactly your situation by return.'

'Written before he received news of our encounter here. He clearly thinks we have a minor skirmish to deal with. Is it time to bring the force back together? Your comments would be appreciated.'

'Very difficult to tell whether there is a major escalation right along the frontier or whether these are war parties, operating as before.'

'Clearly, he may make a different decision once he has digested our dispatch.'

Smith called over the messengers. 'Are you men fit to return to the centre?'

'Yes indeed, sir. We have fresh horses.'

'Then return to Major Doyle that we must keep lines of communication open at all times and trust that the excursion to the north perimeter is a swift one.'

Watching the two riders disappear into the distance, both men considered that their decision not to call for reinforcements might be the worst decision they had made.

***

General Montpellier, commanding the French corps, was furious.

A hastily established, functionally manned outpost had somehow resisted a concerted attack of over one hundred combined cavalry and Huron tribesmen.

Calling Emanuelle Chevalier, his second in command, to him he swiped his white gloves across the man's face. This humiliating act brought no more than a downcast, shameful look of acceptance, as if to be whipped like a dog was all he deserved.

Apologies were offered but Montpellier was in no mood.

'Sacre Vache, you have to be ashamed of yourself! I offer you two choices. One you may return to the garrison fort at Louis and consider yourself under arrest pending court martial, or you can take out a command and achieve retribution and full recompense from our English foe.'

'Pardon, monsieur, I am only so prepared to lay down my life to the cause of victory, but I swear this was no ordinary outpost, we were sumarilly beaten by a force which could

324

mysteriously reproduce itself at will. Unless by gross misfortune the British had an army under march and fully prepared in waiting, or they have an uncanny knack of knowing our movements.'

'Enough, mon dieu, I have never heard anything quite like it! Mysterious? Gross? Uncanny? We are talking about a bunch of backwoodsmen which stumbled upon you just at the moment your force was concentrated in the wrong place, in an uncoordinated attack!'

'Non, monsieur, not uncoordinated. We were applying very sensible tactics against stubborn resistance. I do not know what happened, but it was devastating. Now, monsieur, please with your approval. I will regain the initiative in the region and send ze British back to their stinking urban origins!'

'Take the appropriate course, and I warn you my friend – do not fail. There will be rolling heads if you return with your legs around your tail!'

Chevalier ceremoniously turned on his heels and called to his officers as he exited the Command post.

***

Three hundred well-equipped soldiers marched out of the fort to a pipe and drum accompaniment. Eighty or more Native Indian, Rock, Creek and Cord tribesmen filed out behind the Corps, with twenty more outriders, scouting ahead on magnificently painted ponies.

***

A day's march away, the Lower Creek fort was coming awake and breakfasting whilst replenishing their supplies and ammunition.

Banoldino walked among them and gave a word or two of encouragement but always reminding that there was likely to be a follow up to the skirmish of the day earlier.

Tim Clancy caught his eye, as he cleaned out the barrel of his musket with the ramrod. His cheerful expression and focus on the task in hand impressed Banoldino to the extent that he walked across and sat alongside him on an upended tree trunk.

'Your name, soldier?'

'Clancy, sir, Timothy Clancy.'

'May I ask where you are from, Mr Clancy?'

'Just Tim will do, sir. I am from County Tyrone, in Ireland and wish I was there now hunting rabbit for my mammy for tea.'

'Ahh, yes of course. It sounds like a wonderful way to spend your time. Tell me, if you were not there and could be anywhere else in this big wide world, where would you choose to be?'

'Well if it's all the same to you, sir, I'd rather be right here, with my cousins, Seamus and Kevin, awaiting a chance to hit something a bit bigger than a rabbit.'

'What is it that makes you so happy to be involved here?'

'Well, sir, as I see it, we come a long way to this big open country to find freedom, and I'm damned if I'm gonna let a bunch of pompous, overdressed, French peacocks take that feeling from me.'

Banoldino laughed. 'Your answer does you great credit 'mon ami'! I also am happy to be here with Seamus and you and Kevin. We will all have a drink together when this is over. A drink to freedom.'

'Fine by me, sir.'

Banoldino walked on taking in the atmosphere of camaraderie that had sprung from nowhere to prevail between this dissident bunch.

It occurred to him that no authority could overcome the spirit of these settlers in what they saw as their right to freedom, to choose which Christian doctrine to follow, which king to bow down to, if any, and which law they choose to adhere to.

One day such a people could become a mighty adversary or a mighty ally.

Within a short time, defensive positions were being finalised by George Smith and a final discussion regarding placement of the guns resulted in mounting canon on the roof of the barn with a trestle and decking support, constructed to provide a level platform and allow recoil. Steps were quickly erected for easy access and powder and shot stacked on the roof.

The wagon containing the remaining powder kegs was stowed under canvas at the rear of the barn.

The fort lay quiet for the rest of the morning but scouts returned confirming that a 'substantial force' was approaching from the southeast, and that they had artillery and at least four hundred men.

'Now we know Lieutenant Smith, what we are going to have to face here, I think it is time Major Doyle was acquainted with our position.'

Quickly dispatch riders were prepared and their message was short, 'Come quickly, major attack on Lower Creek. Colonel Don Bosco and Lieutenant George Smith'.

***

Wolfgang Otte circled out of the encampment and made his way into the forested area which flanked the road north. Dodging in and out of the trees he made good time to the top of the ridge and searched around for a suitable place for ambush.

The dispatch riders, mounted on paint ponies, loomed into view one hundred and fifty yards down the heavily wooded trail. Their progress at this stage slowed by the sharp incline and the uneven, wheel rutted surface of the path. As the first rider drew alongside Otte's elevated position he fired off a single round of his Stanley Carbide musket and a puff of smoke blurred his view of the downed man's passage through the air before landing heavily in the thick foliage of the clinging climbers around the base of a large redwood tree.

The second, alarmed at the crack of the shot breaking the silence then witnessing the spurt of blood emitting from his partner's head, was only able to rein in his mount and pulled so hard on the head that he managed to bring the pony down beneath him.

He struggled to raise himself against the slope and the agony of the weight of the horse on a damaged leg.

His eyes opened wide in surprise to see Herr Otte, the 'skilled surgeon' of their own side, waving a pistol ahead of him. Drawing up Otte muttered an apology before releasing the shot which penetrated dead centre between the eyes of the fallen scout.

Stooping and pulling from his waistband a surgical knife, Otte scalped both riders and stuffed the skin and hair into a small pouch.

Pulling on the reins of the pony, Otte managed to right the mount and climb aboard before following the frantic gallop of the first rider's horse, determined to prevent it finding its way back into camp.

Despite his frantic efforts, he was unable to find the pony. Eventually he decided to turn his mount and drive her in a long arch around the Lower Creek encampment before dismounting in a thicket and cutting her throat.

***

Two hours later, Banoldino sitting for a few moments, when all preparations had been made, to reflect on the position. His thoughts turned to Kirsten and he reached for parchment and a quill. He started to write a few lines, before his mind turned to Otte and his reprehensible pursuit of his beloved lady.

Banoldino resolved to slit the man's throat at the first moment he considered it would not jeopardise the mission.

A feeling of uneasiness engulfed him, to the point where he found himself feigning a further tour of the garrison with the real objective of checking the man's whereabouts.

After some moments, and a few vague enquiries, he had drawn a blank.

Alerting George Smith he issued a general order that the surgeon was to be found and brought in for consultation. A dozen or more men searched the encampment, and the perimeter, to establish that no-one had seen or heard of Herr Otte within the last few hours.

Banoldino turned to Smith. 'I fear the worst, Lieutenant. I think Doyle may never receive the dispatch we sent out. Indeed I fear for the safety of the two riders.'

Smith was aghast at the news and begged an explanation. When Banoldino told Smith of their history, the younger man was angry, calling Banoldino to his quarters where he turned on the Spaniard.

'Sir, I understand your motives, but I am damned well annoyed that your actions may have jeopardised our mission. Surely you understand that, had it been common knowledge that there was an issue between you and the surgeon, it could have been dealt with.

'Every member of our force deserved to know about it. A situation that could explode at any time!'

Just at that moment Otte wandered into the camp with a rabbit dangling from his hip.

Both men turned in astonishment at seeing his calm exterior and easy manner.

'Gentlemen, you look as if you haf seen a ghost! Vat can be the matter vith you?'

Smith turned on him. 'Herr Otte, I would like a report of your whereabouts during the past two hours.'

Upon receiving the benign account of Otte's animal trapping exploits, Smith once again addressed the problem.

'Please give me your word that your actions have been in the interests of our mission.'

Otte threw his hands in the air. 'Why, Lieutenant, I don't imagine this little rabbit having much effect on the hunger of the battalion, but I am willing to share as far as it will go.'

'Herr Otte, we have made the barn a temporary field hospital as you are aware. Please confine yourself to those quarters for the duration of the forthcoming encounter, however long it may prove to be.'

'At your service, Lieutenant. I vould not vish to be anyvere else.'

Turning he left, with Banoldino temporarily sheathing the knife he would willingly have used to slaughter the German had he uttered one wrong word.

'Senor, I am deeply suspicious of the man myself. Unfortunately we have no time to pursue the matter, and I would request that you keep your powder dry for the time being.'

Smith turned and left Banoldino to his thoughts.

***

Only a few moments passed when a bugler sounded the alarm. Soldiers had been sighted and the encounter was imminent. The garrison scrambled to its posts and a short silence ensued before the whistle of cannon overhead signalled the commencement of hostilities.

Nine pound shot plunged into the hillside behind the fort, setting fire to dry grass in the immediate areas. The thunder of reloaded guns rumbled in the distance before more shot thudded into the ground before the main gate. A barrage of shot ensued with red hot balls dropping into the fortified areas creating mayhem, setting alight the fortifications and two partially unloaded carts.

In a sense the light numbers involved in the fort proved a blessing as most of the damage was done to property and not to the soldiers.

Fifteen torrid minutes passed before the French advance got under way. Spread out across a quarter mile stretch, each rider was flanked by twenty or thirty foot soldiers. The Indians made up a front rank running swiftly toward the fort, they flung their arrows in an arch across the sky and rained damage down on the defenders.

Going to ground quickly, reforming and firing at will, they made ground to within seventy yards of the perimeter before a shot was fired in response. Two or three regular soldiers manning the front gate were caught in a hail of arrows and were theatrically downed, dropping over the perimeter in full view of the attackers. A cheer went up in the French ranks to witness the Red Coats under attack by long bows something the French always associated with English historical supremacy.

The full advance began to the steady snare drums of the French marching band. The regal nature of the French banners was almost medieval, reminding the well-read amongst them of European chivalric standards.

But now Banoldino ordered his thirteen pounders into action and the defenders watched in awe at the destruction caused to the French ranks. Horses, embattled French cavalrymen, Indian warrior alike, they were pounded into the dirt by the barrage of shot from the barn.

Following each thunderous shot, they were reloaded within seconds, another fierce explosion saw a hot ball scythe into the French ranks.

Banoldino was relentless, he turned the angle of the guns to take in the flanks of the advance and caused similar havoc.

The French Cavalry had had enough of this and decided upon an heroic charge.

They mustered their forces and thundered toward the encampment.

Despite heavy musket fire they lunged on, dust and smoke mingling to create a fiery atmosphere which made it appear that the horses were galloping along on a cloud.

Now they were upon the gates and the reinforced defences. Many of them were able to leap through the perimeter fence scattering the guards landing in the courtyard where they began thrashing with their sabres with systematic skill.

Groups of Redcoats grabbed at reins and pulled down both horse and rider. Other horses were speared on the end of bayonets and riders shot as they leapt.

The fight raged on at very close quarters before the militia reinforcements closed around the French from the sides of the encampment and offered volley fire into their rear. The French Cavalry's effect on the battle was brought to a grinding halt as there appeared not a horse standing. Now they were all foot soldiers fighting for their lives.

The Indian warriors now came heavily into the fray leasing arrows at will to severe impact on the besieged. Banoldino had abandoned his battery, and joined in the hand-to-hand combat. There appeared to be Huron Indian everywhere, their black painted faces making them appear ever more fearsome, they were nimble and acrobatic, evading sword thrusts, even musket shot and arrow. They seemed almost indestructible and the battle raged relentlessly on as dusk began to fall.

The air was full of the smell of sulphur, the battled ground strewn with bodies and dismembered horses. There were wounded stumbling in every direction.

The barn was suddenly overwhelmed by a group of warriors approaching from the rear. They clambered over the far slope and appeared around the gun battery and at the ridge, gaining vantage for their arrows.

Banoldino quickly feared the loss of the artillery or even worse, that the savages might be able to use them. He quickly grabbed two men and lead them around the barn up the steps toward the gun placements. Thrashing at two warriors blocking their way on the steps he managed to overcome them. He sliced one across the neck and thrust a second straight through the abdomen. Tim and Seamus Clancy followed, bayonets fixed, as they reached the top of the steps.

Beneath, dust and fragments of straw fluttered down as the roof above became a battleground. Blood dripped through the shingles on to the floor and on the temporary bunks, arranged now, with wounded and dying.

Otte, quickly ordered all the men that could walk to abandon the barn.

They struggled with some of the wounded but as they were gathered up, Otte showing great purpose, cleared the room but for four or five left behind on low cots, unable to walk.

Otte grabbed a fuse wire and stuffed one end into a barrel of gunpowder. He lit the other end with a burning ember from the smouldering east wall of the barn. Quickly he ran with every last ounce of energy away from the barn as a huge explosion blew the building to pieces.

Bodies of Huron warriors were thrown into the air, the roof crashed down into the building and artillery caved in after it, there was a thirty yard cloud of black smoke and splinters of timber rained down on the entire encampment.

In the explosion there were casualties among the militia. Many French were killed and wounded where they had been swarming over the east end barricade. Those on the roof, thirty or more, were blown to bits.

Some twenty French, outside the fortifications by this time, including Chevalier, turned their horses and tactically retreated the battle ground. Only an occasional musket shot thudded into the ground around their mounts as they made their getaway.

The remaining French, attempting to feign superiority and claim victory, fought on, hand to hand, with the remaining defenders and were brought down almost to a man.

Five or six Huron and a handful of French stragglers made their escape into the woods without fear of pursuit as every man under George Smith had fought himself to a standstill.

The British flag was raised over the fort, and hung limp but proud over the smouldering battleground.

As the night closed in, Smith arranged a perimeter defence, outriders and guards. The forty men remaining on their feet were fed and watered and fulfilled all the orders he managed to issue.

A troop of six men were given the task of disseminating dead from living, seriously wounded from injured and with only slight regard to the colour of their uniform, had performed the task within an hour.

Two hundred dead were lined up outside the fortress. Many more coloured the open ground, too far from the perimeter to be collected safely.

Fifty wounded men of all origins lay around a new 'field hospital', a former cow-pen, on the north perimeter, being handed water and bread and some attempt at treatment from Herr Otte.

The remains of the barn continued to smoulder and an occasional explosion not much more than a fire-cracker, would go off without threatening any of those remaining inside the fort.

It suddenly occurred to Smith that he had not encountered Banoldino for some time, turning to his colour sergeant, he asked, 'Would you find Colonel Don Bosco and ask him if he would be good enough to join me in my quarters?'

Within a few moments the solider returned 'The Senor has been injured, he lies in the hospital.'

***

Smith turned quickly, spotted Otte picking his way through the wounded that littered the area all around the pen, and immediately felt uneasy. He strode over to the area addressing Otte. 'Herr Otte. I understand Senor Don Bosco is injured, would you take me to him?'

'Ahh, I appreciate your concern, Lieutenant. But I regret, there may not be any chance for you to talk with the Senor before...' Otte shrugged his shoulder, but nonetheless pointed out a mound in the corner where Banoldino could be distinguished by his mane of dark hair, now loosely arranged about his head.

Approaching, Smith feared that Banoldino might already be dead.

Upon close inspection, he detected a little movement, and spoke quietly into Banoldino's ear.

The response was a cough, of heavy, wheezing, emitting from his mouth before his head turned, enabling him to look up into Smith's eyes. 'Splendid battle, Senor Smith. A very brave stand I think, on our part, the men were exemplary.' Banoldino coughed heavily again, this time leaving Smith wondering if he would ever catch a normal breath.

'Senor, you are hurt, do you know what happened?'

Banoldino shrugged almost indiscernible but enough for Smith to gleen his meaning. 'The spoils of war, I think. I was fighting on the roof of the barn, I could not let them gain the artillery and the high ground. There was an explosion... the powder kegs secured in the barn must have caught alight and... Banoldino mouthed 'booom', but no sound emitted.

'How badly are you hurt, has Otte offered any assistance?'

Banoldino shook his head. 'He took one look, came up smiling and shook his head. His look was triumphant! But Senor, my friend, I would ask one thing of you. I fear for my wife. I have told you about Otte. He is a dangerous man. Would you do everything in your power to protect... ' Another burst of coughing.

Smith took Banoldino's hand and grasped it in his own. He drew it up so that the back of his hand rested against Smith's breast bone.

'I will protect your wife with my life, Senor, you can depend upon it. But, look, let me see, I am sure we can do something.' Standing back he lifted the blood soaked blanket covering Banoldino from the waist. But seeing the mess of entrails held back by Banolo's other hand, he could barely hide the twitch that started at the corner of his mouth and brought on a deep swallowing action as he fought to keep down the bile.

His mouth then formed a smile. 'Hey, we will have a decent physician take a look at you. Please wait here my friend.'

Walking away Smith knew it was a matter of moments before death took his comrade. He knew not how to handle the situation. Let him die in agony? Relieve him of his pain? Give him a bottle of whisky, but thought again after considering it a waste of good whisky.

Just at that moment a white painted face appeared on the perimeter fence. A woman shrouded in long tasselled garments and long straight hair, with only her face visible was leaning over a stricken warrior.

'Hey! You there. Come here!'

The figure ignored him and continued her ministrations.

'Who gave you permission? What do you think you are doing?'

This time the woman stood to acknowledge him. In a light shaky voice she simply said, 'doctorie'. 'I am doctorie,' she sprinkled some herbs onto the lips of the stricken warrior whose face broke into a benign trance-like state.

'Come! Please come with me!'

Smith quickly dragged her bodily toward Banoldino. Reaching him he stood her in front of the cot, then, leaning, he pulled back the blanket. 'Can you do anything for my friend? Can you help my friend?'

She turned to look mournfully up at Smith. A tear dropped from her eye and ran down the white paint dripping on to her tunic.

Her head moved from side to side. Smith took her hand. 'Please try. Do what you can.'

Another look and this time, she waved a hand. Smith immediately realised that she was calling on them to follow.

'Quickly, you two men pick up the cot and bring Senor Banoldino.'

For more than ten minutes they walked on following the shadowy figure before Smith held her up. 'Er, please one moment. I, am not able to… leave… er my Post. The fort… I cannot leave my men. Do you understand?'

She nodded slightly but turned to move on. Turning to his men,

'Men, Cleary, Johnnson, I can't order you to do this, in fact there is no precedent. But I believe this woman can help Senor Banoldino. He is a man worth saving. All I can ask you to do is take him, to where she commands. Then return as quickly as you might to the fort or to safety. I can only ask you. If you put him down and return to the fort with me, right now, nothing will ever be said of the matter.'

Cleary looked at the woman now just discernible against the dark tree line. With a quick exchange of glances, both men started walking after her, taking care with Banoldino to avoid, if possible, the rocking which was proving his great discomfort.

Smith returned to the garrison and quickly resumed charge. Concluding that the dispatch riders did not make contact or that Doyle had not returned from his own exploits in the north, he began making plans to abandon the post in favour of making for the centre.

***

Deep in the forest, beneath a gnarled and ancient oak, battered by years and years of attrition, the white faced woman knelt over the stricken figure.

337

An hour of diligent stitching had drawn his innards together and despite waste and unrepairable stretch after stretch, she was finally able to push the remaining parts back into the cavity.

With even more diligence, she sewed up his torso until it resembled a human form. She spread a thick paste of herbs and tubers all over the area until his skin was encrusted as it dried, the image of the blackened tree bark beneath which he lay.

Covering his body in broad wet leaves, she settled down again at his side and ground up even more herbs into fine powder.

With the pale burning light of a fading campfire as a backdrop, she slowly and deliberately blew white powdery puffs from the palm of her hand, across his mouth and nostrils making sure that each intake of breath entering his lungs, did so with a strong draught of white powder mingled with the oxygen.

Her ministrations had the effect that was intended, Banoldino hovered on the edge of life, hovered on the edge of death.

His breathing so minor that it was hardly discernible. His pulse hardly detectable, his heart hardly audible. His eyes remained tight shut, his fixed expression motionless. The covers on his body as still as a shroud. And so it remained for hour after hour, turning to a day, then a night, then another.

An encampment had grown up around the witch doctor. Helpers, one providing food and water, another keeping the fires going.

Others chanting outside as if their own lives depended on it.

The old one changed his dressing, covered him again in freshly ground paste, mopped down his broken body with fresh water and lit candles under his nose so that the sacred aromas entered his body.

Two more days in and the delirium started. He began to moan, then to sweat, then to tense and release, stiffen and collapse all his functioning muscle. Blood spurted from him when he convulsed, red tears fell from his eyes.

Then he awoke. At first to the horror of a deadly white-faced spectre, then when he realised that this was his 'carer', the one in whose palm his life was finely balanced, he looked on her as a prisoner might look on a tormentor, a torturer. Grateful when the treatment stopped, hateful when it was needed.

Then the pain. His insides were trying to knit together, but acids burned the new linings and the snake like tubes that made up his innards writhed like eels in boiling water.

She administered all ancient painkilling potions and unctions, she breathed opium into his mouth from her own ancient, parched lips.

He writhed in pain nonetheless and cursed her from the pits of hell.

A week later, he asked her for some food.

'Anything, please, perhaps a broth, or porridge, something that will slide.'

She understood little of what he asked, but returned with a milky broth and fed him spoon by spoon until it was downed.

He suffered when it hit his entrails and thought the process so painful that it would never again appeal to him. Three hours passed and he asked for another bowl.

Another week and he sat for a few minutes. He asked her to bathe him. A day more passed and he asked her to hold up his head whilst he looked at himself. He saw the chequered flesh of his stomach, red and angry here, white and pasty here. He did not like what had become of him. He passed water, and she gently mopped up the mess. He realised that it was not releasing in a normal manner.

She took his hand and lead him to feel around his lower abdomen, there were scars, something told him that everything was not as it should be.

He looked at her and her expression told him all. His reproductive organs had been damaged. Her skilled fingers had done all they possibly could to restore what remained to resemble what had been before.

She held a smooth hand to his face, gently massaging until he sank back onto the straw-filled sack to which he had become attached.

His thoughts raced to a life without physical completion with his beautiful young wife. Then he contemplated life completely without her.

Each alternative was unbearable, unacceptable. He would rather be dead, indeed he now resolved that is exactly what he was going to be. Dead.

***

Kirsten sat with Allison, waiting by the window for news. They had become good friends. Now they were equally anxious for the return of Banoldino. As the days had gone by Kirsten responded to encouragement from Lady Evelyn and from Allison, and tried her best to be cheerful and contribute day to day where she could, for the community.

Many of the inhabitants of the growing community had a stake in the success of the military response. Those already damaged along the frontiers. Those who were hoping to take the journey in the future. Those who were overcrowded now by refugees so that their lives were put on hold. Those who had financial interests in the trading and development of the frontier.

There were those whose loved ones had gone out to turn things around, they perhaps had the most vested interests of all.

Some of the original troop had returned, wounded and unable to make further contribution. They came through confirming what a grand bunch of people they had served with. Smith, Doyle, Banoldino, Jones and Richardson, there were other heros, those who did not return at all.

Kirsten, of all those waiting was concerned, but never for one second doubted Banoldino. He would triumph and he would return.

Now, the seventh week after their departure, the militia was camped a few miles from town. Riders had come in to confirm that the troop would march into New York with some ceremony at noon tomorrow. There was great excitement for many, but now a full toll of missing and wounded was posted and Banoldino's name stood out like a beacon.

Kirsten was stunned. Unable to comprehend. Lord Ranleigh immediately returned from the Court House to talk with her in person. Lady Evelyn sat with them.

'I understand Banolo was wounded, he is being nursed by a witch doctor woman out at McGruder's Creek. She has been with him twenty days and nights and he is still barely able to travel.'

'I must go to him! Why was he left out there? Surely there are enough people in town to manage his ailments?'

Ranleigh intervened. 'Kirsten, please let me go. You must stay here. Look after the child. I will bring him home, I promise.'

Kirsten wrestled with the options and was unable to decide, Lady Evelyn made her point in agreeing with Ranleigh, and carried enough influence to make it a plan.

Her mind was in turmoil. What had happened to him? Why had she not been told.

In agreeing that Ranleigh should go into the wilderness to bring him home, she insisted that Major Doyle come to the house with a report.

Governor Clarke personally accompanied Doyle and they both extended great sympathy.

'We believe Smith did the only thing he could do. He could allow Banoldino to die where he lay, or he could take a chance with this mystical Indian woman.'

'Who was she, which tribe? What skills had she displayed?'

Doyle answered, 'Ma'am this is all we know. It was a tough encounter, many dead on both sides. An epic battle from all reports.

'Your husband was caught in an explosion, when some stores went up in the heat of the battle. It is not certain how the explosion was set off, but the barn in which they were held, was on fire at one end and there was fighting on the rooftops.'

Kirsten's hands went to her mouth as she covered an anguished cry. Allison put an arm around her shoulders.

'So my husband was caught in a burning barn and the whole thing went up in an explosion? My God what has become of him?

'Now we are to bring him back after spending weeks in the forest with some medicine woman! It's all too much, this shouldn't be happening!'

'In times of war, Madam Don Bosco, many sacrifices are made.'

'But I want to know why my husband has made, it seems, all the sacrifices! I want him back, Mr Clark. I want my husband back!'

Kirsten sat and effectively dismissed them. In truth they had no desire to remain any longer and the feeling of guilt and blame was already permeating the atmosphere.

They made a graceful farewell and left.

Kirsten cried openly when they had gone. She knew Ranleigh would do the right thing and could only hope Banoldino was not so badly injured that the journey would endanger him more. She was lost without him. She felt all would be lost if he did not return in good health. For the moment she hugged Allison and bade her go and fetch John

Nathan, that she might hold him and feel that the family was still intact.

Two more anxious days went by before a dispatch rider pulled up at the gate of Ranleigh's town house. Bearing a message for Mrs Don Bosco alone, he was ushered into the sitting room.

Kirsten swept in. 'Is it my husband?'

'Yes, ma'am, Senor Don Bosco, ma'am. He is on his way and will hope to be with you by early afternoon.'

'How is he, is he riding? Is he being carried?'

'Yes, ma'am, he is aboard a carriage and well protected, ma'am. I think he is quite well.'

'Thank you, soldier. Do you need anything? Fresh water? Food?'

'Yes, ma'am, me and the horse need freshening up, ma'am.'

'Allison, would you be so kind as to see that this man has all he needs?' Allison hugged Kirsten and gave her a reassuring look, hopeful for the outcome.

Kirsten quickly removed to her room and did everything she could to make herself ready for his return. News had gone around that the mission had been a great success, that the French–Huron army had been severely dealt with and was moving north to the Hudson.

British forces were amassing there and would be a deterrent to any further escalation of violence.

The homesteaders were safe again and the frontier would once again flourish and push the boundaries as more and more Europeans arrived. Trade with the Cherokee nation would begin again and there was great optimism for the future.

Major Doyle and George Smith of the regular army were commended. So too was Senor Banoldino Don Bosco for his heroic part in the action. There was great interest in the militia with local farmers boys queuing to sign up and considerable commitment to defence agreed by the council.

Banoldino's return was greatly anticipated and people were on the streets. He raised his hand to their greetings and to most of them, his black hair flowing, his cloak pulled up around his face, peeking out from beneath his helmet, appeared normal. He received their acclaim without really showing any emotion.

By the time he reached the Townhouse, Ranleigh and Evelyn had joined Kirsten and the staff on the steps. The carriage pulled up and the crowd drew in around the group.

Kirsten raced down to the carriage and pulled open the door. Banoldino putting on his best face raised his eyes and smiled but the effort curtailed suddenly, his expression turning into a grimace. Kirsten held back, unable to move toward him nor recoil. He was pale, his eyes bloodshot, his skin dry as parchment. His black mane was greying at the sides where it swept passed his ears.

'My darling! It's so good to see you!' Was all he could manage, his voice cracked and low.

'Banolo! My love, come let me hold you.' Her arms reached out and were met by one of his own, a sort of protective shield.

'My darling, wait, a moment, just until we are inside. Please.'

He lurched forward appearing to lose his balance, but corrected just before he toppled. One leg followed the other but painfully slowly. She stood aside to give him room, which he accepted, whilst he manoeuvred himself to face the steps. George Smith appeared from the other side of the carriage and was there to hold out an arm for Banoldino to hang onto.

Making the best of the moment the two managed the steps without any further incident and Kirsten followed with the others behind her.

The gathering of locals closed in on the steps, as if to be near to them, but the door was quietly closed and that's all they saw of the family for some days. Wickham from the

Chronicle watched carefully a scene he would recreate in print during the days that followed.

Inside Kirsten could barely hold herself together. She watched as Smith guided Banoldino to a chair in the sitting room, arranging him until he signalled his relative comfort.

Ranleigh and all the family came in succession to welcome him home, and he held up in good grace until the children and Allison had passed through and were ushered from the room by Lady Evelyn.

Once the room was quiet Ranleigh thanked Smith for making the effort to greet Banoldino and accompany him this far. Meanwhile he offered both a tot of whisky which both declined.

Kirsten sat opposite and held her tongue for the moment.

'Well, old man, how are you feeling?' asked Ranleigh.

'I regret, I am not at my best, Andrew. I have taken a bit of a battering.' His eyes which had been fixed on the fire for some time, now looked fleetingly across at Kirsten to see the hurt expressed across her lovely features and it caused him a deep reaction in the pit of his stomach.

'George, once again I thank you. We will talk soon, I would like to meet in a few days to fulfil my full report on the encounter and put my observations on record. I would like to congratulate you on a very well fought campaign.'

'Sir, we could not have achieved what we did without you. Ma'am, if I may, I will take my leave of you now unless you require anything further. Please call me at any time if there is something I can do for you, anything, I will answer to your call.' With that and a short bow toward Ranleigh he left them.

Now Kirsten rose and went to him, sinking to the floor at his feet. She knelt in front of him and took his hands in hers. 'My love, you must let me help you. Tell me everything. I must know so that I am able to do the best for you.'

'All in good time, my dear. Andrew, may I take it that all is well with the mill? And progress has been as we hoped with the shipbuilders?'

'Banolo, please, no business, you must rest.'

'Kirsty, dear, I will not let him do anything, absolutely anything at this stage. But allow me to answer and I will take my leave. Banolo everything to do with our enterprise is fine. I will brief you further tomorrow, but take my word that everything is just as you would want it. I will see you both in the morning.'

Alone at last Kirsten looked into his eyes. To her he had aged ten years, he looked so ill, thinner and completely changed.

He knew she would have her explanation, now or tomorrow, it would not rest.

'Darling, I have been very ill. I am sure you were told how it all began. All I have to add is that I would be a dead man if it were not for an Indian woman who cared for me, using all her considerable powers to patch me up. The potions she provided actually kept me alive, are keeping me alive right now. I feel perhaps it would be better if I were not.'

'Darling, surely not, you have me and John Nathan, your family, please never say that. You must put this behind you. You will regain your strength. I am here, I will help you.'

'I know, of course you are, but Kirsten please, do not believe a full recovery is possible. I will never be the same man I was. I have taken injuries that should have finished me, but I am here, only because of some mystical power. Something has kept me alive – and it will one day be clear to us why this has happened.'

'Darling, I don't know what to say, your words give me little—'

Banoldino with great effort sat forward in the chair. 'Kirsten, my love, I would never hurt you. I would rather die. But I am unable to be the man you want. For the moment, it is all I can do to simply not let go. It is taking every ounce of strength simply to... be. I know no other way of saying it.'

'Darling, what can I do? Had your leg been blown off, I would know what to do. If you were blind, I would know what my role was. How can I help? What I see is a man who is very tired. My role is to provide you with rest. Until you tell me what you need that is all I can do. Come.'

She led him to their room and with considerable effort, she placed him on the bed and proceeded to loosen his clothing. He stopped her. The hand, although somewhat feeble, was firm enough to leave her with no alternative. She allowed him to do it and watched the painfully slow process of him loosening his clothing, removing his boots until he reached a point beyond which he would not go with her in the room.

At his request she went to fetch him a small brandy.

When she returned he was wrapped up tightly in a night shirt and draped a blanket around his knees. He leaned heavily against a range of soft pillows and although looking slightly unbalanced and anything but comfortable, he let the brandy permeate around his throat for a second before digesting down into his stomach.

'I may sleep for a while, please do not disturb me unless I call.'

Kirsten knelt at his side. 'Banolo, my love, it is so good to have you with me, you mean everything to me.' She slowly rose and without taking her eyes from him, closed the door behind her and retreated to the sitting room.

Finding Allison arranging flowers on the dining table she walked over and with perfect timing Allison turned so that they fell into each other's arms.

Kirsten's head found her shoulder and she buried herself there for some moments whilst her grief poured out.

'I don't know what to do. He... he, this is not the man that lead out an army just months since! He is not my Banolo. What am I going to do?' She sobbed for several moments as

Allison could say nothing to meet so much anguish and sensibly offered nothing but a shoulder to cry on.

Eventually in almost a whisper Allison spoke. 'Come dearest, sit for a while, I will bring John Nathan and Annie. We will watch them at play, I know it will fill your heart to see them.'

Allison was right. Her own child was just a few months older than John Nathan but standing upright whilst John Nathan was only managing to sit. They passed things to one another. A little bell, a rag doll, they found fascination in things that were hardly noticeable.

Annie pretending to sleep, patting a small decorative cushion so that John Nathan would follow suit. Their two little heads would not fit at once on the cushion so that Annie had to try to fix it several times with the same result, one little head would slide off onto the floor.

Allison provided a second cushion so that they could both lay down. They thought this was some achievement.

Kirsten looked on, amused, then sad, sometimes both together. A tear was never far from her eye.

The process of healing went on for some weeks with little improvement in Banoldino. Kirsten made herself busy, working almost to a standstill to keep him in a positive frame of mind, seeing to the child's needs and managing their social affairs. She hardly had time to dwell but she remained desperately concerned for the future and for any real signs of recovery.

Banoldino never let her see him without his long nightshirt. He bathed two or three times a week with the help of Dante, and made sure Kirsten was occupied somewhere else, or simply insisted that she leave it all to himself.

He tolerated her constant chatter, the rigorous way she went about all her chores, as if showing him the way. He began to tire of her words of encouragement – her hopes for the future and her chiding him for his low humour.

He became impatient with her, though neither of them noticed. Others did. Evelyn could see the marked change in Banoldino and Ranleigh consoled himself that things would surely come round.

George Smith visited every other day. He had become a good friend to the family. He was tireless and began helping Banoldino with some elements of the business. Carrying a message for him, attending a meeting upholding his interests.

The moment came when Smith arrived and produced Colonel Doyle, recently promoted to take charge of a full regiment of regulars, recently bolstered by reinforcements from Britain, and the volunteer militia.

They took drinks and Banoldino politely but firmly asked Kirsten to leave the room.

'Well, Senor, I am sorry to see your recovery is slow. We have missed your council. Lieutenant Smith and I would like to go over some of our findings with you and see if you are able to bring anything to mind which would, perhaps fill in the blanks?'

'I will try, gentlemen, you know I will. But... '

'Do not be concerned, we will take things one step at a time. Come again in a few days perhaps.'

'No, please continue. I would like to bring a conclusion as soon as possible.'

Doyle continued. This is what we know so far. George, if I stray at all, please put me back on track.'

'You stowed away some barrels of powder on a carriage which was placed under cover in the barn? A canvas? Sailcloth?'

Banoldino nodded his head.

'Late afternoon a party of Huron approached under cover from the forest and scaled the barn, mounting the temporary stairway and gained position on the roof. There were twenty or more if reports are correct so far?'

Again Banoldino nodded.

'Inside the barn, the wounded were gathered up and shipped out. We have reports of a fire breaking out on the north side, and even burning straw from the roof top filtering down. It must have been a very precarious situation. George?'

'Yes, sir. One of the injured reports that Herr Otte ordered evacuation of the barn and saw to it that every man that could walk or could be carried, was shipped out of there within minutes.'

Doyle continued looking toward Banoldino. 'At some point, you and two or three men rallied to storm the rooftop?'

Banoldino nodded. 'Yes, I saw the Indians had us at their mercy. The small detachment manning the artillery had been removed, either thrown from the roof or taken refuge. One was even fighting a lone battle, wielding a ramrod at the savages.'

'You raced to support him using the stairway?'

'Yes of course, we had no other way, other than to reach the rooftop and try to upset the imbalance of numbers.'

Doyle focused again on Banoldino. 'Were the wounded still inside the barn at that stage?'

'Yes, I believe so... I... '

'Are you certain? Can you recall anything, or anyone in particular?'

'I looked in through the large south entrance as we swept past. I wondered if it would be possible to get some of the wounded to help. There was not time. I considered it my duty to get to the rooftop before the carnage started.'

'Did you notice Herr Otte?'

'Not at that time, compared to the... it was dark inside.'

'Did you realise the barn had been evacuated?'

'No, we were heavily engaged within seconds. All we could do was take on the next, then the next.'

'One of the injured who was removed to safety was certain that five or six men, unable to walk, or raise themselves, were left in the barn when it went up.'

Banoldino looked at both men, from one to the other. 'That is tragic. There mustn't have been time... '

Smith spoke this time.

'Another of the injured who had been carried to a place near the pig pen, reported that Herr Otte was the last man out. That he ran from the barn seconds before the explosion.'

Again Banoldino looked from man to man. 'He went back to help those on the ground?'

'Another of the injured men states categorically that the wagon containing the powder kegs, was nowhere near the fire and in no immediate danger.'

'What are you saying?' Banoldino's expression had changed quite dramatically.

'We have no proof, no absolute proof, but our firm opinion is that Herr Otte ignited the powder kegs.'

'He left the wounded to die?'

Doyle continued. 'It is my view that he intended to blow up those on the roof.'

'But the wounded, surely you couldn't ignite a powder keg with five or six wounded men in the building?'

'There is more. We believe that Otte ignited the powder because he knew you were on the roof. His concern was not that there were twenty natives raining fire down on our defences, nor that the outcome of the battle was in serious doubt, but that he intended to bring about the demise of a mortal enemy. Yourself Senor.'

'You think he murdered six wounded men, two other fighters on the roof, destroyed over twenty of the enemy, all because of his hatred for myself? Gentlemen, this is a heavy burden. Except that it turned the tide of the battle, this is an act of consummate evil! I should have finished him off when I had him in my sights. I will regret to my dying day that I let this man live! That I chose to take him and risk the lives of gallant young men.'

Banoldino sank back in his chair and focused on the flames in the grate. He fell into silence. Smith rose first, went over to shake his hand. 'I am sorry to have brought such awful news. Please let me know if there is anything I can do for you and your family.'

Doyle rose next and saluted. 'You have nothing to blame yourself for. The actions of a mad man – such behaviour is incomprehensible to all decent people.'

'What will you do?'

'The man is under arrest. We will have him shot. Or hang him. Nothing is too good for him.'

Banoldino's head dropped to his chest. His eyes closed and he fell into a sleep.

Doyle and Smith made their way to the lobby where Kirsten emerged from the drawing room where she and Allison had sat with Lady Evelyn talking in hushed tones.

'Ma'am we must take our leave of you.' Both bowed and made for the door. Smith turned taking a long look at Kirsten his eyes filled with sadness 'Ma'am, your husband is sleeping, we er, gave him some news which he found to be stressful. Please accept our deepest sympathies, I'm sure he will explain in good time.'

Kirsten just managed, 'Lieutenant Smith.'

'Your servan, ma'am.'

As they left she looked in on Banoldino and indeed found him in a deep sleep. She was sensible enough to hold her desperate curiosity until he had rested.

***

Wolfgang Otte sat motionless behind bars in the basement of the Council House, where an armed guard checked him every thirty minutes.

His trial had taken only an hour. Seven witnesses confirmed he cleared the barn except for six injured men Richard Lewin, Sean McGurdy, Frederick Blomquist, Anthony Cleary, James Dodd and John Carden who were too badly wounded to move and there was a lack of able-bodied men to transfer them within the moment they were given under Otte's direction.

Six witnesses claimed he ran back into the barn in the region of the powder kegs and came running for his life after a moment or so. The explosion then ripped the place apart.

Otte claimed he did not know members of the militia were on the roof. He claimed he was acting only to do as much damage to the enemy as possible, but leaving wounded men inside with no chance of survival, condemned that as a downright lie.

Other witnesses including Lord Ranleigh and the chief justice himself attested to the fact that Otte harboured a pathological hatred of Banoldino, and was intent on getting rid of his target for reasons which included his unquenchable desire to possess the man's wife.

There were some signs that there remained a lack of absolute proof that Herr Otte could have perpetrated this act entirely with one objective. George Smith took the stand and was asked his view of Herr Otte's actions on the day.

Smith confirmed that he 'believed Otte to be capable of anything.'

Then he produced a small Canvas bag. He probed inside the bag before bringing out a tangled mess of what appeared to be human hair. Separating the two parts and holding one in each hand he announced, 'With the Court's permission, I believe these are the scalps of two of our militia, Stacy Devlin and Jamie Teek.

'These boys were dispatch riders sent to our encampment by Major Doyle. They left to return a message confirming our position to request reinforcements. Neither of these men has ever been seen again. This pouch was found among the belongings of Herr Otte. He had gone missing that afternoon and I believe he ambushed our two riders and prevented the message reaching Major Doyle. Yes I believe Herr Otte capable of any act that may achieve his own evil ends.'

Kirsten did not have to be called. She sat for a few moments to hear the verdict and watched as Otte was lead away with the sentence of being hung by the neck until dead was passed.

Banoldino was not present and Kirsten took the carriage home to tell him the news. News which brought no comfort at all.

Chapter 37

Otte's Legacy

Kirsten lay alone, the arrangements for their stay in town had been extended and Evelyn determined that they both needed to be restored to full health before returning to their own ranch.

During the first days following his return, Banoldino insisted that they have separate rooms whilst he continued his recovery. A nurse attended each day, dressed his abdomen wounds and administered opium for the pain.

His nights were interrupted by delerium and discomfort and Kirsten tried to insist on being with him the whole time, but his resistance became so volatile that she thought it better to keep the peace.

On this occasion, she left him around ten o'clock, kissing his forehead, which she noticed with concern, was covered with a slick layer of perspiration. She made her way along the corridor and quietly closed the door behind her. Leaning for a moment in her despair.

Her room in the town house faced the rear of the building which had a yard and high stone wall, backing onto another building of similar proportions. Below her window was the shallow roof of the garden room, which was used occasionally for breakfasting during the summer months.

There was no view, leaving Kirsten to draw the heavy drapes across the half opened sash window, and recline across the bed for a few moments, in a prelude to undressing for a lasting slumber.

Silence settled upon the building until a distant laughter told that Ranleigh and a few friends were still enjoying a cigar and glass of port, probably over a game of cards, before retiring for the evening.

Her thoughts drifted back to Cashel and the brazen escape made by Banoldino and their flight through the Irish countryside. Arriving at the lake and their first love making in the shallows, she clutched her belly and curled up on the bed.

She came abruptly to her senses with a cold, wet hand pressed hard over her mouth. Sheer panic made her writhe this way and that. She bucked upward, unsuccesfully, at the weight which was pinning her to the bed.

Every attempt to scream was thwarted by the brutal power of the hand over her mouth. She was making as much noise as she might by humming an anguished moan in between deep, panic-stricken gasps.

Suddenly a severe blow to her face brought her to a frozen stillness.

She watched as the hand drew back into a second striking position. It was held for a few seconds, poised to deliver another blow but her stillness proved sufficiently convincing that the hand relaxed and dropped down in front of her eyes. It was held as a threat for a further moment before it began unbuttoning her tunic.

For some moments Kirsten lay quiet and watched intently as her tunic fell away and her shirt was pulled from its fastenings. Her underslip was torn away and her breasts fell free of constraint, her skin gleamed in the moonlight. She felt blood trickle from her nose.

She knew the figure towering over her was Otte. The familiar smells of sweat combined with gin and the rough hair-covered body was unmistakably his. How this was possible she could not begin to know. She had left the

Courthouse, his sentence had been passed and his fate sealed. He should by now have been lying in unconsecrated ground.

Kirsten's terrifying dilemma left her motionless in despair. The consequence of calling out, to bring Banoldino from his drugged sleep, unable to offer resistance in his present state. To try to attract Ranleigh's party through their own jollity, without waking the entire household and bringing the children into danger all seemed out of the question.

She resolved to fight this animal as she had done before, but she had been blessed by good fortune twice before. She had managed to catch him off-guard, in tight situations, now he was invested with almost inhuman power, determination, and everything was stacked this time in his favour.

Feeling her resistance only encouraged him to apply more power. Every time she tried to raise herself he thrust her back down and his weight crushed her entire form to the matress.

His hand slipped away from her mouth as her struggles and the wetness of her tears enabled her to slide one way then the other. But she let out no sound and he knew he had her. Once again she had to put herself in his mercy to preserve Banoldino. His well-being, or his safety. Either way she did not care.

Both hands were now free to explore her body. Falling to her breasts he lingered long, prodding and kneeding and picking at her until she shook her head violently from side to side.

Now he went for her skirt, her underskirt and the drawstrings of her pantaloons. His breath quickened and he finally tore at his own clothing. The matted, spiky hair covering his chest and shoulders rubbed into her face as he positioned himself.

Finally he gored into her. He found himself fully inside her at last, after years of lusting and desire, he had her completely at his mercy.

Kirsten's head went back and she fixed her eyes on a crack in the ceiling. It appeared to be getting bigger, longer. Each time he thrust into her, the crack appeared to widen.

She thought the ceiling might cave in on top of them and she cried afresh and prayed that it would. She thought of a long shard of plaster lodging itself between his shoulders and of his vile face, his smooth, bone hard, hairless head jerking back wracked with pain.

Instead his head did jerk back, his sweat poured in cold uncomfortable drops onto her breasts. His thrusting reached a crescendo before he went limp and collapsed on top of her. 'Liebchen, liebchen ahhh liebchen... '

For some moments Kirsten lay there. Her shame complete, her disgust, absolute. Her head throbbing with pain, from her neck to a point between her eyes.

Her breathing settled down and all sobbing subsided. She wanted him to leave now, without another word, without disturbing the household, without endangering any of her loved ones.

How could she make it so?

'Sir, Herr Otte, please, I am finding it hard to breath.'

A course chuckle emerged from his gaping mouth. 'I too am finding it hard to breath. I have exerted every sinew in our glorious union. Neffer haf I felt such a connection. Never in my life haf I found total perfection in the act of sex. This was loff, an act of loff. Surely you felt it, surely it was the same for you?'

'I felt a very strong, sensation, Herr Otte, it was very powerful.'

'Yes, yes. I knew it, I knew you vould vant me in the ent!'

'Herr Otte, you must go. Ranleigh and his friends will soon be finished and he will come up the stairs. Your escape will be more difficult.'

'You are right, liebchen, You care for me, you vish me to escape to freedom and one day to return to you.'

'Yes. I would wish that, I do not wish to see you hanged.'

Suddenly he kissed her full on the lips and held her for a long moment. She felt the bile rising in her stomach and could only wriggle to control it. He thought she was moving in time with his probing lips and responding equally.

He started again to begin rubbing her bare thighs but Kirsten responded pulling away gently. 'Herr Otte, you are in danger, I hear the others. If they raise the alarm you will be trapped. You must go.'

Mercifully, he pulled away taking her entreaty as sincere care for his survival. Pulling his breeches about him and tugging at his shirt, he made toward the window. Turning he looked once more at her still exposed thighs, her thick hair, shining silver in the moonlight.

'My darlink, I vil return.'

He disappeared throught the drapes and she heard his scramble across the shingles and drop to the firm ground of the yard. He had gone, completely. Somehow she knew it was final and she would never see him again.

She lay back drawing covers around her and sobbed into her pillow.

Crazy thoughts entered her head. Had she allowed him to do that to her a year ago, he would not have attempted to blow her husband to pieces. It was only an act. It was only a few moments. It was nothing.

She let her hands wonder down her still damp body. It felt no worse, no different to her own touch in reality. It was over and she regretted the damage her failure to capitulate had done to Banoldino, to their life together.

She sobbed now with new ferocity. Her body wracked with sadness and regret. Half an hour later a sudden fear gripped her insides. She leapt from the bed and grabbed at the wash basin. Straddling it she sluiced water over her and into herself. She washed and rinsed for many minutes and flung the bowl across the room spilling its contents onto the mat and splashing the walls.

* * *

Months passed and the escape of the villainous German, Otte, was no longer a topic of conversation in society.

Kirsten had stopped dreading the thought of the subject being rasied and her having to think about him afresh. It was gone from her and she felt the fresh air of freedom once again.

Her relationship with her beloved Banoldino was strained and difficult, but she convinced herself that with time, all would be well again.

Kirsten accepted that they would produce no children and that their lives would be changed for ever. Banoldino's health improved and some of his old vigour returned but most of his energy was spent in commerce and making each enterprise acheive the fullest possible profitability.

His business went from strength to strength. Supplying shipbuilders lead to part ownership of ships. Which lead to trading relationships with Europe and England in particular. Everything he chose to pursue turned into a success. Ranleigh, Rickard, many others followed his lead. He had the Midas touch and they all benefited.

Their stock in society continued to grow with equal alacrity. They became the toast of the county. Kirsten was the first guest on every list for every occasion. She even eclipsed Lady Evelyn in celebrity.

Her beautiful complexion, her golden hair, dazzling green eyes. Her easy manner and ready smile enhanced by charming dimples, the intriguing scar across her shoulder, visible when she wore the finest gowns on those special occasions. She was irresistible to men and essential to women of ambition.

Banoldino was still handsome and dashing, having been restored some of his colour and bearing. His hair was even more profoundly white at the temples and his dark eyes always attractive. His temper was the only thing different to the Banoldino of old. Now he did not suffer fools, he had a way of dismissing his entourage in an instant when he wanted to be alone. He spent hours without uttering a word and was broody and impatient.

Their son, John Nathan, grew into a fine looking boy, a credit to his mother in manners and deportment. At four years of age, able to engage confidently in conversation about horses and the merits of fast sailing ships.

Time passed and their world grew around them. The town became a city. The house became a mansion. Their interests grew far and wide and their healthy accounts grew into banking.

The only physical contact between Kirsten and Banoldino was a light kiss each morning and evening as they wished each other the best. Their life as lovers was over. It was never mentioned and played no further part in their relationship.

She often cried into her pillow at night. He would drink an extra brandy whenever he felt sentimental. He was always tired, always in pain and a draught or two at the end of the day was justifiable.

***

Still, there was hope, great prospects for the future. Ambition for their son John Nathan. Huge potential for the riches and glamour to be enjoyed at the very top of society in their fast developing world.

Chapter 38

Beyond the Horizon

Sailing from the Niger River into the Atlantic, once losing sight of land, was a new experience way beyond the imagination. The dark blue-black of the heavy ocean different somehow from the expanse of the Mediterranean, even than the Bay of Biscay, in texture and resonance.

Although Daemon was aware that hundreds, perhaps thousands had already made the journey during the seventeenth and earlier in the eighteenth centuries, it still gripped him in awe and wonderment.

The ship was bound for another world, one he had heard only little about. The imagination began and stopped on a scale which was based on familiarity. It could never have grasped the vastness of the seas that lay ahead, the time it took to cross them or the ferocity of the swell when weather impacted every moment of every day upon their existence.